# DEAD RECKONING

## Lee Ellis

Grosvenor House
Publishing Limited

This book is published by
Grosvenor House Publishing Ltd
Link House
140 The Broadway, Tolworth, Surrey, KT6 7HT.
www.grosvenorhousepublishing.co.uk

This book is a work of fiction. Any resemblance to
people or events, past or present, is purely coincidental.

A CIP record for this book
is available from the British Library

ISBN 978-1-83615-000-8
eBook ISBN 978-1-83615-001-5

# Author's Note

The background to 'Dead Reckoning' is based on events in the Nottingham Blitz in 1941. For this I am indebted to 'Battle Of The Flames' by David Needham. Otherwise it is a work of fiction and any similarity to real persons living or dead, is entirely coincidental.

To the memory of my parents and all other citizens who lived through the Nottingham Blitz and to those who did not survive.

AS the train pulls out of St. Pancras many apprehensive glances are exchanged, the same unspoken question reverberating through every carriage. *Will he appear again this evening?* Women read the same fear in the eyes of other women and watch the male passengers suspiciously. Is it him? They bunch up with unaccustomed closeness. All sightings have been by lone women. Keep together and remain safe. That way I won't see him. Others dismiss the stories, outlandish imaginings by suggestible fools or made up by insensitive mischief makers. But he's been seen for twelve consecutive evenings and always on this same departure, somewhere between London and Nottingham. This will be the thirteenth…if he appears. The buffet and toilets are quiet. For such visits you must leave your seat and the apparent security of fellow passengers.

The man opposite gets up. Where is he going? One of the women is no longer in her seat. She's out there alone, near the buffet, between the carriages, checking on her luggage, waiting at the toilet. She returns, unharmed. Perhaps tonight he won't be seen and this nonsense about the strange predator scaring women on the 5.15 will be scotched for good. The man also returns. At least it's not him. Look around the carriage. Most of these men are too old…or too young…or too wimpy…but appearances can be deceptive. The train passes Bedford. All's well.

People get restive. Fifty miles without visiting the toilet is perhaps taking its toll! While for others the needs of their stomachs become pressing, making the beckoning of the buffet car irresistible. The carriage is less crowded, there are ominous gaps between seats. A perilous complacency pervades, yet people are relaxing, convivial conversation replaces silent anxiety, thoughts transcend immediate concerns. Kettering is passed. It's going to be all right.

The train reaches Leicester. Only twenty five miles to go. Soon it will slide into the familiar surroundings of Midland station and weary, but relieved passengers will stride out with hardly a glance at the Edwardian sandstone edifice, quickly forgetting they've ever been on a train let alone this one. They'll dismiss all talk of the 'predator' without any memory of their fraught journey.

Too busy preparing her report on her London meeting, one young woman has not concerned herself with the stories connected to this particular train. Concentrating and writing in one position, her back aches a little and her legs are stiff. She needs to stretch them. The train passes Loughborough. She'll have to be quick. Some people are already retrieving small cases and clothes from the upper racks. Time enough for a quick cup of coffee before arrival in Nottingham. She gets up and goes through two carriages, passing no one coming the other way. It may be too late. The buffet staff will want to pack up. Maybe she'll just get to the buffet, then return. She looks at her watch. Yes, if they are still serving, she'll grab that coffee. She reaches the vestibule between carriages. Only one more before the buffet car. Someone is coming the other way. She stops to let him pass and turns to the window, lingering for a moment, watching the country flying by.

When she turns back he's still there, hovering at the other window. Perhaps he's waiting to be the first to alight in Nottingham? But it's not the same man. This is someone utterly different. Younger, shabbier, grimmer with steely even threatening eyes and he's looking directly at her! He makes her uneasy. She's no longer interested in going to the buffet. It's time to go back and quickly! She should get away from the window now, but that means moving closer to him. She freezes. He steps forward. He's coming for her. It's him. It's the predator! She screams, a long low wail...

# 1

THE hammering and banging that's dominated the area for weeks has stopped. Local residents come home to a strange, but welcome hush and leave in the morning without the incessant battering of building and excavating to accompany their departure. Only the contractor and the developer do not share the enthusiasm for the 'find.' The new building will be delayed, disrupting the schedule of the one and the financial security of the other. In these straightened times such a construction is risky enough without the complication of having additional works.

For as they dug down to begin the first foundations the ground gave way, revealing a huge hole, deep into the sandstone. The developer blamed the builder who had not priced for such extra works. The builder blamed the surveyor, who had not predicted such works being necessary. The surveyor blamed the developer. His brief was specific, such additional work was not provided for in his contract. It would mean pile driving to reach the bedrock, not to mention the in-filling, the strengthening of walls…and who would be responsible?

Then while they wrangled, in his wisdom the building inspector pronounced the hole was not natural. The city sandstone is riddled with caves and this looked like a new, previously unknown network. There could be medieval connections, immensely significant in the city's heritage. The builder complained of the delay, the developer countered

1

saying they were well north of the city centre so how could this be medieval? No one listened to him and he buried his head in his hands, dreading the inevitably punishing conversation he envisaged with the bank. It was no use. The archaeologists were called in and given time to investigate. Delay heaped on delay as the men and machines were idle.

> ...*The raid was incessant and prolonged. It was the worst attack on the city so far and proved to be the worst in the whole war. Two hundred were killed in that one night including 50 when two bombs hit the shelter at the Co-op bakery. It was the largest loss of life in a single incident, but bombs fell right across the city. Next day fires were still being damped down and firemen had arrived from as far away as Birmingham and Manchester. 272 fire pumps had been deployed during a night in which 424 high explosive bombs and 6,084 incendiaries had fallen. Many of the casualties were children. When war started thousands had been evacuated from the cities, but Nottingham was not considered a likely target and the children remained. It was a decision to be regretted on a night the city would remember for all the wrong reasons.*

Arlene pauses and checks her map of the city in 1941. She's marked all the places known to have received hits on that fateful night. What she writes next is pure speculation, but could be right. After all, an unexploded bomb had lodged in the tower of St. Mary's church, then inexplicably *carried* out by the two fire wardens on duty! Unexploded bombs have been found in other places over the years and there were certainly hits all around Sharp Road. So, who knows what they'll find excavating the caves at the building site? Unless they find something interesting a story about 'medieval connections' can only run for one night. But with a wartime connection it might have a better resonance. She's been working on the article about the infamous air raid for weeks, enlivening it from her interviews with survivors. She makes a note to insert a piece with pictures on the 'then and now' of where some of the bombs fell, then writes:

*"As we look back nearly seventy years and the anniversary of that terrible night draws near it is not just these places that remind us of those perilous times."*

She stops, wondering how best to link the events at Sharp Road with her article on the war. No more than a hint should suffice. After all, this is meant to be an article in a *news*paper. Too much speculation and her hard work could be heading for the spike. But she has to say something...

*"The site, undeveloped since the war is known to be close to where many of the bombs fell. As the archaeologists explore these large holes in the ground they might find much more than relics from the middle ages..."*

Then she remembers what some of the survivors said and randomly includes some of their impressions.

*"There was so little time...we just had to drop everything and run to the shelter...sometimes we hesitated, there was always something to do, to finish off, but always we went...we'd heard the sirens so many times, we were almost immune to them, but on that night it wasn't just sirens...down in the shelter we heard the constant rumble, but it seemed to be getting closer..."*

It doesn't fit. Set the wartime scene first, then link it to the present, the building site, the big hole and the discovery of the caves. Then the subtle hint, past and present coming together, the suggestion will be enough, readers' imaginations will do the rest. A little more polishing and the article will be ready in time for the anniversary of that awful raid. She works on. It's nearly done, but she's not satisfied. Something is missing, one last finishing touch. She has plenty of material from the past, but what of now? She needs to capture the flavour of the moment.

When she arrives, Sharp Road is deceptively quiet. The builders' temporary fencing still encloses the site, but there are no construction activities. Neither are there are any spectators. Arlene doesn't understand. Even the most unexciting development must attract a few gawpers and this will be no small building, five storeys of offices and smart apartments. She shares her curiosity with the man who stops her at the barrier.

"I thought the place would be besieged. Everyone in the city must want to know what you're going to find."

"And you are?" he says suspiciously.

"Arlene Bates, I'm from the *Evening Courier*."

"Reporter," he sniffs as if he's just encountered someone with a contagious disease, "Did you write that piece the other night?"

"I want to follow it up. I'm writing an article on the war and…"

"You can't come in," he says, stepping forward in case she slips between him and the barrier."

"I only want to ask a few questions. Have you found anything?"

"No, not yet, we've only just begun."

"Are you working now?"

"You can't come in, it's too dangerous."

"Dangerous, in what way?"

It's a foolish statement and he hastily tries to rationalise his impetuous reaction.

"I mean we can't have too many people around while the work progresses."

"You are from the archaeology service?" she says.

"There's an engineer on site, he has to assess any potential instability to the foundations."

"You're from the builder?"

"We are still responsible for the security of the site," he says stiffly.

But he's said too much and she continues to chomp at the bone.

"What do you mean about the foundations? Is there a possibility of collapse?"

He desperately tries to backtrack.

"I'm not an expert, but obviously if people are scrabbling around underneath we have to be careful."

"But you said you have an engineer on site. Surely he won't allow anything that could jeopardise the building or at least the little that's here," she says, glancing at the few rows of bricks.

"It's not just what you see above ground."

She scribbles in her pad.

"What are you writing?" he says.

"What you've just said."

"But I was only…"

"What's your name?"

"That's not important."

"Let me see the engineer."

"What for?"

"To get a professional opinion on this unstable building."

"I didn't say it was unstable."

"You said it was dangerous."

"No, I said we have to be careful."

"You said it was dangerous."

"Only if there are too many people below ground."

"How many are down there? What are they doing?"

The increasingly rancorous exchange goes on, he refusing to give way, she refusing to back off.

Meanwhile, four metres below two professional archaeologists and four 'helpers' work away, intent on revealing what lies beneath. So far they've been unsuccessful. No clay pots, medieval coins or any other indications of previous inhabitants. While the two professionals diligently scrape in the main trench, excavated from the first fissure that opened up beneath the foundations, the helpers carefully dig into the side of the hole. Carried away by their enthusiasm they penetrate some distance into the sandstone, away from the others.

They take less care now, digging more rigorously. Suddenly the sandstone wall gives way and a space, at least a metre wide, opens up. For a few moments they stare incredulously through the gap. The others have not stirred, unaware of this new find. The four stare at each other. They ought to stop, call over and get some guidance, but they can't. They must go through and explore further. This is no longer some tedious dig, hours of scraping at the soil for tiny relics from the past. Now driven by some greater force from the past, they scramble into a narrow tunnel, just high and wide enough for them to creep forward. There's barely any light from above and they need their torches.

No one speaks. Speech is unnecessary. Their coalescing thoughts are enough. Ahead, beyond or at the head of the tunnel the same force draws them. They move slowly, silently except for the sound of their feet on the floor. It gets lower, narrower and they have to dig away at the roof and side to get through. It's only possible now for two to go forward at a time. Then a call from behind.

"What is this? Where are you?"

Their professional colleagues have discovered the new hole. A head is poked into the opening. A torch beam strikes their backs and bounces beside and in front of them. Someone calls.

"Come back! You'll destabilise the ground. It's not safe!"

"Let alone destroy the evidence," someone else calls, more concerned with the integrity of artefacts than for their safety!

They don't answer. They don't turn back. They must go on. They are *driven!*

A second head appears at their back.

"Get back here now!"

Still they ignore the call. The tunnel narrows further until only one can creep forward. His eager companions keep scraping the walls and roof to make more space. The young man at the front thrusts forward faster as he's drawn even more. Oblivious to the damage he may be doing to the 'dig.' He has to go on. Desperate to find whatever lies ahead, his companions continue widening the tunnel, possessed by something or *someone* more powerful than the pleadings of those behind. The only sound is their scraping, hollowing and gouging. The scooping and boring gets faster and even more frantic, then suddenly stops as the front man's trowel makes contact and a distinctly metallic sound pierces the heavy air.

As the earth falls away from the object for all to see, no one moves or speaks. The mysterious attraction is lost, replaced by agonising fear and the need to get out as fast as possible.

"It's a bloody bomb," one cries.

"Get out," another shouts.

In the confused twisting and turning as they all try to scramble back down the tunnel they scour themselves against the sandstone, dangerously weakening the walls and roof which split and shake.

"We'll be buried alive!"

"If we're not blown up before!"

Somehow they slither along without serious injury and reach the original hole as loose earth crashes into the tunnel.

Reporter Arlene Bates is still in heated debate with the man at the top trying to get access to the excavations, their argument suddenly stopping as the two archaeologists scramble up the ladder and race across the site towards them.

"Get away, get away! We've found a bomb. It could go off any moment!"

# 2

11<sup>th</sup> April

WALKING quickly through the centre of the city on his way to the police station, Chief Inspector Jenner, detects a change. Even this early in the morning Slab Square is normally thronged with people, but today there are fewer folk and they are less inclined to linger or exchange pleasantries. They hurry on, their minds on work, shopping, daily chores and cares. It's a casual observation, as a detective might make many times in a day, only later looking back and remembering it as the first of many unsettling events. For now, he's one of the few in the city unconcerned by the 'sightings.'

Perhaps that's not surprising. A widower of many years, he lives alone, and in his early fifties is still only a chief inspector. It's not that he lacks the drive and determination for a more senior role. It's irritating having to relate to superior officers of sometimes questionable ability, but he's long ago eschewed further climbing up the greasy pole. It would still mean subordination, only of a different kind to even higher levels of 'authority.' Jenner has never confused respect for order with respect for authority and he's never been a good subordinate. Too independent, too reliant on his individual judgement or as some might say 'too bloody minded,' over the years he's perhaps rubbed up too many the wrong way. Not so much his methods are unorthodox, but more his thinking. Methods and procedures - assuming they can be identified - can be dealt with, thinking cannot. He first got involved in 'peculiar' cases in London, only to find the same reputation following him here. So he's given up worrying about what others think and remained in not so splendid isolation. While he may be 'difficult' he has a record of solving 'difficult' cases.

It's now two tortuous weeks since the 'man' first appeared to those terrified women on the train. It began as a joke, then became a curiosity with gossip turned into nagging nervousness, grist to the steadily rising tension. Few women speak of it openly, but it's there. Almost overnight Nottingham has turned from a vibrant, carefree, self confident city to one gripped by fear. Fuelled by more and more sightings on the same train, unspoken terror has found many voices leading to alarm and at times panic. A pall hangs over the city, dampening people's natural vigour with a sullen wariness. Now no one trusts anyone else – especially women of men. They stare suspiciously at men on buses and trams, even at neighbours and colleagues. Students at the universities no longer stay out late. A practice other younger – and older – women soon copy. The city's social life is severely disrupted.

Everybody says they'll carry on as normal and there's a lot of bold talk. They 'won't be intimidated.' But as days pass, only the sceptical and the brave mean what they say while others say it would be foolish to take 'unnecessary risks.' Those who dismiss the 'sightings' out of hand are either contemptuous or comical, sometimes both. Many others latch onto the 'ghost' as no more than that, a 'spirit' with a penchant for trains, unpleasant maybe, but essentially harmless. None in these groups own up to actually seeing it.

Others ask why he is haunting the train? A troubled soul, revisiting some previous railway disaster, a victim or traumatised survivor of a gruesome accident? A tragic anniversary? Local railway historians delve into the archives, but the only crash remotely relevant on the line from London was back in 1898 and that was some distance away at Wellingborough. It also involved a Manchester train, which would not have travelled through Nottingham and it was in September, not April. So the connection has to be something more individual, the railway only peripherally involved.

The number of female passengers on St. Pancras trains, especially those travelling alone drop off and there's a growing reluctance by many to travel on any train or even trams or buses, even taxis. For if this 'thing' can't be ignored and it's not an innocent ghost, railway or otherwise, it must be a real person. So now come demands for the perpetrator to be found. The sinister word 'predator' creeps into conversation, with no hint of the light heartedness of barely a fortnight before.

## 11th April

The day after the first sighting one local radio station seizes the story for its afternoon phone in programme. It's inundated with calls, which carry over into the second, third, fourth day. Many 'witnesses' call in, eagerly recounting their experiences, which grow more lurid and expansive by the hour. The lines are jammed, people are unstoppable, jostling over the airwaves to get heard with their pet theories, explanations, guidance and homilies for the future. The descriptions of the man are wildly conflicting.

"...*tall, imposing, I felt he would walk all over me...*"

"...*short, grubby, sneaking about...*"

"...*a fat, greasy creature ...he made me shudder...I shudder even now...*"

"...*thin and gaunt, as if he'd not eaten for a week...that I might be his next meal...*"

"...*big and ugly, ready to pounce at any moment...*"

"...*a not unhandsome man, but with his gleaming smirk I felt trapped in his power and had to get away...*"

"...*he was all in black...*"

"...*his clothes were loud and gaudy...*"

By the fifth day the descriptions get increasingly more detailed and intense, but also wide and sweeping. When the presenter challenges these elaborate happenings with "How long was he there?" or "Didn't you try to get away?" he gets meaningless mumbles, evasion or suddenly remembered appointments for which they 'have to get away.'

By the second week the inconsistencies increase, comments and 'reports' contradicting each other even between witnesses to the same event at the same time. The sightings are erratic. Days pass and nothing is reported, then many on a single day. People's memories fail them in ordinary let alone stressful situations. Yet, even if a majority are exaggerations or even fabrications they can't all be discounted. Some were there and did see something uncanny. Those with incoherent fear rather than the more colourful and plentiful reports are probably the more reliable.

Then come the lecturing and the self righteous with varying 'advice' on what to do if the 'man' is encountered.

"…brazen it out, he's an ineffectual nutter…"

Others are less sanguine.

"…don't travel alone…"

Then there are the confrontational.

"…travel and work as a group. If you see him, challenge him, then pounce…"

Clearly such advice is not directed to a ghost who would presumably be indifferent to provocation let alone direct attack. The presenter wonders whether this would be effective or wise.

"What do you mean by pounce?"

The caller hesitates, then blusters, saying 'he should be suppressed,' but offering no guidance on how this might be achieved.

"…Don't be frightened, such men are cowards," another caller says.

The presenter questions the wisdom of a confrontational approach.

"Might that not provoke him?"

The caller doesn't answer directly, merely repeating her assertion that 'such men are cowards.'

The presenter persists.

"But maybe a dangerous one?"

The caller rings off.

## 11<sup>th</sup> April

At the police station Jenner is summoned to his superior, Chief Superintendent Emmins. To his intense irritation and slight alarm Davies, the Assistant Chief Constable is also present. Why are they mob handed? Can't Emmins brief his own officers alone or is it a matter of wider importance? Even now Jenner doesn't connect the meeting with the feverish anxiety sweeping the city. The Assistant Chief begins.

"The situation is getting very delicate, Derek."

Jenner says nothing, unaware a response is expected. After a few moments and an embarrassed cough, Davies continues.

"I am, of course referring to the situation on the trains."

Still Jenner doesn't respond. Emmins nervously fills the gap.

"*Train*, sir."

Davies glowers quizzically.

"That's what I said...on the trains."

"It's one particular train," Emmins continues, already wishing he'd avoided the pedantic interjection, "It's the evening departure from St Pancras at..."

"Yes, yes," Davies barks with an irritable sigh at Emmins and a mystified frown at Jenner, "whatever it is, train or trains, it...they...have managed to scare this city into a state of unrestrained panic."

Jenner finally acknowledges why he's here.

"Oh, *that*," he says with a dismissive grimace and a further correction, "You mean the *man* on the train rather than the train itself?"

Davies glances at Emmins as if to say 'You started this nonsense,' then to Jenner, "Yes, Derek the *man* on the *train*, who's been terrorising these women."

"Allegedly," Jenner corrects.

"What do you mean *allegedly?*"

"There's no definite evidence of any man, only what these women say."

"You mean we've not caught him?"

Jenner pulls himself up sharply. *We* means *him*. He's uncomfortable. He never wanted this case in the first place. It's a low priority, which he doesn't regard as in any way serious. Emmins and Davies are looking at him, obviously expecting a reply.

"At best it's a load of women with ridiculous delusions. At worst it's a fantasist who's committed no offence."

"Not yet," Emmins says gravely.

Jenner doesn't respond. There's a long, embarrassed silence. Then Davies speaks.

"Derek, you of all people know how strange, if seemingly innocuous events can be connected to serious crimes."

Now here it is. My background with 'peculiar' cases. Amazing it's taken them as long as five minutes to get to the point. But he'll be neither apologetic nor aggressive. Stick to the facts, keep to procedures.

"Not without an already existing crime for the connection to be made. In this case…"

Emmins interjects.

"So we wait until a woman is molested…or worse?"

"I didn't say that."

"No woman feels safe on the trains," Davies says.

Jenner can't resist another correction.

"On this particular train…" he begins.

Davies glances irritatedly at Emmins…again the *particular* train…then he turns to Jenner.

"Funny how these *ridiculous delusions* have all been on this particular train that you're so keen to emphasise. At least you've taken that part of the case seriously. Okay, one particular train involved in the sightings…so far. It may change. In any case it's affecting women's security on all trains in and out of the city. We've got to find this man. The press…"

"I don't take notice of newspapers," Jenner says curtly.

"Then it's time you did," Emmins says.

…So, it's your turn now is it?

"…you know how easily public confidence can be quickly undermined if the press aren't handled carefully."

"Not my concern," Jenner says gruffly.

"So you conveniently leave that to others while…" Emmins barks, but Davies puts a restraining hand on his shoulder.

This is not the time for a general discussion on press relations, better to turn it back onto Jenner.

"Derek," Davies says, "some of your previous cases…"

Jenner groans inwardly and stiffens outwardly.

"…when…*extra-ordinary*…forces are *allegedly* involved, press reaction can be helpful or unhelpful, depending on how it's handled. Therefore…"

Jenner only half listens to the rest of the conversation. He ignores the litany of his previous cases in which inexplicable developments were involved, intervening only to point out when his investigations were successful. This is grudgingly acknowledged. Then, in an unguarded moment he admits to not having read all the 'complaints.'

Maybe this is leading to him being taken off the case? But it's not to be and when past success is used to justify him taking a more 'robust stance' he listens more carefully. Though annoyed he agrees to bring his 'individual approach' to bear, particularly updating and reviewing the evidence.

Emmins will liaise with the British Transport Police in placing uniformed and non uniformed officers on trains and around the station.

"That way we might even catch him red handed," Davies says.

Jenner is less optimistic. If he only exists in these women's heads, he won't be there to be caught, red handed or not.

He leaves the station early and walks to the tram stop, carefully avoiding Slab Square. He's seen and heard enough for one day and unlike in the morning takes little notice of people. In the crowded tramcar he's lost in his own irksome thoughts and doesn't hear the fevered discussions, nor sees the rows of upright newspapers in front of engrossed passengers, neatly folded at a particular article.

*'...With no progress in identifying let alone apprehending the mysterious stranger, seen by so many women on the evening train from London, it is not surprising more people are being drawn to a more bizarre explanation. Is the threat from this sinister man drawn not from the present, but from the past? Several witnesses describe his unusual clothes and a dated demeanour, reminiscent of wartime...'*

Jenner would notice the reference to 'witnesses' is vague and unsubstantiated and there's no detail on exactly what are the differences in clothes or an explanation of the man's 'dated demeanour.' But this is not the article that everyone is so avidly reading. If Jenner had troubled to buy a copy of the paper, like them he would have turned to the inside page and the 'special feature' by Arlene Bates, following up the allusion to wartime.

*'...the siren's rhythmic howl diffuses every street, corner, house, pub and vehicle. Everyone knows to get to the nearest shelter as quickly as possible, but some hesitate.*

*There have been so many false alarms, so many unwarranted interruptions without cause. Twenty months into this war and the city has seen some raids, hit and runs, 'mistakes' for other places which have seen 'real' raids. But though there have been casualties, compared to other places Nottingham has been spared. Many times planes have been spotted approaching the city only to continue to some other target. It's bred a slight complacency, a resigned acceptance when the sirens wail.*

*This has been made worse by seven consecutive nights when the population has had to take cover in basements, under stairs and in cold damp shelters as the bombers thundered overhead, relieved when they hear them fade away to their objectives in the north west. Last night they endured air raid warnings for over five hours and now it's starting again. Yet there's no alternative, little comfort remaining in the blacked out streets with their hidden dangers, if not from bombs from those who evade the wardens to pursue their own nefarious ends.*

*A bus has stopped, the passengers joining the driver and conductor as they tramp to the seeming safety of the shelter. A few hold back. Perhaps they've almost reached their destination and could walk on. After all, this may be no more than they've heard before. It's not far and by the time Jerry comes...if he comes...they'll be safe enough. Yet the shadowy buildings along the dark streets could be perilous and even if they're not ordered by the wardens to seek shelter, what if this is the night when the bombs do fall?*

*Then they hear the first explosions in the distance and see the tell tale yellow plumes in the sky. This is not like any other night. This is no false alarm, nor a hit and run raid and the city will not be attacked by mistake. This will be sustained and heavy bombing. People scurry for the shelter, the strengthened basement of a large house. It's crowded, dark and smelly, but offers some precarious safety.*

*Now comes the continued drone of the planes, the thundering rumble of distant bombs, then the occasional bangs of closer ones. It may be a long night. Best settle down and try to ignore the noise. Everybody is here, the young, the old, the hushed, the rowdy, the stylish, the scruffy, confined together for a few hours, ignoring their differences, secure in their immediate protection from crumbling walls and flying debris. Others arrive. It gets even more cramped. The ominous rumbling of the bombs and the droning of the planes get louder, sometimes muffled by distance, sometimes heightened by nearness, but always unrelenting. Those that discounted shelter realise this is no night to be with those that must fight the flames and try to rescue the trapped. Then a droning even closer than before, the baleful whistle a few moments later and the enormous ear splitting bang as the bomb falls...'*

The fabricated allusions of the past tail off as abruptly as they began and the article reverts to present 'disturbances,' drawing parallels between wartime and the dark nights on the train.

*'...not surprising accounts of some witnesses to the predator have mentioned fleeting, ghostly images, seeing the carriages momentarily transformed into those of the 1940s and heard sounds similar to the ominous rumbling, droning and explosions of the Blitz...'*

Again no detail about the 'witnesses' and how such 'accounts' of the past were obtained, while Arlene further fuels speculation on the real or imaginary 'ghost.'

*'...The assistant chief constable assures us 'appropriate resources and the most proficient and experienced officers are engaged on the enquiry.' Yet, despite the alarm in the city there is still virtual inaction by the police. Maybe they*

*should call on a different kind of resource, one that can tap into the past and extra normal forces?'*

## 12<sup>th</sup> April

Jenner is thoroughly irritated and bored. He spends the best of the next day wading through the statements of the 'sightings' on the train, but closer scrutiny only reinforces his scepticism. How could Emmins seriously consider this farrago of emotional drivel as evidence? His sergeant has very thoughtfully appended notes taken from the many callers to the radio station. Reading through these does nothing to lift his irked disbelief. Some of these women might be better in the hands of a sympathetic psychiatrist than a crusty detective...no, that's going too far as his sergeant will be quick to remind him. He agreed to go through this exercise and he has, but he could have better spent these hours... tidying the office, helping the cleaner empty the bins, directing traffic at some remote rural intersection...

Emmins and Davies are overly swayed by newspaper reports and sensationalised radio phone-ins. He wasn't forceful enough and should have been less compliant. On the other hand, with so many 'statements,' can they all be wrong?

He closes the file, then tips out the contents. It's no good. If...*if*...this is a real case, subjective impressions won't be enough. He needs 'hard' evidence, but the officers on the trains have got nowhere, seen nothing, heard nothing...so, back to the beginning.

Sergeant Jennifer Heathcott is at the door. In her mid thirties, she's an experienced detective sergeant and has worked with Jenner on several of his 'peculiar' cases. They are a contrasting and complementary team His sometimes unorthodox approach, which irritates other officers doesn't bother her. She has a lively interest in the past, making such unusual cases all the more fascinating and quickly recognises the exceptional and mysterious. On the other hand he's steered by necessity rather than innate preference. Though experience has taught him when intuitive leaps into the unknown are necessary he still approaches 'strange circumstances' with continuing scepticism.

He looks up. She says nothing. She's seen that look too many times before. He waves her to sit down. She notices the radio 'reports' on the desk.

"Are the phone-ins consistent with the statements?"

"Consistent?" he grunts, "I suppose so. Consistently deluded, consistently emotional, consistently indefinite, consistently…"

"Alarming?"

"Probably," he says guardedly, "at least to some of these women."

He turns over several of the statements, depositing them in a neat pile, dismissed like a detention class for recalcitrant children.

"There's more to this than a load of hysterical women," she says.

"I didn't say they were hysterical."

"You said they had delusions."

"At best."

"And at worst?"

"A…"

"A fantasist is responsible?"

"Possibly."

"Or more likely a deranged killer?"

Jenner sighs resignedly. It's bad enough having to sit through the agitated whinging of his superiors, but when his own sergeant allows her emotions…

"I've had a difficult meeting with Emmins and Davies."

He pauses. She waits, then fills in the gap.

"They weren't satisfied with progress, so…"

"No extra resources, of course."

"…they referred to previous cases in which you…"

"In which *we…*" he corrects pointedly.

"…were involved…"

"They even listed some."

"Let me guess," she says, "Local disturbances in the 1840s…"

"Resulting in the successful resolution of a recent murder."

"Fourteenth century criminals?"

"And naturally, modern equivalents."

"So, they accept the closure of those cases are relevant to what's going on in the city."

"Not in the city, on trains… allegedly on *a* train coming into the city."

"But still involving…"

"…extraordinary forces."

He almost spits out the words. She ignores his grimaces and shaking head, saying "All the more reason to be sympathetic to the case."

"On the one hand we have a dangerous prowler cum predatory attacker. On the other…ghosts and spirits."

"Did they say that?"

"Not as such, but otherwise why involve me?"

"Better to…"

"Set me up to fail?"

"…cover all eventualities."

He waves his hands across the papers on the desk.

"I have to bring my *individual approach* to bear, use my *particular talents* with *peculiar cases* and take all this stuff seriously."

"Which is why you've been re-examining the statements."

"They are concerned there's too much…"

"Alarm?"

"Stirred up by that scurrilous rag."

"You've read the latest article?"

He grunts derisively, picks up last evening's newspaper and turns over the offending pages before consigning them to the wastepaper basket.

"The paper's exceeded even its own depths of inane excess. If people consume such ludicrous drivel, no wonder there's panic. What on earth has the wartime blitz got to do with these crazy...incidents...and now this...(he retrieves the paper, checks the author, then throws it back down again)...Arlene Bates, thinks we should be 'tapping into the past and extra normal resources,' whatever that's supposed to mean."

"Have you studied all the press reports?"

He points to a pile of press cuttings at the far edge of the desk, placed where they are liable to fall on the floor.

"And they are...?"

"Even more vague than these so called 'sightings,' more dramatic, more *alarming*, but less productive as hard evidence, probably because what they profess to report has been deliberately exaggerated and distorted. Who is this Arlene Bates anyway?"

"She seems to be drawing some interesting parallels with the war."

"Absolute gibberish."

Jennifer hesitates. He's not going to like this. With a sharp intake of breath she continues.

"Is it a real man or a ghost?"

Jenner groans, then glares at her with unconcealed incredulity.

He almost says 'Not you,' but sighs deeply, then says, "At this stage we must assume it is a man."

"Even so..." she begins.

He glowers with pouting irritation.

"...it would be intriguing."

"Would it?"

"I mean, who is he, why is he appearing?"

In previous investigations Jennifer's fascination with such things has been of value. Jenner doesn't feel this is one of those occasions.

"As yet no one has been attacked," he says.

"As distinct from being merely frightened?"

"I suppose so."

"Maybe we should call in a professional adviser."

He looks at her disdainfully and groans again.

"You have someone in mind?"

"Ettie Rodway."

"You contacted her about the case?"

"It was a social call."

"Somebody stoking it up?"

She ignores the question and says, "You...we...all worked well together in the past."

He considers this for a moment, then says, "On occasions when there was an actual crime."

"Yes, but even so..."

"Sergeant, I don't believe in worrying about suppositional crimes..."

"Well, suppositional could become actual and if..."

"...or calling in additional resources to help solve them when they are clearly not required."

Suitably rebuked, she slightly changes the subject.

"What about the officers on the trains and around the station?"

"Nothing."

She nods.

"You're not surprised?" he says.

"Only women see him."

"Precisely."

"Because only women or a woman is involved."

"Exactly."

"Whenever another man is around he doesn't appear."

"There were some female officers."

"But not alone, they were always accompanied by a male officer."

"It wasn't considered…"

"Safe?"

"Male officers were not acting alone either."

"But neither they nor any other men have reported seeing him."

"No."

"Women shouldn't always have to be in the company of a man to be safe."

"No, of course not."

They are silent for several minutes. Then he pushes half the statements to her side of the desk, snorts and grumpily starts reading the remaining papers again. She picks up her pile, smiles to herself and starts reading.

## 13th April

In the old days when its longer distance trains had been taken out and the very existence of the building was threatened St. Pancras station had a lonely atmosphere of living on in only ghostly magnificence. The great roof protected increasingly deserted platforms. Intent on getting to their train, few passengers lingered to marvel at the mid Victorian splendour. But now revamped, the old arching steel and glass look down on the sumptuous modernity of the Eurostar concourse with its bustling shops and unrelenting hurriedness. Someone plays the piano. He's rather good and attracts a small band of admirers with time to spare, keen to bask in an easy calm amidst the bustle.

Beneath the platforms of the old station, in what was once the basement storehouse for beer is the new realm of the modern travellers. Hectic shoppers grab welcome bites and drinks for the immediate journey. Some may have more pricey purchases in mind. A last minute surprise package to impress a new liaison or reactivate a too long suspended friendship or smooth the closure of a long, regretful absence? Eager tourists and weary workers queue for tickets to far flung or commuter destinations. Others while away a spare hour or so relaxing in bars and cafes. Then there are those for whom the delights of the new station have no more attraction than the mundane ones of the old. Their sole purpose is to find their departure and get on the train as soon as their racing legs and the crush will allow.

When the old station was redeveloped and much of the platform level gouged away to refurbish the basement into the new concourse, the new Eurostar platforms left no room for the remaining national distance trains. A new airier extension, as big as the original station was built to the rear to accommodate them. So, further along the concourse, continental and domestic travellers diverge. Those for Paris and Brussels turn to check in and wait while those for Leicester, Derby, Nottingham and Sheffield make for the escalator. While the platforms and the train are new the destination is the same as it's been for a hundred and fifty years. Most pause only to confirm the right platform and find their trains, but more sensitive souls might be aware of earlier times. Long gone platforms that occupied the great space above the Eurostar concourse, steam hauled trains purring impatiently ready to set off. Perhaps such fleeting but sharp images are all the more reason not to linger even though the train is not immediately departing. Few want to remain alone on the platform. Those that dawdle or wait around are all men. Women need to be together or close to a man they already know.

They are a mixed bunch. The subdued, lost in thoughts or fears look around uneasily or bury themselves in newspapers or the suddenly fascinating view from the window. Others are voluble and excited, though that could be concealing apprehensions. Lone passengers choose not to sit more than spitting distance from others, attaching themselves to whatever company is at hand. All long for the doors to close and the train to depart, hoping no sinister person has boarded, sure only of those immediately close to them. It's a moving, transient refuge, but a refuge nevertheless. Didn't someone say there are police on the train?

Within minutes of the train's departure the swiftly formed groups open up conversations on the flimsiest foundations, engaging in intense and garrulous chatter as if they've been friends for years. There's safety in numbers and talk binds them in a precarious safety. Most men, except those who are with a woman are shunned and rigidly kept apart. A gender distinction is formed creating women only carriages

St. Albans is passed without incident. The mood lightens and an unspoken comfort courses through the train. But when it stops at Luton there's a collective inspection of who gets on. Pairs of women go to the open doors the better to scan the platform. When they return to their seats and pass on a cautious reassurance the relief improves. The journey seems secure, the train relaxed and insulated from the fear and stress in the city, to which they get ever closer. Women, previously concerned now seem heedless of danger, but are nervously talkative. Some say the whole story of a predator or a malign ghost is a 'non event.'

One says, "Do you think it's been put around as a prank that's got out of hand?"

Intent looks are exchanged. Is this a bold dismissal of two weeks of angst or a tremulous plea for others to help excise her anguish? Should she be reinforced or challenged? No one is quite sure and a long silence threatens to crack the fragile confidence. Then another woman, sharing the same need for solidarity, speaks up.

"Oh yes, that'll be it."

The dam bursts and a desperate interchange follows.

"You can't believe all you read in the papers."

"They always blow it out of proportion."

"But what about those who've rung the radio?"

Another, shorter silence, then a vigorous spirit asserts.

"Attention seekers, some folks'll say anything to get their names read out."

Much nodding and assenting. But other women, while listening don't join in, remaining suspicious and introspective. Reassurance from such lively babbling doesn't cheer them. It's skin deep at best, the product of a nervy confidence. When the train stops at Kettering the edgy scrutiny of passengers getting on is resumed, but now no one takes up observation at the doors, unwilling to stray far from the safety of their seats.

"No one suspicious?" someone whispers as the train pulls away.

Her companions smile nervously.

"No, not getting on," one replies quietly, then adds ominously, "nor got off."

At Leicester the mood changes again, more sombre with less talk. Almost the last place an unwelcome traveller might come aboard and while there's the same monitoring of passenger movements on and off the train, it's undertaken in silence. As the train departs no one comments. If a potential threat has been detected it's not shared with others. Left to wonder, imaginations concoct something dire only to dismiss it because nothing suspicious has been noticed. Or so they believe. If it's not mentioned might it go away?

At Loughborough the carriages are pervaded by an eerie silence, pierced by staccato, jittery prattle from a small group of young women making their way to the buffet car. Few have bothered to make the short trip during the journey and sales are well down. As they enter the last carriage before the buffet car one stops suddenly and grips the edge of an unoccupied seat, staring fixedly into the distance. One of her friends turns and calls out. She doesn't answer and still stares intently. Her friend looks back, but seeing nothing untoward, calls again.

"What is it, Janine?"

"Don't you see it?"

"See what?"

"No, it's gone."

"What, there's nothing…"

Janine suddenly runs to her friend, collides with her, slips and almost knocks her over. Her friend grabs her and asks again.

"What is it?"

"Nothing, nothing. Come on, let's get a drink."

At the buffet the other friends are waiting and have already got in the drinks. They want to immediately return to their seats, but Janine is badly shaken, pale and reluctant to move away from the counter. She swallows her drink in one gulp.

"What's wrong?" one says.

Janine doesn't reply at first, then orders another drink, which she puts away a little less quickly, almost gasping for breath between gulps.

"I'll be okay in a minute. It's just…"

"She's had a shock," her friend says to the others, "Go back, I'll stay with her for a while."

The others pick up their drinks and somewhat bewildered make their way along the carriage back to their seats. Janine stands for a few moments by the buffet counter, then turns to look back down the carriage. Her friend waits patiently. Janine turns back.

"I'm okay now."

"So, we'll…"

"It's gone, you see," Janine says, lifting her arm and slowly pointing towards the end of the carriage, "It's normal now…the carriage, I mean, the seats are there and the colour and the windows."

"What did you see?"

"It was only for a moment, a couple of seconds. I couldn't come through because I couldn't get…I was in…a compartment."

"A compartment?"

"Yes, you know like trains used to be."

"But these are open carriages, there are no compartments."

"I know it's like that *now*, but then...and it was dark, everything was red...red everywhere...so dark...because the windows were dirty...smoke I suppose."

"Smoke?"

"Yes, from the engine."

"Janine, what are you talking about?"

"Crazy isn't it, even now I can't believe..."

She steadies herself, pulls up straight and in a firmer voice looks her friend directly in the eyes for the first time.

"I stepped out the compartment and into the corridor."

"Corridor?"

"Stop repeating what I say," Janine snaps, "Yes, of course there was a corridor, how else do you think people got along the train?"

"Yes, but..."

"I got to the window, in the corridor I mean and looked out and then..."

She stops suddenly. Her friend waits expectantly.

"Then I was back...here, I mean, in the carriage...the *open* carriage."

"Are you alright now?"

"Yes. It was very quick, I suppose all this talk, I let my mind run on and..."

"I didn't think you thought much of all the talk."

"I didn't. Oh, it's all nonsense, come on, let's get back."!

The colour has returned to Janine's face. She seems better and they start back along the train. Their other friends have almost got back to their seats. As they pass through the connection between carriages there's a smartly dressed young woman, around their ages, standing alone by the window. In the prevailing atmosphere of the train this seems so unusual, one of them is forced to speak.

"Are you alright, duck?"

She looks up.

"Yes, yes of course," she says, rather bemused.

"Just been to the toilet, eh?"

"Yes, yes," she says, rather flustered.

"If you like you can walk back with us."

She looks at them bewilderingly. In the present mood of most passengers, it's a reasonable and helpful suggestion, but she's clearly averse or not aware of that mood.

"No, no, I'm fine…thank you," she says curtly.

"As you like then."

They pass on into the carriage and leave her alone. The others have reached their seats, but are quiet for a time, Janine's bizarre outburst suddenly bringing the reality of the 'talk' to mind. Then one speaks.

"Someone else is on the train."

The others look at her incredulously. One titters nervously.

"Of course there is, a whole train full of people."

The others make noises, subdued, not quite a laugh, somewhere between apprehension and mirth.

"No," the first says emphatically, "I mean there's someone on the train for *us*."

The tittering stops. Her friends stare at her fearfully for a few seconds. Others in the carriage have overheard and all conversation stops. Everyone turns and looks to the end of the carriage through which they've just come.

Beyond that carriage Janine and her friend are making their way back towards their seats. The carriage they pass through is not busy and they swing from seat to seat on either side. Then Janine stops.

"What's up?" her friend says, "You've not seen again that…"

"No, no," Janine says, but doesn't move.

"Then why…?"

"Shush! Listen!"

Her friend cranes her head sideways, unsure what she's supposed to be listening for. The few other passengers, having heard Janine's cry are also listening.

"There's someone up ahead," Janine says.

"Of course there is, this is a…"

"I mean, someone…different."

"Not again, you've seen that old carriage and…"

"No!"

The train jolts, passing over some points and as it starts to slow down they are pushed back into the seats. But Janine is up again quickly and edges towards the end of the carriage. Her friend follows, shaking her head. Then they hear a cry ahead, piercing…terrifying…superseding mere fear, demanding their attention and help.

Then a resonant bump that transcends the whole carriage, followed by a dreadful slithering as if someone has fallen down…a few footsteps. There's a moment's hesitation. The realisation of what has happened is inescapable, but the shock is paralysing. In a few seconds their minds pass through the inevitable stages.

…The predator has actually struck. They should do something. But then they would be in danger caught between the two carriages. No, everybody has heard that awful cry. They won't be alone and must rush to assist…

And so they do. They are the first to arrive at the connecting corridor between the two carriages and the sight they see produces another guilty hesitation. Their other friends enter from the other carriage. One screeches in alarm.

"What's this? another says.

Janine is kneeling down, gently cradling the prone young woman on the floor. Blood is trickling from a wound on her temple.

"Is she…?" someone says.

Janine shakes her head. Someone checks the woman's pulse, but is unsure. The train is already slowing down and enters the station in Nottingham.

# 3

**14<sup>th</sup> April**

*'IS NO WOMAN SAFE?*

*After last night's terrible attack on the London train, disturbing questions have to be asked. Not just is any woman safe, but is any woman safe anywhere? For the odious fiend responsible for the sickening battering of an innocent young woman is still at large. Despite carrying out the assault in a public place on a busy train with plenty of other people about, he managed to get away. It has also emerged that a number of police officers were on board the train, yet were unable to apprehend the villain, let alone prevent the attack in the first place. So, where is he now? What will the authorities be doing to make the city safe and protect women from further attacks?*

*The police are not divulging details. At the very least it is a case of attempted murder. Fortunately, other passengers came to the poor woman's aid within minutes of the attack and were able to immediately summon further help. If they had not arrived at the scene so quickly such help might have been too late. With the train already slowing down and arriving in the station, the injured woman was rushed to hospital without delay. So, with so many emergency service personnel in the station, how did he get away, apparently unhindered and unseen?'*

The arresting headline is startling even to readers used to the sensational stance taken by the *Evening Courier*. By two o'clock most shops and news-stands have sold out. With the wholesaler besieged by feverish messages the paper has to print its next 'edition' before the evening rush. This is big news and not only for the newspaper. The incident is mentioned in the national news bulletin while local television leads with the story in its lunchtime programme. Those not at home crowd into electrical shops and pubs to watch and listen. The chief local reporter stands in front of the station as disconcerted travellers walk by with worried expressions. She soon gathers a motley gaggle of mischievous teenagers and unruly children, leering and waving, anxious to be seen on the 'telly.' A few are unceremoniously carted away by embarrassed parents or more responsible friends.

Unaware or contemptuous of their antics she carries on regardless. This is no mundane midday item. It's the most sensational story of her career and all eyes in the city are on her. Like the newspaper she must first 'set the scene' in suitably dramatic fashion.

"From where I'm standing, the sandstone grandeur of Nottingham's Edwardian station frontage is unchanged. Inside, the station also seems unchanged. Departing travellers still queue in the booking hall for their tickets, expectant friends, relatives or business colleagues wait to greet arriving ones, the platforms are still thronged with passengers, patiently waiting for the trains that still arrive and depart in the same way as any other day. But all is not the same nor will it ever be again. For yesterday, after two weeks of torment and anxious waiting, what too many expected, what none wanted and all dreaded finally happened.

'At first, all we heard was congestion and a huge crowd at the station. Everyone from the London train was milling around, getting more and more annoyed, shouting at the police and demanding to be allowed to go home. Then we learnt the dreadful news.

'On the evening train from London as it pulled into the station, a young woman was brutally attacked almost within view of hundreds of her fellow passengers. Fortunately the emergency services had been alerted and on the train's arrival she was immediately rushed to hospital. The police were reluctant to allow anyone to leave while they tried to detain the attacker. Then there was general alarm. Some said the attacker was still on the station, that a demented fanatic was at large and there could soon be more victims.

'I've spent most of the night here and the station has been packed until the early hours. Added to the terror of those who had been on the London train was the consternation of people arriving from other trains and those arriving to catch departing trains. Eventually the police let people go, but then the chaos spilled onto the streets outside as people jostled for taxis, buses and trams, desperately anxious to get away as quickly as possible."

'Despite the presence of dozens of police both on the train and within the station, the assailant escaped. Enquiries are ongoing. A vast manhunt is underway and police are appealing for witnesses to come forward. Meanwhile the consternation remains today. This morning I've been talking to people and how they feel about travelling. I have some of them with me now."

She turns to a small group of three women and one man and talks to each in turn. She gets a mixed response, though all express a general concern with 'the situation' and - with a little prompting - the need for 'the predator' to be quickly caught.

"We're here to meet my daughter. She's due to arrive shortly on the London train," one woman says.

"Naturally, we're concerned," her husband says, "We've drilled into her she must be careful, stay with other people and make sure those around her are...safe."

He pauses, turns over his thoughts for a few moments, then says "We don't know what is best. She could be in danger on the train...but if what we hear is true and the man got off the train last night and into the town then she may be in the safest place."

His wife shudders. The reporter turns to two other women.

"I'm here to see my daughter off on the London train," one says, glancing at her daughter, who smiles slightly, though more from her mother's reassurance than any real confidence.

"Her father offered to drive her," the mother continues, "but she was insistent and so are…"

The reporter cuts in abruptly.

"But if this man is in the city, then as this gentleman has said, she may be safer on the train, especially if it's going *to* London?"

This does nothing to ease the woman's nerves. Other interviews follow until the presenter in the studio finally cuts her off so he can deal with 'other stories.'

She's so engrossed she continues to interview other people at the station after she's ceased broadcasting, despite the crew shouting and gesticulating wildly to that effect! On returning to the studio she gets a dressing down for 'going too far,' monopolising the limited time available for a midday report, making assumptions about events without checking reliable sources and speculating on the safety or otherwise of particular trains. But she's not be chastened.

"You're missing the point and need to get up to speed on what's going on. This event is such a vital and gripping story the whole programme should have been devoted to it."

She gets her wish later when a half hour 'special' is hastily arranged for the evening, including her 'extra footage,' recorded after she went off air at lunchtime. Already her report has struck a chord with terrified viewers throughout the city.

In the meantime the presenter switches to another correspondent, waiting patiently at the hospital.

"The situation remains the same. Last night a young woman was admitted to the hospital via the emergency department following an incident on a train. The hospital will not comment on her condition."

"Do we know the woman's identity?" the presenter asks.

"The hospital refuses to say. I get the impression on direction from the police. We can only assume publicising her name could be sensitive."

Viewers are left to ponder on the implications. The reporter only has the 'official bulletin' from which the hospital 'spokesperson' is unwilling or unable to amplify. It amounts to a news blackout and his frustration reflects a greater one sweeping the city. People are scared. A young woman's life possibly in the balance while a dangerous predator is loose in their midst. In the febrile atmosphere wild rumours spread, the story dominating local radio all morning and into the afternoon.

The callers reflect the frenzied mood, the widespread fear felt by almost as many men as women with incoherent demands for 'action.' One man sets out 'more reasoned measures to tackle the situation.'

*"There should be a special force established to hunt down this slug. The authorities have to recognise they are dealing with a major emergency. We need a rigorous sweep of the city...with enough officers it shouldn't be that difficult to find him..."*

"You think it will be easy to apprehend this man?" the presenter says.

*"Of course. As I said with sufficient resources it..."*

"Assuming he's still in the city."

The caller is thrown off balance, but stumbles on.

*"He got off the train...disappeared into the crowd...so he must be somewhere in the city."*

"Not necessarily…" the presenter begins, but the caller won't be put off. If you're in a hole, keep digging.

*"He won't have time…to escape…he'll know the station and the roads will be watched…"*

"As you said," the presenter says provocatively, "If the police put enough officers…"

*"He's still in the city…somebody knows…somebody's seen him."*

He's rings off abruptly, but the next calls vindicate his adamant stand.

*"He's definitely in the city."*

"You're sure of that?"

*"Oh yes, I've seen him!"*

The presenter tries to get the caller to amplify, but she's reluctant to be more specific.

*"I'll only say I've seen him in the city…I have to think of my own position."* (she's previously refused to give her name)

"Have you informed the police?"

But she's already rung off. Yet within seconds another caller has information on the whereabouts of the 'predator.'

"Where?"

*"In the city."*

"You've seen him yourself?"

*"No, not me, but several people have told me they have."*

And so the vague assertions go on. A torrent of other callers declaring they or other 'reliable people' have seen 'the predator' in the hours immediately after the incident. A few give specific locations, but the sightings crammed into such a short time and spread over such a wide area means the man has either moved at breakneck speed or there's more than one man.

Jennifer is first at the railway station until Jenner arrives to coordinate the investigation. He sends her to the hospital where Karen Renshaw lies under constant surveillance. Jennifer remains all night, hoping for an opportunity to talk to her. The medical and nursing staff watch and wait. At this stage there's little more they can do. The young woman's injury is serious and she lies inert, with a drip and her head bandaged.

Jenner is insistent.

"Tell the press nothing, no name, nothing for the attacker to know."

So nothing is said about the victim and her injuries. Nor about the state of the investigation, though at the moment there's little that can be said. Jenner comes to the hospital in the morning, complaining of the 'chaos' at the railway station, giving the press a wholly uninformative statement and asking when Karen is likely to regain consciousness."

"It's difficult to be precise," the consultant says.

Jenner sighs. He hates the perennial imprecision of doctors.

"Any likelihood of me being able to question her today?"

The doctor sighs. He hates the perennial impatience of policemen.

"Chef inspector, as I said I can't predict she'll even be awake today let alone capable of being subjected to interrogation."

"Not interrogation, doctor, questioning, there's a difference."

"Either way, I can't be sure she…"

"This is a natural coma, isn't it? It's not been medically induced. She's got to wake sometime."

"Her coma has not been induced. It's a result of the severe injury she received and as such it's impossible to be precise. Last night her condition did not improve, but neither did it deteriorate. We will be monitoring her very closely during the next few hours. It's touch and go."

Jenner persists.

"It's absolutely vital we talk to her as soon as possible. If she wakes…?"

"I understand your position, but at this stage I cannot be confident she will even wake at all."

"Bloody hell," Jenner says quietly.

"Precisely," the doctor says and turns away.

"Can I see her?" Jenner says.

The doctor is amazed at Jenner's persistence. Hasn't he made the position clear enough?

"Not until she's awake and recovered sufficiently to face questions. Even then…"

"Yes, but we need to keep an eye on her."

"That's our job, chief inspector," the doctor says firmly with an icy glare before walking resolutely up the corridor.

"Not much hope there," Jenner says grumpily,

Jennifer knows they don't need to be in Karen's room until she wakes, but frustrated by the need to quickly gather vital evidence Jenner has no time for medical niceties.

"She's not moved all night," she says, shaking her head, "Anything new at the station?"

"A lot of panic and overstated vagaries."

"What about Janine Thompson who first found her? She was in a right state when I saw her, understandably worried about Karen. Afraid he was still around she…"

"Pity he wasn't, we might have got the bastard. She couldn't add anything to what she initially said to you."

"She said she interrupted the attacker."

"She said she *might* have interrupted the attacker. It was conjecture. She *assumed* he ran off, away from the corridor and up the train. In which case other passengers in the next carriage were bound to have seen him, but no one admits as such. At least, no one in that exact location."

He opens out a sketch map of the train carriages and the buffet car, with the connection between carriages where the attack took place.

"Useful device," he mumbles, "One of the officials at the station provided it. At least someone showed some initiative."

He points to the various locations.

"Here is where Karen was discovered. Janine and her friend came from this carriage, through which, according to her, the attacker ran to where other passengers…"

"Does it matter?" Jennifer says.

"It wouldn't matter if we had a clear description. Janine Thompson can only recall a 'disappearing shape up the train.' However, it does matter because other witnesses reported seeing him in other places…(he gets out the plan of the train again)…here and here and here…this one at the opposite end of the train!"

He folds up the plan and stuffs it in his pocket, saying "Which is tantamount to none of them seeing him at all!"

"Or all of them seeing him run through the train?"

"*If* it's the same man. When pressed, Janine Thompson only *assumed* 'a disappearing shape up the train' was a man. We have another who *may* have seen a male figure slinking away. She's sure he wasn't there before the attack – though at her position in the train how would she know when that was exactly? Anyway, *slinking* away, not running. There are others. It's like these idiots calling the radio. No viable description we can work on, no reliable information on time and direction, which might help us track him down."

"Janine did her best. She first thought the woman was dead and was terrified. Then she realised, though badly injured she was alive."

"Why didn't someone activate the alarm?"

"They acted as fast as they could. The train was already entering the station. They dialled 999, so emergency services were quickly on the scene."

"Not fast enough. We didn't get him. He was one step ahead of us."

"He was bound to be. It was carefully planned. He'd worked it out after travelling on previous trains. He must have followed her, then timed the attack just before the train was coming into the station, so he could escape quickly in the crowd."

"So it wasn't random," Jenner says, "If it was a random attack it could have taken place any time during the journey from London. It was the *right* train, coinciding with most of the sightings, so the attack was the conclusion of the pattern."

"His previous appearances were threats, warnings?"

"Maybe."

"He must have been travelling on the same train for at least two weeks. He was playing with us."

"And we…I…didn't take it seriously."

"You weren't to know."

"A particular train, but was she a particular victim?"

"Why go to all that trouble if he was just after her? You'd only do it…"

"…if there was no particular victim. It could have been anybody."

"You think the attack was opportunistic, unconnected to the sightings of a predator?"

"Predator," he snorts, "Perhaps it was only opportunistic in making use of those damned reports in the paper."

"Otherwise pre-planned, fitting in with his playful scheme. The process is more important than the act itself?"

"In which case it's not over."

"He'll do it again?"

"He'll do something. It depends on whether she lives… whether his intention was murder. As you say, is he playing…as a cat does with a mouse?"

"So Karen was in the wrong place at the wrong time?"

"If it's the same man who's been on the same train these past weeks, then he's familiar with the journey, the arrival, the station. If you're right, she was in the wrong place, but not the wrong time."

"But the train terminates in Nottingham. He'd know everybody would be getting to leave. So not necessarily a good time."

"A *risky* time perhaps."

"So many people about."

"Which it seems concealed his escape."

"So it was all part of the buzz, the thrill of the game so to speak."

Jenner isn't sure.

"Perhaps. Again, it all depends on whether she really was the intended victim."

"And if he was interrupted by Janine Thompson and the others..."

"You heard what the doctor said. This could be a murder investigation."

They are silent for some time, then Jennifer says, "If she lives what will he do then?"

Jenner shakes his head, then says gravely, "Or if she's not the specific victim, will he attack again on the train?"

"With more officers on the train, we'd be sure to catch him."

"He'll know that by now."

"So, another train, another place?"

Jenner shakes his head again.

"This was our chance, we should have got him."

"On the train?"

"A carriage is a sealed unit, what could be easier? He got off and into the station. If only we'd moved quicker, sealed the exits earlier..."

"We got there as soon as we could," she says stiffly.

"I'm not blaming you. It's me. Utter bloody chaos, people milling around everywhere, the platform packed, total panic. We were overwhelmed, people demanding to be let out of the station. We started talking to them, but we didn't have enough officers. By the time we managed to close the station, he'd got away."

"Perhaps, but he could still have been in the crowd. Even if we got him, how would we know it was him?"

"So he escaped as one of the passengers even after the exits were being controlled?"

She nods.

"No. He got away earlier. By the time we were controlling those barriers we would have picked up anyone suspicious."

"What about forensics?"

"Nothing yet. Our best chance is for her to wake up."

He steps to where a constable stands at the door to Karen's room.

"Absolutely no one to be allowed in there," he says.

"Just doctors and nurses?" the constable says.

"Only those you know. Anybody you don't know, you keep out."

"But, if there's an emergency?"

"If there's an emergency you'll know them."

"And relatives?"

"What relatives?"

"Her father is here."

"What, in there?"

"No, there's a relative's room."

"Bloody doctor," Jenner says through gritted teeth, "told me I couldn't see her."

"And another man has been," the constable says, anxious to make sure all visitors are taken into account.

"What man?"

"Didn't give his name."

"Young? Old?"

"I didn't see him. One of the nurses said he was young."

"So he didn't stay?"

"No."

Jenner turns to Jennifer.

"Did you know about this?"

"The doctor said a man was enquiring last night. I took it to be the father."

"You didn't see him?"

"No."

Jenner turns to the constable.

"Nobody's been in the room?"

"Nobody."

"Keep it that way," Jenner says, then to Jennifer, "See what you can find out from the doctor about this other man. For the moment there's nothing more to be done here. Go back to the railway station and see what information you can find on the movement of passengers on the train. How many got on in London, how many got off and got on at intermediate stations. It's a long shot, but something useful might turn up. In the meantime, if they're still here, talk to the father and follow this other character. We have to concentrate on Karen Renshaw and her background."

## 15th April

Jenner is not in a good mood. He's just returned from a meeting with his superiors. Again Chief Superintendent Emmins has seen him mob handed, Assistant Chief Constable Davies doing most of the talking.

"Bloody spare part," Jenner mutters, "Emmins might as well not have been there. If I was to be hauled over the coals, could have been done in Davies office alone. Protocol, though and of course, respect for the hierarchy."

"Not something you've ever considered important."

He looks up suddenly to see Jennifer in the door.

"You crept up very quietly."

"Hard meeting?" she says, sitting down opposite him.

He stretches back in his chair, assuming an unnaturally haughty expression.

*"Absolute frenzy in the city. In all my years in the force never seen anything like it. Can't go on like this,"* he says, mimicking Emmins, then switches to the tone of Davies, *"I know manpower is stretched. I've already spoken to the transport police and they've undertaken to increase their patrols. Likewise, we will do what we can in the city, but at the end of the day..."*

He breaks off.

"At the end of the day?" she says.

"You know the rest," he says, then assumes the familiar intonation of the assistant chief constable.

*"Women are virtually boycotting all forms of transport. Quite apart from the fear and panic, the knock on economic consequences – I'm told employee absenteeism has skyrocketed – is a disaster in itself. However, our gravest concern, the man responsible for this vile attack is still on the loose, ready at any moment to strike again..."*

"Sounds like the newspaper," Jennifer says, shaking her head.

*"...This man has got to be found, the investigation must be ratcheted up several gears...* Why do they state the bloody obvious when they're kicking you from pillar to post?... *There's a need for a coherent plan..."*

Jennifer winces. This is reminiscent of some of the radio phone-ins.

*"...with enough officers...a rigorous sweep of the city..."*

Has Davies internalised the half baked views of every saloon bar worldly wiseman in the city? Meanwhile Jenner chunters on.

"I've not got the resources for a major manhunt and in any case by now it's a waste of time. Most statements we took at the station made no reference to anyone. We have no clear description. Those we have are utterly contradictory. Emmins wanted to expand the investigation well out of the area, nothing specific, just a general extension without any lead. Fortunately Davies quashed that one. Anyway, this is a local man. I know it, got a feeling in my water."

He stops at last, drawing breath. Jennifer slides the *Evening Courier* across the desk.

"Have you read the latest article?"

If he's bent on venting his ire, it might as well all be released in one session. He looks at it quizzically.

"Yesterday's?" he says, but already knows the answer as he sees the different headline.

*'ATTACK VICTIM REMAINS IN HOSPITAL.'*

"Today's," she says,

"Yesterday's was bad enough."

He starts reading. The front page report is heavy on slick and punchy sentences, but short on detail. A rehash of the previous day's piece, larded with sensationalised, but vague accounts of the general fear in the city *'spilling over from the terrible happenings at the railway station.'* He clicks his tongue as he reads through, repeating the more ridiculous phrases.

"*...a debilitating resignation...fortitude faced with this fiend... coming together for collective defence...*" then a particularly infuriating one makes him snort indignantly, "*...acceptance by the authorities...*acceptance by the authorities! Who's written this trash? (he reads the journalist's name) Who is this Arlene Bates?"

"She's the one who's been..."

"Bloody scurrilous hack!"

Jennifer gulps resignedly and says, "You need to look inside."

Jenner turns over the pages. She waits for the onslaught.

*'Even at a very busy station like Nottingham, a train disgorging its passengers doesn't usually cause more than a passing stir in the lives of several hundred people, but two days ago it was the scene of pandemonium and terrible calamity...'*

"Utter nonsense," Jenner sighs, puffing irritatedly before reading on.

'After the poor woman had been taken to hospital, passengers were marooned in the station, unable to leave while those arriving for other trains were unable to get onto the platform. The lucky ones had already left…'

"Lucky ones!" Jenner cries, "Including the bloody attacker, I suppose. Does this wretched woman have anything between her ears?"

'People were shouting and screaming to be allowed to leave, only to be told the station was closed 'pending enquiries' even though nothing was being done. As women demanded explanations and children cried, police simply stood around…'

"Stood around? Trying to safeguard the scene and take meaningful statements."

'Eventually the tormented people were allowed to leave the station, only to enter frighteningly dark streets and a city on a knife edge of terror as they nervously struggled to get home as quickly as possible, constantly afraid they could be the victim of the next attack.'

"Not exactly liable to calm down people's fears," Jennifer says.

"Calm down?" Jenner thunders, "If she was being paid by the bloody attacker she'd hardly be likely to have done a better job and…" he breaks off, then says, "Now I don't suppose…?"

Jennifer whistles.

"Come on, you're not suggesting Arlene Bates is connected to the crime itself?"

Jenner says nothing, then shakes his head before picking up the newspaper again.

"No of course not, but…anyway, even if she's not it still doesn't excuse…good God, she's at it again, just listen to this…

'…absolute chaos at the station. So many crammed into the narrow space it was a miracle no one was pushed onto the tracks'…of course they weren't, there was a bloody train standing there… 'at the far ends beyond the train where so many *had been forced to go'*...nobody was forcing them... *'It was only the quick thinking of the railway staff, realising the immediate danger, that avoided a catastrophe, by shepherding people back, away from the tracks'*...of course, nothing to do with the coppers who were making sure they were safe though that meant more crowding near the train, she wants it both ways....oh, no she accepts... *'Admittedly this meant the crowding on the platform was increased'*...Naturally, oh wait for it... *'though if the exit gates had been opened'*...which of course would have defeated the whole purpose of the exercise, but that's too much for this pernicious hack to understand...oh, here we go again... *'having spoken to so many of those incarcerated'*...Incarcerated!... *'at the station, we have been able to put together a trail of the events that evening, this'...'*

He shakes his head, then splutters on with the quote.

*'...includes interviews with the public, which has produced reports of even more sightings of the attacker to add to the ones already reported to the police...'*

He breaks off again, then says, "Further useless information, some of this stuff even more outlandish than we've already got in the file...anyway, all gleaned from prattling fools *after* the incident, speculation and exaggeration at best though I suppose we'll have to look at it. She should have sent it to us when..."

"She has. It's just come in."

"And?"

"It's the same as in the newspaper report. You're right, there's nothing reliable we can use."

"Names?"

"No. I rang her. She says it was the best that could be done in the middle of such a chaotic scene. There wasn't time to get names and anyway people were getting away so quickly."

"While they were incarcerated in the railway station! Spare me from the wiles of so called investigative reporters."

"The chief superintendent takes them seriously," she says mischievously.

"Too bloody seriously. I shall have to see this damned woman."

"She wants to see you too. She's rung back several times while you were with the super. Says she 'needs a response from the police following her continuing requests for meaningful updates on enquiries. I said you were unavailable."

"Well, I'm available now. I can…"

"She's coming into the station."

"When?"

"Didn't say. I got the impression it wouldn't be long."

"I want to be informed immediately she arrives."

He returns to the newspaper and reads some more paragraphs, then explodes again.

*"It must be assumed the attacker was disturbed on the train for other passengers were quickly on the scene. With the station closed off to innocent passengers, how did he manage to escape?* Bloody obvious. She's answered her own question. He got away in those first few chaotic minutes, before *we* arrived."

He puts the paper down, thinks for a moment, then turns to Jennifer.

"Karen was attacked in the connecting corridor between two carriages and stayed there until she was taken off the train to the ambulance?"

"Yes."

"And there's a toilet in the corridor?"

Jennifer thinks for a moment.

"Yes."

"Obvious then, isn't it? He slipped into the toilet as soon as he heard the others coming, waiting until the train pulled into the platform, then slipped out while everybody was seeing to Karen. Nobody saw him?"

"He must have moved quickly."

"No, if he'd run along the platform he would have drawn attention. Somebody would have noticed and remembered. They can all be questioned again, but I doubt if we get anything. With all the speculation and especially this Bates woman *having spoken to so many*, but to no effect he might as well have been invisible."

He reads on.

*"It gives us no pleasure to see this terrible incident as the unfortunate culmination of all we have been warning against.* Scurrilous bloody hack! *Our campaign...*Campaign, what bloody campaign?"

He puts it down, snorts derisively and turns to Jennifer.

"Have you read it all?"

"Only the..."

He picks it up again.

*"Further activity can be expected, but* ...di dum, di dum... bloody hell!"

He looks at the paper, then pushes it away, his eyes widening in disbelief. He picks it up again, then puts it down and pushes it along the desk as if it's contaminated. He explodes.

"She's published Karen Renshaw's name! How the hell did she find out? I gave strict instructions..."

His telephone rings. He picks up the receiver and barks at the unfortunate officer at the other end.

"Yes? Yes it is Jenner. Is she? Yes, yes. You can send here up."

He bangs the receiver down.

"That infernal reporter is here. Wants to see me. She's coming up."

"Do I stay?" Jennifer says.

"You bet you stay. I want a witness to this."

Arlene arrives, ushered in by an officer from the front desk. She introduces herself. Jenner doesn't respond and points to a vacant chair.

"Chief inspector, I was wanting to…" she begins.

"Are you responsible for this?" he says aggressively waving the newspaper in front of her.

"Yes. That's why I have come in. Thank you for seeing me," she says, a little warily.

He says nothing, but Jennifer can feel his fury as if she sits next to a blazing fire. Arlene glances at Jennifer, but she knows better than to show any sign of sympathy. A more amenable approach might come later, but inscrutability is the best option for now. Arlene continues.

"What will the police do now the predator has made his first attack?"

"You expect further…attacks?" he says airily.

"Well, obviously I don't know, but as there have been a number of warning signals before…"

"Imaginative assertions you mean?"

"I wouldn't necessarily describe them as such. What the women said they saw on the train were more than assertions. They were positive sightings, so…"

"Vague and contradictory. At the moment they provide…"

Jenner breaks off. Jennifer is relieved. He's about to say the stories, circulating for the past two weeks give little evidence on which to base their enquiries, but that would be interpreted as incompetence. He mustn't let his anger overreach itself.

"But what are you going to do?" Arlene says.

"Enquiries are ongoing," he says guardedly.

Jennifer is more helpful.

"We may know more when we can to talk to the…(she hesitates) …victim."

"You mean Karen Renshaw?"

"How do you know her name?" Jenner says.

"I'm not aware that's a problem?" Arlene says, "Why should her name be concealed?"

"So you won't tell us?"

"Anyone who has information on Miss Renshaw might assist our enquiries," Jennifer says.

"What sort of information?"

"You have a duty to pass on to us any information you have or are likely to receive," Jenner says.

"Of course. You've already spoken to the family?"

"I cannot comment on the details of our enquiries."

"But now the victim's identity is known, you expect further information?"

Jenner says nothing. He's tempted to ask again how Arlene found out about Karen Renshaw, but lets it go. The rest of their conversation is a series of platitudes and exchanges of thinly concealed belligerence. Eventually, realising she'll get nothing any more meaningful, Arlene leaves.

"Bloody rag," he mutters.

"I think she'll tell us if she obtains any further information," Jennifer says.

He picks up the newspaper again and reads the final two paragraphs of Arlene's article. Then tosses it down again.

"Are they all the same? Maybe this Bates woman is no worse than all the rest."

"Maybe just doing her job," Jennifer says tentatively.

"I mean all of them on that rag, in fact all the papers as well the radio and television reports. Innuendo, sensationalising, making the trivial into matters of 'fundamental significance' and exaggeration, always exaggeration, exaggeration. Listen to this. (he picks up the paper again) *Perhaps because of the police's belated concentration on these matters* – cheeky bloody hack – *they are at last taking the threat seriously and undertaking a* – wait for it – *vast manhunt*. Vast manhunt! What's she talking about?"

"It's only an expression."

"We can't mount a manhunt when we haven't yet got a man to hunt."

"It's understandable. After this first attack people will be concerned to…"

"First! First? That's what she said. Are *you* expecting more?"

"That's the general view in the city."

"There's something about her."

"You don't like reporters."

"It's not that. Okay, I'm annoyed with these articles, but there's something more. She's not just coming at this as a reporter. I've got a feeling in my water and it's not right."

"Will it matter she knows the name?"

Jennifer is surprised he doesn't immediately sound off again.

"You mean will it matter *everybody* knows the name? I'd certainly like to know how she found out. Some stupid sod in this station…well whoever it was isn't likely to own up and she certainly won't tell us."

He breaks off, thinks for a moment, then says, "It now means the attacker knows, assuming he didn't already know."

"If he already knows then it was a targeted attack?"

"So the case is just about Karen Renshaw and all this jiggery pokery about a predator is…"

"If it's only about her then why go to all this trouble on the train with plenty of witnesses?"

"None of which can give us any definitive information."

"Then there will be no second attack?"

"Maybe not – at least not on anyone else. He will already know his attack was unsuccessful. With the name out in the open he can be sure."

"So he might attack again?"

"Assuming his intention wasn't just to frighten her."

"She was pretty badly beaten."

"Could be the whole thing went too far. He only meant to rattle her and got carried away."

"Or not far enough."

"He meant to kill her?"

"With her name out in the open we might learn more."

"What do we know?"

"The family have been informed. Her father, Keith Renshaw has been to the hospital."

"Follow up the family background. She was returning from a meeting in London. We need to know more about that."

"She's a marketing consultant."

"Go and see the firm. Another thing, check out Arlene Bates, her background, who she knows, especially any connection to the Renshaws. And no one is to see Karen Renshaw."

"Just immediate family?"

"No more contact than we get. That includes the father. What about the mystery young man. Did you get anything out of the doctor?"

"He didn't remember him at first. Said it was all a bit rushed. When I prodded he did remember somebody, probably young, but..."

"Did he give a name?"

"No."

"Security is vital. The guard on Karen Renshaw has to be effective."

"So you *do* believe there could be another attack?"

"That depends on what we can find out about Karen Renshaw. If this man is desperate, he'll try again...and soon."

## 16<sup>th</sup> April

It's been a long shift. The constable at the hospital is tired and bored. His break has not turned up and is over an hour late. In that hour he's seen no one except a solitary nurse who ambled up from the nurses' station twenty minutes ago to routinely look in on Karen. That same nurse is leaving for her break and talks to a colleague who is relieving her. He looks over to them wistfully. He could at least do with a change of scene let alone a decent cup of tea. They have their backs to him and are engaged in intense conversation interspersed with occasional titters and nodding of heads. It must be interesting. Otherwise the ward and the corridor is quiet. He moves around to stretch his legs and glances into the room. There's no change. Karen hasn't moved, but is stable.

In the half minute while he looks in the room and the nurses are deep in conflab, a woman sneaks past them and along the corridor. By the time he turns the woman is standing beside him. He looks towards the nurses, but they've left, one to her break, the other to check on other patients. He should challenge the woman, but merely stares awkwardly at her.

"I hope I didn't startle you," she says.

She's in her early fifties in a plain blue dress, which on a too brief glimpse by tired eyes could be seen as a nurse's uniform. The reassuring smile and the confident air reinforces this impression. It's as if the woman has read his thoughts and cocks her head to one side, much as an authoritative, but indulgent superior might issue a kindly rebuke.

"I can see you are tired. I have taken charge and won't report you."

He has the impression he has done - or shortly will do - something he shouldn't and that she exercises a higher command in the ward. A nursing officer on her rounds perhaps? Maybe the nurse has been instructed to perform an important procedure elsewhere? The ward is safe in her hands. While she's here Karen Renshaw is safe from harm. *He* will be safe…from censure. He can get his break. He's deserved it and has a right to it. It's as if he's been expecting her and her next remark comes as no surprise.

"Your superiors understand."

It's enough. A reassuring tranquillity surrounds the woman and her composure is infectious. Afterwards he'll be amazed how it was *he* that suggested it, but now it seems the most natural thing to do.

"You'll be looking at Miss Renshaw?" he says.

"She's in here?"

The words are a question, the tone confirmatory. His nod is all she needs.

"A most unfortunate occurrence. You must be more concerned for her safety."

"She must be watched at all times," he says, then conceitedly, "but she'll be safe while I'm here."

"I'm sure you will find the man. He's been seen so many times by so many women. You have the matter under control."

She emphasises *you*, concentratedly staring into his eyes. It could mean the police force as a whole or just him and he's pleased to take it as the latter.

"Have *you* seen him?" he asks.

"No, but I believe those that have."

"Some say he's really just a ghost."

She smiles indulgently and shakes her head.

"There's no such thing as *just* a ghost."

This unsettles him, but her tone is disarming. She must be listened to for she has unique knowledge.

"You've read the newspaper reports?" she says.

"Who hasn't?"

"Did you find the article about the war, the blitz and the bombing absolutely engrossing? I did."

"Yes, fascinating, but also...disturbing."

"I know what you mean. Such matters of life...and death...close reminders of what that poor girl in there has been through...(she nods towards Karen's room) and the... situation in which we all find ourselves."

He imbibes her ever word, delivered slowly and intensely, but without any hint of reproval. There's been too much criticism of the police in recent days. Her approach is reassuring.

"Have you been listening to the radio?" he says, "People are worried. The whole city is very stressed."

She doesn't commit herself.

"You look tired. You need a break."

As she speaks he looks in on Karen.

"She'll be all right while I'm here," she says.

He looks back at her. The kindly face is mesmerising.

"I'm due a break. A colleague was meant to..."

"I understand. I'll be happy to oblige."

He thanks her and goes down the corridor. No one is at the nurses' station. She's alone and immediately enters the room. Karen Renshaw is unconscious and doesn't stir. The woman leans over the bed and studies the face.

"I can see your injuries are real," she says, "You've been most grievously assailed."

She sits down beside the bed. Without hesitation or questioning she recounts much from Arlene's article though dramatised even more than the original. She could have gleaned it all from the witnesses as reported by Arlene, but talks quietly and directly to Karen as if she was there and is reliving the experience.

"You're not alone on this train. There are those who've heard your cries for help. They are coming to your aid. I see them now, running down the train. They are desperate. They know, they have heard. For two weeks women have had to endure the visitations of this creature. He is of your time, but brings with him the images of the past. For he too is not alone. There is another. You will not see him, but his time too will come."

She pauses, stands up and checks on Karen. She's not moved and appears not to have heard. The woman nods her head and resumes her seat.

"Do not be afraid. I have heard. I know. I am here. I will help you. I will ensure what is coming to you is delivered. Resolution will not be by him."

She pauses again as if expecting an answer from Karen.

"I know through someone else. What they call the ghost is speaking to you...to me...*I am coming, I will*...no he is gone and so we must..."

She stops abruptly and listens for a few minutes. There's no sound other than Karen's deep breathing. She gets up.

"Now I must..."

She breaks off again as the room suddenly gets darker. The lights quickly dim and are gone. The bed and Karen's form are indistinct, but can still be made out. Yet there's no illumination from outside the room even though the corridor lights are still bright. Neither is there any light entering from the window. It's as if the room is encased by an invisible shroud, letting nothing in...nothing out!

Then the silence is breached. A dull thud...someone knocking...no, it's too deep. Not a knuckle on a door, more like a spade or a pickaxe thudding into stone...or the earth. It gets louder...closer. More thuds as if two people are working together, deep, hollow sounds, muffled through the ground, but louder, louder. It stops.

The silence is just as unnerving, but doesn't last. The thudding begins again, but faster and faster until merging into one continuous drone and louder, louder. Then it stops again, but only for a split second.

Then an ear splitting bang that simultaneously expands around the room and sucks everything within it.

# 4

## POLICE INACTION CONTINUES

*We are now into the third week of* Predator *on the train crisis. One young woman has been hospitalised as a result of her injuries. After committing his foul attack on an innocent woman this dangerous man was allowed to escape. The whole city is in terrorised ferment. Despite the numerous sightings and descriptions the police have made no progress in tracking down and apprehending him. Additional officers have been put on the trains, providing some reassurance to female passengers, but this is closing the stable door after the horse has bolted. Police enquiries are 'ongoing.' A better description would be 'Continuing Inaction.' They are going nowhere. Why are they not following up the vast information at their disposal? When we say 'Is any woman safe?' are those leading the enquiries listening?*

No longer roused to fury by Arlene Bates and her scurrilous articles, Jenner puts down his copy of the *Evening Courier* with a deep sigh of resignation. There remains an inner resentment, not so much on the reporter herself, but on the effects of her 'campaign' on others, especially his superiors. Yet even this pressure is relatively small compared to what he puts on himself. She may be right. He dismissed the sightings of the 'predator' as the trivial

60

fantasies of over imaginative women. Then Karen Renshaw was attacked, proving he'd been considerably *under* imaginative. The words of Assistant Chief Constable Davies reverberate.

*'You of all people know how seemingly innocuous events can be connected to serious crimes.'*

Words he was only too keen to dismiss now make him shudder. He was reminded how the *inexplicable developments* of his previous *peculiar* cases required his *individual approach*. When he said he didn't take notice of newspapers, Emmins had said *'it's time you did.'* Now he does.

He pulls out a previous copy of the *Evening Courier* and Arlene's 'special report' on wartime Nottingham. He brushed over it at the time, not being 'news' at all, more overly dramatic imagining. Now he's not so sure. For the article was triggered by alleged comments by some of the witnesses to the 'predator.'

*'There has been much speculation the threat from this sinister man...is drawn not from the present, but from the past...his unusual clothes and dated demeanour...'*

*Not from the present, but from the past* is especially apposite, like a voice bringing experiences of past investigations, adventures some might say for they were certainly more like quests. Yet however unorthodox, however inexplicable, those investigations were successful. Criminal activity was curtailed, villains brought to book. What more might an honest policeman want? Yet he hates being reminded of those *peculiar* cases, never entirely comfortable with their remembrances. Emmins delights in revisiting Jenner's times in the Met as if his work there has a distinctly unsavoury resonance. 'This isn't like the Met' is one of his favourite phrases though to Jenner advantages and disadvantages flow both ways.

His mood changes. Hitting the bottom of confidence leaves only the way up and he'll not be beaten. He goes through Arlene's article again. His anger hasn't entirely gone away. Something not quite right still nags him. Not just the article, something is not quite right about her. It pains him, but she'll have to be seen again. Not just an irritating journalist, she's part of the case itself.

He doesn't have to wait long. In the afternoon, seemingly bent on direct confrontation, Arlene arrives at the station, asking to see him without even the courtesy of a telephone call. Perhaps he's less likely to avoid her if she's already on the premises. He could send her packing. He's a busy man after all, but he *wants* to see her and is ready. Jennifer is out. This time he'll see her alone. Perhaps better. Choice language on either side is best not witnessed.

Arlene asks for an 'update' on the investigation as if her latest article has not been written.

"We are assiduously analysing our *vast information*," he says sarcastically.

"So no further or immediate progress?" she says, blandly ignoring the swipe from her article and refusing to bite.

He continues in the same vein.

"We are *listening*."

She stares quizzically.

Then, realises he's playing with the article, says "I was only pointing out…"

"Our *inaction* in not finding the *bolted horse?*"

"Amongst other things. I'd be only too pleased to publicise something people in the city could feel progress was being made."

"Such as?"

"A description of the man who attacked Karen Renshaw, an appeal to the public for help in finding him. Somebody must know something."

"I've no doubt *somebody* does, but the fact we've not received any definite information means they're either unwilling or unable to assist us. With only vague and contradictory statements from the *numerous descriptions* to which you refer it's difficult to make an appeal on the lines you mention."

"Even so…"

"Even so, Miss Bates, you and your newspaper with the constant castigation of the police are doing nothing to assist our investigation. By continually whipping up panic you're seriously undermining it."

Jenner tries to remain calm, but the anger in his voice is clear and he glares at her sullenly, dismissing her with a curt, "I've nothing more to say."

"But *I* have," she says, "Just before she was attacked on the train Karen Renshaw rang the paper and asked for me. I was out at the time so…"

"Information relating to her should have been divulged to us before now."

"Karen left her name and number and asked me to contact her mobile. I got no answer because by then she'd been attacked. As soon as possible I will interview Karen. It will form the basis of an article about her dreadful experience."

He replies stiffly.

"Assuming you're able to do so, which I doubt, I'll take that as a threat."

"Why should you feel threatened? Once recovered she'll be free to speak to whomsoever she pleases. I'm sure she'll be very keen to speak to me first."

"The first person to speak to her will be me."

"I didn't mean to…"

"Undermine my investigation?"

"Of course not."

"Were you acquainted with Karen before the attack?"

"I don't see the relevance…"

"Answer the question!"

"I didn't know her and for obvious reasons don't know her now."

He picks up the previous edition of the paper.

"You say *the threat...is drawn not from the present, but from the past*. What did you mean by that?"

"I said there was *much speculation*."

"If you're in possession of important information it's your duty to inform us."

"As I said, I was reporting on speculation."

"I do not deal in speculation."

"Neither do I...normally...but without official hard information..."

"People will take this as emanating from our enquiries."

"It's reasonable when passengers report seeing a ghost for them to assume it has its roots in something in the past."

"*Unusual clothes and dated demeanour*. Where did you get that from?"

"I did say it was a bizarre explanation."

"Those aren't the words of women on the train."

"They are a summation of what they saw."

"What's your connection to Karen Renshaw? What about her past is so important? If this information is relevant to my enquiry..."

Arlene thumps the table angrily.

"I don't know what you're talking about!"

"You're aware that withholding information from the police is an offence?"

"I'm not withholding information relevant to your investigation."

"Why was Karen trying to contact you?"

"Are we having a normal conversation or am I being interrogated?"

"Don't be ridiculous. Answer the question."

"I don't know."

"You must have some idea."

"You want me to speculate?"

"You obviously regard her attempt to speak to you as important, so I'm asking you to conjecture a possible explanation."

She gets up and turns to the door. She's about to go out, but then stops.

"She would have read my piece about the sightings of the ghost on the train. Perhaps she expected something to happen, a fear, an inkling that arose out of the ghost. There's something about her life which is crucial to this whole business."

"Which she was going to share with you in particular?"

"Only because she knew of me through the newspaper and – unlike others – might expect a sympathetic ear to what she had to say."

He shakes his head.

"All right, then," she says, "What do you think she was going to tell me?"

"If I knew that, I'd hardly be asking you."

## 18<sup>th</sup> April

Arlene's contact at the hospital hasn't been in touch for several days. Knowing it may be difficult Arlene's avoided calling during working hours, but each time only gets the voicemail message. Tanya is a domestic supervisor. She frequently moves around the hospital from ward to ward. She's a useful source, but perhaps has little to report. Maybe it's getting too difficult. She may be distrusted or has just lost interest. Surreptitious messages to the press have an exciting appeal, but the novelty can wear off and then…

…the telephone rings. It's the phone call she's been awaiting…Tanya.

"I've been trying to get you. Is there a problem with…?"

"Something you ought to know. It may be nothing, it may be important."

"Karen Renshaw has woken up?"

"Not that I know of."

"You've got to the ward where she is?"

"I was there this morning."

"No change then?"

"I was talking to a couple of the nurses. There's a rumour, only a rumour, mind. You'll have to take it as it is. Two nights ago a woman came onto the ward. She may have gone into Karen's room."

"But aren't the police guarding her?"

"There was a short time when the nurses noticed the policeman wasn't there."

"So they saw the woman go into Karen's room?"

"Not exactly. Around the same time a woman was seen rushing along the corridor away from the ward. No one knows who she was. When the policeman came back they asked him if he was expecting a policewoman coming into the ward. He said not. Then they noticed the door to Karen's room was open. Both the nurses and the policeman were adamant it had been closed. They checked on Karen and she was all right."

"Has anything been done?"

"Apparently not. One of the nurses or the policeman might have left the door open."

"And the woman may have been completely unconnected with the ward."

"I suppose so. You don't seem surprised."

"I've come to expect almost anything...it doesn't matter. Can you find out more?"

"I'll make sure I regularly visit the ward."

"Keep your ears to the ground. Let me know if you hear anymore."

"About the woman?"

Arlene hesitates.

"No, not specifically about her. Anything else, especially if Karen wakes up."

Jennifer is on her way to the hospital. All day she's had a feeling she should be there. There's no pressing need.

If Karen wakes up the constable will advise her immediately, but she can't shake off the sense she has to be near Karen. The closer she gets to the hospital the stronger it is until by the time she pulls into the car park it's overwhelming. She sits in the car, eyes closed, hoping it will soon subside, but it grows stronger, while fleeting visions jumble confusingly.

She's on a train. There are others. It's crowded. Most of the passengers are women. At first it's quiet. No one is speaking. It makes the sound of the train wheels more distinct. Then it's very noisy, rumbling, clattering and banging, the carriage swaying slightly. They must be passing over points. The train slows. But now it's changed again, an old carriage with a corridor. Then another sound, higher, piercing, someone is screaming!

It fades and she's on a building site. There is scaffolding and unfinished walls. It must be the end of the working day for no one else is around. She's walking along the side of the works past a cement mixer, stacks of bricks and unopened bags of cement. Then she hears a heavy, loud thud from somewhere inside. She looks across, sees nothing, then the image is gone.

Now it's very noisy, chatter and laughing all around. It's very hazy, only blurred shapes, moving across and beside her. It gradually clears and the shapes sharpen. She can hear the chinking of glasses, there's a table…no a bar and a man is pulling pints. It's a pub! She's in the midst of the activity, but no one notices her. She's merely a spectator, invisible to them all. A man brushes past her. She turns to face him. He's gone. No one else is around. The noise is gone. There are only the blank, brown walls of the pub, but they are fading.

She opens her eyes. She's still in the car. People are wandering across the car park. There's no building work going on, she's at least two miles from the railway station and no pub for a quarter mile. Maybe she nodded off and was dreaming or at least day dreaming, though how could a train, a pub, a building site be on her mind? Too vivid for a reverie, too short for a real dream.

She gets out the car and walks to the entrance. It'll pass. But while the visions are gone the need to get to Karen is still with her. She walks faster. She has to get to the ward. She hurries past the nurses. There's only the constable.

"Everything all right?" she says.

"Yes, sarge."

His voice is muted and he has a sheepish expression. She goes to the door.

"You're not supposed to go in," he says, "The doctor said…"

She looks at him sternly.

"Something is bothering you."

He says nothing, but is still uncomfortable.

"I'm going in," she says, "I'll be very careful. You'll say nothing and when I come out you'll tell me what's wrong."

Her supposition is correct. He doesn't argue.

Despite his bland assurance, after her experience in the car and the continuing draw to be here, she half expects some dramatic alteration in Karen's condition. She's still unconscious, but seems peaceful. Jennifer glances at the various instruments. There's nothing untoward, no warning lights or bleeps. She sits beside the bed and watches Karen's immobile form for a few moments, listening to her deep, regular breathing.

Then it begins. As she stares at the pallid face it's as if she sees beyond the closed eyes and the exhaustion of fraught activity, into her troubled mind. Someone is running. Who is it? She closes her eyes as she did in the car. She sees a building again, not the construction work, a solid structure, but it's burning and it's her that's running! She runs and runs, faster, faster. She has to get away!

She opens her eyes. There's no noise, no heat, no fire…the room is unchanged. Karen lies motionless. Jennifer is seized by a sudden panic. All is not…cannot be well. She gets up and leans over, at first not hearing the tell tale breathing. Then her hearing adjusts. Karen *is* breathing. She turns and staggers to the door, unnerved and confused. Then her policewoman's grit and even temper returns. The constable is outside the door, gesticulating anxiously. She opens the door, steps out, glances down the corridor, then closes it quietly.

"I saw the doctor," he says, nodding towards the nurses' station, "He's gone now, but if he sees you…"

She knows his nervousness is more than the prospect of a reprimand from the doctor.

"What's happened?"

"The doctor, he…"

"Not the doctor. What have you been so anxious about?"

His face has turned ashen.

"Whatever it is cannot be the end of the world," she says.

"Not the world, but it could be the end of me."

"What is it?"

"It was my fault. It was time for my break. Constable Edwards was long overdue."

He tells of the mysterious woman seen near the ward.

"One of the nurses thought she saw her leaving the room."

"*Thought* she saw?"

"She wasn't sure."

"But Karen was unharmed?"

"They checked everything. It was all right and has been since. I've been extra vigilant. No one has been near except the staff."

"Let's hope you'll continue to be especially vigilant," she says sternly, "Why didn't you report this immediately?"

He hesitates and scrapes his boot along the floor. She reads his mind.

"Chief Inspector Jenner will have to be told."

"That's what I was afraid of."

"I know you didn't see her, but did you get a description of the woman?"

"Yes, from one of the nurses," he says, then explains what was seen.

Jennifer listens carefully, then says, "A good job there was someone around here with decent observational skills."

"It won't happen again."

"It better not. I want to know immediately if she comes back. That means if she's seen without twenty miles of here."

As Jennifer returns to the car she mulls over the description of the visitor. There's something oddly familiar about the mystery woman.

## 19th April

Arlene is more than irritated with Jenner's attitude. Despite a woman being seriously assaulted he's giving little priority to the only solid information he has, casually dismissing the witnesses on the train without a rigorous analysis of what they saw and heard. It's not just those that were close to the attack on Karen, but the many more who reported sightings of the 'ghost' over the previous two weeks. If they were all thoroughly interviewed a detailed picture could be build up to launch a major hunt for the attacker.

She fiddles with another censorious article, exhorting the police and particularly the 'senior investigating officer' to take up the mantle the *Courier* 'has so long been demanding.' She abandons it after a few paragraphs. It's too long and repetitive. Readers have absorbed much of this before. The emphasis has to shift. The campaign will have to go beyond 'mere speculation,' something substantial that galvanises the public, stimulating agitation to force the police to act.

She writes a new opening paragraph. It needs an arresting headline, a phrase that captures getting the evidence, then acting on it!

*'Investigate to Hunt.'*

She writes a further paragraph, then stops again. Campaigning is not enough. There's work to be done. 'Hard core' information has to put Jenner under pressure. She goes over her material, examining the many statements. She'll see them all again, this time conducting in depth interviews.

## 20<sup>th</sup> April

With other lines of enquiry yielding little of value, Jenner concentrates on Karen's background. Jennifer is looking at her work and movements immediately prior to the attack. She's already seen the family, but he needs a more substantial picture. He'll begin with her father.

The Renshaws live in a suburban detached house, typically built just before or after the Second World War. The front garden tidy, the house in good repair, though with no outstanding features, which might well indicate the inhabitants. Keith is like his house and his garden, neat, respectable, mundane, a man without fervour or fury. But first impressions can be deceptive.

Keith answers the door. He's in his mid fifties, dressed casually with plain, but good quality trousers and jacket. He's unsurprised to be visited by a detective chief inspector. Maybe the rank impresses him as a mirror to his own. To be interviewed by a mere constable or even a sergeant would not be appropriate. The house is silent. Mrs. Renshaw or anyone else is out. Jenner is ushered into a spacious rear lounge with French doors leading to the garden, a twin to the one at the front, orderly and unimaginative. Yet the room is not as Jenner expected. Newspapers and magazines are scattered across the furniture, which Keith quickly scoops up and dumps on a table, which is just as untidy. Within his own confine Keith is unconcerned by appearances. Perhaps few outsiders venture into his realm and for whom he has no interest in pandering to conformity.

"You are here about Karen?" he says abruptly.

"Purely routine," Jenner says.

"I was here all night," he says aggressively.

"Sergeant Heathcott has already confirmed your movements, Mr. Renshaw," Jenner says, trying to put him at his ease, "I'm not here to substantiate what we already know. Unfortunately your daughter is still in a coma. We are unable to talk to her."

"She will recover?"

"I hope so...I believe so. In the meantime it would help us to get a sense of her background. She lives alone, I understand?"

"She has her own place. She's a professional woman and has done well."

"I'm sure she has. Do you see her often?"

"Every week. She's a very dutiful daughter."

"Did she have any enemies?"

"Only the same as we all have."

"Meaning?"

"People envious of her success. Real proficiency in any walk of life always appears easy to the incompetent. Jealousy is a terrible affliction, Mr. Jenner. Then there are the weak who always prey on the strong."

"Indeed? How might that affect your daughter?"

"It affects anyone who makes a success of their life, whether high or low, born into wealth or poverty. Those spending their lives talking rather than doing are always keen to blame those that make the most of what they have without relying on others."

Keith's voice, normally high pitched gradually reaches a crescendo. Though he speaks in general terms Jenner detects an inner struggle, a determination to bring down some object or adversary, which he has transferred on to the plight of his daughter. Yet another person pursuing a 'campaign.'

"Anyone in particular who might wish to harm your daughter?"

At first silent, Keith shakes his head and turns his hands over palm up in resignation before he speaks.

"No one immediately comes to mind."

Jenner looks at the clutter on the table. There are box files, old newspaper cuttings and notebooks.

"You've been undertaking some research?" he says.

Keith glances towards the table, gets up and tidies the clutter.

"It's a continuing project. I've been working on it for some time."

He returns to his chair. Jenner is curious about the 'project,' but for now doesn't pursue it.

"What about relationships, anyone Karen was seeing?"

"No significant relationship" is the ambivalent reply.

"No one at the moment?"

"No one...at the moment."

"So there have been relationships in the past?"

"She's an attractive woman. It's inevitable."

"No one who might retain feelings...not reciprocated... someone who might bear a grudge?"

"Not from any romantic involvement."

Again the equivocation, the half answer, implying if the question is differently put...

"Could someone harbour a grudge from a different cause?"

Keith points to the table and rises in his chair, then sits back with a sigh.

"It's all there. Reports at the time, the law, my own researches, statements from others."

Jenner waits. There's more to come.

"You ask if anyone might wish Karen harm. I know of no one who would directly wish her harm."

Another pause, another implied answer.

"Not *directly*?" Jenner says, "but indirectly?"

"You've not asked me what I've been working on."

"I assume you'll tell me if it's important and relevant to my enquiries."

"Karen bears her grandfather's name, Renshaw. To someone, that might associate her with something of which they would rather not be reminded."

"Someone?"

"I cannot give you a particular name."

"Yet this is someone who...*indirectly*...would be prepared to kill her?" Jenner says bluntly.

"A killing is what it is all about, Mr Jenner."

"A criminal matter?"

"It should be."

"You will have to be more specific."

Keith gets up, picks up some files and hands one to Jenner.

"Karen's grandfather was killed on a building site in 1965. Here are the press reports of the time and the coroner's judgement."

"Accidental death," Jenner mutters.

"It was no accident."

Jenner studies the press cuttings. It was a major story in the local press for about a week, then as so often happens with newspapers it faded away as they moved on to more immediate or interesting matters. There's a voluminous file of correspondence over many years, conducted by Keith with almost everyone with an interest or influence. Then there are his notes on the law.

"It was a wholly unnecessary so called accident," Keith says bitterly.

"All accidents usually are. Otherwise they wouldn't be accidents."

It's an insensitive if accurate comment to which Keith bridles.

"Accidents that are caused by blatant negligence are not true accidents."

"What were the circumstances of your father's accident?"

"He was working some thirty feet above the ground. The safety arrangements on the scaffolding were ineffective. He slipped and fell to the ground. He was killed instantly."

"He slipped, so…"

"It would be more accurate to say he miss-stepped. The scaffolding had not been properly secured to the already constructed wall and the boards were loose. If the proper procedures had been adhered to at worst he would have grazed his ankle, not fallen thirty feet to his death. The builder was at fault for poor safety provision, but was never prosecuted."

Jenner skims through the correspondence file.

"I see you've raised the matter…exhaustively…with the coroner, many newspapers, the BBC, ITV, the Health and Safety Executive, your MP, the building employers organisation, the Business Department, the prime minister…"

"You name them, I've raised it with them."

"Has your agitation had any success?"

"If you count success in the number of sympathetically useless letters and promises to 'look into the matter,' then I've been immensely successful. It's all in there."

"Yes, very interesting," Jenner says.

For appearances sake he spends a few moments scanning the files before handing them back.

"As a policeman, this should all be of great interest to you," Keith says, flinging the files back onto the table.

"It's really a civil matter," Jenner says pointedly.

"Not if he breached health and safety legislation."

But Jenner is not going to get into a debate about the priorities for police investigations.

"In which case it would be a matter for the Health and Safety Executive."

Keith ignores the pedantry.

"You'll see the builder hit back in some of the newspapers."

"So you feel the builder or his relatives are still smarting about your campaign?"

"It's possible. George Dugger made a lot noise at the time. He's a vindictive man. My only consolation is that he too went before his time though it wasn't an accident in his case."

Jenner looks quizzically.

"Heart attack," Keith says, "too fond of the sauce."

"But his dependants?"

"It's possible. If they can't get at me…They tried in the press and even stirred up local politicians and other people of influence, trying to put me down even after it was obvious I was getting nowhere. But that was years ago. You'll see I've had more success lately…"

Keith pulls a more recent newspaper cutting from his file and hands it to Jenner.

"One of the Sunday papers have been doing a piece on construction safety. They picked up my father's case and got in touch. George Dugger will be turning in his grave…"

"He has relatives?"

"Oh yes, his son Henry and a grandson, Malcolm, then there's his daughter Margaret and her children."

"They are still in the business?"

"They are."

"So you believe, with this more recent publicity they'll want to make trouble?"

"If they can't get at me…they failed for so long and now…they might well go for Karen."

"I take it she has no connection with the building trade?"

"No. John Renshaw, my father, was still a relatively young man, only about my age."

Jenner tries to change the subject, but Keith holds his ground. If he can't succeed in his campaign, he can at least explain every intricate detail of it to a captive policeman. After finally exhausting this to a wearied Jenner he talks more generally though soon latches on to his favourite subject by talking about his father.

"He was originally from Nottingham, but went abroad after the war. I think it was Brazil."

This part of John Renshaw's life is not dwelt with at any length and Jenner remains unclear what exactly he was doing in Brazil. It makes Renshaw senior all the more interesting, especially with Keith's next remark.

"When he returned he was not well off."

Jenner's curiosity is aroused. He takes 'not well off' to mean John Renshaw was destitute. What happened in Brazil? Was he involved in some precarious business venture that failed or something nefarious perhaps?

Keith skims over his father's first years on his return to England. He met Keith's mother and 'drifted into the building trade.' Jenner suspects Keith applies a liberal meaning to 'trade' and doubts if John Renshaw had ever served an apprenticeship in any skilled building occupation. More likely he needed to find any job and could only get employment as an unskilled labourer. Jenner is tempted to probe his precise duties at the time of the 'accident.' He thinks better of it. He doesn't want to encourage further details of Keith's campaign, but he'd like to interrupt the monologue. Eventually there's a lull and Jenner steers the discussion back to his real interest. Fortunately Keith is happy to talk about Karen.

He's very proud, extols her achievements, fulsome and congratulatory, but adding little to existing information. Jenner listens patiently and is finally able to prod Keith onto more specific matters.

"She works for a firm called Alpha Consulting. They're involved in all sorts of advisory services and the like. Most of it's beyond me. Karen is a marketing consultant. You know, helping people to sell things to other people, things they don't need."

He laughs. It's the first time Keith's taut mood has relaxed.

"No seriously, she's very good at her work."

"Has she been long with the firm?"

"Five years. She's highly regarded."

"I understand she was returning from a meeting in London?"

"She's often in London. She gets around a great deal, meets a lot of people, though she's not really a people person."

"Isn't that unusual for someone who is advising people?"

"Oh, I don't mean in her work. She's very professional. Easy with clients, but that's…what would you say…a concentrated time. You have a job to do, they understand that and respect her, but…"

"Outside of the job?"

"Like I said, not a people person, quite reserved really 'till you get to know her."

"Is that what you meant about relationships?"

Keith has to consider this.

"I suppose so. But she was very comfortable in her job."


## 21st April

*'At last a picture is emerging of the predator and the evening train 'ghost.' Following intensive interviews with the women who have seen the man it is possible to put together a description.'*

Jenner puts down Arlene's latest article. 'Put together' is the operative phrase. She's allegedly interviewed dozens of 'reliable witnesses' or 'trustworthy observers' to the strange happenings on the train over the last weeks, contriving a 'generic description' of the 'foul marauder' on such flimsy information. Unfortunately her 'forensic analysis' doesn't stand up to critical assessment. Dissipated across several paragraphs the descriptions contain contradictory elements. Arlene makes no comment on such flaws. She has a greater project to promote rather than such humdrum matters, which a detective cannot ignore.

But a few consistent traits emerge from her interviews. The man is 'quite young,' of respectable if dull appearance, decently dressed, but his clothes seem 'old fashioned,' slightly less than average height though from experience 'average' tends to be a moveable feast. He has bright eyes - staring or shifty depending on taste - and likewise a grin which is either unsettling or disarming. Mr. Ordinary, he could fit the inclination, delight or distaste of virtually every woman in the city, which is precisely the point. He's what any woman might want or fears to see rather than what she actually sees.

Arlene makes much of the different classes and occupations of the women, reinforcing her contention he's a threat to them all, irrespective of age or background. Convinced the assault was neither random nor the first of a sequence of unprovoked and seemingly motiveless attacks, Jenner rejects this. This is no serial killer. This is all about Karen. Other women, even those who might look like her are not at risk.

This is beyond Arlene's sphere of interest. Though the article doesn't always make her position clear she's more interested in the 'ghost' than the 'predator' – assuming they are not one and the same. So, she brushes over the incongruous statements and unbelievable attempts to fit the inconsistent facts to her preconceived and dubious notion. Everything builds up to her final sentences which form her 'extensive research' alluding to a 'common thread of experience' linking all the women. She doesn't mention what it is, but at this stage Jenner is unconcerned with journalistic deficiencies. The fact she's mentioned it at all is unnerving.

What does Arlene know?

Jennifer goes to see Karen's employer. Alpha Consulting is located in a smart new building close to the canal area. She first sees her boss, Ralph Tuckwell, the Marketing Team Leader. He's around forty, tall with a wide moustache, much in the style of a Mexican bandit and sporting a wide gaudy tie, rather 1960s psychedelic and oddly out of place with his trendy shirt and smart, casual trousers. She half expects to see a sombrero perched on his cabinet. He asks about Karen and learning there's 'no change' moves with relief into his normal management speak.

"We have an immediate resource deficiency in her team, but with some careful reallocation of priorities I believe we can continue to deliver our objectives within the scheduled timeframe."

He explains in unnecessary and confusing detail Karen's 'prime duties,' before finally emerging from the verbose fog to make clear she's a key worker and well regarded.

"Karen is missed already. Her principal relationships are of course with our clients. In that sphere she enjoys an outstanding reputation. She has the twin abilities of conveying to clients the fundamentals of required changes to their strategies, especially where they have unfortunately been following familiar, but dare I say it, outdated practices, yet communicating these sometimes delicate messages with clarity and sensitivity."

"So, no dissatisfied clients, no one who complained of the service they were getting? From what you say, I assume it's sometimes necessary to be candid. She's not overly blunt, for example, to which some, perhaps unjustifiably, might take offence?"

"Definitely not."

"Does she get on well with her colleagues?"

"She enjoys excellent relations with all her colleagues."

"So you know of no one who might wish to harm her?"

"Definitely not. This terrible thing has rocked the organisation to its foundations. I can only assume Karen has been the unfortunate victim of some deranged nutter. You must find him."

"We will do our best."

Ralph Tuckwell might well be describing a saint. Jennifer puts it down to the optimistic babble, irrespective of reality that he constantly projects from the synthetic bubble he has to inhabit. Jennifer talks to Karen's other, closer colleagues. Most she sees reinforce, albeit less gushingly, Tuckwell's view. The shock of the attack on Karen has permeated the office and they may be unwilling to criticise her while she lies in a coma at the hospital. No one can think of potential enemies who might wish to harm her. Only one man, James deviates slightly from the general consensus.

"She's a good woman, always willing to help with advice, especially the juniors, but on occasions she could be sharp, even aggressive."

"She's aggressive with you?"

"Not with me, but I've noticed she has been with others."

He's reluctant to mention names, but firm in his opinion, though vague about particular incidents.

"Is she always like this?"

"Not all the time. Maybe only when she's under pressure."

"What sort of pressure?"

"You know, usual work pressures."

"Only work pressures. What about outside work, personal matters?"

"I couldn't say. I don't know about her private life."

"This aggression, is this just your opinion or a more general view?"

"I'm sure I'm not the only one who's noticed."

"You make it sound as though it's a recent thing."

"It is."

"Why is that?"

He shrugs.

"Could she have made enemies recently, perhaps with clients?"

"I can only comment on the office."

It's not very enlightening and despite what he says maybe James has been on the receiving end of a sharp tongue and harbours a grudge.

"Anyone else I should speak to?" she says.

"You could try Annette, her secretary."

The secretary is a mature woman, who's been with the firm for ten years, working directly with Karen for five years, the whole of her time as a marketing consultant. Like the others she speaks highly of her abilities.

"She's very incisive and imaginative, skills greatly valued by clients. Her reports are always succinct, precise and constructive. It's a pleasure to work for her."

"You must know her very well."

"I believe so."

"I'm trying to get an all round view of her to help with our enquiries."

"As I said, her work…"

"It's not just about her work."

"She was coming from an important meeting in London. There was…is…no one in her professional relations that would have any reason to do this dreadful thing."

Annette is very loyal. It won't be easy to prise out broader, but Jennifer persists.

"I've heard that though she was popular she could be truculent?"

"I wouldn't describe it like that."

"How would you describe it?"

Annette says nothing, but is obviously thinking. Jennifer suspects she may launch into another discourse on her work, the glowing testimonials, her indispensable position in the firm, but…

"She could sometimes be rather short with people, but it was only because she's so conscientious and cannot accept less than the highest standards."

"Very commendable, but has this resulted in her making enemies?"

"Not enemies as such because until recently she was extremely likeable, courteous and patient."

"But that has changed?"

"She has many contacts, knows many people. No one can please everybody all the time."

"But...?"

"She's been all right with me, but lately...some people in the office... there've been altercations with a few."

Even stronger than from James and unlike the general office line.

"You've been very frank about Karen," Jennifer says, "You are sure?"

"I have great respect for her, but I can only say what I see."

"So, is there anyone who might harm her?"

Annette has been calm, precise, concentrated, but suddenly becomes very agitated.

"Oh you must find him!"

"That's why I need to know anything about Karen that could possibly give us a lead."

"There is no one I know for certain who would harm Karen."

"Anyone for whom you are *uncertain?*"

"I don't wish to indulge in speculation."

"No one in the office?"

"Certainly not. However miffed they might feel, there's no one here who would even contemplate such a dreadful thing."

"Away from work, personal relationships?"

Annette stiffens.

"I know nothing of that nature and in any case it would be none of my business."

"On which you cannot even *speculate*?"

"No."

"Well, you have been most helpful. If…"

Jennifer gets up to leave.

"There's one thing. It's just a thought. It might not be anything."

Annette stops. Jennifer waits. Annette stares at her absently. Jennifer gets to the door and Annette speaks.

"I'm surprised the *Courier* hasn't picked it up. They seem to be mentioning everything else with little foundation. I don't believe any problems Karen may be having with her colleagues has anything to do with anyone here. That said, she was under pressure of some kind. I'm not sure why, but the way she's been in the office is the result not the cause of it."

Annette scribbles on a paper and hands it to Jennifer.

"It may be of use to you. These are all the companies and specific individuals Karen has been working with in the last year."

"Is there anyone with whom she has had difficulties?"

"I'm not suggesting anything. It's only a list. It's all I can give you."

"And the *Courier* has not…?"

"Karen's father has been engaged in a long standing… I can only describe it as a crusade."

She explains about John Renshaw's accident in 1965 and Keith's attempt to expose the builder, George Dugger as responsible.

"Mr. Renshaw has managed to get his views aired recently in the newspaper, yet they haven't made any connection with the attack on Karen."

## 22nd April

Annette was clearly irritated by the *Courier* articles, which in her view missed the point about the attack on Karen.

Jennifer goes to see the Duggers, but interestingly none are at home. She follows up on some other names on Annette's list, but nothing significant emerges. The firms in London and elsewhere are delegated to other officers.

Today she returns to the hospital. Her peculiar experience with Karen weighs heavily on her mind. If her condition has not improved she might be able to sit with her again. Something might turn up. The same constable is on duty. It reminds her she's not yet had the opportunity to mention the mystery woman to Jenner. It could be a serious matter, but whoever she is, Jennifer is sure she poses no threat to Karen. If she can be found she might even be of help.

The constable remains uneasy.

"Will Chief Inspector Jenner be in today?" he asks anxiously.

"He might," Jennifer says, "How about Karen?"

"No change, but the doctor says she's stable. He's sure she'll come round…eventually."

"I'll go in."

She expects him to object, reiterating the ruling that only medical and nursing staff should enter the room, but he's obviously more fearful of Jenner than them.

It's as if she was last here only a minute ago. Karen still motionless except for her soft breathing. She reminds Jennifer of those effigies over tombs in churches. They seem to have been asleep for hundreds of years. Could Karen be the same in reverse, not really sleeping, but…

Jennifer sits beside her, staring for a few moments into the closed eyes. Then she closes her own. Perhaps she can make contact again, absorb another vision, a new message that might break the logjam of their enquiries, something pointing to her attacker. Nothing comes. No image, no sound except Karen's breathing, even her own which now seems much louder. Concentrating on your own breathing may be good for meditation, but it's an impediment for receiving transmissions from others. There'll be no expansion of her earlier 'contact' today. She opens her eyes, takes a long lingering look at Karen, then leaves.

The constable is talking to the ward sister. He notices Jennifer, but the ward sister does not. Jennifer wanders in the opposite direction. If the ward sister sees her she'll want to know where she's been. An embarrassment to her, but even more for the constable and she doesn't want to increase his anxiety. Jenner could arrive at any moment. She looks into the 'visitors' room.' It's empty. She goes in and sits down. She'll wait until the sister moves off or the constable comes to say it's clear. This is ridiculous. She feels like an unapproved interloper.

She doesn't have long to wait. Jenner arrives. He skirts past the constable and the ward sister, wanders along the corridor and seeing Jennifer enters the visitor's room. He asks about Karen, then erupts into another furious condemnation of Arlene's latest article. He's especially critical of her reference to the 'common thread' that 'all the witnesses have mentioned.'

"Does she go into detail?" Jennifer asks.

"No. It could be just conjecture. This Bates woman is pretty good at that. On the other hand…what does she know? Probably saving up the details for her next scurrilous piece. Hardly likely to lessen the panic she's already stoked up."

Jennifer is tempted to say Arlene, although sensationalising is only 'doing her job,' but thinks better of it. Instead she mentions her visit to Alpha Consulting and particularly her conversation with Annette. They exchange information on their respective enquiries especially about the 'accident' and how both Annette and Keith Renshaw have made the same connection with the attack on Karen.

"Seems a pretty tenuous connection, may amount to nothing," he says, "but we'll have to follow up on the Duggers."

"There's another thing," she says, "I haven't had a chance to mention it before…"

...Jenner explodes when he hears about the 'mystery woman.'

"Where was that damned constable?"

"...I think I know who she is..." Jennifer begins, then notices the constable is not at his post, leaving Karen's room unguarded.

"Stay here," Jenner calls, then he's out of the door, striding down the corridor in search of the constable.

"If he's lucky he'll be directing the traffic," he thunders.

Jennifer goes into the room. Karen is safe. Outside she can hear Jenner shouting.

"Where have you been? How long have you been away?"

The constable is panting heavily.

"One of the nurses saw a...man. She was...suspicious..."

The constable points to the entrance.

"Here, on the ward?" Jenner barks.

"Outside the ward."

"Was nothing done? Where were you, sloping off again?"

"I was here. Sergeant Heathcott was along the corridor. She went into Karen Renshaw's room. I was talking to the ward sister. Then one of the nurses came running over and called out. It was him...the same man as before. I ran outside. He was at the far end of the main corridor. I went after him, but it was busy with visitors and trolleys and..."

"You lost him?"

"Yes."

# 5

THE 'mystery woman' has not been seen again at the hospital, but she's not gone away. She's still in Nottingham. She arrived by train from her base in Gloucestershire a week ago. It was not a comfortable journey. The closer she got to Nottingham the pull grew stronger and so too the foreboding, but it was only when she arrived that its source became clearer.

She's always had the gift. When she was a child her mother said it was 'being aware of presences.' As a teenager and a young woman her powers of prescience continued to grow. Now in her early fifties she has the fine tuned skills and experience of what she calls a 'time link consultant.' It's served her well over the years, gaining her a reputation for thoroughness, accuracy and insight. But she's not here to see a particular client or follow up the many local enquiries. Her visit is less specific, but no less directed for she's drawn by a strong sense of the past, which she's been unable to shake off.

She's used to coping with strong, but vague or confused sensations. They can emerge during consultations. She becomes suddenly aware of something beyond what's said, a significant undercurrent of which the client is totally unaware, but crucial to the advice she must give. It may come after the consultation, while she mulls over what's been discussed. If it's benign she can offer reassurance and hope, but if disturbing it has to be handled with delicacy and tact. Then there are times like this. A strong feeling unconnected with anyone, the only sure foundation the need to get to a city over a hundred miles away

She knows Nottingham well and has been here many times. She has friends and acquaintances in the city. She's heard of the disturbances on the trains and the attack on the young woman. What she doesn't know, she soon picks up from the recent *Courier* reports, the phone-ins on the local radio and conversations with almost anyone she meets. She finds the articles by Arlene Bates particularly interesting especially the tantalisingly enigmatic references to a possible link to the past. She suspects Arlene has been stoking up and exaggerating the story, but even allowing for journalistic hyperbole it chimes well with her own feelings and confirms the connection with recent events. The how and why is not evident. That means getting back to the hospital.

She finds the ward and quickly gets the opportunity to approach the constable on duty. She's used to avoiding obstacles, official or otherwise and has perfected a persona of both innocence and authority. She plies this to good effect and gets in to see Karen.

The sensation of slipping through time is immediate, but quickly passes for Karen is in the present and silently cries for help. She reassures her, telling her she's not alone just as she was not alone on the train. For in her mind she is there and everything is as vivid as Karen and the others saw it.

Karen is still and silent, but in the vision she speaks again. *Where is she?* The plea is confused. Is she on the train? No, there's more. Then *'Who is this man?'* She tells Karen he is of her time, but now she sees another and he's not of her time though his time will come. She hopes Karen understands for he only speaks to the woman and Karen can only know through her. She reassures again. Then the room is plunged into darkness. There's no light from outside either through the door or the window. All she sees is the motionless form of Karen.

But she has little time to be frightened before the charged silence is shattered by a constant rhythmic thud, as if a giant thumps on the door. Now more a hammering than a thudding...a digging perhaps? Then it stops and the weighty silence returns. She can get out! But she can't leave Karen alone, entombed in this looming stillness. It lasts only a few seconds, then the awful hammering begins again, louder and faster, faster, faster! Now a deep, deafening rumble until her eardrums are assailed by a thunderous eruption bursting all around the room. Yet not from outside.

It's here! They are at its core and it's sucking them within itself. She must break free and run, run, run. Somehow she gropes her way to the door, grabs the handle, pulls it open and staggers into the corridor. She expects the awful boom to follow, but the corridor is silent and deserted and she hurries along, avoiding the staff, quickly hurrying through the main corridor and out into the car park.

From there she runs and runs until well clear of the hospital, utterly exhausted by her panic driven sprint. She catches a bus, unaware of its destination. Anywhere to get away from the source of the noise and confusion. She reaches the city centre, wanders into slab square and settles onto a vacant spot on one of the benches. For some moments she just sits, staring at the Council House, her agitation gradually subsiding. She's not alone. There are plenty of folk about, sitting like her or scurrying across the square. Her only interest in them is that they are here. She closes her eyes for the first time since she left Karen's room. It might mean the visions and worse the noise returning, but has to be faced. She sees nothing and hears only innocuous chatter, footsteps and the pigeons. She calms further, opens her eyes and retires to a suitable hostelry.

A couple of drinks and surrounded by innocent company the tensions are gone, but she's filled with fear, guilt and remorse as she remembers her time in the hospital room. Fear for Karen, still lying in a fearsome void in the midst of the terrible noise and darkness. Guilt she ran away and left her. Remorse for deserting a client alone and vulnerable. But Karen is not a client, she didn't approach her...but she did...in her coma she appealed for help! She must get back!

No, she was the catalyst. On her own Karen will not be troubled by fearsome visions or battered by terrifying noise. She will be safe. Yet safe only in this time...but what if, in her coma she relives the past? It's impossible. She can't go back...not yet... she must first think out what it means and what must be done.

Instinctively she puts a hand to her head, meaning to take off her hat. It's helps her to think. But her hat isn't there. It's a large hat. She's had it for years. It's like an old friend, always with her, something which must be kept close. Her agitation returns. Then she remembers. Thinking it would draw undue attention, she took it off when she entered the hospital and quickly stuffed it into her shoulder bag. She pulls it out. It's crumpled. Her foolish escapade has ruined it. But just like an old friend it's resilient. She lays it down and smoothes it on the seat. It reassumes some of its familiar shape. Battered old thing, it's been through many scrapes, but like its owner it's hardy. It takes only a minute to be as new or as nearly new as any aged creature can be. Now that's settled she can think again.

She ran away. How now can she approach her friends in the city? What would she say to them? That she's come half way across England because of an indefinable 'awareness' she can't explain except by dubious impressions beside a hospital bed in a room where she should never have been? She smiles to herself. They'll understand. They've heard such things before. She'll redeem herself.

Away from the immediate scene she's detached and can think more clearly. She goes over what she 'saw' and 'heard.' The darkness encloses, the noise echoes, the men appear...the *men*...not the man. Is this a false memory, did she really see *two* men? She goes through it again and again, disciplining herself to remember accurately what she saw and heard, not what she *thinks* she saw and heard. There were definitely two separate men. She told Karen one was of her time while the other was not of her time. Not of her time because he didn't speak directly to Karen, only to her. Of her time because many women have described a 'ghost.' Such things are easily dismissed by the sceptical and observations can be embroidered by overpowered imaginations, but in this they are right. The past is with the present, inextricably linked, but how and why?

A couple of young women are sitting nearby. One has the latest copy of the *Courier* and they are discussing the 'sightings' and the attack. She listens for a few minutes, then there's a pause in their conversation.

"Excuse me," she says, "I couldn't help overhearing. I've come to meet friends and have heard a little of what's been happening in Nottingham."

The young women are only too pleased to 'fill her in' on recent events and show her Arlene's latest article.

"This is very critical of the police," she says, "Do you think this is right?"

They are non committal and much more interested in the 'ghost.'

"You believe it?" she says.

"Many have seen it," one says, "There's got to be something in it."

They are sure the ghost is real and though intrigued are fearful of the implications.

"What do you think?" the other says.

"You're right to take the ghost seriously," she says, reflecting her troubled state, then lightens up, "But I don't believe he's a threat to…"

"But that girl was attacked on the train."

"Of course. I didn't mean you shouldn't be on your guard."

"Some girls are frightened to go out."

She's about to say the ghost and the attacker may not be connected, but they might not understand any more than she would be confident of explaining it. They discard the newspaper when they leave. She picks it up and reads Arlene's article in full, intrigued as much about the journalist as the story. She must find out more.

She goes to the city library and gets all the recent copies of the *Courier*. Now she's as conversant with events as the women in the pub and understands the panic in the city. Arlene's approach may be exaggerated and overly dramatised, but it's more than pure sensationalism. There's a personal interest. Her article about the war has a nuanced sensitivity, lacking in her pieces about the ghost, the attack and her criticisms of the police. This resonates with her own feelings. She goes back to the newspaper records and delves into wartime editions. At that time there were other local newspapers as well as the *Courier*. She scours them all and makes copious notes. Time moves on. It's early evening and the librarian interrupts her concentration to say the library is closing. She goes back to the same pub and gets a meal before booking into her hotel. Tomorrow there'll be work to be done.

She sleeps fitfully, continually mulling over the wartime newspaper reports. Visions of air raids, hapless citizens running to the shelters, fire appliances roaring through the streets including brigades from other areas as the city is pounded, fronts of weakened buildings disintegrating as the fires overwhelm their structures. She forces the drastic pictures from her mind and wills herself back to sleep, but they soon return and she's jolted into a dislocated wakefulness. Around four the battles of the flames sweep away any hope of sleep and she gets up.

She studies the notes she made at the library, hoping they might induce sleep, but they do the opposite and she's soon immersed in the detail reports. After an hour she lays on the bed, her back and shoulders aching from the constant leaning over to read the notes. She closes her eyes and feels drowsy, but sleep still eludes her as her mind translates her handwriting into more fearful images of smoke, fire and water. Hose pipes laid along the streets, feeding the men who fight the flames, in turn fed directly from the river as normal supplies are quickly reduced to a trickle. Did it ever run dry on one of those harrowing nights?

She gets up and returns to the notes. Better a crick neck than the traumatic visions. Is her imagination working overtime or is it more? How much of what she 'sees' is sparked by her disturbing notes, fuelled from the feverish reports of eighty years ago and fanned by more recent embellishments? It's been a crammed and demanding seventy two hours. Until today she knew little of the war years in the city, but what she's read coincides with the growing feelings she's harboured since she left home.

The inexplicable encounter in Karen's room chimed so completely with the pull that brought them together, the thought of the blackness and noise chilling her still. But if the source of that extraordinary draw was in the room it suddenly reversed and she had to escape!

She studies her notes again. One particular place resounds. The time for listening to others is past. She'll read no more. She's impelled by a force from within. Tomorrow she must go to Sharp Road.

Then she sleeps soundly until breakfast.

## 24th April

Most of Karen Renshaw's local clients have been contacted and nothing significant has emerged. They all speak highly of her abilities, praise her work and enjoy good relations There are no indications of animosity towards her. Contacts in London and elsewhere are being seen separately. Meanwhile Jennifer calls at the office of 'George Dugger and Son.'

It's in a smart new business estate, though its own window to the world is far from prepossessing. Under the main sign in bright red letters prospective customers are encouraged to 'Let Duggers Do The Digging.' The crass sign accords well with the ambience of the office. Rather than let Duggers do anything, let alone digging there's an air of irritation that anyone should invade their inner preserve. The receptionist, when she deigns to recognise a visitor, is curt and unsmilingly aloof. Assuming him to be the head of the firm, Jennifer asks to see George Dugger only to be informed 'old Mr. Dugger passed over' at least ten years ago.

"Then perhaps his son," Jennifer says.

The receptionist tells her Henry Dugger is 'out of the office,' implying no one else could possibly be of assistance. Jennifer wonders if they ever get any work with this attitude. Anyone wanting an extension built will presumably decide they would rather put up a tent in the garden.

"Then whoever is in charge?" Jennifer says.

The receptionist ponders for some time as if grappling with a particularly abstruse problem.

"There is Mr. Malcolm," she says at last, quickly adding, "but he's out on site at the moment."

"Then in his absence, is there...?"

"There's no one else of the family. There is..."

But Jennifer won't be fobbed off with a minion. It's only 'the family' she's here to see. She turns to leave and almost collides with a young man rushing in the opposite direction.

She steps back to avoid him. Rather than apologise he glowers belligerently. The receptionist is thrown into immediate confusion.

"Oh, Mr. Malcolm...you're back. I thought you were out on site."

"I was," he says gruffly, passing around her desk, "Bloody architect didn't turn up. If I'm wanted..."

"Malcolm Dugger?" Jennifer says.

"Yes, who are..."

Jennifer thrusts her warrant card at him.

"Detective Sergeant Jennifer Heathcott. I can see you are free to answer a few questions."

His eyes narrow, his mouth tightening as he reads the card.

"What about?"

"I'm investigating the assault on Karen Renshaw. You may have read about..."

"You'd better come through."

He leads the way along a short corridor and into a small office, where he stands defensively behind the desk.

"There's nothing to say. I was at home that night and so was my father,"

"This is purely routine," Jennifer says, "I have a list of firms with which Karen Renshaw had dealings and..."

"Karen Renshaw has never had anything to do with us, so we couldn't possibly have appeared on any list. I know nothing about her."

Without being asked Jennifer, settles into the chair opposite the desk.

"So, if that's all," he says, remaining standing.

"It was a most vicious attack," she says.

He says nothing, no expression of sympathy or concern.

"There's a lot of understandable anxiety in the city. Obviously we're following up any..."

"I've already told you I was at home all night."

"What time was that?"

He sits down. This isn't going to be dealt with as quickly as he would have liked.

"All evening, as I said. I got home around five thirty. My cousin Arthur Palmer and his wife came round about seven and stayed until after midnight. My father and mother also came round. We can all vouch for each other."

He stands again and glances at the door. Jennifer remains seated.

"I understand your company has had dealings with the Renshaws in the past. There was an accident…"

"I know nothing about that," he snaps.

"Before your time, but you must have heard…"

"It's ancient history. Keith Renshaw has been stirring it up again recently, but there's nothing to it. It was an accident. His father was…"

"Yes?"

"Nothing. It doesn't matter."

"Your parents, your wife and your cousin will need to make statements to verify what you've said about your movements. As I said, it's purely routine."

"Naturally. Now, if you don't mind, sergeant, I'm very busy…"

"I may need to see you or your father again."

He doesn't respond and Jennifer is peremptorily ushered out the office, the receptionist only too pleased to escort her completely off the premises. It may be nothing. It may be everything. Jennifer came with only mild curiosity, but leaves with a strong suspicion surrounding the objectionable Malcolm and the whole Dugger clan.

The rest of the morning passes uneventfully as Jennifer works through the last of the contact firms supplied by Annette, Karen's secretary. Only one remains, the Wallace group. It's a collection of stores, originating as a single furniture shop. Since those early days over fifty years ago it's extended in scope with carpets, curtains, floorings and other 'household' items, taking in and opening more stores with names such as 'Home Stage' (*Make your home a stage which everyone will admire*) and 'Home Everything' (*'Turn your home into everything you could possibly want)*. The final name of 'Home Comfort' has been very successful.

The contrast between the Dugger and Wallace head office couldn't be more marked. Jennifer is shown (not led as with Malcolm Dugger) into the office of Simon Wallace, where she's offered a drink (which she declines) and invited to sink into a stylish and comfortable armchair. Like Malcolm Dugger, Simon is the grandson of the founder of the firm and around the same age, but that's the limit of their similarity. Simon is polite and amiable, only too pleased to 'assist the police with this terrible enquiry.' He sits opposite Jennifer, avoiding the barrier of the desk. He smiles warmly, but his mood changes immediately.

"I can guess why you are here," he says.

"It's a routine enquiry. Your firm and your name in particular came up…"

"As a client of Karen Renshaw."

"You knew Karen?"

"Knew? Don't you mean *know?*"

"Of course."

"She's still all right, isn't she? I heard she was in a coma. Has she come round yet?"

"No, but the doctors are hopeful."

"I can't imagine who would do such a horrible thing. It's…"

His voice wavers and cuts out.

"I'm sorry, it's the shock. It's so terrible."

He touches his eyes and sniffs.

"It's okay," Jennifer says, "Take your time."

"I'll be all right in a moment. I just need to adjust. Even now I find it difficult to believe. Karen was…is…a precious person. For anyone to attack her. Why would anyone want to harm her?"

"That's what we want to find out."

He talks about Karen's work. Much the same as Jennifer has heard from other clients, but Simon's praise has a particularly personal edge.

"She had...has...an immense warmth. Nothing is too much trouble, taking time to explain things, patient and indulgent to those of us who are not perhaps always too quick on the uptake."

He chuckles slightly and seems about to speak, but nothing comes out and his eyes are full. He takes out a handkerchief and dabs them quickly.

"She's obviously more than a valued marketing consultant," Jennifer says.

"A real friend, yes a true friend. I was distressed when I heard she'd disappeared."

"Disappeared?"

"I rang her the next day...the day after the attack I mean. All they said at Alpha Consulting was she'd not come in. Then I heard about the attack. They didn't give out the name of the woman. At first I didn't connect it to Karen. Yet I had this feeling. It was as if..."

"Yes?"

"Oh nothing...well...I know it sounds crazy, but it was as if Karen herself was telling me. Not that she was actually talking to me, that would be ridiculous, but before her name was divulged I just knew. Please don't think I'm mad to say such things."

He cannot know his admission jars with Jennifer.

"I don't think that at all," she says.

"The announcement of her name just confirmed what I was feeling. I was distraught. I suppose I still am."

"You thought she was missing?"

"That's what I mean about feeling something from *her*. She was missing, but not really if you see what I mean. Before the announcement I *felt* she was missing and she was...to me."

"Did you try to reach her when you thought she was missing?"

"I...I don't know what you mean."

"Did you contact her family?"

"No...that would have been an intrusion."

"But if you were as close as you say..."

He stiffens, saying "We have a *professional* relationship."

She's hit a raw nerve, all the more reason to persist.

"You don't get that concerned about someone disappearing if it's only a professional relationship."

He hesitates. She stares questioningly.

"Well, all right, she's also a friend. I was concerned as a friend."

"What sort of work did she do for the company?"

He relaxes. This is a more comfortable line of questioning.

"General advice on marketing our products, how to pitch ourselves in the market, presentation, special offers, logo design..."

"And the different trading names?"

"Yes. You've obviously come across 'Home Comfort.' All our new stores will carry that name. We may also rename some of our existing ones," he says eagerly.

"*Home Comfort for home comforts?*"

"Yes. It was Karen's idea. It's been very successful."

"It must be much easier to forge a successful professional relationship when you enjoy such a good personal one."

He hesitates, unsure how best to reply.

"As a friend," she adds.

"There were things I needed to talk to her about...about the firm, I mean. We were planning a new initiative for the spring season. When I couldn't immediately contact her, naturally I was concerned," he says earnestly, then trying to make light of it, "Time is money as they say."

"Time and money seem to have gone hand in hand with the group."

As she expects he's keen to talk about the business.

"It all started with my grandfather, Albert. He had a small shop on Mansfield Road. It was just a general store, but he made the wise, but bold decision to specialise in furniture. A lot of it was second hand. Money was tight after the war. He saw a gap in the market, but it wasn't easy. He could have got it wrong, putting all his eggs in the one basket so to speak. But his gamble paid off."

"And the firm now?"

"Has grown and grown. Though I say it myself it is a prosperous enterprise."

"You have a particular interest in marketing for the firm?"

"Amongst many others. I try not to be away too much."

"It's just routine. Can you tell me where you were on the evening Karen was attacked."

"One of the few occasions when I was away. I was at a meeting in Leicester till quite late. We're hoping to open a store there. Something of a new departure."

"It's only twenty five miles away."

"Ah yes, but another city. You know how it is between rivals."

"You drove there?"

"Yes. The traffic on the M1 was awful."

"You have a good memory."

He shrugs and smiles indulgently.

"I like to be precise."

She returns the smile.

"Yet you're not really precise about everything, are you?"

"I don't…"

"Karen Renshaw is more than a professional colleague or even a good friend, isn't she?"

He doesn't answer immediately. It's enough.

"I've told you," he says.

"You have a relationship much more than you…"

"I have no *relationship* with Karen Renshaw."

"Did you go to the hospital to see her?"

"I've told you. I didn't know it was her that had been attacked."

"…after you knew she was there?"

He hesitates, conscious however he answers will not look well.

"I didn't see her."

"You were at the hospital?"

"I did go there. I had to be sure it really was her. But I didn't see her."

"You *had* to know."

"All right, all right. Karen and I were…we…but not now. It's over."

"Did the relationship end amicably?"

"It's hard to say it ended when it didn't really begin."

"I don't understand."

"I mean it didn't develop into anything…serious."

"But it remains serious enough for you to try and see her at the hospital."

"As a friend and colleague."

The 'mystery woman' gets to Sharp Road in the morning. It's quite unlike what she expects. The road eerily quiet, builders' equipment still in position even though there's been no work for several weeks. That's not surprising, but where are the archaeologists? She walks towards the site, but there's still no one around. She checks her map and goes over the route again. She's convinced this is the right place and connected to the 'ghost.' Yet no one else has drawn a similar conclusion, not even the otherwise perspicacious journalist on the *Courier*. If anything the lack of activity increases her conviction. She walks on. There's no one to ask. The children will be at school, but surely there'll be some movement at the houses? People are always coming and going.

She comes to a barrier across the road and can go no further. Why do they need to close the road for the archaeologists? Has the 'dig' extended under the road? She peers into the space, but can see no excavation other than a large hole at the side of some minor new building work. There are houses on either side. What was here before the site was cleared for redevelopment?

There's a sign. 'Danger. No admittance.' It would be comparatively easy to get through for a closer inspection. She edges aside the barrier, exhilarated at getting closer, but also uneasy. She glances at the houses. Are eyes watching from behind net curtains? What if she's caught? There could be someone behind the building work. Sensing an unknown danger, she replaces the barrier and walks back down the road.

It's nearly twelve o'clock. She's hungry and needs a drink. She continues for a quarter mile, walking without hesitation as if she's been here many times before and knows every street and corner. After turning several times she finally arrives in Kingston Street. A little further it's crossed by Winsford Street. She's suddenly gripped by an inexplicable anxiety and stops at the corner. She can go no further The crossing holds her. She has to be here, but isn't comfortable. It's a place of hope, but also intense sadness, simultaneously attracting and repelling.

There's a pub called 'The Grapes' at one of the other corners. It looks welcoming and is advertising lunch. She hurries over. The menu is unimaginative, but the place looks clean and tidy.

"I'll have the chilli con carne," she says.

"Be about a quarter hour," the landlady says.

"That's fine."

"Sit where you like, before the rush."

"Does it get crowded?"

"Hopefully," the landlady laughs, then says, "You're not from round here are you, duck?"

"I was trying to find the building site in Sharp Road. I'd heard they'd discovered something interesting, but it was closed off."

"That's because they discovered something more than old bits of pottery and the like."

"What have they found?"

"An old bomb, unexploded, from the war. They called in the bomb disposal people, but they suspect it's a big 'un so they have to get a more specialised unit to deal with it. In the meantime, some families have been evacuated as a precaution. They've been put up in the school over the street."

She finds a comfortable table by the window. The landlady comes with her meal, then hovers.

"That's the school over there. In the old days they used to have a name for these cross roads. Come over and I'll show you."

They stand together by the door.

"We're on one corner. There's always been a pub here," the landlady says, then points in turn to each of the other three corners of the cross roads, "The school, still is. Then over there a local shop, but it used to be a pawn shop and over that side where that house is…"

"Its quite new, post war I'd say."

"That's right. A church hall used to be there. So, originally, the church hall, the school, the pub and the pawnshop. So this cross roads was called *salvation, education, intoxication and damnation.*"

They laugh.

"But not anymore," the mystery woman says, "No pawnshop and…"

"…no church hall."

"Do people still call the cross roads by those names?"

"Some of the older folk do, but for others it's not really funny."

"How do you mean?"

"Let's hope the people who've been evacuated to the school from their houses on Sharp Road will soon get home."

The mystery woman shudders.

"You all right, duck?"

"Yes, yes…I…just felt a shiver."

"I'll shut the door."

The mystery woman sits down.

"Why don't some people think those names are not funny?"

"Everybody finds *damnation* funny and of course *education* and *intoxication*…Well, we're still here, aren't we? But where the church hall was is a sad story…"

"It was bombed."

"How did you know?"

"Oh nothing…well a post war house in the middle of pre war ones…"

"Yes, I suppose so. The church hall was being used as a shelter. Got a direct hit. Everybody inside was killed."

"That's why you said you hoped the people in the school will soon be able to go home?"

"Yes."

She finishes her meal and leaves. She's drawn to the house where the church hall once stood. As she crosses the road the draw gets stronger, but it's too akin to a moth drawn to a flame. Outside the house it becomes intolerable and she quickly re-crosses back to 'The Grapes.' She stands there immobile, frequently having to step aside as the lunchtime customers arrive.

She can't get the bombs out of her mind…the unexploded one in Sharp Road and the one that destroyed the church hall and all those within it. One long gone, the other unearthed, an old danger and a new one. She can't stay, yet knows she'll be back.

*'After extensive interviews with dozens of women The* Courier *can now reveal a major clue, which should be further investigated. All on the train saw a message left by the mysterious ghost. Memories can be distorted over time, descriptions may differ, but all consistently reported seeing the same collection of numbers, without variation, always in the same order. 8541. What does it mean?'*

Jenner screws up the paper and tosses it in the bin, but that's like the ostrich burying its head in the sand. His fury won't change the facts. Arlene is certainly adept at the water torture. First there was a 'common thread.' Now that infernal strand is exposed. He already knew, of course. He has his own witness statements and some contain allusions to these numbers and usually in the order Arlene mentions. But she exaggerates (not every witness mentioned seeing the numbers) and bends the truth. (some put the numbers in a different order such as 4518 or 4158) She's also circumspect about her so called 'interviews.' Either she didn't explore the context or chooses not to mention it. Some were vague as to when and where they saw the numbers during the train journey and none offered any explanation. Most were also vague about the 'what.' Some said they saw the numbers fingered in window condensation, others said they were pencilled on tables or on paper napkins or on seat reservations. Interestingly Janine and the others who came to Karen's aid didn't mention the numbers at all.

At least now Arlene admits to general contradictions in witness statements. That's new. Perhaps there's more to come. The water pressure will be turned up during torture. Arlene implies the numbers are important and will be of *immense value* to the investigation. That assumes they contain something more than idle doodles, a specific clue linked to the attacker. The numbers may have no significance beyond a single simple scrawl, repeated by stupid or vindictive copycats. Such persons will be laughing how seriously Arlene has taken their 'joke.' Even worse, what of her loyal, but hoodwinked readers?

Yet, what if it's genuine? What could the attacker be saying?

He tries to get Arlene at the paper, but she's out. He'll try many times during the day, but she'll always be out. Then the inevitable call he's been expecting comes through just after twelve and he leaves for the chief superintendent's office.

Emmins begins affably enough, but Jenner is not fooled.

"Just want to get up to speed on the investigation, Derek."

"It's proceeding," Jenner says guardedly.

"You've seen the latest article in the *Courier*, I suppose. It's in the early edition."

"I've read it."

"Is there anything in what Arlene Bates says?"

"I've been trying to contact her, but she's out or at least that's what I'm being told."

The assistant chief constable comes in.

Having caught the tail end of the conversation, he too is intrigued by the article, saying "Doesn't let up on us, does she?"

"Sells papers," Jenner says gruffly.

But Davies is not amused.

"Also puts us in a doubtful light. Not good for PR."

Jenner is tempted to say he's not interested in 'propaganda,' but fortunately Emmins gets in before him.

"It's got all the flavour of one of your peculiar cases."

"What do you mean by that?"

"Well, you know, extra sensory activities and all this ghost stuff."

"It's got nothing of the kind except what this damned journalist chooses to dramatise and fabricate."

"Maybe, but you have to admit it's got the same ingredients as that business down south with the film about, what was it about...? Any way, there were what you might call echoes of the past. Then there was our own one, you know, the canal and the missing man and then you found..."

"None of that has anything to do with this," Jenner explodes, "Here, we have a real assault."

"Exactly, that's what I mean, but there are still these... esoteric elements."

Sensing Jenner's short fuse has almost reached its explosive end, Davies intervenes.

"What Charles means is that with your previous experience of these matters, you should be able to bring your...expertise to bear. After all, we're not making much progress otherwise while this journalist, what's her name...?

"Arlene Bates."

"...is running rings round us."

Jenner bites his tongue. Emmins comes in again.

"What about this numbers business, Derek? This *8541*. What's it about? Is it true what she says?"

Jenner plays it down.

"It's just a crazy story the paper has picked up and exaggerated."

"But is she right? Have witnesses on the train seen these numbers?"

Jenner grumpily assents, admitting many of the witnesses have referred to it and the essence, if not the letter of Arlene's story is substantially true.

"I didn't want it to be publicised. Ribald rumours soon flourish. We could get copycats, deflecting the investigation from the real predator."

The meeting ends with Davies and to a lesser extent Emmins expressing continued if lukewarm confidence in the conduct of the enquiry while Jenner promises to pursue all avenues, 'however unconventional.'

Though coming away apparently displeased he takes his chiding more to heart than his superiors realise. The issue of the 'numbers' is bound to return and he'll have to quickly re-examine their significance.

The witnesses were as dumbfounded as he was, only one whimsically saying 'could it be a phone number?' She couldn't be serious. If it was a phone number it was a very short one. Assuming it to be prefixed by an area code such as 0115 it would still be three digits short. Could it be part of an address? Perhaps a lottery or some other ticket number, a keypad number, a PIN number, the last four digits of a credit or debit card number or computer password number? But what would be the point of any of those? Who willingly divulges such things?

He doodles around with more alternatives, each one more obscure than the one before, concluding they're most likely part of a phone number. A chilling reminder. I know your number. I know you. I know you're on this train and where you live. I'm coming to get you. He's already checked Karen's phone number. It's not the same. He's still fiddling with possibilities when Jennifer joins him.

He points to the bin and Arlene's submerged article, saying grumpily, "Have you read it?"

"Yes."

"I've been trying to get hold of her all day."

She waits for the latest diatribe, but he returns to his scribbles, saying "Any more thoughts on 8541?"

She hasn't and reverts to Arlene.

"It's probably better you can't get her."

"Why?"

"Because you only rub her up the wrong way. It doesn't help us."

"That's what Davies said. I'm not concerned with the delicate feelings of suspects," he says sarcastically.

"You regard Arlene Bates as a suspect?"

He shuffles uneasily.

"Can't rule anybody out."

"She's a reporter. However much you dislike what she writes, she's only doing her job."

"Terrible position the fine tradition of English journalism has descended to."

"How is she connected to the attack on Karen Renshaw?"

"Don't know yet, but she is. I'm sure of it."

They move on to a more general discussion of suspects.

"The 'attack' on Karen," Jenner says, "could it have been retaliation for something she did to someone else? Something in her background, someone she provoked?"

Jennifer is sceptical and a little shocked, saying "And it went too far?"

"It's possible."

"So, whoever set up all this 'ghost' stuff, it was part revenge for some real or imagined slight?"

"Not necessarily set it up, but he could have used the hysterical nonsense as a smokescreen."

"It's not necessarily hysterical nonsense."

"Okay, we'll have to agree to differ on that point, but I still feel he used whatever it was for his own ends."

"And his own ends were Karen Renshaw, meaning there'll be no more attacks?"

"Unless it's on Karen again. What about her contacts? We've got all the reports back on the non local people. Nothing significant," he says, "What about the locals?"

They work through the list of clients supplied by Annette, assessing their respective dangerousness, but before finishing Jenner suddenly changes the subject.

"Then there's the family. I saw Keith Renshaw four days ago. He was very supportive of his daughter and clearly concerned, but he has a peculiar attitude. He said Karen is a 'dutiful daughter.' Odd way to talk of your daughter who might be at death's door in hospital."

"Perhaps there's a story there."

"Could be," he says thoughtfully, "Anyway, about Karen's local contacts, there's the Wallace group."

"I saw Simon Wallace, grandson of Albert Wallace, the founder of the business. Apparently started out with one small shop and built it up. Rags to riches type of thing."

"You're doubtful the grandfather really was a self made man?"

"Sounded a bit pat."

"Anything more?"

"He was very complimentary about Karen. Perhaps too complimentary."

Jenner savours a possible development.

"Something beyond a purely professional relationship?"

"He was distraught at the news of Karen. I had to prise it out of him and he still maintains they were just friends, but I suspect there is – or was – something much closer. He said she was 'a precious person."

"Hardly what her father called her. Could he have been the mysterious male visitor at the hospital?"

"He matches the description given by the constable and, more importantly the nurse. He also admitted – after a lot of probing – that he went to the hospital, though he denies going to the ward or her room."

"So there's a connection?"

"Yes, but I think he can be discounted as a suspect. He has an alibi. He was at a meeting in Leicester, drove there and back. I've checked it out."

Jenner is unsure, then wonders about the recent change in Karen's behaviour as described by Annette and James at her work.

"What was the change driving Karen's recent aggression?"

Jennifer doesn't comment. Jenner moves on to John Renshaw's death and the 1965 'accident.'

"Both Keith Renshaw and Annette drew attention to the Duggers and your meeting with one of the Duggers fits."

"Malcolm Dugger was very defensive. As soon as Karen Renshaw's name was mentioned he came out with an alibi without being asked, which he used to distance the whole family."

"A convenient alibi provided by and for each of the family. You've only seen Malcolm, the grandson. We need to see Henry, the son and then the cousin...what's his name?"

"Arthur Palmer."

"And his mother. They all sound like a bunch of rogues."

"But after all this time, would they really pursue a vendetta with the Renshaws to the extent of attacking, maybe trying to kill Karen?"

"According to Keith they killed her grandfather."

"It was an accident."

"That's what I told Keith," Jenner says, then after a long pause, "What about the mysterious woman at the hospital? She could be connected to this damned reporter."

"About her..." Jennifer begins.

The phone rings. Jenner answers, says 'bloody hell,' then bangs down the receiver.

"We've got another one and this time it really is murder."

# 6

**24<sup>th</sup> April**

ON the north side of the railway station, a woman in her late fifties lies crumpled against the wall in Station Street. Blood has trickled from the side of her head, but is quickly congealing. The wound is fatal. Several passers by discover her. Police and ambulance are called. This is a busy street. The main entrance to the station is around the corner. A crowd quickly forms. Police arrive, clear the crowd except for those that discovered the body and the street is closed. This is now a crime scene.

Jenner and Jennifer arrive. The discoverers are questioned. There are no witnesses to the murder. The doctor confirms death occurred very recently, maybe only minutes before discovery, ten minutes at most.

"The murderer could have been waiting or she was followed, in either case this was pre-planned," Jenner says.

"Is this connected to the attack on Karen Renshaw?" Jennifer says, "After all this is the side of the station."

"The train has just come in."

"Then we need to see everybody."

They race round the corner with as many officers as can be spared. News of 'another attack' has already got out and the station manager, perhaps remembering how valuable time was lost eleven days before closes the exits. Jenner is impressed and commends his 'intelligent precaution.' Passengers leaving the London train are less understanding as they are corralled in small groups and questioned by officers. It will be a long process. There are only a few officers available to question hundreds of passengers, but Jenner is determined to gather as much information as possible before events go 'cold.' Fortunately, in response to his request additional uniformed officers arrive to supplement his own team of detectives. He flits between the various interviewing groups, impatiently assessing the emerging information, but also carefully looking over the passengers, assessing potential suspects, hoping the age old gut feeling kicks in and he can look the 'predator' straight in the eye. It doesn't come, but at least they have a comprehensive dossier of everyone on the train, where they've been and where they live. It might be useful later.

The murdered woman is identified from her belongings as Sarah Murrell, later confirmed by her brother. She's divorced with one daughter, who's abroad back packing. The timing of her murder is consistent with the arrival of the London train, but she wasn't carrying a train ticket. The machines at the barriers don't always retain tickets. If she still had a ticket she might have discarded it on exit. More importantly, the station manager is sure no one was able to exit the station before he was aware of the 'attack' and deployed staff to close all exits. So, despite Jenner's rigorous and extensive interrogation of passengers she doesn't seem to be directly related to the 'ghost' train.

Enquiries with staff and passengers are mixed. Some say she could have been in the train, though the statements are far too vague to be reliable. British Transport officers on the train have no recollection of her. So, although Sarah was attacked near the station Jenner is sure from the swift action by the station manager that she was definitely not on the train. Initial investigations also reveal no immediate connection between her and Karen, though Jenner is not convinced.

## 25<sup>th</sup> April

The press go wild. To grab public attention national as well as local papers and broadcasters attach the 'ghost train' cliche. Radio phone-ins reach fever pitch, quickly ramping up panic throughout the city. Reports connect the murder to the earlier attack and the details of Karen's ordeal are painfully repeated. Jenner makes the usual appeal for witnesses or information, concentrating solely on Sarah Murrell without mentioning Karen. He's bombarded with questions implying a connection, but refuses to be drawn on any possible link. The press think otherwise and speculate on an even more serious undercurrent. Naturally the *Courier* leads the pack.

*'IS A MANIAC LOOSE IN THE CITY?*

*Quite apart from the horror for her family, friends and the city's wider population last night's dreadful murder of an innocent woman close to the station raises the terrible prospect of even more horrendous events. First there were strange 'happenings' on a London train. Innumerable people reported sightings of a weird stranger, some said in old clothes. There was talk of a 'ghost' inhabiting a 'ghost train.' Then, twelve days ago Karen Renshaw was viciously attacked on the same train and now lies in a coma in hospital. Twelve days in which no progress has been made in the hunt for her assailant. Now another woman has been attacked and murdered at a time and place close to that attack twelve days ago. Otherwise it seems the two women are unrelated.*

*This is now more than lurid stories of a ghost train, easily dismissed by sceptics, much more than a mere 'predator,' serious as that is. This newspaper has warned throughout of the need for women's fears to be acted upon with comprehensive and diligent investigation. Extra patrols and officers have been put on the trains, but last night there were no police in or around the station. A deranged attacker could be at large. His murderous intentions must be quickly brought to an end with a swift and early arrest.'*

Jenner has become accustomed to a sense of resignation when he reads these articles, but he's irritated by the repeated references to twelve days, pointedly emphasising the lack of progress. He's also aware of two other things. Arlene Bates' byline doesn't appear at the head of the article and she didn't appear when he gave the press statement. Neither has she, unlike others, tried to contact him about a link between the two women. Maintaining that there's no obvious link only fuels the salacious theory of an indiscriminate 'maniac,' but he's only half sincere, convinced Karen Renshaw is the key to unlocking the investigation.

Forensics turn up nothing. The doctor confirms the cause of death as a heavy blow to the head with a blunt instrument, probably by a right handed person.

"That leaves us with ninety per cent of the population," Jenner says gruffly, "Man or woman?"

"Probably a man, though a strong woman is not impossible."

"Thank you, doctor...very helpful."

After he's identified the body, Jenner talks to John Crendell, Sarah Murrell's brother.

"You've travelled from Derby, Mr. Crendell?"

"Yes."

"And your sister also lives in Derby?"

"Yes."

"She lives alone?"

"Yes."

"Does she have any other relatives other than yourself and her daughter?"

"No, about my niece..."

"You've been unable to contact her?"

"I'm afraid not."

"I don't suppose you have a telephone number?"

"No."

"Your sister was carrying a recent postcard from Australia. We have contacted the Australian police. I'm sure they'll quickly locate her. I have to ask this purely routine question. Where were you last evening?"

"I was in a pub in town with friends from work."

"In Derby?"

"Yes."

"We'll need the details. Now, do you know anyone who might have wished her harm?"

"She had no enemies of which I am aware."

"Do you know what she was doing in Station Street at that time yesterday?"

"I assume she'd just come off a train."

"You assume?"

"Well, I don't know, but it seems the most likely."

"Or she might have been on her way to catch a train?"

"Possibly, but as she lives in Derby..."

"She might have been going home?"

Crendell hesitates.

"Not at that time in the evening," he says at last.

"You're sure she was arriving rather than departing?"

"Yes."

"Why so? She had friends in Nottingham she was visiting?"

He hesitates again.

"I wouldn't describe them as friends exactly, though I suppose...yes friends of a sort."

"She came regularly from Derby to Nottingham to see these friends of a sort?"

"Yes."

"And she always travelled by train?"

"Yes...where she goes...it's not good for parking."

"So, she made regular trips to Nottingham in the evening and always travelled by train from Derby. Where was she going?"

"My sister has…had…a weakness. Well, it could be a weakness, in her case it was not, she was good at it."

"Good at what?"

"Gambling."

"What sort of gambling?"

"All sorts, but she was particularly partial to cards… poker."

"On line?"

"Oh no, nothing as mundane and limited as that. The real thing."

"So she came to Nottingham where there was a regular and serious card game?"

"Yes."

"You say she was good at it. So, she had no money troubles?"

"No. She liked to gamble, but wasn't addicted. She knew when to stop, though in her case there was always another day when she could recoup her losses and more."

"I'll need the address where she played…names of those involved."

"Of course."

"She would have travelled on a local train from Derby?"

"She usually took the same one. It gets into Nottingham around ten minutes before the London train."

"You're aware of the recent attack on a woman on the same London train?"

"You mean Karen Renshaw?"

"Did your sister know her?"

"I don't know. I wouldn't have thought so."

"I assume that while she was a successful gambler, she didn't make a complete living out of it?"

Crendell almost chuckles.

"Who does? No, Sarah had a full time job. She worked for a firm called Draycon. She was their finance officer."

As Crendell is leaving Jennifer comes in.

"Mr. Crendell, the police in Melbourne have come back to us. They have found your niece. She's cutting short her trip. She's coming home. I have a number if you wish to speak to her."

Crendell is thankful, but crestfallen. After he leaves Jennifer reports on the first enquiries.

"No link with Karen Renshaw, I suppose?" Jenner says.

"No one with an obvious motive."

"So, as yet we have nothing. It's hard to believe. A busy street, a busy time of the day, somebody must have seen something."

"What about the brother? Anything emerge?"

Jenner updates her on John Crendell.

"Follow up where Sarah Murrell worked. Then there are the gamblers..."

"Sounds quite a girl," Jennifer says admiringly.

Jenner snorts derisively.

"Perhaps, but what sort of people was she mixing with? Her brother says she was a successful gambler. I've yet to meet one. What if she owed a lot of money and couldn't pay up?"

"Her brother said she wasn't addicted."

"No, but she regularly travelled fifteen miles for a card game. Is gambling the link to Karen Renshaw?"

"We've no indication Karen was a gambler."

Jenner muses for a moment.

"But I'm sure there's a connection between them."

"And if there's no connection..."

"We've got a serial killer on the loose?"

"That's what the papers..."

"I don't need reminding about the bloody papers," he thunders, then says contritely, "I'm sorry, Jennifer. It's just...did we...did I get this wrong from the beginning?

Now not just a serious assault, but a murder. Could it have been avoided with a different approach from the start? If I'd taken seriously…"

"No! Blaming yourself won't do any good," she says vehemently, then more considered, "We've been assuming the assault on Karen Renshaw was solely about her."

"And now when an apparently unconnected woman is murdered."

"But you believe there is a connection?"

"Karen Renshaw is the pivot, but it's only a gut feeling. We've no clear evidence the two women are linked in any way."

"We've only just begun."

He picks up the newspaper.

"The *Courier* isn't alone. All the papers are stressing there are no links to Karen. In other words…(he reads from the article)…*A deranged attacker could be at large.*"

"Sensationalism and very irresponsible."

"Maybe, but what I said to the press will only confirm what they're saying."

"You had to say *something*. Besides, if we said there was a connection they'd only pester us even more and…"

"At least Arlene Bates has been quiet."

"…if you're right and there is a link the killer will believe we're on to him when we're not."

"That article was not written by Arlene Bates."

"She's not been heard of."

"Small mercies."

"No, she's gone missing. I checked with the *Courier*."

Jenner is keen to pursue this intriguing development when there's a knock at the door. He sighs and shouts 'Enter.' Constable David Warren enters sheepishly, hovering beside the door unsure whether to speak or wait until given leave. Jenner doesn't immediately recognise him.

"Yes?" he barks.

"PC David Warren, sir. You may remember…I was at the hospital…"

"Oh yes, the one who let that damned woman get in to see Karen Renshaw when you were supposed to be guarding…"

"Excuse me, sir, but we don't know that she got into the room. She was seen in the ward, but when I left…"

"Exactly…when you left. Yes, yes, all right. We can be pretty sure she *was* in the room, but no matter. What is it?"

"I've just seen the picture of the woman who was found near the station…"

"Sarah Murrell? What about her?"

"I recognised her. She's the woman who was in the ward."

"Who went in to see Karen Renshaw?"

"Well, as I said…"

"Don't start all that again. You saw this woman, spoke to her?"

"Yes, sir."

"You spoke to Sarah Murrell on the ward and she asked about Karen Renshaw?"

"Yes."

"You're absolutely sure about that?"

"Yes."

After Warren leaves Jenner claps his hands.

"I knew it! I knew there was a connection."

Jennifer shakes her head.

"I don't believe Sarah Murrell was the woman who came to see Karen in the hospital."

"Why not? You don't trust Warren. I give you he was most remiss when he was supposed to be guarding…"

Jennifer is adamant.

"Sarah Murrell was not at the hospital."

Jenner looks at her quizzically.

"From the descriptions of the woman at the hospital I can see there's a similarity in age and maybe appearance with Sarah Murrell," she says, "but it's definitely not her."

"Why?"

"Because…"

The phone rings. Jenner answers with 'yes' then 'of course' followed by 'now' and 'right away.'

"I have to go," he says, "Emmins wants to see me."

He gets up. She's about to speak, but he cuts her off.

"Remember to follow up the firm, Draycon and the gamblers."

He's not in the best of spirits when he arrives in the chief superintendent's office. This should be an 'updating' meeting and he expects nothing less than a critical reception, but he's unprepared for what he faces. The presence of the assistant chief constable should be a warning, but Davies has been here before. Jenner summarises the initial enquiries. They listen patiently, asking a few innocuous questions for clarification and he concludes with an indication of further investigations.

"Something may emerge from the firm she worked for, then there's the gambling mentioned by her brother. When we have…"

Emmins intervenes.

"That's all very well and good, Derek. Obviously those enquiries have to be pursued, but everything you've said assumes the murder of Sarah Murrell is a continuation of the attack on Karen Renshaw even though you've not drawn any link between the two victims."

"The one doesn't necessarily follow the other, but we can't rule out any potential lines of enquiry. If we pick up anything from either her place of work or any nefarious activity associated with her gambling…"

Now it's Davies's turn to intervene.

"I assume you've seen the latest copy of the *Courier*, Derek?"

Jenner inwardly groans 'Not again' as he nods.

"Implying no connection between the attack on Karen Renshaw and the murder of Sarah Murrell reinforces, however inadvertently, the press contention there's a serial attacker, indeed killer. It changes the whole nature of the investigation."

Jenner tries to repeat his point, though aware the words sound hollow and are falling on deaf ears.

"Despite what I said, I believe there could...there has to be a connection to Karen Renshaw."

"That's not what you said to the press," Emmins carps.

Jenner's about to speak, but Davies intervenes again, this time with a firmer and truculent tone.

"The newspaper is right. You were wrong from the beginning and have continued to be so."

The put down is blunt, final, brooking of no response. Most of all it jars so exactly with his own dispirited evaluation. Jenner is utterly dejected. Emmins continues.

"You can't have it both ways, Derek. If there's a link between Karen Renshaw and Sarah Murrell then they are entwined with some aggrieved enemy. If they are not it can only mean these attacks are random, which means the paper is right and no woman in the city is safe."

"That's a somewhat sensational assessment," Jenner says pertly, recovering some self possession.

Emmins reacts forcefully.

"I didn't mean we should *say* that."

"But it's okay to criticise me for saying something I don't mean!"

There's a longish silence. Jenner should not react too quickly. After all, Emmins is only articulating his own fears and therefore... Then Emmins charges in again.

"It's the same MO, Derek and this time it's been successful."

"How so?" Jenner says.

"Both women were attacked around the same time on the train, so..."

"Sarah Murrell was not attacked on the train."

"All right, she was at or near the station and Karen Renshaw was on a train coming into the station. You have to admit it brings all the stuff the paper has been peddling into sharp focus, the so called ghost and the predator, both on the train."

Jenner can't resist upbraiding him.

"Now who wants it both ways?"

"Meaning?"

"Meaning such common factors – if they really are common – could point to a link between the women."

"All carried out by someone with a grievance against both women?"

"Possibly."

"Why would he go to so much trouble?"

"Why would a serial killer? Surely he'd make his move at a time and place convenient to him not to some bloody railway timetable!"

"But we're talking about different things!"

No one speaks until Jenner wearies at the embarrassing silence.

"I'll follow any legitimate line of enquiry, including a motiveless attacker, but there is still a need to pursue other matters including the meaning of '8541."

"You said the number was not found anywhere near the crime scene," Emmins says.

"That's not the point. There were some sightings on the train."

"Which I recall again you dismissed at the time as 'foolish imaginings."

"Until it was picked up by the *Courier*," Davies says darkly.

Jenner squirms a little, then says, "If that wretched number hadn't been divulged the investigation might have progressed more effectively. There's always the danger of copycats, confusing the evidence."

"We don't know what it means," Emmins says.

"We need to analyse its meaning…if there is one."

"That sort of confusion is typical of a serial killer playing with us."

"Okay, it could be muddying the water, but…"

"The only mudding of the water now is the one you're looking into."

The third silence, shorter than the others, but much more ominous. Emmins and Davies exchange knowing glances. The time for decision has arrived. The fraught meeting must be concluded. Davies speaks.

"Derek, the press coverage, especially since the murder is having an adverse effect on the force's relations with the public, which can't be ignored. However, it's a symptom of a wider problem."

He pauses, clearly uncomfortable with what he has to say and exchanges another meaningful look with Emmins before continuing.

"The point is, I know you've had successes in the past – some of them significant – but we're of the view that at times you can be too steeped in your own theories, especially when they relate to past events and that…"

Davies breaks off. Emmins assists.

"…this is one of those occasions."

"I'm not steeped in the past," Jenner says, "It so happens the cases have involved relevant past events, which had to be considered. I didn't impose such matters on investigations, they imposed themselves on me."

Emmins is ready to respond, but Davies, having recovered from a temporary loss of nerve is quicker.

"Therefore, I am relieving you as SIO for both the attack on Karen Renshaw and the murder of Sarah Murrell. Inspector Williams will take over the case…"

"Williams…*Inspector* Williams has insufficient experience. He's only…"

"...while overall control will be exercised by Chief Superintendent Emmins."

Jenner says nothing at first, but glares pugnaciously, turning his head slowly between them.

"Is this a permanent deployment?" he says finally.

"It depends on the length of the investigation," Davies says, "To begin with we can consider it ...(he glances at Emmns, who scowls)...there's no fixed timescale, but there are plenty of other cases on which you will be assigned."

"I'm not interested in other cases."

"Look upon this as being for your own good."

"You might consider taking some leave," Emmins says.

The intervention is intended to be helpful, but has the opposite effect.

"Might I?" Jenner says, "Is that all?"

"Unless you have any questions," Davies says with a half smile.

As he walks along the corridor anger, sorrow, frustration, self reproach and a rising rebelliousness compete with a deep sense of duty. They're right to be concerned with the lack of progress, but that's not necessarily down to incompetence on his part. They're driven by obsessive sensitivity to scurrilous and unwarranted press coverage and a sacrificial victim at the altar of public relations is needed. They'll rue the day they've removed him from the investigation...Inspector Williams...a rookie nonentity still wet behind the ears and as for Emmins in 'overall control'...

By the time he reaches his office his more extreme grumbles and assumptions have subsided, leaving a profound emptiness. Is he getting too old, too stuck in his ways? Is it time to retire? He brushes it aside. The milk is spilt. Nothing to be gained fretting about it...at least not now...that's for another day. He may not take leave, but he can't concentrate here. He starts collecting a few things as Jennifer enters in a perky mood.

"You were right," she says, "I had an interesting conversation with the general manager at Draycon. Sarah Murrell was acquainted with Karen Renshaw through the firm. Karen handled the company's marketing. As the finance officer Sarah would see her when she came in. He said that…"

Jenner is only half listening.

"Good work, Jennifer. You'll have to advise Inspector Williams."

"Williams? Why him?"

"Because for now he's in charge day to day for the investigation. Emmins is in overall control."

"What's happened?"

"They've took me off the case. Apparently it's for my own good. You know where to find me. I'm going home."


## 26<sup>th</sup> April

*'What is the real significance of 8541, the collection of numbers scrawled in various places on the London train, which has now become notorious as the 'Ghost Train?' Everyone is guessing, kindling much talk in pubs, bus and tram queues and supermarket check outs, let alone the booking office at the station. The order of the numbers has been switched around in every possible combination, but still the meaning is unclear. Or perhaps there is no meaning? Is the predator deliberately amusing himself with us in this horrid way? The speculation surrounding the mysterious digits does nothing to soothe the panic gripping the city. If this is a joke it's in poor taste.*

*The police have ruled out any connection between the ghost and the numbers and between the two unfortunate victims, one lying in the morgue, the other still in a coma.'*

Jenner puts the *Courier* down. The blatant inciting of the city 'panic,' so piously regretted and the unwholesome references to the fate of Karen Renshaw and Sarah Murrell annoys him, but he's in accord with the main thrust of Arlene Bates' argument. He's no evidence, but the persistent conviction the 'ghost' and the numbers are linked. Meanwhile, Jennifer has discovered a connection, albeit a slight one between the two women. There is more to come and his gut feeling won't go away.

He's not been into the station since the agonised meeting with Emmins and Davies. Officially on leave, in practice he's in retreat. His flat is airy and bright, but seems a very dark place. Forebodings and fears on past and present, exacerbated by the drubbing from his superiors, seriously undermine his confidence.

The past, not just his past, but *the* past dominates. Even Arlene's absence puts her in the past. Her article *comes* from the past and she's now no more than the ghost train and the ghost man she writes about. The article, obviously published in her absence, does nothing to alleviate his blackness, but gradually it has a recuperative effect and natural resilience kicks in.

He rings the newspaper. She's 'not available,' meaning they've no idea of her whereabouts. He goes to the kitchen where he keeps papers ready to be put out with the bins. He's not touched the pile for a couple of weeks and rummages through old copies of the *Courier*. He finds Arlene's article about the war and it incites pictures in his mind.

The dark streets, the sirens, people moving quickly, traffic coming to a halt, much scurrying, running towards the shelters or at least something that will pass as one, the drones of the bombers, getting louder, nearer. Maybe they'll pass tonight as they have on other nights? But it's not to be. Tonight they have come for us. The raid begins.

He opens his eyes. This is foolish. He puts the paper aside. He must dismiss the pictures, but the wartime experience remains, sadly remembered though he's far too young to have known those times. He closes his eyes again.

The pictures return, but now his policeman's take supervenes. What of those that didn't hurry to the shelters when the raid began, who saw the blackness and the vulnerability as an opportunity?

Maybe his superiors were right? He shouldn't be sensitive of past cases. That past, *his* past is not gone and he knows someone who could help.


The mystery woman gets the call at her hotel.

"Ettie Rodway?"

"Yes."

"My name is Arlene Bates, I'm a journalist on…"

"The *Courier*. I've read your articles. How did you know I was here?"

"It's my job, finding things out."

"How can I help you?"

"You'll understand. It's connected to my article. Can we meet?"

"You'll have to be more specific."

"Things have arisen which need exploring."

"I'm not really into publicity."

"I'll respect your privacy."

"Will you come here or will I come to the paper?"

"Neither. I don't want to meet in the city. Do you have a car?"

"Yes, but not here."

"I'd like to meet you at my aunt's house."

"Where is that?"

"North, twenty miles."

"That's quite a way from the city. Can you pick me up?"

There's a silence. Ettie asks if Arlene is still on the line.

"I don't want to come into the city."

"You mean you don't want to be seen?"

"I know it's inconvenient, but can you come to Mansfield? I can pick you up from there. You can get a bus. I'll meet you at the bus station. Say, at twelve?"

"Well, if this is important…"

The line goes dead. Ettie is mystified, but intrigued. Why can't they meet in the city? What's Arlene afraid of? How will she know Arlene? How will Arlene know her? She rings the newspaper, but they can't help.

'Miss Bates has not been in the office for several days.'

It's a straight choice. Ignore it or go to Mansfield, at worst, a wasted journey and bus fare. She gets her coat and hat and goes to the bus station.

It's a long journey. Mansfield is only fifteen miles from Nottingham, but passing through every suburb and village it seems more like sixty. With doubts about the venture she tells herself she can still make the most of the day. Sherwood Forest is not far. She'll go there and visit the haunts of the famous outlaw. She's so convinced there's no alternative she gets off the bus and looks around for another to take her to the Sherwood visitor centre and doesn't notice the young woman coming up behind her.

"Miss Rodway, my car is just around the corner."

As Ettie turns Arlene is already walking away.

"Yes," she calls, "You are Arlene Bates?"

"Yes, of course," Arlene says, hardly turning to face Ettie, "We must hurry. I'm on a double yellow line."

"How long have you been waiting?" Ettie says, catching her up.

"About three minutes."

"But the bus…"

"…is always on time."

Fortunately, Arlene has avoided a parking ticket, though a traffic warden is bearing down from the other end of the street.

"You were cutting it fine," Ettie says as they speed away.

"Car park's too far," Arlene says.

Ettie tries to open up a conversation, but Arlene only responds with occasional grunts and neutral comments. They travel east towards Ollerton, but then Arlene turns along a series of minor roads and Ettie quickly loses any sense of direction.

"Your aunt must live in a very isolated place?" Ettie says.

"It serves a purpose," Arlene says cryptically.

There's no mention of how Ettie will get back to the city.

"Why are you so concerned not to be seen in Nottingham?" she asks.

Arlene doesn't answer immediately, eventually saying, "Soon be there."

They pass through a hamlet of a dozen houses. There's no name sign. A half mile further they stop at a lone bungalow of 1920's vintage, though well maintained with modern windows. Arlene opens the door and leads the way into an airy lounge. The chintzy curtains, the many pretty if unsophisticated ornaments and the picture crammed walls are testament to an older woman of respectable taste. Arlene relaxes a little and disappears into the kitchen to make tea.

"You aunt is away?" Ettie calls.

"Yes, for a couple of days. She has friends in Sheffield."

"Your uncle…?" Ettie begins when the tea arrives.

"My aunt is a widow."

"Your father's sister…?"

"My mother's."

Ettie can hardly believe she's travelled half way across the county to meet a complete stranger for reasons as yet unclear. Yet curiosity and the need to explore beneath Arlene's articles drives her. She has many questions, but for now an obvious one must suffice.

"Why me?" she says, putting down her tea cup and staring piercingly at Arlene

"Because of your background. You have experience of these matters."

"Matters?"

"You've read my articles. For three weeks or more the city has been in ferment, strange things seen, a woman attacked and all pivoted on the London train and the station.

You have exceptional knowledge of paranormal activity and have worked with the police in the past to great effect, both here and in London and elsewhere. You don't like to be called a psychic or a medium, but you have a particular gift making contact and drawing links between past and present."

"I'm flattered. You are well informed."

"Like I said. It's my job."

"And how might I be of assistance?"

"The police have been less than diligent in their enquiries."

"I gathered that from your articles."

"It's not just the failure to make progress and bring the perpetrator to justice, it's their refusal to acknowledge that other…"

"…less conventional?"

"Yes, less conventional elements could be involved."

"I should tell you I'm acquainted with the senior officer leading the investigation."

"That can only be advantageous," Arlene says, airily dismissing it, "The predator, the man on the train, there are differing descriptions…"

"Which makes the police job more difficult."

Arlene doesn't like being reminded of police 'difficulties.'

"Yes, but there's consistency about the train and the man's appearance. They talk about an old train and the man wearing old clothes. It's in the past, the war. I've written about those times. You've read that article?"

Arlene launches into an impassioned account of an air raid, becoming a longer, more prosaic version of her article. It's some time before Ettie manages to intervene.

"You feel these appearances on the train and the attack on Karen Renshaw are connected to events in the past?"

Arlene refers again to air raids. Ettie talks about the train. Arlene makes no connection and goes back to the air raids. Ettie jolts her out of this obsession.

"What about the murder of Sarah Murrell?"

Arlene looks at Ettie blankly.

"Sarah? There's no Sarah in the air raid."

"No, no, the woman who was murdered outside the railway station."

"The raids continued. At first the authorities hadn't considered Nottingham as a target for the luftwaffe, but how wrong they were. Then..."

"But how is the murder of Sarah Murrell connected to the war?"

Arlene looks at Ettie confusedly, then says, "Sarah Murrell? Yes, maybe she was one of those I interviewed."

"When did you interview her?"

"I don't know. I saw so many...for the article...the police hadn't seen them all."

Ettie tries once more.

"I'm not talking about your article and what the women saw on the train. It's about Sarah Murrell. She's dead."

"Dead? Oh yes, there were many dead, hundreds in one night."

"Not the war," Ettie says emphatically, "You didn't publish the names of the women you'd interviewed, but did you tell anyone? Did you mention Sarah Murrell to anyone?"

It's no good. Arlene is back in the war. Is she deliberately blanking out Sarah Murrell's murder? As Arlene chunters on Ettie wonders what's behind the approach to her. A cry for help, unsure what to do? What more does she know?

Then Ettie is seized by a more sinister thought. Is this all a malevolent charade? Is Arlene more involved than she cares to admit? Why does she not want to be seen in the city? Why reluctant to talk about Sarah Murrell? Is she prepared to tell or so overloaded with information she's losing the power of coherent speech and seeks refuge in this obsession with the war? Are the content of the articles directing the journalist rather than the other way round?

*Could she have done it?*

Arlene stops talking and looks at Ettie quizzically as if expecting a response. Ettie doesn't want to engage in further fruitless discussion about air raids. She believes the origin of the ghostly 'appearances' including the 'the man from the past' have been activated by the archaeological dig at Sharp Road. It could provide a useful change of subject. Tiring of Ettie's lack of response Arlene begins again.

"I have a personal interest in these things. There are memories of those days in my own family."

She pauses. Then, in case Ettie hasn't realised says, "I mean the war."

Ettie nods politely.

"My great uncle Wilf talked of one particular raid. He didn't go into details, only saying it was very bad. Many were killed and there was great destruction."

"Was this that inspired you to write your article?"

"I wanted to write a follow up feature with more details. I kept meaning to go through it with him in depth, but things came up, I put it off."

"It would be interesting to see him."

"It would, but I can no longer talk to him."

Arlene stops abruptly, then says "He died."

"I'm sorry to hear that. Was this recently?"

"10th April."

Ettie's thoughts about connections resound.

"Isn't that the day archaeological work at Sharp Road stopped?"

Arlene has to think about it.

"I'm not sure. I'd have to look it up. You seem to know."

"Yes. There's a…"

Ettie stops herself. She's not yet ready to draw her conclusion openly. Instead she jokes about Arlene's skilful research, yet not knowing the date. Arlene laughs. It lightens the mood.

"There's a bomb, isn't there?" Ettie says, hoping Arlene will make a connection.

"Not for certain," Arlene says.

"But I thought that was why the archaeologists had to pull out."

"I've heard work has stopped. There's supposed to be something metallic, but it could be anything, even a medieval artefact," Arlene laughs, "Wouldn't that be ironic? Anyway it's irritated everybody, those that were evacuated, the archaeologists, the army disposal team."

"It was the breakthrough," Ettie says unguardedly, then quickly, "breaking through to the object I mean."

Arlene carries on, oblivious to Ettie's concerns.

"Just before he died uncle Wilf told me more about that night. It was a story he'd bottled up for many years. He was meant to be meeting someone, but he was late, so they never met up. He spoke very movingly. I wonder now if he had some sort of premonition that he'd never see me again. Yet if he did, don't you think he might have told me more? Or perhaps what he told me was enough and it was too painful to tell more. I'm sure he needed to speak and...anyway, I never saw him again.

'He said he was always shameful after the air raid. I took it to mean he was ashamed of surviving when so many others didn't. It's a common reaction among those who survive some terrible ordeal. He talked about going to a bombed out church hall and he saw a man leaving."

"Who was this man?" Ettie says, anxious for more specific information that might link with what she's learnt from the landlady of 'The Grapes.'

"He didn't say and I'm afraid I didn't ask, but I can tell you what he said about him."

Ettie listens carefully to Wilf's description. She commits it carefully to memory. She may need the details in the future.

"Since I spoke to him, I've gone over it a hundred times" Arlene says, "I believe he felt more than the shame of a survivor. Wilf felt a great guilt."

"Why would he feel guilty?"

Arlene shakes her head.

"I don't know. Because he was late for his meeting? Could he have done something bad, which he couldn't tell me?"

"Is this why you're afraid to go into the city?"

Ettie is getting used to Arlene waiting, then speaking as if she's answering a completely different question.

"I too feel guilty," she says at last.

"Why?"

"Because I wrote about the number '8541.' I didn't mean it to appear in the paper. I wanted to think about it first, but they published it anyway."

"Is that bad?"

Arlene does it again, talking about everything except what she's asked. Ettie persists until Arlene drops her vagueness.

"I knew the police wouldn't have wanted it in the public domain."

"Because?"

"Because it may be connected to the ghost and the attack on Karen and…(after a long pause) the murder of Sarah Murrell."

"I must soon get back to Nottingham," Ettie says.

"It's getting dark," Arlene says, suddenly concerned for Ettie's welfare, "I'll take you back to the city…to your hotel."

Little is said on the journey and however hard she tries Ettie fails to make sense of the route they take. It will be very difficult to retrace her steps to the lonely bungalow. Even in Nottingham Arlene takes a wide circuitous course, making it impossible for Ettie to surmise what direction she's come from. They arrive at the hotel and with a curt 'goodnight' and 'keep in touch' (with no indication how Ettie will achieve it) Arlene speeds away. Whatever she's afraid of the darkness provides some comfort.

It's been a long day for Jenner, busily doing nothing, but while physically inert his mind is racing. He continually returns to Arlene's *Courier* article on the war, picking it up, ostensibly reading it through though by now he knows every word by heart, then throwing it down, thinking, imagining until the whole process begins again. It's a fascinating subject and he wonders why he's never explored Nottingham's wartime experience before. Perhaps it's good to sit back without daily pressures, allowing disparate thoughts to coalesce...maybe into something worthwhile? The same thoughts and ersatz memories are rerun like an old film, then he's engulfed by overwhelming guilt, but though it's strong it's not his guilt. He is the accuser.

*You are responsible. It's because of you that it happened.*

Is he in the interview room, interrogating a suspect, putting to him the real facts as distinct from his implausible excuses? Is this one of the usual villains or some new entrant on the local criminal scene? It's not clear of what he's accused, but his guilt is undeniable. You know the place. There are no excuses. What place? Where the crime was committed? A lonely, dark place where a crime can be easily concealed? No, Jenner doesn't know what or where, but it's not a hidden or unfamiliar location. It's somewhere crowded, there are many people and...then it's gone...a fleeting vision...no more than a conjuring trick of his imagination...concocted memories just like the 'ghost.' What ghost...ghosts? The ghosts the women saw on the train, the ghost of Arlene Bates...his ghosts? If he identifies the ghosts...could that be the answer?

His reveries are suddenly interrupted by the telephone. He ignores it. Someone from the station...maybe his successor, Inspector Williams? He'll give *him* short shrift.

Perhaps he's expected in. How long did he say he would be on leave, a day, two days, a week? If he doesn't answer they'll go away. But they never do. He gives up and answers. It's Jennifer.

"I've followed up that card game. The house where they meet is quite a swish place on the edge of West Bridgford, owned by a Cud Fenton, owns a couple of car showrooms, trades as 'Best Buys in Town'…"

"Second hand car salesman," Jenner grunts.

"I checked him out and the other regulars. No record, the business is legit, no financial problems."

"Did anyone owe money?"

"Nothing significant. 'You win some, you lose some,' he kept saying."

"What did Fenton say about Sarah Murrell?"

"He met her some years ago. His accountant was on holiday. She stood in, found they had a mutual interest, went on from there."

"So no one with a grudge connected with her gambling?"

"No, at least not with their regular games."

"Meaning?"

"Fenton got the impression she had other gambling connections, but he has no details. He said she was a good player and will be missed except by those who lost out to her."

Jennifer chuckles.

"Thanks for telling me," Jenner says.

"How are you doing?"

"Surviving."

"Are you coming in soon?"

"Sometime. How are you getting on with Williams?"

"I've managed to keep out of his way so far."

"Don't jeopardise yourself on my account."

"Have you had any more thoughts or would you rather forget it?"

"I've forgotten nothing. Maybe something will come up, nothing specific yet."

"In which case there's something else you need to know. The number '8541' has been discovered scratched on a wall just outside the station."

"But surely the whole area was examined thoroughly?"

"It was. There was a rigorous search during the initial investigation, thorough forensics. We had the road closed for two days. I'm absolutely certain nothing was found. It's appeared since the murder."

# 7

*THAT day the BBC News reported Liverpool had been raided again, but did not state how serious it had been. Those outside Liverpool were unaware how close the people were to breaking. They had endured a massive raid during the Wednesday night and Thursday morning with 232 tonnes of high explosive bombs and over 29,000 incendiaries. As the weather over Liverpool deteriorated part of the bomber force was diverted to Hull and unloaded 110 tonnes of high explosive bombs and over 9,500 incendiaries over the east coast city. Hull's misery slightly spared Liverpool.*

*In Nottingham the people were tired after seven consecutive nights sheltering in basements, under stairs and in cold, damp Anderson shelters in gardens. They heard the bombers making their way north west, knowing the likely target and relieved it was not them...for now.*

*One of the bombers was shot down over Nottinghamshire. Four of the crew offered no resistance and were captured. The body of a fifth was discovered. His parachute was unopened. The newspapers, restricted in their reports, merely said at the bottom of a column:*

'NIGHT RAIDER DOWN. An enemy raider crashed in flames in the North Midlands early yesterday morning. Four members of the crew who had baled out were taken prisoner.'

*It was a fine warm day, very welcome after the seemingly endless nights of winter. Nottingham people were making their way home, unaware that this night the Luftwaffe bombers would not just be passing over. Already at airfields in France, Belgium and Holland final preparations were being made for the night's mission. A total of 210 aircraft would be sent to Hull, Barrow in Furness and Nottingham – its share would be 107 with the target area in the south east of the city.*

*The night was clear and brilliantly lit by a full moon. The raid would begin with incendiaries, starting many fires, followed by high explosive bombs, which would drive civilians into the shelters. More bombs would keep them in the shelters while the fires spread and destroyed the city. More bombs would be aimed where the fires burned, pounding the firemen with the intention they would be driven to seek shelter from the explosions. Not all civilians would go to designated shelters. For some the basements of a pub or a church hall would suffice.*

*The rising and falling sounds of the sirens mingled with the unmistakable engine noise of the bombers. The terrible long night begins…*

## 27<sup>th</sup> April

Like Jenner, Jennifer is fascinated by the potential connection between wartime and the sightings of the ghost and the vintage train. Continuing to keep out of the way of Inspector Williams she uses every bit of spare time investigating the basic facts of the air raids and delves into all the newspaper and official reports she can find. Her collection of cuttings, photocopied archive reports and her own notes quickly expand into a bulky dossier. She's wary of this work being seen. It would mean batting away problematic questions and she's taken to heart Jenner's warning not to expose herself by being too closely associated with her old boss. She won't desert him for she knows his 'gut feeling' is based on insightful judgement and attested experience over many years. She'll pursue similar lines of enquiry, but until she's ready and has more robust evidence she'll keep shtum. She keeps the dossier in a locked drawer in the office and transfers it to her bag before going home.

This evening she makes a detour to visit Karen Renshaw at the hospital. PC David Warren will be on duty, still smarting after being on the receiving end of Jenner's tongue. She's sympathetic to his predicament and in any case has a good idea how he was so easily enticed from his post, allowing the 'mystery woman' to get in to see Karen. Whatever he says, she knows that woman was not Sarah Murrell.

She asks a few standard questions of the ward sister before moving up the corridor where David Warren stands in a state of desolate boredom outside Karen's room.

"Any change?" she asks, though already knowing the answer, but it's a way of putting him at ease.

"No, sarge," he says stiffly, "She's still in the coma, but stable."

"You look like you need a break. Go on, get down to the restaurant. I'll keep an eye on her."

He looks at her with puzzled embarrassment. He's obviously not heard.

"Chief Inspector Jenner is on leave," she says with a wink, "He'll not be coming in here today."

"Thank you," he says, then as an afterthought, "There's been no one to see her except her father. He spoke to the doctor and was allowed to look through the door, but not go in."

"Take your time," she says as he walks off, "a good half hour, you need it."

He ambles down the corridor, hovering at the nurses' station to talk, a little over long, with one of the young nurses. Any advances in that quarter he should have made already, Jennifer thinks, impatiently waiting for him to get away. Eventually he turns and with a slightly nervous glance in her direction, leaves the ward. The young nurse also watches him, then goes into one of the other rooms. Jennifer wastes no time and quickly slips in to see Karen.

She's in a deep coma, just as Jennifer last saw her. As before, a distinct 'feeling' permeates the room. She doesn't sit by the bed. That seems presumptuous and she might want to leave quickly if someone comes in. Instead she stands besides the head of the bed where she can see Karen as if from a position even higher, looking down not just on her but on anyone or anything that might be influencing her, perhaps another watcher or director. It's uncanny and disturbing, as a spectator might feel witnessing some terrible yet magnetic event.

All she can hear is the soft rising and falling of Karen's breathing, deep, seemingly strained yet oddly reassuring, a rhythmic continuum with no clear ending. Is this Karen's fate, to lie in this sterile demi-existence, neither living nor dead, unable to go back to the one or truly enter the other? The respiring pace is tranquillising. Jennifer shuts her eyes, but it's no empty daze and doesn't last. Fragmentary thoughts jostle for attention, but with their flitting imprecision her mind wanders aimlessly into a disturbing blackness. A sound rather than an image dominates, at first soft, dull, distant but then a higher note, whining up to a piercing howl. It's a sound she's never heard, but has imagined countless times and jars with the work she's been pursuing disjointedly throughout the day. It's an air raid siren.

It gradually wanes as an orchestra might close the overture before the performance begins. Now on the stage of the mind, pictures cluster erratically with disparate visions. People crowded in a darkened room, others running from a building, explosions, fire, water, then sounds of scrabbling through debris, shouting, screaming and the smell, then silence, but only for a moment until other images occupy the now empty stage.

She's in a train, the soft rattling of wheels on rails beating out a different rhythm, but no ordinary train. It's *that* train and from the grip of whatever extra sensory power pulls her in she knows what must come. It's a corridor train, many compartments crammed with noisy folk in a steaming smokiness. Walking smoothly through those standing she sees a man at the junction of two carriages. The chatter of the other passengers is less intrusive now. He slides his finger through the condensation on the door window. She moves closer, straining to see what it is. She's almost upon him. He turns to her plaintively. She's not afraid, but desperately curious to know what he's formed on the window. Could it be…?

…the predator! She's about to turn and run back along the corridor to the safety of the din of the crowd, but cannot move. Something stops her. She dare not go on towards the man, yet neither can she go back. For while the noise from the compartments has faded she knows she's not alone. Someone else is there, but *there* is no longer on a train, but here in Karen's room. Someone else is in the room!

With the sight and sounds of the train now faded she's in a blackness, interrupted only by Karen's dull breathing and the slight perceptible sound of another. Whatever it is she must see. She opens her eyes. The room is hazy, with indistinct shapes. The sense of immobility continues, her feet as rooted as her eyes are blurred. Gradually through the muzziness the bed, the window, the chair are defined and then beside the door a shape becomes a person. Jennifer is looking directly at the 'mystery woman.'

"So, you've returned," Jennifer says.

"Not quite the scene of the crime," Ettie Rodway says, "You don't seem surprised."

"As soon as I heard about the mystery woman I knew it had to be you."

"Does Jenner know?"

"He's not given it much thought. Just lately he's had other things on his mind."

"I was going to get in touch..."

"But you too had other things on your mind."

"Something like that."

"How did you get in here?"

"The same way you did."

"I'm a police officer."

"But not one the doctor allows to come into the room."

"So when you came before...don't tell me...you charmed that young constable who took you for one of the senior nursing staff."

"He was very trusting."

"And this time?"

"Things have turned up. I had to come back....I saw you at the main entrance. I thought if you could get in, I could get in."

Jennifer glances at the bed. Karen has not stirred.

"Come," she says, "As neither of us are meant to be in here, we must go outside."

"In a moment," Ettie says, "I need to spend a few minutes beside Karen."

"How long have you been here?"

"Long enough to know you were making contact."

"What do you make of it?"

"In a moment."

Jennifer pokes her head around the door, nodding to Ettie the corridor is clear.

"I'm supposed to be standing in for the PC. So don't be long."

"You can stay," Ettie says.

"No, I'll wait outside. If I knock three times..."

"All right."

Jennifer stood beside the head of the bed with her back to the wall, from which she could see anyone entering. Partly apprehensive, partly enquiring, she had to be ready for any power that might be guiding or directing Karen. Ettie is less concerned for her own safety, but just as curious. With Jennifer on guard she needn't protect her rear so takes up position with her back to the door, resting the water jug on the bottom of the bed, gripping it firmly in her left hand. From this position she can look directly at Karen, project any persuasive power and quickly receive any responses.

At first nothing happens. Karen remains comatose. Ettie is frustrated. She hasn't much time. She knows Jennifer was receiving some communication from Karen. Why doesn't she see nor hear anything? After all her years of experience her powers cannot be less than Jennifer's. The ambience is unchanged, nothing to disturb receptivity. Except a change of recipient. It's her. She will have to speak, stimulate Karen into opening the portal.

"I understand, Karen. I'm here to help you. Open the door of your mind, allow what you see, you hear, you feel to come through."

Karen doesn't stir. Ettie tries again.

"If you can disgorge your burden it will help you recover. Then we can…"

"What are you doing?"

Jennifer is behind her.

"You can't talk like this. She's a sick woman."

"She's not sick," Ettie says defiantly, still staring intently towards Karen.

"But you can't interfere with her treatment."

Jennifer is beside her, talking directly into her ear, but Ettie doesn't flinch from her vigil on Karen.

"I'm not interfering. She's been disturbed by the trauma."

"The attack."

"No. That's merely physical. I'm concerned with her inner health."

"Her physical health is also her inner…"

"Quiet! I must get on."

Not used to being put down Jennifer would ordinarily object, but shocked by Ettie's forthrightness she's silent. Ettie continues with a mixture of reassurance and provocation.

"I can see what you see, the man running from the building. I can hear the noise. It's deafening. You must be…"

Karen's head moves slightly and her lips quiver as if she's about to speak. Ettie stops. Jennifer is fearful and looks nervously towards the door.

Ettie closes her eyes, saying "I know, but where is this building. Is it…"

She stops, opens her eyes and says "Yes, but try to remember."

Karen directly faces Ettie. Her eyes are closed. Her lips move as if she's talking, but there's no sound. Ettie waits. Jennifer is very agitated and wonders if she should intervene.

"But the building," Ettie says, softly, but emphatically.

Karen speaks, very quietly. Ettie and Jennifer lean forward to catch her words.

"Him…him…train…he coming…the woman he…"

She stops and is impassive again.

"This is dangerous," Jennifer says, "We should call the nurses."

"No," Ettie says, "She's calm now."

"But she's coming out of the coma."

"She's not. She's in no danger. I must get on."

"You must not say anymore. You must stop this."

Ettie closes her eyes and waves for Jennifer to be silent and not interfere. Amazingly, Jennifer complies. Ettie doesn't speak. Jennifer quickly gets in front of her at the side of the bed. Ettie's eyes are closed, screwed tight in deep concentration. This continues for some moments. Karen doesn't stir. Jennifer gets more alarmed. Should she cast discretion to the wind, jeopardise her own position, drag Ettie from the room and call the nurses? If this gets out of hand…she glances again to the door, then at Karen and finally back to Ettie, for whose welfare she's now deeply concerned. Ettie's eyes open.

"The connection was breaking. That's why she appeared to be speaking."

"She *was* speaking."

"I tried to get the connection back, but she reverted to the ghost appearances and the attack on herself. I was trying to get her to expand on the building, but no matter."

"She mentioned a woman. Could it have been one of the women on the train who came to her aid?"

Ettie grimaces.

"Perhaps…perhaps not," she says quietly, then turns to Jennifer with reassuring smile, "We can leave now."

They return to the corridor. It's empty. Jennifer sits at one of the chairs and taps the next one for Ettie to join her.

"I thought I was your friend," she says reprovingly.

"You are, so all the better that you understand."

"Well, what did you achieve?"

"Much the same as you did, I guess."

"How can you know what…?"

"You saw the train, the so called ghost?"

"Yes. Did you?"

"I didn't need to. I knew already. Did you see Karen running from a building?"

"Yes and the noise."

"And the building was burning?"

"Something was. I could smell burning."

Ettie nods knowingly.

"I was partly successful. Karen is struggling. Her pain is very great."

"But the burning building?"

"Karen sees someone running from a building."

"While in her coma?" Jennifer says, struggling to comprehend.

"The coma is only her state of being at the moment. Her inner self lies beneath that veneer. Her essence is within and it's with that we must commune."

"Is it wise to badger her this way? Should we say anything to the nurses?"

"And admit we broke their rules and entered the room? I think not. In any case Karen is in no danger, at least no more than she was before."

"You cannot know that."

"If I were to unnaturally bring her out of the coma that could be dangerous. But that's not what I'm doing. The only danger in stimulating her inner self would be in suggesting things outside of her perception and I'm not doing that either."

Jennifer is neither understanding nor pleased.

"Now I know how you were able to get past the PC," she says, shaking her head disapprovingly.

Ettie is about to respond when she sees PC David Warren approaching. They both get up. When he sees Ettie he slows down and proceeds cautiously. Jennifer seizes the initiative.

"There's no reason to be concerned. I assume you know who this is?"

He stares incredulously at Ettie, then says, "She is…"

"The mystery woman has returned, but she's not who you thought she was."

Jennifer shows him a picture of Sarah Murrell. He stares at it intently, looks across at Ettie, then returns to the picture before glancing at Ettie again. Jennifer takes the picture back.

"There is only a slight resemblance," she says, "They're about the same age and when you're tired and…unduly persuaded…it's only too easy to assume a similarity."

David Warren knows Jennifer is letting him down softly. He can see now the two women are not alike.

"Are you going to say anything to Chief inspector Jenner?" he says anxiously.

"Of course. He'll understand. This is Ettie Rodway. She's assisted us on previous enquiries. DCI Jenner knows her well."

"So you knew she was going to be here?"

Jennifer hesitates.

"I think we've all been a little confused. Karen Renshaw has not been disturbed. Least said, least mended, shall we say."

Only David is confused.

"Well, now that's cleared up, we'll be on our way," Jennifer says.

"No change then?" he says.

"Change?"

"With Karen."

"No, you told me when I arrived."

"Oh yes, so I did. I thought perhaps you might have seen the doctor."

"I had a brief word. Nothing new, except…if she does come round, you'll ring me immediately…any time."

Jennifer and Ettie leave. They say nothing as they make their way along the corridor. Even in the lift they remain silent, even though they're alone, both unwilling to speak within the hospital boundaries. Jennifer breaks the silence only when they leave the building.

"Ettie, we have to talk."

"We do indeed. We'll go to my hotel. I assume you're off duty now. You probably need a drink."

On the way they talk of old times and previous enquiries on which they've all worked together.

"It's given the DCI a reputation he'd rather not have," Jennifer says.

"For solving otherwise unfathomable cases?"

"This is beginning to feel *unsolvable.*"

"Even less so than other cases."

"There's much adverse press coverage."

"I know. I've had..." Ettie begins, then breaks off.

"Two days ago he was taken off the case. They've used his previous unusual cases as an excuse."

"So he's the scapegoat for the lack of progress and the flak in the *Courier?*"

"It seems so. What were you going to say?"

"Never mind, I'll tell you later."

After a few drinks in the hotel bar they start to relax and Jennifer opens up the conversation.

"You came about the case?"

"I'd heard of it. So I came."

"Then why didn't you call us?"

Ettie hesitates, thinking how best to explain her initial reluctance to see her and Jenner.

"You see it was more than normal curiosity and the prospect of meeting up with old friends. All the way I felt driven to get here as soon as possible. When I arrived, saw the local paper and spoke to locals I went straight to the hospital and got into Karen Renshaw's room."

"By brazen subterfuge."

"Yes, I'm ashamed to say. I don't normally do such things, but being able to get round that poor young policeman was as if I was using powers way beyond what I can usually deploy. Yet it wasn't me. I was just the vehicle. Just as I'd been driven to get to Nottingham, then driven to get to the hospital, enabled to see Karen and learn what she was experiencing."

"That's exactly what I felt," Jennifer says excitedly.

"After a fitful night's sleep, I was driven again next day. This time to get to Sharp Road and the archaeological dig."

Ettie explains her time at Sharp Road, the 'Grapes' pub and where the church hall used to be.

"You see now the significance of what we both felt when we were in communication with Karen?"

"The burning is the war?" Jennifer says.

"Exactly."

"It was so vivid, as if I was actually there."

Jennifer recounts all she 'saw' and 'heard' in Karen's room.

"But how can it be? If I was picking up...communicating in some way...mind to mind with Karen, how could she have seen such things, she's younger than me?"

"She's not *seen* these things any more than you have. You...and I...have been enabled to communicate with what's been communicated to her."

"But how? She's in a coma."

"Whatever...whoever...has communicated with her it was before she was attacked. We're only able to share in her experience *because* she is in a coma. Those memories, experiences are locked in by the coma. It protects her."

"Protects her from what?"

"That's what we have to find out."

Jennifer shudders.

"I don't understand. You're experienced in these things, but I am only a police sergeant. I respect what you say, what you can discern and, though I don't yet know how, that these things may help the enquiry, but why am I making contact with...the past?"

"You've always had an interest in historical matters, Jennifer."

"But this is different."

"It gives you an advantage, a tool that makes it easier to get contact, a key to the door as it were."

Jennifer is perplexed. She gulps down the last of her drink and orders some more.

"I'll have to get a cab home," she laughs, then more seriously "Can these things only be seen by women - Karen, you, me, the women on the train?"

"Very probably, but remember it's a man on the train. The message at the heart of all this, if that's what it is, must be from a man."

"You seem very sure."

"Let's say I have suspicions."

"And what are these *suspicions* based on."

"I've seen Arlene Bates."

"She's disappeared?"

Ettie recounts her meeting with Arlene, her obsession with the war, the memories of her great uncle Wilf and her peculiar reticence to talk about Sarah Murrell.

"Where is she?" Jennifer says.

"I don't know. I had to get to Mansfield, but I don't know where we went from there. She brought me back from her aunt's house, but it was late and dark and we came into the city from such an unfamiliar direction. I got very confused."

"Sounds like she did it deliberately. Why is she afraid of being seen in the city? What's she afraid of?"

Ettie doesn't answer.

"You think she's implicated with the attack on Karen?" Jennifer says.

"It's possible."

"It doesn't make sense."

"It might if she's desperate."

"She has to unburden herself?"

"Perhaps."

"Does she know you have a connection with us?"

"I told her I was acquainted with Jenner."

"Then it makes even less sense. The clandestine meeting away from the city at the house of an aunt who's conveniently somewhere else. Picking you up at a bus station in Mansfield, running around the countryside, creeping back into the city at night by the most roundabout route she can devise. Not wanting to talk about the murder of Sarah Murrell."

"She's obsessed with Karen Renshaw."

"And the war."

"I think she had to talk to someone independent, unconnected with the city, her work, her family."

"She'd done her homework on you."

"She has more to tell."

"You were trying to get out of Karen about the building… from which she saw a man running."

"We must find out more."

"You can't go back to the hospital and see Karen again."

Ettie says nothing.

"You know where this building is?" Jennifer says.

"I suspect where it is. It's a place to which I *will* return."


## 28<sup>th</sup> April

Laid up in his flat Jenner is not idle. The mysterious number '8541' discovered scratched on the outside wall of Nottingham railway station galvanises him into further enquiry. He doesn't doubt what Jennifer said about the number appearing *after* initial enquiries following the discovery of Sarah Murrell's body, but he has to satisfy himself. He always likes to get a 'feel' for a crime scene and he won't be denied this one.

He gets to the railway station and finds the place. It's on the wall in the same street where Sarah Murrell was found, some fifty yards further from the main entrance to the station. He's surprised to find the area has not been secured. Presumably the relevant forensic examinations and photographs have been taken. The number is clearly visible, about five centimetres in height and well formed. This is no capricious act of drunken vandalism. Someone has gone to some trouble to leave a neat and legible impression. The numbers were meant to be found.

A couple of workmen are standing by the wall with brushes and canisters.

"What are you doing here?" Jenner says gruffly.

"Could ask you the same thing, mate," one says.

Jenner shows his warrant card.

"Your lot have been and gone," the other says, "Haven't you heard?"

"Heard what?"

"We were told to shift this off the wall. Orders from the police."

"Yes, of course," Jenner says, "I just wanted a final look before it was removed. Do you know which officer gave the order?"

"Don't know. You'll have to see't station manager."

"Of course."

Jenner takes a photograph, then goes to the station. The manager is a little surprised to see him.

"Your senior officer, Mr. Emmins, insisted the damage was removed without delay. Something about not wanting to unnecessarily alarm the public and avoid a spate of similar copycat activities. Ordinarily we'd deal with it as part of routine maintenance of the building anyway, but as he was so concerned I arranged for it to be dealt with immediately."

"Quite right," Jenner says.

"Was there any special reason for your visit...er...chief inspector?"

"Nothing important. I've been away on another case. I was in the area so I thought I'd come and see. Well thank you, good morning."

Jenner gets away before he's assailed by any more embarrassing questions, leaving the manager shrugging in puzzlement.

Of course, if the story about '8541' being seen on the train had been kept under wraps none of this would be necessary. Copy cats indeed, isn't that what he told Emmins and Davies? That wretched journalist Arlene Bates again...

He goes to the central library and like Arlene and Jennifer works through all the material he can find on the Nottingham blitz. Then he draws up a timeline from initial incidents in 1940 right through to the end of the war, though he soon concentrates on the heaviest period in 1941. It's then it comes to him.

How could he have been so stupid? Why didn't he immediately see what was staring him in the face? Not a pin number or an address or a truncated phone number or somebody's birthday, but definitely a date. '8541.' 8th May 1941! Up to that time the city had been relatively unscathed, but then all changed. It was the worst night of air raids.

Great swathes of the city were engulfed with incendiaries and high explosive bombs. The attack and subsequent damage was so severe fire crews were overwhelmed and police were closing streets to ensure public safety. Station Street, temporarily closed as the site of Sarah Murrell's murder in 1941 was completely blocked and remained so for some time because of debris from the collapsed Boots Printing Works and an unexploded bomb at the railway station. In the goods yard 100 wagons and coaches were on fire.

With so many calls for assistance many fires burned unchecked. Fire crews were so stretched they continually had to decide which fires to tackle and which to leave. More and more incendiaries were being dropped while other fires were fought.

Many churches were damaged. One, St. John's was entirely gutted by fire. As soon as the one at St. Peter's Church was brought under control they had to immediately transfer their wheeled ladder to the roof of a bank, then heard an explosion only fifty yards away where a paper company had been hit. The fire at St. Mary's church was particularly hazardous. Firemen were hampered getting to the church because of other crews fighting fires all around it. Then they found the fire was raging at a place where it was difficult to gain access with the appliance. Fighting the fire from the turntable ladder was dangerous and largely ineffective. The fire was too deep rooted. They would have to tackle it from inside only to find they had insufficient hose and spare pumping capacity. In the Lace Market area fires were spreading and in danger of joining up to create one massive inferno. Water was in short supply. Crews had the lengthy job of relaying from underground tanks. Elsewhere water was taken directly from the canal.

Jenner ploughs through the long list of destruction – gasometers (two received direct hits), railway lines, shops, works and factories, the constant threat from collapsing buildings, bomb craters in many roads impeding the emergency services, fractured water mains, gas mains blazing fiercely. Both football grounds and the cricket ground were embedded with incendiaries. The noise was incessant – the roar of the fires and the constant reverberating bombers and engine noise of fire pumps, the muffled thump of bombs and the pounding of anti aircraft shells.

Church bells were heard peeling at a village nine miles away, which was strictly prohibited. When people went up the church tower to investigate they found the drone of the aircraft engines approaching the city for over an hour had become a constant roar which made the bells vibrate with a ringing sound. Across the fields an orange red glow could be seen on the skyline as far away as Macclesfield.

Many fire crews had been sent elsewhere, especially to Liverpool and Hull and on return to Nottingham were exhausted. Many firemen in the city would come back to find their houses had been burnt to the ground while they were saving other properties. Unexploded bombs were a continuing menace. 59 were reported in the city area. During the night over 400 high explosive bombs and nearly 7000 incendiaries were dropped. Over 200 incidents were logged. Casualty services were overwhelmed.

Now Jenner reaches the most harrowing part of his researches – the human cost. Many surface air raid shelters were destroyed and rescuing survivors was hampered because they were buried under debris. Well over 5000 houses were damaged, nearly a thousand people rendered homeless. In all, 200 were killed. The greatest tragic incident was three direct hits from high explosive bombs on the Co-op bakery on Meadow Lane while the night shift was still on the premises. Flames shooting from gaps in the rubble, fed by fats used as part of the baking process meant the fire brigade was unable to make much impact. The death toll was 50.

The aftermath of that dreadful night would go on. The following day people went to see the crater left by the impact of an unexploded bomb. When it went off 5 were killed and 28 were injured by the blast. Ten days later when an unexploded bomb was detonated it started a fire. While it was being extinguished another detonation was heard. It was another bomb no one knew anything about.

Typical of the time one newspaper with clinical understatement merely reported 'Sharp Raid on Midland town. Widespread damage.'

Jenner is exhausted. Even from the vantage of eighty years the dispassionate official records shake him to the core. He leans back and closes his eyes. He needs a recovery spell. After a few minutes rest he puts away the documents and his notes. Only now does the full impact for his enquiries sink in.

His interest in the war is well founded. What the women saw on the train – an old train with compartments, compatible with a train in wartime, the crowds, the noise and the man...the 'ghost,' the 'predator'...above all a man in 'old' clothes...could it be the clothes a man would typically wear in the 1940s? The number clinches it. Even allowing for Arlene's exaggerations, it was seen by many women at various places on the train and is then scratched on the side of the station where the same train terminated its journey. That, more than anything else is what links the attack on Karen Renshaw to the murder of Sarah Murrell. Somehow they are both related to that infernal night of the blitz. But there's a difference. The number appeared on the train *before* Karen was attacked while the number scratched on the wall definitely appeared *after* Sarah was killed. The connection is an uncomfortable one and he shudders.

Are there two killers, with the second copying the first? He has rejected the possibility of a killer or killers without a clear motive other than their own deranged satisfaction. But if he's right and the connection is merely the number being repeated, then it becomes a real possibility that at least the second killer is such. Yet Karen and Sarah are otherwise connected as Jennifer has discovered. They knew each other. That must mean Sarah is no random victim. Are there two villains? After all, Karen was only attacked albeit viciously whereas Sarah was deliberately and expeditiously killed.

His fixation on the date brings everything together - the air raid, the sightings on the train, the 'ghost.' It strengthens his resolve. He no longer questions his own abilities. His critics may say he's too obsessed with 'the past' and 'pseudo investigations.' Maybe that's an obsession he should have cultivated earlier in the investigation.

He finds a contemporary official assessment, not wholly reported in the newspapers, which sets out the extent of damage as well as casualties on that fearful night of 8th / 9th May. He makes a list of the terrible toll in property and lives. It's a depressing paper. The bleak numbers enliven his imagination and he has to stop. War is a horrible business. The vindictive deployment of incendiary bombs lighting up the path for more obliteration, the misery, the destruction, the slaughter of the innocent.

He returns to the records and completes his list. One place catches his eye. A church hall receives a direct hit. The basement was being used as a shelter. He skims over the grisly catalogue of casualties and notices the location, a short distance from the archaeological exploration at the building site on Sharp Road. He lingers, reading again the address as if it contains a connection to his enquiries. The sightings, the ghost, the attacks on Karen and Sarah come to mind, but as it has no obvious significance he returns to the records.

The newspapers were not wholly concerned with the war and the air raids and his natural inclination soon homes in on the criminal activities of the time. He's surprised by the amount. Rather than diminishing during the war certain criminal pursuits actually increased. This was especially the case with house breaking, general robbery and petty crime. The blackout and deserted streets acted as a welcome shield to such villains just as the black market and illegal trading flourished during the rationing and scarcities of goods. The 'wartime spirit,' of solidarity, fortitude and altruism did not extend to all citizens. In all times there are those willing and able to exploit the weakness and vulnerability of others.

There are references to a persistent and successful run of robberies and he's amused to find the local newspapers were as quick then as they are now to lambaste the police's 'lack of progress.' One name keeps cropping up, a petty criminal called Ronald Calthorpe who is charged a few times, but never successfully prosecuted. He suspects the detectives at the time knew who was responsible, but were unable to assemble sufficiently damning evidence. It's fascinating, but at best only tangential to the work in hand. He'd like to take it further, examine police records, but that would divert him from the main investigation. It's only then he remembers that he's been taken off the case. But why should a minor matter like that get in the way of some 'good coppering?'

The 'other cases,' which the powers that be have so graciously assigned to him stretch neither his intellect nor his time and he's already concluded most of them without giving Emmins the satisfaction of bestowing even more detritus. As such, at least for a few days he's free to pursue his own enquiries unhindered. Bundling up his extensive notes he walks across town to the police station and instead of going to his office, slips down to the archives. There's plenty of material extending over the whole wartime period. He concentrates on matters more directly connected to the air raids and particularly the grim night of 8$^{th}$ / 9$^{th}$ May 1941.

As an emergency service the police were inevitably involved with the terrible carnage, assisting the fire and ambulance services as well as ensuring public order was maintained in such traumatic circumstances. To his surprise there are detailed reports concerning the direct hit on the church hall near the junction of Wisden and Kingston streets. There were few survivors to be evacuated, most work concerned with the grim recovery of bodies. Important and necessary, but why was it recorded in such harrowing detail? Other places were hit that night, for which there are extensive civil defence and fire service accounts, but less so police ones. Why is the church hall disaster different? There must have been something of broader criminal interest.

He trawls through the reports for any reference to crimes associated with the area. A particularly cunning villain might have taken advantage of more than the blackout. During an air raid houses would be left unoccupied as people went to a local shelter, providing a profitable opportunity for an unscrupulous and enterprising burglar. Someone like Ronald Calthorpe perhaps? Then he finds it and the police interest is clear. Among the unfortunate victims killed by the direct hit on the church hall was Ronald Calthorpe.

He feels a twinge of disappointment. Calthorpe was such an interesting character. He was looking forward to following up his later exploits and discovering whether he was ever subsequently brought to book. But his criminal career was so abruptly cut short and he's never heard of again.

Then he's suddenly wrenched out of his brooding.

"So this is where you're hiding."

He looks up to see Jennifer.

"I'm not hiding."

She closes the door carefully and comes over.

"How did you know I was here?" he says sheepishly as he closes the files.

"Not difficult to figure out," she says, sitting down in the opposite chair, "I was told at the desk you'd been seen entering the station, but as I couldn't find you in the office, where else could you be?"

"You know me too well."

"Found anything interesting?"

"You need to be careful. If Inspector Williams comes down and finds you talking to me…"

"He's out and anyway, you're only off the case, not off the force."

She fingers the files and skims through them.

"Wartime records, very interesting."

"Taking your time," he says.

"You're not the only one with an interest in the war."

She explains Ettie is in Nottingham and has been contacted by Arlene.

"She's been very busy," he says, "Pity she couldn't have got in touch earlier."

"I've told you. She had to follow up Arlene."

"So we now know where Arlene Bates is."

"Not exactly."

Jennifer explains Arlene's secret location at her aunt's house, her reluctance to be seen in the city and Ettie's confusion during the journey.

"There's a rabbit off here."

"There's more."

Jennifer recounts her visit to the hospital and their experiences with Karen Renshaw. He whistles.

"Oh dear, contravening doctor's orders, potentially undermining not only the recovery of the victim, but also the investigation itself. Whatever would Inspector Williams, let alone Chief Superintendent Emmins say?"

"Much the same as they would say if they knew Chief Inspector Jenner was still engaged on the enquiry and wasting his time trawling through eighty year old files with no obvious relevance."

He chuckles.

"Maybe you didn't come down here just to find me."

"I *did* come to find you, but I say again, have you found anything interesting?"

He explains the significance of '8541,' the $8^{th}$ / $9^{th}$ May air raid and the direct hit on the church hall. Now it's her turn to whistle.

"Ettie said she suspected the location of the building where she felt Karen saw someone running out. It could be the church hall. It's also close to the building site where the archaeologists were working and now there's an unexploded bomb scare. There used to be a pub on that site called the 'Cross Keys."

"A pub," he says, remembering the crowded place in his imagination, "Wasn't that also what you and Ettie got from Karen?"

"Yes, it fits. Ettie went in a pub across the road from where the church hall was. It was called the 'Grapes."

"Two different pubs."

"I know it'll sound crazy..."

"Don't stop. It all sounds crazy. I've been thinking crazy things too. It's best to get it all out. Perhaps then we can judge what's really crazy and what's not."

"I was wondering. What if the 'ghost' - or whatever it is the women saw on the train – was set off by the work on the site of the pub, but that doesn't work if it's a different pub."

Jenner considers for a moment.

"But you say the 'Cross Keys' was destroyed by a bomb."

"Well, partly, what was left was demolished."

"And there could have been another bomb, an unexploded one."

"If you're thinking around that air raid and the direct hit on the church hall, another bomb a quarter mile away doesn't explain the ghost."

"I suppose not."

While Jenner lapses into another reverie about the war with visions of the terrible air raid, Jennifer examines the records of the destruction of the church hall. Lost in their own concentrated thoughts, they're silent for a few minutes. Then Jenner emerges from the fire and a running man.

"Whoever is on the train – ghost or otherwise – he must have a connection to the air raid. It has to be someone in the church hall, a victim or a survivor."

"I don't know about the ghost, but there may be a connection. Did you check all the names of the people in the church hall?"

"I skimmed them," he says vaguely, not wanting to admit it was the information on petty thief, Ronald Calthorpe that really took his attention.

"The survivors or the victims?" she says.

"There weren't many survivors," he says, meaning he was concentrating on a particular victim.

"I've been through all the documents. One of the survivors has an interesting name – John Renshaw."

"What? Let me see," he says, grabbing the file.

"Do you see?" she says.

"I do. Could John Renshaw be…?"

"Karen Renshaw's grandfather?"

"One and the same John Renshaw who left for Brazil after the war who, according to his son Keith wasn't 'well off' when he returned and drifted into the building trade."

"And was killed in an accident on a building site in 1965."

"Not an accident at all according to Keith."

"He blames the Duggers. I didn't see a Dugger on that list of survivors."

"Nor on the list of victims. Just as I missed John Renshaw as a survivor, I think you may have missed an interesting name amongst the victims."

"It's a long list. I was just about to…"

"What do you make of this?" he says, passing back the file with one name he's ringed in pencil.

"Hilda Wallace?" she says.

"Another coincidence? Could this unfortunate woman be related to the Wallaces?"

"Simon Wallace mentioned his grandfather Albert, who started the business after the war."

"But nothing about a Hilda Wallace?"

"No."

"Looks like we…you…will need to go back and interview Simon Wallace again."

"He was reluctant to go into details, but eventually he admitted he did know Karen."

"And he was at the hospital. Maybe their connection goes back much further."

"Then there's John Renshaw. I've not seen him."

"But I have. I should go back and see him."

"You're not supposed to be on the case."

"Is that right? Then I shall have to go as someone with a particular interest in wartime Nottingham."


## 29<sup>th</sup> April

The uncertainty at Sharp Road continues. A structural engineer, examining the integrity of the building work discovers certain metallic objects. The archaeologists, desperate to be allowed back on the 'dig' gleefully seize on the finds, only to disagree amongst themselves on their origin and significance. They argue about whether the finds are medieval or early modern, finally reaching a loose consensus that they're not especially old artefacts. One of them turns over an unfamiliar shape.

"It's an alloy," he says, "I don't like the look of this."

He returns it to the site and asks the engineer where it was found. The engineer, more concerned with getting the building work restarted is unsure and points vaguely to the hole where part of the cave network can be seen.

"Was it on the surface or deep down?" the archaeologist says.

The engineer shakes his head.

"If it was deeper is it more likely to be old?" he says, then jocularly, "Tell you what, I'll say it was found on the ground so it's not so old, then there'll be no point you being here and we can start building again!"

The archaeologist is not amused.

"Tell you what," the engineer says, trying to be helpful, "some of those things were definitely found deeper even if this one wasn't."

"We're not interested in the others."

"So you do believe this is older?"

"It's not that old, it's an alloy."

"Is it now?" the engineer says, carefully turning the metal over in his hands, "That could mean…"

He's interrupted by the sound of movement. They both step closer and peer down. Small piles of loose soil have appeared around the edges of the bottom of the hole. They stand stock still, watching and waiting, then there's a slithering sound.

"Get back!" the engineer shouts, "It's not stable."

It's as well they do for the ground previously beneath their feet suddenly opens up, then collapses into the hole. This is followed by deeper openings and rumblings, the ground cracking and louder sounds of falling rock. Fearing the whole area could open up they run further back, only stopping at a good distance at the edge of the site. They wait again for the sounds of movement to subside.

"Is it safe to go back?" the archaeologist says.

"Carefully," the engineer says and leads the way gingerly to the side of the now much larger hole.

Fallen soil and rock has filled in part of the hole, but also exposed more of the caves. The archaeologist leans over and stares down.

"Don't get so close," the engineer says, gently pulling him back.

"Those caves could stretch for miles," the archaeologist says.

"Don't even think about it," the engineer says with a wry smile, "You're not going down there to ferret about after more bits and pieces."

"The caves in the middle of town were inhabited in medieval times. These might have been too," the archaeologist says, savouring further explorations, "this land fall is excavating it for us."

"Oh yes? And holding up this development even further?"

The engineer gazes down disdainfully.

"If these caves are as extensive as you say, we'll have to abandon the project altogether even if we're not held up again by you lot digging around and subverting our schedule. Then we'll have to…wait a minute, what's that?"

The archaeologist leans over again.

"What have you seen?"

"There, look, near the bottom on the right side, that smooth bit between the rock, it's metal and it's big. Bloody hell, it's a bomb!"

The few houses in the street that escaped the first fears are now evacuated and specialist bomb disposal officers are recalled. By the time they arrive there are further earth falls, concealing the metallic fragment seen by the engineer and the archaeologist. Major Phillips, the officer in charge finds it difficult to accurately identify the probable area in which the supposed bomb is likely to lie. As the engineer and archaeologist have remained near the site he seeks their help, but it's not easy. Since they were last at its edge the hole has changed area, depth and shape. They describe the movements, the exposed caves and the 'side of what looked like a bomb.' Phillips is dubious. There's already been one 'false alarm' and he hopes he's not been called out unnecessarily. Then the archaeologist produces the alloy fragment.

"Where did you get that?" Phillips says.

"We're not sure. When we thought the site was safe we came back to retrieve some metallic objects for further analysis. Unfortunately they weren't especially old and therefore…"

"It's old enough," Phillips says, "You didn't find this in the hole, did you?"

"With all the excavation both by us and the archaeologists," the engineer says, "a lot of material has been displaced. I think it was probably found on the surface. So, it's nothing to do with the bomb?"

"I'm afraid it is. It's an alloy…"

"Like I said," the archaeologist chips in.

"…and it's definitely part of a bomb. There are three parts, nose, body and base, welded together, but the tail fin is made of a lighter alloy attached by screws or rivets. See here."

Phillips turns it over and shows the damage to the side of the metal.

"Tail fins were often torn off on impact. So, it's a definite sign. There is or was a bomb near here. I would say it's between 50 and 500 kilograms."

"So it could be a big one?" the engineer says.

"The only problem now is finding it," Phillips says.

They insist on accompanying him to the hole. Ordinarily that would be out of the question, but his cursory inspection failed to find the 'smooth metallic surface' they described. So he agrees and after firmly instructing them to stay close to him and make no sudden movements he leads the way carefully to the edge of the hole. Even then they can only provide vague directions.

"So much has moved," the archaeologist says.

"Then we'll have to dig down," Phillips says, dubiously scanning the hole.

The two 'helpers' are safely moved back. Then Phillips returns with his team and they delicately excavate the fallen soil, and rock. No matter how cautiously they work several times they break into more caves and pull back anxiously until the rubble has settled. It could be a long job. Hours pass. Yet no matter how warily they proceed and how tired they become, they work with energy beyond mere professional commitment. For despite the danger they're impelled to find the bomb whatever the cost. It's as if some unseen force draws them wider, deeper, closer to where it lies.

By early evening the hole is very deep and they still haven't found anything. Then one sapper, softly striking the earth hears the telltale slightly ringing sound that he knows is neither soil nor rock. He stops immediately. Phillips comes over, gently scrapes some loose soil and exposes a wider section of metal, recognising it as part of the body of the bomb.

"It's big," he mutters, echoing the engineer, "I hope it's not one of them."

He means a bomb with a delayed action fuse, which can be activated if disturbed.

"We'll have to find it. Get to the nose. Now, very, very steadily."

Working through the earth from both ends, the men gradually reveal more and more of the 'big 'un' until Phillips is sure there's enough room to tackle the fuse. He orders all but a few of the men up the ladder and out of the hole while he makes a careful examination. He's ready to open up and retrieve the fuse when they feel a movement beneath their feet, followed by a slithering above. Then with a sudden jerk the bomb drops down.

"Get out!" Phillips shouts, "Quickly, quickly!"

# 8

## 30th April

ANY hope the 'disturbances' on the London train will abate soon fades. Though nothing is reported for a couple of days, anxiety and alarm in the city remains and passenger numbers are well down. It's always on the evening train from London. No other services are affected. Some wily travellers take an earlier train or one much later, but not everyone can do this and a few take the bus. It takes longer and is less comfortable, but what's comfort in the face of such a dreaded prospect? The fear of what *might* be seen or heard is too much for too many. A few young women, courageous or reckless depending on point of view, choose to travel on the 'ghost train' as 'a bit of a lark' in which brazen curiosity overrides prudence, but they keep in tight groups for protection. They see nothing, but their disappointment is quickly forgotten when on the third day some passengers stagger from the train on arrival in Nottingham quaking and distressed.

The agitation continues into a fourth day. Despite police presence there are still sightings of the man in the odd clothes, visions of an 'old' train with compartments, shabby upholstering and the noise of many more passengers than are actually on the train. If anything the sights and sounds are more wide ranging than before and although no one is attacked or even feels directly threatened by the 'man' talk of a 'predator' picks up again. There's chaos on one train with women screaming and shouting in one carriage, but despite an extensive search police find no one suspicious.

Once more the media panic machine accelerates into overdrive and Inspector Williams is forced to make a feeble statement, regretting the 'latest upset' and promising 'rigorous action.' Predictably unimpressed, the *Courier* mercilessly criticises the 'woeful lack of progress.' Jenner wonders what Emmins will make of that.

Then there's a lull. Nothing is reported for a day. Many believe the 'visitations' have ceased, but Ettie is sure this is only a pause and the apparition - if that's what it is - will quickly return. She makes her plans accordingly. Noting that ghostly activity is primarily seen and heard between Leicester and Nottingham she catches an early train for Leicester, from where she'll join the down train from London.

Not many other people wait on the platform and when it arrives many more leave than join the train. There are plenty of available seats, yet women bunch up in close clusters. Ettie deliberately avoids these groups. It's more likely she'll see or hear something when she's alone. She finds a completely empty carriage, which in 'normal' times would be unknown. A couple of young women walk through on their way to the buffet car. They look at her bewilderingly.

"Are you all right, duck?" one says.

"I'm fine, thank you," Ettie says, smiling reassuringly.

"You can come and sit with us if you like," the other says.

"Thank you, but no."

They hover, obviously concerned for her welfare.

"You know about this train, don't you?" the first one says, "It might not be safe to be on your own."

Ettie thanks them again, confirms she knows about the train and reiterates she's 'perfectly all right.' They're unconvinced. Ettie is solidly emphatic. She 'knows what she's doing.' After they've gone she glances around the bare seats. Is she wise to reject their help? If anything is to happen might it not be better if there are witnesses? This is a lame excuse. If she moves it will be out of fear rather than professional acuity. It passes. She's alone out of choice and isn't afraid. Whatever is to be revealed will be benign. But...can she really be sure?

At Loughborough more get off and hardly anyone gets on. She settles down for the last few miles, disappointed and a little annoyed. What right has this apparition to ignore her? Maybe it knows her special sensitivities and is determined not to be unmasked. Perhaps it's a mischievous presence, delighting in unnerving the innocent, playing with gullible imaginings, but avoiding anyone who'll not be easily fooled. No. If it's real it's serious. It has a message to convey, however muddled and incoherently communicated.

Then she sees him. A cloudy form, slowly coalescing into a recognisable shape. A man stands at the far end, near the connection to the next carriage, where there's now no automatic door, but a wooden one with a handle. She looks around. The modern open carriage has disappeared and she's standing rather than sitting in a corridor, as so many women described, old, worn, very 1940s.

He looks directly towards her. She concentrates keenly. She must remember every detail. His clothes are old in time, but not in condition. He's not shabby, dressed simply in a neat suit, which may have seen better days, but is clean, pressed and relatively smart. He's young, in his late twenties. He doesn't move, but continues staring. Will he come closer?

There's the beginning of a slight smile at the side of his mouth, but it doesn't broaden, instead it's nervously stilted. Could he be more fearful of her than she is of him? He turns to his side and points a wearied arm towards the window. He turns back and nods just once. He keeps staring, but still doesn't move and then, very gradually his form becomes hazy again until it's gone. She looks around and behind. There's no one else. She's still in the old train though now she hears the rattling of the carriage and the rumbling of the wheels.

She walks towards where the man was standing. He'll not return tonight. She stops where he stood and looks back along the corridor. There's still no one with her, though for the first time since the man appeared she hears chatter from the next carriage. Gradually the corridor and the old compartments fade until the vacant seats of the modern open carriage assume their place. She turns back to the window. It's an old window, which she could open by pulling down from the top. It's as it was. She's back in wartime. She turns again and looks back to see the modern seating, then turns again to face the old window. One way she's in the present, the other she's in the past.

She stares hard at the window. It's misted except four numbers have been cleared with a finger. '8541.' She looks closer, her breath condensing on the window. She curses herself. She'll cloud over the numbers. She leans back. The numbers are still there. She shudders with fear. She wipes away the condensation, gliding over the numbers, but when she takes her hand away they are still there. She clears the window again, but the numbers remain. She rubs them vigorously several times. It's no good. No matter how many times and with increasing pressure she wipes, the number '8541' won't be rubbed off the window.

At Sharp Road the initial shock passes, but the whole area is evacuated, disrupting many more people than previously. The residents and the public at large are advised the inconvenience is 'purely precautionary' and there's 'no immediate danger.' It has the opposite effect to what's intended. If the bomb is not so dangerous why is it necessary for so many to be kept away? Newspaper and broadcasting reports only exacerbate the situation, especially as they receive few, let alone explicable, answers to their questions.

A view circulates the bomb isn't immediately likely to explode (a more cynical interpretation that if it was going to explode it would have done so by now!) and therefore it should be moved quickly to a safe place for detonation. The archaeologists, who have been attracted to the site like hungry vultures are very happy with this proposal. The sooner the bomb is got out of the way the sooner they can resume their excavation as the 'moving bomb' and the disposal team have already done most of the hard work.

However, Major Phillips is uneasy and far more concerned than the official information implies. Since the bomb 'slipped' there've been more earth and rock falls, making it difficult to formulate a clear plan of action. A bomb that's prone to 'slipping' only avoids detonation by good fortune. Helping it on its way by loading on a lorry and transporting it out of the city could be tempting a dangerously rickety fate. Before he calls in further men and equipment he'll make one more careful examination.

Even though he's only been away from the hole for a short time the bomb already appears to have moved yet again. Or do his eyes confuse him? The longer he looks he wonders whether it's actually moved! He shakes himself. This is ridiculous. Tiredness and an over active imagination need to be curbed. He gets down closer. The whole bomb is not exposed though from previous examinations he knows it's a large one. It's lodged in sandstone rock, which will have to be carefully supported during removal. Best to first excavate beneath so the bomb can be propped up, but that's precarious in itself. Even then it'll need significant preparatory work to ensure the bomb is reasonably stable before being moved.

Phillips imagines all the pitfalls as he emerges from the hole. There are potential disasters at every stage from first digging under and around the bomb to eventual arrival at an appropriate and distant place for it to be safely detonated. He walks around the hole for several minutes, apparently examining the area, but really mulling over all the hazardous eventualities that could beset them. It's no good. This big bomb is going to be too problematic to move.

There remains only one viable alternative - a 'controlled explosion' on site. He talks it over with his team, the engineer from the builders, representatives of the local authority and the emergency services. The police very reluctantly accept the prospect of a complicated and distressing scenario. It's bound to mean the evacuation of an even larger area. The local authority officers are extremely concerned at the possibility of collateral damage to surrounding properties. The archaeologists are predictably furious. Excavating, however indelicately carried out is one thing, but an explosion of any kind is bound to destroy any archaeology.

"Surely it can be moved," their leader says, despite having received a full explanation of the situation.

Phillips doesn't immediately comment. Moving it would be preferred, but he's unsure of its stability.

"It might go off anywhere between here and the detonation site," he says bluntly.

The archaeologist turns very pale. He says nothing for some moments, then remembers his principal priority.

"There could be invaluable medieval remains down there. It's even possible there's a lost monastery. We know of incidental references in several fourteenth century documents. The caves, which proliferate at this end of the city, are also of immense historical significance. If they're lost..."

"I'm not concerned with *incidental references*," Phillips says dryly, "We are dealing with an extremely dangerous high explosive, whose behaviour is to say the least highly erratic."

"Behaviour?" the archaeologist says incredulously, "You make it sound as if the damned thing has a mind of its own!"

Phillips says nothing and goes to speak to the police superintendent. The archaeologist retreats to talk to his colleagues.

One of the sappers has overheard the conversation and turns to his companion.

"For sure, this is a rum 'un."

"That archaeologist" the other says, "He could be closer to the truth than he realises. It's not sure what it wants to do."

"Did you feel it too?" the first sapper says, "When we were down there? I've never felt this way before even so close to one."

"You mean as if we weren't alone?"

"...and it's thinking."

"...or someone is."

While the discussions continue on what action to take the people evacuated from their houses get more disgruntled. Groups of unhappy residents gather in all the surrounding streets, moaning and groaning. With no information speculative rumours multiply rapidly.

"Why is it taking so long. Surely they would have dealt with it by now?"

"Maybe it's more serious than we've been led to believe."

The most chilling remark mirrors the concerns of the disposal team.

"It's not yet decided what it wants to do."

Hours pass with no news and no action. A peculiar calm pervades the area. Earnest discussions continue in private, but to outside observers all is quiet and at the perimeter there's an unguarded complacency. Then the silence is suddenly broken as one of the barriers crashes to the ground.

A policeman rushes over, but he's too late. Someone has got through and is racing towards the hole.

"Stop! Stop!" he calls.

"There's a bloody bomb in there," someone else shouts.

The superintendent joins them.

"Who is it? Get after him?"

One of the policemen gives chase.

"It's a woman, sir," the other says.

"Man, woman, what does it matter? Go on, stop her for God's sake!"

The persistence of the number '8541' finally unnerves Ettie. It's her. She's allowed fantasy to eclipse fact and like all the other women what she's imagined has taken over. Perception has become reality. She closes her eyes. When she opens them it'll be gone. She'll return to her seat and it'll pass. But it doesn't. It's still there. A tenacious writing on the window that won't go away. No matter, she'll get back to her seat. But when she turns she's horrified to see she has no seat for the 'old' carriage has returned.

She calls out. Her voice languishes in its own echo. The chatter from the next carriage is no more. She's entombed in unnerving silence. Then, very faintly comes the rattle of the carriage, the rumbling of the wheels, getting louder. Now the bouncy clatter of points and the old di di di dum, di di di dum of the expansion joints on old track long since superseded by continuously welded track. She's back in the 1940s!

Yet there's no sound from within the carriage. No one else is here. She calls again, this time louder though less fearfully. She staggers back along the corridor past empty compartments to the far end. She tries the door. If she can get through she's bound to enter a modern open carriage, mix with real people and escape the unpredictable prospects of a perilous past. The door sticks. She pulls it vigorously. It doesn't move. She tugs it again, then loses her grip and is thrown back against the wall of a compartment. She tries again, but it won't move. She's marooned in the 1940s in a closed carriage, alone with an unknown shade of dubious intentions.

"Help, help!" she screams.

The words fall like leaden weights against the windows and compartments as if she's sealed in a deep freeze. No one answers. No one hears her. She looks back down the corridor, fearful of seeing the man again, but there's no one. She turns into the nearest empty compartment and sits by the window. At first there's only blackness outside, but then she sees distant lights and dull shapes of buildings flitting by. It's impossible to tell whether they are of her time, but at least there's something beyond the confines of this carriage. They must soon arrive in Nottingham where the train terminates. Then the past will be wiped away, the carriage returned to its modern state and she can escape!

She calms. Then sees it. '8541' fingered on the glass. Not again! The infernal number can't be wiped off the window! She jumps up and dashes back into the corridor. All her strength is wrenched away and she has to lean against the compartment door for support. She looks to where she saw the man, but there's no one. Then the wheels screech loudly and the carriage sways from side to side. The train is slowing down. They must be coming into a station. Arrival in Nottingham is imminent.

At the far end of the corridor there's no door, only a spinning brownness coalescing together the floor, walls, roof and upholstery as if the carriage is being pulled into a narrowing cloudy vortex. It draws her. She's getting closer though she hasn't moved. She's light headed and unsteady and grabs the side of the corridor on the window side. The haze clears. The man reappears. She steadies herself, ready to run even though her legs are transfixed.

He stares directly at her as before, shaking his head intermittently. One hand is on the ledge of a window while the other is also shaking. His mouth opens, but there's no sound beyond the rumbling of the train. She's reminded how Karen 'spoke' to her in the hospital. This is surely no more than what the other women saw or heard? No. He's here because *she's* here. She must use the gift she's had since she was a girl. Surely it's as strong as ever!

She closes her eyes to concentrate. The sounds of the train fade. For a few moments she 'sees' only blackness, but then a shape moves rapidly towards her. She's tempted to open her eyes, but remembers again Karen in the hospital. Don't break the connection. Keep concentrating. If it's real the vision will present itself.

She's in a street. It's early evening and still quite light. A man rushes towards her. He's a little breathless, brushes past with a quick apology and hurries away. He stops occasionally and looks at something. Perhaps his watch? He's racing for something and is late. There's a large building ahead and though some way behind she can see him galloping up the steps. It's an old building, tall and imposing, red brick, Gothic. Could it be a church? He's late for a church service? Must be a very important service for him to be so agitated. She knows this place. She's been here before. Not a church. A railway station. St. Pancras in London, where trains depart for Nottingham.

She's in the station. The man has gone through the barrier. She hears the steady beats from the locomotive. They quicken. The man runs. The train accelerates. If he's lucky he might catch a door at the rear and get on the train. He's not lucky. The locomotive's cylinders are pumping rapidly. Great grey puffs of smoke are thrust to the station's roof. He stops running, hangs down, his arms almost at ground level and gasps great gulps of air in exhaustion.

It's the same man Ettie saw earlier. Now more agitated, he paces up the platform as if by doing so he can summon the train to return. He gives up after twenty yards and desultorily walks slowly back towards the barrier. As he nears the ticket collector, he throws his arms in the air in enraged impotence. They exchange a few words. The man shouts. She can't make out the words. He passes through the barrier and sits at a seat on the concourse, shaking heightened agitation. He must wait for the next train, arriving much later in Nottingham. He'll be too late…

Eventually he looks up at the station roof and calms. Ettie follows his gaze, but as she does the great iron arc flickers and fades. The train's wheels rumble and squeal. They pass over more points. The vision is gone. She opens her eyes and returns to the compartment only to find the same accusatory number on the window. 8541. She rubs the window with her hand, but it stays as the train pulls into the station in Nottingham.

The woman runs faster than her pursuers and reaches the edge of the hole before they catch up with her. As she peers down a policemen brings her down with a soft, but accurate rugby tackle. She shrieks as she bumps onto the ground.

"Get off of me, you great bully!"

He puts out his hand to help her up, but she slaps it aside.

"Get your filthy hands off me, you maniac. You could have pushed me down. You know there's a bomb down there?"

"It was to stop you falling in."

"I'm not going to fall. I'm not that stupid."

The superintendent arrives with another two constables, one of them a woman.

"Get her away and be quick about it," he barks.

"In a moment," she says, brushing down the dust, "I just want to…"

"You're not going to *just* anything. This is an extremely dangerous place. Any slight movement could set off the bomb."

"Like thrusting me over the edge?"

"The constable was only doing his duty. Now, madam if you'll…"

"Don't now madam me. I am a journalist. I have a *duty* to report on the situation here."

"Get away from the edge!" the superintendent says, nodding to the constable and the policewoman, indicating for them to be ready to forcibly remove her.

She glances at the constable and steps a few paces away from the edge.

"This is a restricted area," the superintendent says, "You're not permitted in here."

"Restricted? On whose authority? This is a matter of considerable interest to the whole city. Do you realise how many people have been displaced because of your restricted area?"

"It's not *my* restricted area. It's to safeguard those people and yes I'm fully aware how many have had to be evacuated."

"I have a story to write. I need to be able to describe the area."

"Then you'll have to do your describing from a safe distance. Where did you say you were from?"

"I didn't say, but I'm from the *Courier*," she says, thrusting her press card in his face.

He studies it carefully.

"Arlene Bates, the *Courier*, eh?"

"Is that a problem?"

"You should know better. Now, come along."

He motions towards the barrier and she reluctantly moves away, escorted by the constables.

"Your actions are highly irresponsible," he says, "You realise I could charge you. Now, if you please leave the site without further ado we'll say no more about it. This bomb is extremely unstable. It could go off any minute."

"Could it now? That could be useful for my story."

"There've been adequate press releases," he says curtly, suddenly realising he's said too much.

"What about the pub?" Arlene says, "it was called the 'Cross Keys."

"This is a building site, not a pub."

"But the pub was on this site, it was lost during the war."

"Is that important?"

"It's everything."

Ettie is ready to leave the train. Will she emerge into a modern station, yet from a 1940's compartment? Assuming she'll be able to leave the train. Will the doors be locked? People are waiting on the platform. They don't look like they've just stepped out of a wartime musical. Will everything outside be suddenly blown away as she's unable to wipe away the number on the window? She gets to the compartment door. The train stops. She glances back. The window looks distinctly clearer. Is it a trick of the light? No. There's no number smeared on the glass.

She turns back to the corridor. But the corridor isn't there. She's in the middle of an aisle with seats on either side. The upholstery, the lighting, the luggage racks, a modern open carriage. There are no compartments. It's over. The old carriage, the 'ghost' train is gone. The man is gone. She gets to the connecting section between carriages. She goes to the door, but can't open it. Other passengers are waiting from the other carriage. She tries the door again.

"Press the button," somebody calls.

Yes, of course. This is a modern train. The doors are electronically controlled. She has to press the button to release them. How wonderful!

"It's green," the voice says again, "Press the button."

The button has changed from red to green. The door can be released. She's confused and fumbles ineffectively. Someone leans over and presses the button. The door slides open. She stumbles onto the platform. People pass her and walk to the exit stairs.

"You all right, duck?"

It's one of the two young women who offered to help her.

"Er...yes, I'm all right, thank you."

"It's that bloody train. All that way on your own, not surprising you're feeling a bit muddled. Should've stayed with us. Anyway, goodnight."

"Yes, thank you. You're probably right. Goodnight."

She waits and stares through the train window. Still the same modern carriage. She turns away and closes her eyes. Will it change? Is she really back in the present? She opens her eyes. Nothing has changed. She's definitely in the present. The platform is deserted except for a couple of police officers, a man and a woman. They must have been on the train. She doesn't remember seeing them, but apart from the two young women she doesn't remember seeing anyone on the train...except...

She walks along the platform and passes the police officers. They don't speak. She's reassured. She goes through the ticket barrier and into the street. She turns to her right and then right again with no clear intention of where she's going. Perhaps she should've spoken to the police. But then what could she have said?

*"I have seen a man from eighty years ago and he smeared a number on the window. Then I saw him in London. He missed an earlier train. He was very agitated and I was on this old train with him, but then it vanished and I was back here."*

Gradually she remembers. She caught the train at Leicester and saw other passengers. Everything is clearer now. Or at least as clear as travelling in time as well as distance can ever be. This is Station Street. Why has she come along here? Then she sees him some fifty yards ahead. The same man from the train. He hurries. Where is he going? She walks faster. He stops. He doesn't look round, but she's wary and also stops. He looks at the wall of the station, then moves on. She follows and reaches the place where he stopped. She does not yet know it, but this is the place where the number '8541' was found scratched on the wall, but it's no longer here. She looks round. The man is gone.

Jenner feels let down. Taken off his own enquiry, he was looking forward to pursuing an ersatz one, following the further career of the reprobate Ronald Calthorpe. But the death of the petty thief and burglar in 1941 wrenched it away, like getting engaged with an intriguing novel only to find the last couple of chapters missing. It's not just professionally disappointing. Even though Calthorpe was killed long before Jenner was born he feels he knows him.

He muses again on what he knows. Calthorpe was presumed killed following the air raid in 1941 when the church hall he was sheltering in received a direct hit. Relevant papers were found on his body so there can be no doubt of his identity. *Presumed*. The word resonates irritatingly. But it's only a word. Only two types of people emerged from that direct hit, survivors or dead bodies. Calthorpe was presumed dead because his body was found in the church hall. It can't be anything else.

Yet his fascination with the persistent villain continues and he delves deeper into his notes. It was an impressive record. Whatever else, Ronald Calthorpe was nothing if not industrious. If the suppositions of Jenner's wartime predecessors are correct he was active for a good five years although his exploits seem to have significantly taken off in the first two war years and especially during the blitz. Would he have had the same difficulty ensnaring him as they did? He studies the 'evidence' carefully, imagining how he would put together a feasible case bearing in mind he would not then have had the advantage of modern investigative techniques. Interviewing him would have been an absorbing task.

Most of the unsolved thefts follow a definite pattern with a regular MO to the burglaries. Those that don't can't have been Calthorpe's work. Others must have been responsible. Whether that was the conclusion drawn by detectives at the time is unclear. If not, then they were wasting part of their time trying to pin them on Calthorpe.

The similarity of his operations covers the types of property, the time of the day (or more precisely the night), the mode of entry and the chosen areas of the city. With detailed intelligence of the city might it have been possible to predict his next moves? If so it doesn't seem to have happened. Jenner even contemplates setting a trap for him, but rejects it. Calthorpe would be too wily to be easily 'set up' and at that time police resources would be too stretched to indulge in anything beyond purely reactive detection. In such dangerous times, the strained atmosphere of the blackout and air raids, the dismal streets suddenly punctuated by the terrors of fire and explosions, the empty properties...

...empty, deserted, an exploitative advantage, to be taken as it was by so many others? Crime increased during the war, the darkness providing perfect cover for shrewd operators like Calthorpe. He must have tramped through shadowy areas, casing potential targets, even entering damaged properties before the residents or emergency services were on the scene, slipping away with his booty as deftly as he arrived. With good knowledge of streets and alleys he could avoid embarrassing questions let alone capture. Such a rogue would have little to fear from air raid sirens. Not for him scuttling to the safety of shelters. Confusion and dread meant opportunity and profit. But there was always the chance he'd be caught by the very dangers he sought to exploit. Did his luck run out on that fateful night? Maybe he'd had one near miss. Did he enter a house only to find a bomb dropping too close for comfort and sought shelter, which was then itself a target, bringing his criminal course to an abrupt and hideous end?

The detailed police file on the hit on the church hall had to be because of their interest in Calthorpe. They had to be sure he was gone. It seems no one asked after him. A loner, without friends or relatives, a predator preying on the already battered city. Did the detectives thank the luftwaffe for inadvertently clearing up a seemingly insoluble case or were they like Jenner, a little saddened by the gruesome finish of a worthy adversary?

Jenner moves on from Calthorpe and examines the individual stories of all those killed in the church hall. Hilda Wallace is intriguing. John Renshaw was one of the few survivors, his subsequent life, the apparently unsuccessful expedition to Brazil, his penniless return and eventual recovery only to be killed on a building site in 1965. Is there more to this coincidental connection between Karen and the Wallaces? He doesn't relish another diatribe from Keith Renshaw about the 'accident', but it'll have to be faced.

The official reports and statements of the fire and ambulance services include some interesting background information, but are gruelling reading and wearying of carnage and misery Jenner is ready to put his notes aside. Then he finds a short witness 'statement' taken on the night itself. It's an account of a conversation between a constable and a young 'lady of the night,' presumably she too found more profitable business during the darkness and mayhem.

Her name was 'Milly.' A later appendage describes her as an 'experienced prostitute,' in her late twenties. Her full name was Emily Fielding. She frequently worked when the sirens signalled an imminent raid, but for some months there were few real attacks. It made her blasé and she took advantage of the deserted streets to ply her trade with less likelihood of brushes with the police. However, the ferocity of this night forced her to what she considered safer 'areas,' away from her normal territory in the south east of the city near the river.

Unfortunately on 8<sup>th</sup> May there were no real 'safe' areas, only those less dangerous. She was close when the church hall was hit, but unlike Calthorpe was outside and avoided the explosion though she was blown against a wall by the blast. When the policeman found her she was unhurt apart from shock. She described the sudden explosion, for which she said there was no prior warning.

*'It came out of nowhere. There's been nothing like it round here before.'*

She'd been in the area for some time, the constable delicately avoiding any reference to her precise activities, further background provided by a colleague the following day. She mentioned seeing a man running from the building and was able to provide a brief description, which was presumably John Renshaw.

Jenner closes his dossier and reluctantly concentrates on one of those 'other cases' assigned to him by Emmins. It's monotonous work. He leaves the station relatively early and manages a short, largely unproductive visit to Keith Renshaw. After that he stops off at his favourite café for a meal before going home to enjoy a relaxing moment listening to the local radio.

Jennifer has promised to come round. When she arrives they swap the information gleaned from their separate enquiries, though being unable to pursue separate interviews outside of the remit set down by Inspector Williams, she's made little progress.

"So you've not seen Simon Wallace?" he says.

"No, but I will. What about Keith Renshaw?"

He scowls.

"I could hardly get a word in edgeways. He kept gibbering on about that wretched accident to his father. The man's obsessed."

"It might be important."

"Perhaps, but I wanted to talk about his father's early life. I put it to him that John Renshaw was a survivor of the direct hit on the church hall. He appeared to know nothing about it. Said his father never talked much about the war. He was in a reserved occupation, so he was denied – as he put it – the glory of being directly involved in the fight."

"Did you mention Hilda Wallace?"

"Yes. He knew nothing about her being killed in the same raid. He was also vague about his father's life just after the war, about him going to Brazil and so forth. Kept saying 'I was very young at the time.' Apparently that was something else John Renshaw didn't talk about. I prodded him about his father's financial position after he came back from Brazil. Gave me one of those non committal shrugs and said 'You know how it is out there. Everybody's corrupt. You either know the right people or you don't…'"

"Yes?"

Jenner mimics Keith, throwing his hands in the air and shaking his head.

"…you don't get the work."

"What sort of work?"

"That's what I wondered. Keith had another attack of amnesia. The 'work' was probably closer to the what the 'right' people were doing."

"I don't want to pour more cold water on everything, but have you seen this?"

She drops the day's *Courier* on the table. He scans the front page.

"Page four," she says.

He groans, guessing what may await him on page four.

*'WHAT SECRETS LIE UNDER SHARP ROAD?*

*While hundreds of people are confined, frustrated and fearful, away from their homes in uncomfortable detention there is still no progress at the great hole in Sharp Road. Is there or is there not a dangerous bomb lodged beneath the workings? Apart from the inconvenience the new building development is seriously held up with expensive implications in time and money.*

*The excavation gets bigger and bigger, deeper and deeper. Yet the work gets no closer to extracting or at least making safe the supposed bomb. 'Supposed' because the authorities were earlier denying there was a bomb there at all. Residents rightly complain it is taking so long.*

*Now we are told* 'the bomb is unstable and could go off any minute.' *Yet little action is taken to avoid such a calamity. They are not even giving precise information on the size of the bomb, only that it is between 50 and 500 kilograms. The potential damage a 500 kilogram bomb can cause is clearly much greater than that of a 50 kilogram bomb. So, what now?*

*Irrespective of the size there is no decision on whether and how the bomb should be moved. Getting it out of its subterranean hiding cannot be easy otherwise it would have been done before. If it is moved, where to? How far into the country must it go to be safe? The longer the distance the greater hazard to areas through which it would have to pass. The alternative is what is called a* controlled explosion. *There is little sign at the moment of control by anyone and an explosion of any kind doesn't bear thinking about.'*

Jenner pauses and puts the paper down

"This is really going to calm people's nerves," he says," At least this hysterical gibberish isn't on the front page."

"There's a signpost for the article on the front page."

"So there is," he says, picking up the paper again, then immediately discarding it, "*No progress* is her catchphrase. Nice to see it's not just the poor old coppers who get it."

"There's more. Read on."

"Must I?"

He opens the paper again.

*'But there is much more to the gaping hole than an unexploded bomb and the disruption to the whole area. There was once a pub on the site, the 'Cross Keys' which was partially damaged during a terrible air raid in 1941. The place was never the same again and the remains have had to be demolished in preparation for the new development, but the 'Cross Keys' may have been no ordinary pub. The removal of its remains coinciding with the peculiar happenings on the London evening train may be more than coincidental.*

*A possible connection between the two should not be so sniffily dismissed as were the women's reports of strange happenings on the train. Some of the bomb disposal team have expressed concerns about the elusive bomb, not just its size, but also its apparent ability to 'move' within the soil and rock.'*

Jenner throws the paper down.

"Can't miss the chance of sniping at us, can she? *Sniffily*? I'm never *sniffily* about anything. *'Some of the disposal team?'* How did she get hold of that? Or did she just make it up? I don't suppose there's been any statement from the army about this bomb?"

"Not yet."

"That damned woman, she'll be…"

His rising fury, ready like a kettle to blow off steam is suddenly interrupted by the announcer on the radio.

*"And with that piece by the lesser known Russian composer Gretchaninov, tonight's 'New Explorations' ends a little earlier…"*

"Damn," Jenner says," what are we going to get now?"

*"…as we have an exclusive interview with the campaigning journalist on the Courier, Arlene Bates."*

"I thought she'd disappeared? Did you hear that? '… *leading the campaign to get to the bottom of what is really going on in the trains?* He's introducing her as the *rising star* of local journalism? If she's the rising star, I shudder to think what a falling star is like!"

"Turn it up," Jennifer says.

*"Your articles have created quite a stir in the city and beyond, even national newspapers have been quoting from them. Do you think at times you might have gone too far in your assertions?"*

"That's it, give it to her!"

*'In what way have I gone too far?'*

*'Your criticisms of the police for example?"*

There's a slight pause before Arlene replies.

*"I've merely voiced the concerns of many people. I don't believe the police took the incidents seriously. It was only when Karen Renshaw was viciously attacked…'*

*'And now the murder of Sarah Murrell?'*

*'I've not commented on the murder investigation.'*

*'Nevertheless, your criticism of the police…'*

*'My views are a matter of record. There's no point in going over old ground. I don't wish to dwell on that."*

"She can't justify herself, that's the truth of it!" Jenner says.

*"It could be said your articles, if not actually causing… unease…in the city have certainly fuelled the flames of …'*

*'…panic?'*

*'I didn't say that.'*

*'But it could be said?"*

Arlene laughs.

"She's playing with him," Jenner grunts, "Of course she fuelled the flames, damned irresponsible journalism. If it wasn't for her…"

Jennifer turns up the volume on the radio.

*"Okay' the interviewer says, 'Let's move on. I understand there are other matters about the assault of Karen Renshaw and the murder…'*

*'No, not the attack on Karen and…the murder…It's what's been happening on the train that concerns me and the authorities are ignoring what's staring them in the face. What's happened in the last few days cannot be ignored.'*

'You mean the mass evacuation at Sharp Road, the excavation of...?'

'...an unexploded wartime bomb? Well, of course.'

'How is that connected to the disturbances on the train?'

There's an audible sigh, then Arlene answers emphatically.

'Countless women have seen a mysterious man on a wartime train."

"Hardly countless," Jenner says, "Her usual exaggeration."

"But I still don't see...?'

'Wartime train, wartime man, unexploded wartime bomb. The connection is obvious. Everything is connected to the war.'

He doesn't immediately pursue this line of questioning, but instead goes back to the work at Sharp Road.

'Do you think you were wise to go to where the unexploded bomb is located?'

There's a pause. Jenner and Jennifer wait expectantly.

'Why wouldn't I go there?' she says guardedly at last.

'It's a restricted area.'

'It's a place of concern to my readers. They have a right to be informed.'

'You had to be ejected.'

'I was only doing my job.'

'Was it necessary to break through the barrier and try to get to where the army were excavating?'

Arlene's voice is louder and even more vehement.

'I didn't enter the excavation! I was only at the edge and it's not an excavation. It's a landfall. There's a difference.'

'Even so, were you not putting yourself and others in danger? We understand the bomb is unstable.'

'You understand because I've reported it. Someone has to get to the bottom of things and expose what's going on."

"Which of course can only be her," Jenner says.

Frustrated by his interruptions, Jennifer tells him to shut up, which to her great surprise, he does.

"I don't believe the disturbances on the train and the discovery of the unexploded bomb happening at around the same time is a coincidence. They are connected.'

'Because of the war?'

'Obviously, but there's much more to connect them."

Jenner and Jennifer gasp. The interviewer lets her carry on, probably as staggered as they are.

'There was a pub on the site called the 'Cross Keys.' It was partially demolished after bomb damage. That air raid was on the 8th May 1941. '8-5-41.' The same unexplained numbers that have been seen on many occasions by women on the London train.'

'There was a great deal of damage throughout the city on that night. Your own article…'

'You're missing the point. That date is clearly related to what has been seen on the train.'

'The man was travelling on the train on the night of 8th May 1941?'

'Precisely and on the same night the 'Cross Keys' pub was destroyed. The man must have been going to the pub that night."

"Well, go on, say to her…" Jenner says, but breaks off.

The interviewer is at last starting to do his job.

"This is all speculation. The date, the train, the man, the excavation, they're not necessarily connected.'

'But they are, they are! You've forgotten the vital element.'

'Which is?'

'The bomb! You've forgotten the bomb. That links everything together. Like I said, the bomb, the train, it's not a coincidence. They both happened on the same night of that terrible air raid. The bomb was not discovered because of the building works. The bomb is a relic of that night. It knew what was coming, what is coming."

Another slight pause into which the interviewer should intervene, but he says nothing, bewildered and astounded by what he hears. Everyone listening will be similarly amazed and will wait in trepidation for what Arlene will say next. She doesn't disappoint them.

"It's now only eight days to the 8th May. The bomb has brought everything together. It will happen.'

'What will happen?'

'They will not be able to disable the bomb. Not yet, it's not the time."

Recovering from some of his shock the interviewer thanks Arlene for her 'contribution' and hastily announces the commercial break after which programmes will continue with 'Smooth Hits For The Night.' Jenner turns down the volume and sighs thankfully.

Jennifer expects him to shout 'poppycock' or something similar, but he only says quietly "Is she a nutter?"

She shakes her head.

"Whether she is or isn't, she can't be ignored. Every newspaper, television and radio will repeat her wildest claims

"The news gatherer becoming the news, eh?"

Jennifer considers for a moment, then says, "You can no longer say 'the ghost' is a put up job by Arlene."

"Surely *you* don't believe all that stuff?" he says incredulously.

"I didn't say that, but not all the women who reported seeing him and the train can be wrong or deluded."

"So Karen Renshaw was attacked and Sarah Murrell murdered by a ghost?"

"She wouldn't talk about Sarah Murrell anymore than she would with Ettie."

"Maybe this ghost business started out as publicity stunt. After all, it's successfully flogged a lot of papers."

Jennifer thinks this is weak.

"How so, all those women?"

"No, not all of them. Just a few mates of hers to begin with. Then as the story gets legs and women are apprehensive the collective imagination takes over and it gets out of hand."

Jennifer looks at Jenner dubiously. He no more believes what he's saying than she does. Just like her, Arlene's assertions have made him think along lines he can neither explain nor know where they might lead.

"Arlene didn't arrange the vicious attack on Karen," she says.

Jenner says nothing.

"Anyway, Arlene hasn't got many mates. Where were they when she wanted to get away?"

"Why did she want to get away?"

"If we knew that we might get a bit nearer to the answers. She had to unburden herself and rather than friends or colleagues she chose to speak to Ettie, a complete stranger."

"It could be useful if we knew what Ettie thinks now."

## 1st May

Once more Jenner leaves the police station early. At home he sits in silence, then puts on the radio. His first reaction on hearing there will be another news report is to immediately turn it off, but finds it difficult not to listen.

"Reports are coming in of further developments in the continuing disturbances on the evening London train. Yesterday there was a dramatic increase in the number of women reporting seeing the mysterious man in old clothes. Police protection on the train has been stepped up, but the so-called 'predator' has still not been apprehended. This evening, any hopes this was a one-off event have been dispelled.

Many more women, leaving the train in an agitated and traumatised state were able to describe both him and the train in great detail. The appearance of the mysterious number 8541 has also been reported. Some tried unsuccessfully to remove it. Yet a thorough examination of the train has revealed no graffiti or damage. Therefore whatever the number is it can only be transitory.

Is the persistence of the number the same as the man and the compartment train? Such speculation has grown after our *interview last night with local journalist Arlene Bates. Is some kind of extra sensory activity at work involving the train, the man and the unexploded bomb at Sharp Road? To add to such startling possibilities, passengers arriving in Nottingham have for the first time reported seeing the inexplicable man leaving the train. This means any threat he poses is no longer confined to the train. Now he has definitely arrived in the city."*

Jenner sits in silent gloom, tossing around alternative explanations. *'Speculation has grown after last night's interview.'* The announcer's gift of understatement is unparalleled!

He thinks over past cases, how the unbelievable became the believable and he'd had to work with someone with special skills... He needs to speak to Ettie. Meanwhile, what's really happening in the city? He rings Jennifer for the latest position.

"I've just heard it on the radio. Is it really that bad?"

"There's great disquiet throughout the city," she says gloomily, "I don't know whether the media is driving the people or the other way round, but the temperature's rising."

He groans.

"Maybe that damned woman was right. *'It will happen... brought everything together.* She said there were *only eight days.*"

"Only seven now."

He rings off and turns on the radio, hearing the tail end of another bulletin.

*"...the consternation on the trains has now spread throughout the city. Women are demanding to leave work early, travelling home only in groups or arranging to be picked up by male relatives. We've been inundated with calls from frightened people everywhere..."*

The broadcast switches to snatches of earlier phone ins.

*'...we usually go to the pub after work, but now no one does... we only want to get home as quickly as we can...He's somewhere*

*in the city…I'm trying not to panic…when will this end?…when will we feel safe again?…he has to be caught…"*

The telephone rings.

"Derek?"

"Ettie? I was going to…"

"Something has to be done. Karen Renshaw is in immediate danger."

# 9

2<sup>nd</sup> **May**

JENNIFER has chosen a bad time to talk to Inspector Williams. The enquiry is stalled and his mind is fixed on how best to proceed, but she can't put it off. It's been on her mind ever since Jenner rang last night.

"We need to consider Karen Renshaw's position at the hospital."

Williams looks at her coldly. He's only been her boss a short while and has not yet got used to her directness, thinking her argumentative and mildly insubordinate.

"It's not a high priority," he says.

"She's still our only witness. If anything should happen to her..."

"The doctors say it's only a matter of time. She'll come round."

"They say it will be fairly soon *if* she comes round. Anyway it's not her medical condition I'm concerned about, it's her security."

"We have a man on duty 24 hours. That's expensive enough already. We can't spare further resources. Haven't you noticed the city is in ferment following these reports of a dangerous man leaving the London train?"

"But what I'm talking about is *real*."

"We have to take account of the *reality* of a threatened predator at loose in the city. We've already got extra patrols."

"That's to reassure the public. In any case you can't patrol every street while Karen Renshaw's whereabouts are too well known."

"Do we suggest to the doctors she be moved? They'll be receptive to that idea," he says sarcastically, "Apart from anything else, how far away is the nearest hospital with similar facilities, Derby, Sheffield, London?"

"She could be in great danger."

"Have you completed that check on Sarah Murrell's background and movements?" he says gruffly.

She ignores the question.

"One officer might not be enough. We have to think about general security. Hospitals are open places. Someone could gain access posing as one of the staff and…"

"In which case he would be challenged by the officer on duty."

"Easier said than done when…"

"You feel one officer's guard can be easily breached?"

"That's my point. We need…"

"And Sarah Murrell?"

"It's in hand."

"But not completed?"

She tries to fob him off.

"I'm working on it…there are a number of people to be seen."

"Then get on with it and don't waste my time with pointless requests to intensify perfectly adequate security."

"I only…"

"I think we've finished, sergeant. Unless there are more specific issues you've not mentioned?"

What more can she say? That her concerns are based on a vague and second hand warning from someone outside the case, relayed to her by the previous SIO?

"No, sir," she says and returns to what he terms her 'more immediate enquiries.'

But Jenner's message from Ettie, chiming with her own misgivings about Karen, nags her all morning. At the first opportunity she makes an excuse about having to see one of Sarah Murrell's 'contacts,' and gets over to the hospital. She hovers in reception and meanders suspiciously around the public areas watching staff, patients, visitors alike, wondering how easily an attacker might assume an innocent identity for nefarious ends. It's a futile exercise. Someone with murderous intents is unlikely to reveal himself, nor hang around for long before going to the ward. Should she talk to the hospital administration, discover how staff are recruited, examine recent records? Even if it's feasible she can't do it alone and Williams has already dismissed any hope of more resources. It demonstrates Karen's vulnerability. Without greater vigilance a determined attacker is bound to get through. Filled with these bleak impressions she goes up to the ward.

The constable on duty is not David Warren and is rather more stiff and formal. He's surprised to see her and tries to pre-empt what she might say.

"All correct, sergeant. There's been no change in Miss Renshaw."

"No visitors?"

"No one."

"Nobody unofficial?"

He looks at her blankly.

"Unofficial?"

"Someone unknown to the staff, who might try to see her."

"That unknown woman's not been back," he reassures her nervously.

"I don't think she'll be back," Jennifer says, "She's been eliminated as a suspect."

"Just a busybody?"

"You could say that. The important thing is to keep alert. Treat everybody, even staff you're not familiar with as someone who could do her harm. Let no one pass you under any circumstances."

"I understand. I know PC Warren…"

"This has nothing to do with him and that woman," she snaps.

"Are you expecting a specific incident?"

"It's always best to be prepared."

She glimpses through the window door. She's tempted to go in, satisfy herself all is well with Karen, but it would be pointless and only draw undue attention. She leaves him a little bewildered, unsure if he's fallen down on his duties and being given an oblique warning. Jennifer seeks out the ward sister, asks about the staff and even examines the duty roster. The ward sister is similarly nonplussed and also asks if a specific attempt to harm Karen is expected. Jennifer is reassuring, but reminds her 'it's always wise to be constantly watchful.'

Back down at reception she's still nervous and can't resist scanning everybody, wandering back and forth, examining exits and entrances much like a criminal might case a place for a job. She's reminded of her brief unsatisfactory discussion with DCI Williams. Is what she's doing any more *real* than his extra patrols?

Ettie insists on seeing Jenner away from the police station. They meet in the same pub where she spoke to the young women when she first arrived in the city. They've not been in touch for a long time. It's good to go over old times. Both are reluctant to move the conversation along. She's not sure how to begin and he's not sure he wants to begin. Gradually the discussion of past 'cases' gets closer to the present, though he lingers on those immediately prior to the disturbances on the train and then to the current cases set by Emmins.

"None of it sounds like the sort of work you normally undertake," she says diplomatically.

"So mundane they'd bore a simpleton."

She senses his distress. It's much more than being assigned to 'lesser projects.'

"Has there been much progress since you were taken off the...other case?"

"Ghosts and predators?" he says bitterly.

"I mean the attack on Karen Renshaw."

"And the murder of Sarah Murrell. You really shook me up when you rang last night. What's it about? I told Jennifer. I think she was shaken even more than me."

Jennifer joins them.

"Have you been to the hospital?" he says anxiously.

"There's been no change. I tried to convince DI Williams to increase security, but he wouldn't hear of it. It's all about budgets apparently."

"Or he thought I'd put you up to it."

"He never mentioned you."

"Lost without trace," he mumbles then turns jokingly to Ettie, "You see what you've caused, all this talk about Karen Renshaw? What makes you think she's in immediate danger?"

Ettie hesitates. He persists.

"What sort of danger? We've assumed someone will try to attack her at the hospital. Who is it? How will they do it?"

"I can't be sure. I only have the feeling and it's very strong."

He sighs and shakes his head.

"I'm sure it is. Now I know why I get so much flak about peculiar cases," he says, then turns to Jennifer, "Is Karen safe?"

"As safe as we can make it with just one constable at the scene. I spoke to the nursing staff. I might have spooked them. It's difficult without being more specific."

She and Jenner look expectantly to Ettie.

"I'm sorry if I've caused consternation," she says, "Perhaps I should have kept quiet."

"No, no," Jenner says, "When you've had these feelings before they've been borne out by later events. Ignoring them has never been wise."

"I wish I could say more."

"You said immediate," Jennifer says, "Does that mean today, tomorrow, this week?"

"The feeling was strongest yesterday. That's why I said immediate, but today it's not been… not quite so strong…so not today."

They are silent for some moments, then Ettie says, "But it's been getting stronger. I thought, maybe after…what happened on the train…it would go away, but then…"

"We've all heard it on the radio," Jenner says, "More sightings of the ghost. It's understandable it was preying on your mind."

"Some reported seeing him *leaving* the train," Jennifer says, "so obviously there's been panic in the city. It's made our job…"

"It's nothing to do with the radio reports!" Ettie says vehemently.

Several people nearby turn to them. Ettie lowers her voice.

"I knew about the sightings and about the man leaving the train before it was reported. *I* saw him leaving the train. I was there. I was on the train."

"When was this?" Jenner says.

"Two days ago. It reinforced what I'd been thinking. At root, the attack on Karen is connected to events in 1941."

She recounts what happened on the train. They listen closely, interrupting only for further details of the man and the train. After she finishes, no one speaks until Jenner breaks the silence.

"Ghosts, predator, attacks, it's all there."

"It's at the heart of your investigation," Ettie says, "Don't ask me how or when, but the past weighs heavily on the present."

"So if we unravel the past we'll break the impasse, discover who attacked Karen and murdered Sarah Murrell?"

Ettie hesitates.

"Not sure about the murder, but definitely Karen."

"You're sounding like Arlene Bates," Jennifer says, "Wasn't she reluctant to talk about Sarah Murrell?"

"I'm not influenced by her," Ettie says sharply, "I don't know about Sarah Murrell. That's for you to find out, but with Karen…she's connected to…"

"The night of the air raid, 8th May 1941?" Jenner says excitedly.

"You've been investigating the war?"

"Is this all connected to that night?"

"Let me tell you what I've worked out. Arlene talked about the war…"

"Articles, radio interviews," Jenner grumbles, "She talks a lot about the war."

"…especially about her great uncle, Wilf Sanders. Just before he died he talked to her about that particular air raid. It was the first time he'd spoken of that night. He was supposed to be meeting someone. I assume he didn't get to see them. Perhaps he was late. No, I now know. He *was* late."

"Did Arlene say that?" Jennifer says.

"No, but I know."

Ettie explains the 'visions' she experienced on the train and of an agitated man who arrived too late at St. Pancras.

"You think that man was Wilf Sanders?"

"I'm sure of it. Anyway, he told Arlene he went to a bombed out church hall and saw a man leaving."

"Who was this man?" Jenner says.

"I don't know. Wilf didn't know, but he gave her a description, which she passed on to me."

After Ettie has repeated Wilf's description Jenner cries out.

"It's John Renshaw! Wilf saw John Renshaw."

He explains what he's discovered from the wartime records including Milly Fielding also seeing a man, which fits with Wilf's account.

"So now we have a connection not only between the Renshaws and the Wallaces, but also between the Bates' and the Renshaws," Jennifer says.

"Arlene said she had a personal connection," Ettie says.

"She went much further in her latest article," Jenner says, "The train, the ghost, the bomb in Sharp Road and the 'Cross Keys' pub that used to stand there."

"The pub where Wilf Sanders was meeting someone?" Jennifer says, "Arlene said the bomb brought everything together."

"Perhaps," Ettie says, "Wilf died on 10th April – the same day the archaeological dig was abandoned because the bomb was discovered…"

"On the site of the 'Cross Keys' pub, the place of his meeting…" Jennifer says excitedly,

"Wilf was always ashamed of the night of the air raid. He was on a journey to the 'Cross Keys' pub, but his objective was never achieved. Dying with that guilt…such a strong emotion…it could do peculiar things. I think it set off his appearance on the train, in fact the train itself."

"So his ghost or his presence - call it what you will - returned to the site of the pub and disturbed the bomb, which was then discovered?" Jennifer says.

"It's the same train he'd taken that night from London. He'd missed the earlier train. He was afraid he was going to be late. He was very agitated when I saw him on the train. Then, with the number smeared on the window…"

"Agitated on 8th May 1941," Jennifer says, "reliving the memory as he died?"

"Yes."

Jenner is sceptical.

"These are tenuous connections and even if correct, where do they take us? Are you saying Wilf Sanders or some…extra normal manifestation or ghost or whatever… attacked Karen Renshaw?"

"I can only say these connections were triggered by Wilf Sanders' death on 10th April. What Arlene said about the bomb site and the pub resonates with my own view. Obviously she felt something very strongly when she visited the site which must have been connected to the 'Cross Keys' pub."

"You've been to Sharp Road?" Jenner says.

"When I first arrived. If Arlene felt anything like I felt then I believe she's right. I went to where the church hall used to be and the feeling there was even stronger. Wilf went there. Both he and this Milly saw John Renshaw running from it…"

"Running," Jenner repeats softly.

"…which also resonates with what Jennifer felt when she was with Karen at the hospital and what I also heard from Karen…a man running from a burning building. These things are all connected."

"Running," Jenner repeats again.

"Which means?" Jennifer says.

"Nothing. I was just imagining it. You're sure you saw a man *running* from a burning building?"

"Yes," Ettie and Jennifer say together.

"So now we have the Wallaces, the Renshaws and the Bates connected, the common link being the church hall, destroyed on the night of 8th May 1941. John Renshaw and Hilda Wallace were both sheltering from the air raid in the church hall. One was killed the other survived. That we know for sure. As for Wilf Sanders, I appreciate what you've both said, but his presence there is only conjecture and why would he or his ghost attack Karen? Renshaw was getting away from what was left of the church hall...running...how does that fit with Wilf?"

"He was late for his meeting," Ettie says.

"So he went to the pub to find whoever he was meeting?"

"Yes."

"You say there's a pub at the cross roads where the bomb fell on the church hall, but it's not the 'Cross Keys,' it's called 'The Grapes.' You were in it."

"That's where I learnt about the church hall, all of which coincides with your researches into the wartime records."

"But Arlene Bates talks of the bomb site and the 'Cross Keys.' If Wilf Sanders was there for his meeting, how did he get to the church hall?"

Ettie doesn't answer his question.

"You're confusing the sequence. The spirit of Wilf Sanders is very troubled. He's also muddled. All these incidents on the train are repeats of his search. I believe he's searching for a woman."

"So my superiors keep reminding me," Jenner fumes.

"No, in the past...Wilf was looking for somebody..."

"You'll be telling me next he's now looking for Karen."

"I can only say Karen is in immediate danger," Ettie says.

"From Wilf?"

"Events are moving rapidly to their conclusion. Today is the 2$^{nd}$ May."

"And the 8$^{th}$ May is the air raid?"

"Precisely."

"So Wilf...a ghost...will attack her?"

"You don't believe me?"

"I don't believe she'll be attacked by a ghost."

"As I said before. The current investigation, the attack on Karen can only be solved in the past."

"But these things can't be perpetrated by a ghost," he says incredulously.

Ettie is adamant.

"Someone will attack Karen."

"On the 8th?"

"Probably."

"Then this *someone* must think she is this…other woman in 1941."

# 3rd May

Jennifer can't avoid to further delay the work assigned to her by DI Williams. She must further investigate Sarah Murrell's background. Her head still spins from the session with Ettie and Jenner. They were so engrossed with the link between Karen Renshaw with Arlene Bates and the Wallaces she's given little thought to any connection between Karen and Sarah. Initially it appeared they were not acquainted, but then she discovered Karen handled Draycon's marketing work and as finance officer Sarah had known her. Are the Renshaw/Bates/Wallace links coincidental? A good copper doesn't believe in coincidences.

She's already pursued two lines of enquiry – the firm, Draycon and the gambling connection with Cud Fenton, the car dealer. She'll go back to them both. She begins with Fenton, tackling him at his work and without warning. He has two showrooms, one in Carlton in the east of the city, the other on Castle Boulevard in the west. She opts for the west, sensing it's probably the larger and more prestigious. She's right. When she enters the well appointed reception area a salesman sprints across to assist her.

"I'm not here for a car," she says quickly before he can get into his sales patter, "I would like to see Mr. Fenton. Is he in?"

Denied a lucrative transaction the young salesman's thrusting ebullience suddenly evaporates and he's more akin to a junior, apparently unaware of the most elementary office procedures.

"Mr. Fenton?" he repeats unnecessarily while searching for an appropriate response, "Not about a car?"

"It's a private matter."

"I see, then...could you tell me what it's about... (he reads her expression)...no perhaps not...well..."

"Has he a secretary?"

"Er, yes, but I don't know..."

She could introduce herself, but prefers to keep that between her and Fenton. If this man knows she's from the police he'll draw conclusions surrounding the 'disturbances' and there are already too many groundless rumours running around the city. She meets a similar barrier when she confronts the secretary.

"Just advise him Jennifer Heathcott wishes to see him on a private matter."

"I could make an appointment."

"I must see him today."

The name works and Jennifer is ushered into the private office. Fenton looks up and for a moment looks puzzled, then his face gradually registers recognition.

"I wasn't sure, but now I see. You're from the police, aren't you? You came to see me."

"It's about Sarah Murrell. I didn't want to advertise why I'm here."

"I understand. I read the *Courier*. Terrible business. Is what happened to Sarah really connected to the attack on that other woman and the peculiar things on the train?"

"Enquiries are ongoing. We're trying to form as wide a picture as possible of Sarah's contacts. When we last spoke you mentioned she had other gambling contacts as well as your own group."

"I didn't mean she was involved in any illegal activities," he says defensively.

"I'm not concerned with gambling matters. This is a murder enquiry. I'm just interested in her contacts."

He's visibly relieved.

"She sometimes joked about her winnings and losses. She was a very precise person, you see. She was an accountant you know."

"Yes, I know. These other contacts, do you have any names?"

He screws his eyebrows in concentration, shakes his head, turns to the window, then looks back with a chuckle.

"There's one thing. I don't know whether it's of any use, but she joked about *'digging* for money.'"

"What did she mean?"

"I don't know, but I think it was something to do with her other gambling contacts."

Jennifer goes on to Draycon, on the way amusingly reflecting on the muddled defensiveness of Fenton's staff. It must be the way he operates, directing his deals from a bunker. His office had windows on three sides, from which he could see the whole forecourt. He was very touchy about his gambling. Maybe another team should look into his activities?

He said Sarah was very 'precise' as if that was unusual and she was a joker...*digging for money*...obviously an in joke that even he didn't understand. *Digging*. The word resounds. It reminds her of something...digging...of course...*Let Duggers Do The Digging!* The vacuous slogan of the Dugger company. She was described as a successful gambler. Was she whimsically referring to them digging out their money for her? Was one of the Duggers another 'gambling connection?' She turns the car around and heads for the Duggers place.

She gets a slightly less frosty welcome than on her previous visit. The receptionist is as cheerless as ever, but faced with Jennifer's steely presence avoids any futile blocking tactics. Jennifer is shown into Malcolm Dugger. She comes straight to the point.

"Were you acquainted with Sarah Murrell?"

He repeats the name. Jennifer waits.

"The name is not familiar."

"I assume you've read the newspapers. She was the woman found murdered near the railway station about a week ago."

"Oh yes, I recall the name now. I'm not sure how…"

"Are you a gambling man, Mr. Dugger?"

"That's not a crime, is it?"

"Not necessarily."

"What has that to do with Sarah Murrell?"

"Just answer the question please."

"I've been known to have an occasional flutter on the horses."

"What about card games?"

He hesitates, wondering where her questioning is leading.

"Sometimes," he says guardedly.

"You've played with Sarah Murrell?"

"The name as I said it's…"

"This is a murder enquiry, Mr. Dugger."

They exchange glances, hers very hard, his decidedly nervous. He blinks first.

"All right, all right. I had a few games with her, but only a few mind you. She was too good for me."

Jennifer can't resist saying with undisguised schadenfreude, "You had to dig deep?"

"It's a mistake to mix business with pleasure. I met her when she did some financial work for us. A few card games followed."

"How long did she work for you?"

"She was never employed by us. She was a good accountant. She had a full time position, but managed to do freelance jobs as well. It was lucrative for her and economical for us. Everybody gained."

"Except her main employer."

"Not a problem as I remember."

"When was this?"

"Couple of years ago."

"What was the name of her employer?"

"Don't remember. In fact she may not have told us. I probably didn't ask."

None of this surprises Jennifer. Malcolm Dugger is unlikely to be meticulous where such details are not central to his main advantage.

"Anyway she changed her job not long after and I've not seen her since."

"Do you know where she went?"

He pouts and appears to be thinking. It's not clear whether to recall the name of the firm or to cover his own tracks.

"Went to work for some firm, what was it Draper or was it Conn or some such name?"

"Draycon?"

"Could be."

"So how did you hear about her? Was it from her employer at the time?"

He hesitates, carefully formulating his reply.

"No, like I said I don't remember who they were. Sorry."

He's far from sorry, but can't or won't provide any further information. Sarah Murrell's recent employment history seems somewhat complicated. Jennifer goes on to Draycon and sees the general manager again. He checks their files. Sarah came to them from a firm of printers called Edward Taylor and Son.

"She came with excellent references."

Jennifer goes on to the printing company. The manager remembers her and confirms that she did leave them for Draycon.

"She was a good worker, but wasn't with us long. I think we were a bit of a stop gap."

"How so? A gap between what? Where she before?"

"She'd been working for herself. I don't think it was paying as well as she hoped."

"How long was she with you?"

"Four months."

"Then she went to Draycon?"

"That's what I mean about a stop gap. I'm afraid we really couldn't afford her. Draycon offered her more money."

"Nothing else, no difficulties?"

"Not with us."

"What about references?"

"She gave us excellent testimonials from her private clients. We followed them up, there were no problems."

"I understand that although she'd been undertaking private work, she was previously employed full time."

"Yes. It only emerged over time. She talked about where she'd worked before. I don't think she'd been there long before she branched out on her own. Everything was okay, but I got the impression she wasn't happy in that employment. As we had good references from elsewhere and we were totally satisfied with her we didn't follow it up."

"Do you know the name of her previous employer?"

"It was a chain of shops…Wallaces."

At Sharp Road the situation is not improving. The continuing changes to the state of the bomb fuels Major Phillips' indecisiveness. This is an unprecedented disposal operation. Unsure whether to go for a controlled explosion or chance removing it, he opts to widen the excavation so more can be exposed. This only reinforces his fears. This is definitely a 'big 'un.' All the while he's harassed by the police, local authority officers and the archaeologists. Escaping beyond the barrier to where his men are working offers some respite.

As a precaution, reluctantly enforced by the police, the evacuation area has been widened yet further. This further exacerbates the unrest among the local population. Arlene talks to large numbers of people, the fruits of her interviews appearing in the *Courier*. There are two pages of 'vox pop' nuggets from the disgruntled residents with a concluding summary in which she lambastes the unfortunate Major as well as the police.

> 'The inconvenience, frustrations and fears of the people of the Sharp Road area can only be swelled by the army's lack of activity. Why hasn't the bomb been moved to a safe place or if necessary detonated on site? Anything that at least purports to be a decision would be welcomed.'

Jenner throws the paper down in disgust.

"*Detonated on site,*" he mutters, "...*if necessary*...if necessary? What does she think this is, putting on a marquee for the village fete in case it rains? Her thoughtless clever dick remarks will really alleviate the residents' anxieties!"

His fury abates slightly and he picks the paper from the floor to read the full article again. Why does she continue this obstinate feud? Her onslaught on the bomb disposal team is particularly annoying. They're only trying to maintain some semblance of order in all the confusion and potential disaster. It's probably good for selling newspapers, but is it also a convenient diversion from herself? She's hiding something. She was peculiarly secretive with Ettie about her aunt's house. At least in this latest piece she's not battering the harassed superintendent, trying to keep people safe while she breaks through a barrier, putting herself and others in peril...Then he reads the last sentence of the article with her final swipe at the police.

> 'Meanwhile the police are making heavy weather of the ever extending evacuation of more and more streets.'

His fury erupts again. Communication through scurrilous newspaper articles is far from ideal. He'll have to find an excuse to talk to her, but no one knows where she is. At the

*Courier* they say she's never in the office, but despite this keeps sending in her material. Even Ettie can't help.

"If only I could remember how to get to where her aunt lives, but I doubt if Arlene Bates is there."

"You think the story of the aunt is false?"

Ettie shrugs.

"Perhaps."

"So, whose place is it?"

Another shrug, Ettie doesn't consider it important.

"It'll be better than nothing," he says and bullies her persistently until she provides an imprecise and contradictory trail of the possible location.

It's of little use and of doubtful reliability. He gets an officer to follow up the vague information. The officer spends a day. It's the most that can be spared without alerting DI Williams to such an unauthorised expedition. He does his best, but returns with nothing definite.


## 4<sup>th</sup> May

Jenner is still concerned about Arlene. It's more than her disappearance. Her unfair and distasteful criticism of the police in general and him in particular is a smokescreen. She knows much more and her connection to the case goes way beyond journalistic curiosity. Then there's her obsession with the war and the bomb. She's now a suspect and has to be found. It might also be the means of him getting back officially into the investigation. He approaches DI Williams with his suspicions.

"We have to find that damned woman."

Williams is amused.

"You can't let your irritation with a reporter get the better of you."

Jenner says it's 'more than irritation' and explains how 'an old associate' was taken to a secret location with some wild story about the war. Williams is unconvinced and wants to know more. Jenner can hardly go into further detail without making a fool of himself and reinforcing his reputation for 'unconventional approaches.' He goes higher.

"It's more than giving us a bad press. Her disappearance has to be investigated."

Emmins listens with avuncular indulgence.

"No one is worrying about her, not her family or the *Courier*. We have plenty more important matters to take up our time."

But Jenner is dogged and eventually Emmins gives in.

"You can follow it up," he says resignedly.

"Does that mean I'm back on the case...officially?"

"I suppose so."

Jenner's obstinacy may be successful, but he doesn't return as senior investigating officer. Much to DI Williams' chagrin, another DCI is drafted in. With studied impertinence, Jenner ignores them both and immediately sets to work further investigating Arlene.

He'll play her at her own game and spends a few hours more at the library trawling through old copies of the *Courier*. He learns a lot about local events in the last ten years, but nothing jumps from the page. He's ready to give up and return to the station, then notices Arlene's by line starts to appear about five years back. There's a reference to a planning proposal in the city centre. Arlene penned a typically opinionated attack on the developers, but what particularly catches his eye is the interest of local television news. With Arlene's recent radio interviews he wonders if she went to the airwaves over the issue. In any case he's had enough of ploughing through pages of old newspapers and needs a break.

He contacts the BBC and draws a blank. Their only recollection of Arlene concerns recent 'problems on the trains' and the murder. Someone comes to the phone anxious to speak to Jenner about 'progress with the investigation.' Jenner quickly excuses himself.

"I'm not involved in that investigation. My interest is in Miss Bates herself. I've been trying to contact her."

He explains about the press article and the reference to television news. The man doesn't understand how they can help and Jenner hastily terminates the conversation. Maybe all this is too long a shot and he should return to the library?

"You could try commercial radio," the BBC man says.

At the local commercial station a helpful woman vaguely remembers the controversy five years earlier, but can't connect it to Arlene. She also wants to talk about 'the train' and 'tensions in the city.' Jenner makes the same excuse and is about to ring off.

"You could try *East Midlands Today*," she says, "They might have something."

Jenner desultorily makes the call to the ITV station and checks his watch. He could fit in another hour at the library. He asks again about the development five years ago. The only person who might know about it is out. Someone will call back. Jenner collects his library notes and gets his coat. The phone rings. It's a man from ITV, John Dennison, an older, more experienced reporter. Jenner dimly recognises the name. Dennison remembers the 'dispute.' It was an interesting story at the time. He interviewed them both.

"Both?" Jenner echoes.

"Yes. They were from opposite sides of the argument. Arlene Bates was one. I can't recall the name of the other woman, but it doesn't matter. We'll still have the footage. You're welcome to come and view it."

"I'll be with you in a matter of minutes," Jenner says eagerly.

It's a fruitful visit to the television studio. The clip is short, but revealing. Two women are being interviewed. One is Arlene Bates. Jenner immediately recognises the other.

"Karen Renshaw."

"Yes, that's the name," Dennison says, "My God, isn't that the woman who was…"

"…attacked on the train? Yes, I'm afraid she is."

Arlene and Karen are on opposite sides of the proposed development. Arlene argues for the preservation of old buildings, which are of 'architectural and historical significance,' while Karen advocates their demolition to make way for an 'exciting modern development, which will rejuvenate the whole area.'

"We did subsequently report on the outcome of the dispute," Dennison says, "I could show you…"

"Who won?"

"Karen Renshaw."

He has enough. Arlene and Karen were well acquainted and there's a history of conflict. He returns to the station and looks through the files. He's not sure what he's looking for except the off chance he might find something relating to Arlene. Jennifer finds him. He tells her of the TV footage, then sends her away again.

"Go over Karen's contacts again, however collateral, use your imagination, anything that might indicate a connection to the past," he says, then adds with gleeful self satisfaction, "There's no need to look out for Williams. I'm officially back on the case with special concentration on Arlene Bates."

Drawing a blank with police files he returns to the library to further check the newspaper reports. He finds another piece a couple of years ago in which Arlene was making much of another development, which would 'compromise the city's unique character with more losses to its diminishing architectural heritage.' There are updates on her 'campaign' in later editions with references to earlier battles, going right back to the conflict over the bulldozing of historic premises by cutting through Georgian streets to make way for the Maid Marian Way in the 1960s. She appealed for a 'positive and successful campaign' like the successful one, which led to 'the protection of the Lace Market.' It's a rerun of the TV debate and Karen is again on the opposite side. Arlene labelled her as like the 'destructive advocates' of the earlier conflicts. Karen counteracted, saying Arlene was using 'older disputes, irrelevant to present arguments' to justify her current flawed campaign, which was 'out of touch with reality' and could only lead to the blocking of 'legitimate development and regeneration.' She said some of the buildings Arlene was trying to preserve were 'at best of mediocre quality and lacked significant historical or architectural merit.'

Interestingly one of the areas involved included the remains of the 'Cross Keys' pub where the unexploded bomb has now been found. Arlene's intervention was a partial success. Other elements of the development went ahead, but she managed a stay of execution on the demolition of the pub, at least until the present new development. So she has form not only in her conflict with Karen, but with a special interest in the bomb disposal site. In the three years after their first confrontation her grudge could have simmered and festered. The second time around she may have been even more determined, but apart from the temporary reprieve for the pub site, Karen won.

How serious were these confrontations with Karen? At best Arlene is an odd character, at worst something more sinister. Has she been waiting to even up the score? Did the so called ghost and the peculiar happenings on the train provide the opportunity to attack Karen under the guise of some mysterious malevolent force? He could be charitable and say she may not have acted with the intention of serious injury, perhaps only to frighten Karen, but it all went wrong. What then? Events moved at a frighteningly rapid pace. She had to deflect attention elsewhere. What better aunt sally than the police?

Then there's the connection with the 'Cross Keys' bombed out pub. A coincidence or a continuing fixation? Is it the source of her obsession with the war? The current development demolishes the last remnants of the pub after the air raid. It's a reminder of past defeats at the hands of Karen, the third in a row. The discovery of the unexploded bomb could be yet more salt rubbed into the wound of her twisted mind? It explains her reckless behaviour, breaking through the barrier, getting dangerously close to the excavation and defying all authority. Again she dips her pen into her vitriol of revenge, aiming it at the man, unwittingly opposing both her and the bomb - Major Phillips. Maybe she doesn't even want the damned bomb made safe at all, but left to suddenly explode and destroy all her imagined enemies!

He returns to the station. Ettie talked of a 'traumatic event' in the past. What if it was Calthorpe's death or, more to the point, his 'murder?' He goes over the police files, but finds nothing. He's not satisfied. Something relevant to Calthorpe's death is missing. If only he could go back and investigate…But perhaps there is a way? What about those mysterious robberies *before* Calthorpe's death? They were investigated. No proof emerged to show he was responsible, but what else might those investigations reveal?

He returns to the much older files back in the 1940s, not just examining them, but working out how *he* would have carried out the investigation. What might he have found that his predecessors of eighty years ago missed?

## 5<sup>th</sup> May

Next day he calls at Ettie's hotel before going into the station. She speaks her mind immediately and Jenner is taken aback.

"It was the 'ghost' that *saved* Karen."

"But she wasn't saved, she was…"

"She was injured, not killed. If he hadn't appeared as he did she would have been killed."

"Then why didn't he save Sarah Murrell?" he says whimsically, "Surely if he's in the business of *saving* women…"

"It's not as simple as that. You're not taking me seriously."

She's annoyed, but he won't be put off.

"If the ghost had intervened outside the station as well as on the train he could have intervened, leaving her maybe injured, but not killed."

She thinks for a moment.

"Sarah Murrell had no connection with the past."

"By the past you mean events in 1941?"

She nods.

"So, what's Karen Renshaw's connection?"

"You've already discovered her grandfather was caught up in that terrible air raid. He was a survivor of the destruction of the church hall disaster."

"Where you felt a particular affinity at the site," he says more sympathetically.

"There's much more to be found and you are the detective."

Ettie's slightly asperous words galvanise and direct what he must do. At the station he avoids the office and returns to the files. It may take hours, even days, but he'll trawl through everything pertaining to the war up to the fateful night of 8th/9th May 1941. As he works the infernal number – 8541 – resonates irritatingly. It's been like a barking dog since its ubiquitous appearances on the train. He now knows what it means. Could it now be his guide like some distant signal, calling him towards greater understanding?

He works relentlessly, unaware that two hours have slipped by and he might be missed. Then the door of the filing room opens. He looks up sharply, glances at his watch edgily, then relaxes when he sees Jennifer.

"I thought I'd find you here."

He closes his notes instinctively.

"I was only...I didn't realise the time. I'll be up in a moment."

"Be prepared before you do. The powers that be are accepting you were right to concentrate on Arlene Bates."

"How so?"

"Because she's just been attacked."

# *10*

ARLENE is soon discovered, unconscious but still breathing. Her injuries look serious. An ambulance arrives and she's taken immediately to the hospital. Jennifer ensures the area is cordoned off and witnesses are interviewed. The assault must have been carried out at lightning speed as she was quickly found only a few minutes later, but no one was close when she was attacked. While not directly disturbed, the assailant must have known he might not have much time.

Arlene had just emerged from the newspaper office after depositing her latest article. It's become her usual practice, flitting in and out in a matter of minutes. No one has the faintest idea where she's living and the editor doesn't seem to care.

"It's fine as long as she keeps producing her copy."

"But surely you need to know where she is," Jennifer says.

"Not necessarily and she'd normally be out and about in any case."

"So you didn't see her?"

"No."

Nor has anyone else. Jennifer goes to the hospital, but cannot see Arlene. She's receiving emergency treatment and no one will be permitted to see her until at least the morning.

## 6<sup>th</sup> May

The attack changes everything. Not least on Jenner, shaken both psychologically and literally out of his peripheral situation

Many regard his approach as 'unconventional' especially with his many 'strange' cases. He also has an unfortunate disregard for public anxieties, not helped by his hostility to the press. But that's now of little importance. His main antagonist is in hospital, though he's uncomfortable with her as a victim, an injured player rather than a spectator constantly shouting abuse at the referee. At least it vindicates his insistence on her seriousness to the investigation.

Emmins acts quickly. Desperate situations require desperate remedies. Jenner is confirmed as senior investigating officer, responsible for all aspects of the case except – for now – press relations. DI Williams is transferred elsewhere.

Jenner imposes a news blackout, though with little confidence it'll have any effect. A bland statement stating a young woman has been attacked near the city centre without any opportunity for questions will not hold. A brief bulletin from the hospital states her condition is 'serious but stable' without giving out her name, but there are bound to be leaks. It will be easy to work out the location outside the *Courier* office. Reluctantly, the editor agrees to respect the silence 'in the interests of the investigation,' but no longer than a day and not even that if another outlet picks up the story.

Jenner normally clears out old newspapers very quickly, but the three days old *Courier* with Arlene's article about the bomb site remains like some awful artefact from a long unsolved case. A reminder, not just of her irritating jibes, but of her mysterious disappearance and now the third victim of what his colleagues continually call the 'peculiar case.' Until this morning it's remained folded on the table of his flat, undisturbed by crockery or other papers, solitary and pristine as if it's just come off the printing press, more like a decorative yet useless antique that's been a family heirloom for countless generations. It can't remain. He picks it up and scans the article with none of his previous anger, taking in her words more carefully.

After her attack on the police *'making heavy weather'* of the evacuation she wrote: *'If the authorities cannot deal with the bomb, it might even be better to leave it alone.'*

He's sure he's not read this before. He must have passed over it in his haste and anger. He reads on, but the intriguing comment is unexplained as she returns to the general attack on Phillips, the police, the local authorities and anyone else her censorious pen can spear. Then there's more bellyaching from the residents. His thoughts of yesterday return before he learnt of the attack on Arlene. Did she really not want the bomb made safe? After all she did report the device had a mind of its own!

On the way across the city he picks up an early edition of today's *Courier*. To his relief and surprise the report of the attack doesn't reveal Arlene's identity. The editor has kept his word, but this must be the calm before the storm. Someone will talk. Other media will break the story. He must make sure he sees the lunchtime local TV news. Then, at the bottom of the page he sees it. Another article by Arlene, the one she must have dropped off yesterday just before she was attacked. Mainly a rehash of her earlier material with the usual barbed castigation of everybody involved and some updating on the current situation at Sharp Road, except for the last sentence.

*'There is something the police ought to know.'*

Curiously ill fitting and left without explanation. Another meaningless sideswipe or something the smartypants reporter has discovered which is beyond the ken of Mr. Plod? Why can't she just say what she means? He's amazed it got past the paper's sub editor. Surely they would have demanded further exposition? Perhaps in the confusion of last evening's event it was missed just as he'd missed that other statement of hers three days ago? Maybe the article was put out as a commendation to an unfortunate colleague without proper scrutiny? But despite her recent misfortune, it does nothing to dispose him towards her. She may now be a victim, but that doesn't mean she's blameless.

By the time he gets to the station he's reverted completely to his old scepticism, not just about Arlene, but everything else and immediately inveighs to Jennifer.

"I'm not convinced the mysterious man on the train really exists and – before you say anything about a so called 'ghost' – it's only a figment of hysterical women's imaginations, exaggerated and whipped up by an unscrupulously ambitious journalist."

Jennifer is gobsmacked. It's as if all that's occurred since the middle of April has never happened.

"Unscrupulous she may be, but she's just been viciously attacked, almost as badly as Karen Renshaw."

"Maybe, but it doesn't alter the facts. Arlene Bates lacks the integrity of a genuinely investigative reporter."

"Like who?"

"My old friend David Farley on the *Mercury*. He wouldn't have lowered himself to her level."

"He's in London. He's not here and she is. I can't believe this. Okay, until the attack on Karen I might have been willing to go along with you. The whole thing could have been a publicity stunt engineered by Arlene, but I don't' believe all those women have been making up seeing the ghost."

"She could have put them up to it, friends, acquaintances with more levity than responsibility and…"

"You've said that before and it's not borne out by my enquiries. In any case, you're stretching Arlene's abilities well beyond her capabilities, especially if you're right and she's not particularly stable."

He considers for a moment, then says, "It's a kind of group think, perpetuated through her groundless articles. Hysterical people see what they think they ought to see. Arlene Bates…"

"Why would Arlene attack Karen?"

"She's known Karen for at least five years. The so called telephone message was not their first contact."

"So Arlene knew exactly why Karen wanted to see her?"

"Or the telephone message is a complete fabrication."

"But why would she admit to any contact at all?"

"To put us off the scent. She thought there was every likelihood - quite rightly as it happened - we would sniff out something else. They've been in conflict for five years or more."

"All right, she didn't immediately come clean about how she'd already known Karen and they'd been opposing each other a couple of times about building developments – innocent or disastrous whichever way you view them. There've been plenty of people on opposite sides of those sorts of things without resorting to assaulting each other. What you're saying is just supposition. Anyway, the attack on Arlene changes everything. Karen couldn't have done it from her hospital bed and Arlene can hardly be a suspect if she's been attacked herself."

He doesn't immediately respond and they are silent, both in concentrated thought. Jennifer is about to speak, but Jenner gets in first.

"Okay, she's been attacked, but could it be a blind to curry sympathy and deflect attention from her? No direct witnesses. As if she was waiting for the right opportunity."

Jennifer is amazed.

"As could her attacker."

"Even so…"

"You think she attacked herself?"

"She may have gone too far. Villain becomes victim. There are plenty of examples of that."

Jennifer shakes her head.

"It's a bit more than that."

"All right, but it's the before and after I'm concerned with. If she was involved in the attack on Karen this is very convenient. Let's consider the attack on her. She's attacked just outside the newspaper office, a place she's not been seen for about a week."

"I admit that's odd. She was seen at the unexploded bomb site and was interviewing local people."

"Of which the paper denied any knowledge."

"Until she submitted her article."

"Have you seen today's paper?"

"They've not given out her name?"

"No, but it's only a matter of time. Look at this."

He points to the short article and repeats the final sentence.

*"There is something the police ought to know."*

"What does it mean?"

"That's what I intend to find out. It's a damned strange way to behave even for a reporter. She was in hiding. Then lo and behold, outside the *Courier* office she's attacked. No one else knew her movements. She covered her tracks when she saw Ettie. We couldn't find her. She didn't want to be seen in the city, creeps into the newspaper, drops off her articles before running away again. Scarlet bloody Pimpernel, but her attacker must have known her movements and where she was. Would he have really waited so long?"

"It's still unthinkable she would attack herself."

"But not impossible."

"You'd have to ask the doctors."

"I intend to. She's in the hospital. That means she can't slip away and I can see her at last."

"Be careful," Jennifer says, "Don't over do it."

"I never overdo anything."

"No, of course not."

"Past and present, three families linked, Renshaw, Bates and Wallace. That means piecing together how Karen Renshaw, Arlene Bates and Simon Wallace are connected. While I'm at the hospital, see Simon Wallace again and then the Duggers. We need more on that supposed accident in 1965. Who did you see before?"

"Malcolm Dugger."

"Let's see, he's the…"

"Grandson."

"...of George Dugger?"

"Yes."

"Try and see the son, Henry Dugger."

"Try and be pleasant to the PC on duty," she says.

"If he's been doing his job properly," he grunts, then only half jokingly, "More to protect the rest of us from her than the other way round."

On his way to the hospital Jenner mulls over what needs to be discovered. From background enquiries he believes Simon is something of a Lothario and they know Arlene had contacts with him. From the start, despite initial denials he's been very attentive about Karen. Maybe in the past he was just as interested in Arlene? Whether she was receptive is another matter, but a feisty reporter might not meekly accept a rival, especially one with whom she's already clashed over the 'city's heritage.' Some men – like Simon Wallace - revel in the competing attentions of different women. Rather than avoiding such complications he might delight in stoking up the fires of contending passions. Playing such a dangerous game in an unstable triangle could lead to disastrous consequences.

Arlene is on a different ward to Karen. Jenner introduces himself to the ward sister and the doctor.

"She's conscious now. It's not life threatening," the doctor says, "but it was a nasty assault, couple of broken ribs, some bruising and a head wound that should heal quickly. We saw her in time. I'd say she was lucky."

"Lucky?"

"If the attacker had continued it could have been very different."

"These injuries...I suppose there's no possibility they were self inflicted?"

The doctor looks at him incredulously.

"Only with great difficulty even if she was some kind of latter day Houdini."

"No, of course not. Is it all right to see her?"

The doctor frowns.

"She slips in and out of consciousness. I've already turned away her father and some of her colleagues from the newspaper. She needs to rest. Maybe tomorrow."

"You say this was a nasty assault and you got her in time. A few more minutes delay before treatment…"

"Could have been fatal."

"Exactly. This could easily have become a murder investigation," Jenner says, "It's vital we get something from Miss Bates as quickly as possible. You're aware of the intense distress throughout the city. The other young woman attacked, we have men guarding them both…"

"All right, Mr. Jenner, but not too long."

The PC on duty looks bored and has nothing to report.

"Has she been any trouble?" Jenner says.

The PC is confused.

"She's in her bed, she can't…"

"Okay. I'll just go in."

"The doctor's not been allowing any visitors."

"He's made an exception in my case."

Arlene lies like Karen, quiet, unmoving, quietly breathing, eyes closed but as he steps across the room they open and she stares at him puzzlingly.

"You're the last person I expected to see," she says softly, "or hardly the first to arrive."

"I'm the most appropriate. At the moment you're the centre of my attention."

Her lips curl slightly.

"Tell me you've come to wish me well - though I don't see the usual bag of grapes – and you'll not be asking me any questions."

"I can't help you if you don't help me," he says, grabbing a chair and sitting beside the bed, "What can you tell me about how you came to be in here?"

"Very little. One moment I was walking along, innocently minding my own business, then a hard sharp pain in my side, then my head and then…nothing."

Jenner isn't sure Arlene ever does anything innocently and is as unlikely to mind her own business as he is.

"You were attacked from behind?"

"Yes."

"So you didn't see your attacker?"

"No, after a split second I didn't see anything until I woke up here. Thank you for asking and I am told I should be okay except for some discomfort for a while."

"I've already spoken to the doctor."

That will be the limit of any bedside manner.

"You were attacked quite late at night. What were you doing there?"

"It's hardly surprising. I work at the *Courier* office."

"You've not been *working* there for some time."

She doesn't answer and turns to face the wall.

"Where have you been for the last week?"

She turns back, now with more of her customary fervour.

"How is that relevant to me being viciously assaulted in a public place?"

"It might help us find who's responsible."

"I've been out and about. Nowhere anyone who doesn't know me would guess."

"You believe your attacker didn't know you?"

She hesitates, then says, "I don't know."

"Do you know anyone who was against you?"

"Only you!"

He doesn't even smile.

"You know the area well. Is it normally busy at that hour?"

"No more nor less than any other part of the city centre. Why is that important?"

"If it's not normally busy you're more likely to have noticed someone. Did you see anyone before you were attacked, someone who could be following you or just hanging around?"

"I've told you I didn't see him."

"But he could have been lying in wait. You're a reporter, an observer, used to noticing things, hearing things."

"Like I saw and heard at Sharp Road?"

"The attack was not at Sharp Road."

"There was no one I recall."

He sighs deeply and grimaces.

"Is that all?" she says, staring intently at him.

"Not quite. I want to talk about your relationship with Karen Renshaw."

"I should have thought that was obvious. Suddenly we have much in common, both recently attacked, though much more serious for her."

"Your relationship is much more than simply being patients in this hospital."

"Well, obviously with me writing about her situation and by extension the predicament of all vulnerable women in…"

"You've had a more direct relationship with Karen Renshaw long before the recent…difficulties…and I don't mean her supposed telephone call to you just before she was attacked."

"*Supposed* phone call?"

"Tell me about your previous contacts."

"I don't know what you're talking about."

"Karen Renshaw imparted some information of direct personal relevance."

She almost laughs, but it would be too painful.

"I've no relationship with Karen Renshaw which could possibly be termed 'personal.'"

"But you've known her for at least five years."

"That's impossible. I only…"

He spells out his recent discoveries from the newspaper reports and the television clip.

She listens impassively, then after a long pause, says tartly, "I wouldn't describe any of that as constituting a relationship of any meaningful kind."

"You've contended with her in ways way beyond that of a journalist."

"A meeting of minds," she says playfully.

"Forceful exchanges of information, but did it go much further in recent times?"

"No it did not," she says firmly, "If you mean about the ghost and the predator I can see where you're going, but as I've said my interest has been purely professional."

He notices the strict formal response, no more than 'purely professional' interest in the ghost and predator, but what's she really denying? Her articles about the war, the mystifying references to the bomb, what Ettie has gleaned through Karen, all resonate. He suspects a link to the Wallaces, but without concrete material he can only probe tangentially.

"Tell me about your relationship with Simon Wallace."

"Who?"

"You must have heard of him. His family own a chain of well known local stores."

She pretends to be trying to recall the name, finally saying, "Yes...the Wallaces...they..."

"They trade under various names...*Home Stage...Home Everything* and...oh what is it...yes...*Home Comfort*...very appropriate don't you think. Then..."

"Yes, all right, I've heard of them."

"He had a relationship with Karen Renshaw and naturally, with your own relationship with her over the same period of time...mutual acquaintances, shall we say? I thought it likely that..."

"What Karen Renshaw does in her personal life has nothing to do with me."

"Quite, but it remains to be seen..."

"This is nothing to do with what you came here to talk to me about."

"I will be the judge of that, Miss Bates."

"I do not and never have had a *personal* relationship with Simon Wallace."

"So you say, but with your interest in the war and especially that horrendous air raid in May 1941, you must be aware how the Wallaces and the Renshaws were brought together on that terrible night?"

"That has nothing to do with me."

There's a long silence. He notes she doesn't ask what he means by 'brought together.'

"Your latest article - which you were desperately keen to deposit at the *Courier* so late at night - it had an intriguing sentence…"

"It was a draft, not yet intended for publication in that form, but the paper published it anyway. I needed to do more interviews, but with the accident…"

A pungent response. It's too convenient. He doesn't believe her. He's about to intervene, but the door opens and the doctor enters.

"You've been here some time, Mr. Jenner. I did say Miss Bates should not be over tired."

"Yes, indeed. There's just one more question before I go," Jenner says, then turning to Arlene, "That sentence in your article…*There is something the police ought to know* …what did you mean, what is it we should know?"

Until now Arlene has shown no sign of tiring and appears perfectly capable of continuing the interview.

"I'm tired now," she says.

"Go now," the doctor says.

At the Duggers', office Jennifer receives the customary blocking from the receptionist.

"Mr. Malcolm is out," she says without being asked.

"That's all right," Jennifer says with her best plastic smile.

"And if you want Mr. Henry…"

Jennifer is amused by the rather old fashioned references to 'Mr.' this and 'Mr' that.

"I don't want to see either of them but I'm sure *you* can help me."

More plastic smile, even wider than before. The receptionist remains impassive, but wonders what Jennifer will say next. Surprisingly, she's enlivened, even voluble when asked for information about the firm's professional associates. Jennifer has inadvertently pressed a winning button. The root of the woman's aggression is a lack of perceived usefulness rather than a defensive wall. This is her preserve and she delights in demonstrating her knowledge. Names of architects, specialist trades and sub contractors pour out and she writes down a list for Jennnifer's consideration.

"Is this what you're after?"

"Are these all long standing people? I'm particularly interested in what firms or specialists the company used some time back, say the mid 60s?"

"Well, I don't go back quite *that* far," she says with something vaguely close to a smile, "but I can check the files."

She scurries into a back room, taking the list with her. She returns in a few minutes with some names crossed out and others added.

"I can't be sure all these people are still in business, but I've added the last addresses and phone numbers we have."

"Thank you, you've been very helpful."

"It's my job," the receptionist says, her lips quivering, even closer to a smile.

"Oh, one last thing," Jennifer says at the door, "Henry Dugger, is he around?"

"He'll be in the office at midday, but he'll be out again by two."

It's a long morning. As predicted, some of the firms have either gone out of business or there's no one now employed with knowledge of activities more than fifty years ago. Then Jennifer strikes lucky. Douglas Cunningham is the semi-retired head of 'Cunningham and Associates,' a firm of architects. Though now in his eighties his faculties are unimpaired and his memory is as sharp on matters so far back as if they were yesterday. He remembers the accident that killed John Renshaw in 1965.

"Unfortunately construction is still one of the most dangerous occupations and in those days many of the safety provisions we now take for granted had yet to come, but any accident resulting in a fatality is always tragic for everyone."

"Was your firm connected with the site?"

"Yes. We were directly involved in the plans and implementation or rather *I* was. It was one of the first site jobs I undertook on my own. My father was then head of the firm, of course."

"Did you ever see the client, someone from the Wallace shops?"

"Occasionally. My role was primarily dealing with the builder, in this case Duggers, but I do remember seeing Albert Wallace on site sometimes. I believe he was a regular visitor. I didn't want to get involved in discussions between him and George Dugger."

"What do you mean?"

"We were receiving our fees without any difficulty so there was no need to become concerned."

"Concerned?"

"The contract – that between the client, the Wallaces and Duggers, you understand – provided for periodic payments. It's not unusual. Anyway I picked up from people on site there'd been delays with some payments. One sub contractor was especially worried as of course it knocked onto his own position. A lot of sub contractors fail through no fault of their own, you know. A couple of unreliable clients or a builder going bust, a perfectly well managed sub contractor can be hit by a cash flow crisis and down they go. It can be very sad."

"But that didn't happen in this case?"

"Well, the Duggers are still around and so are the Wallaces, but it was looking quite precarious at the time."

"You've been very helpful, Mr. Cunningham. One last thing, when you visited the site whom did you meet on the building side?"

"George Dugger was the head of the firm in those days."

"What about his son, Henry Dugger?"

He considers this for a moment.

"He's in charge now. Cutting his teeth back then. Yes, he did visit the site."

"Regularly?"

"Fairly."

"You saw him?"

"Yes."

"On his own?"

"Yes."

Jennifer arrives just after twelve at the Dugger's office.

"Mr. Henry is expecting you," the receptionist says, "I told him you were coming."

She beams. Jennifer doubts Henry Dugger will be quite so enthusiastic. He stares expressionlessly as she enters, not even bothering to stand. If anything he's even less amenable than Malcolm and clearly resents the unwarranted interruption to his day. The receptionist will likely rue her cooperating with Jennifer, a significant departure in an otherwise flawless adherence to the company's obstructive culture.

"Haven't you already spoken to Malcolm?" he begins, "What more can I tell you?"

"Your son is too young to remember the unfortunate fatal accident in 1965."

He scowls and shuffles in his chair. She takes the uninvited seat opposite him.

"I thought you were investigating the attacks on that woman on the train."

"I am...among other things. The woman's name is Karen Renshaw. It's important for us to get as full a picture as we can of her background."

"We've already said what we know."

"But your company is connected to the Renshaws. The accident in 1965..."

"There's nothing more to say."

"We're also investigating the murder of Sarah Murrell. You may have read in the..."

"Never heard of her."

"You should have done. She worked for your company for a time as an accountant. Then she went on and worked for the Wallaces in a similar capacity."

"I've still no recollection of either of them. If you say..."

"You see how your company is connected to both women."

He's still gruff, but less comfortable.

"Your point being?"

She asks the usual questions about his whereabouts at the times of the attack on Karen and Sarah's murder. Eventually after some evasion he admits to remembering Sarah, but can add nothing to what's already known. Then she switches to John Renshaw.

"Never met the man."

"Really? He was working on one of your sites back in the sixties."

"What site?"

"The development for the Wallaces."

"Don't remember it."

"You don't remember anything about the accident?"

"I wasn't very old then."

"Perhaps not, but you must know about when a man was killed on your site."

"There was an investigation. We did nothing wrong despite what Keith Renshaw says."

"So you do remember?"

"I said I never met John Renshaw. I can hardly not know about the accident. Keith Renshaw's been stirring up trouble about it for years."

"Even though you were young, you did visit sites."

"Well I was learning…"

"But you did visit the site on your own?"

He hesitates, finally saying, very softly, "At times."

"Were you on site on the same day one of the Wallaces visited?"

"The Wallaces?"

"The clients."

"Don't remember."

"You don't remember the Wallaces visiting the site or you don't remember the Wallaces at all?"

"I remember they were clients."

"So you remember the site, you remember the accident, you remember the Wallaces were the clients. So, do you remember seeing one of the Wallaces on site?"

He's silent, then says, "Obviously clients occasionally visit sites, but usually for a specific reason. It's a long time ago. I can't think of anything particularly important."

"Would you count not being paid in accordance with the contract as important?"

"We were paid for that work," he says defiantly.

"So now you do have a good recollection of something that happened fifty years ago?"

He's silent again.

"Were you paid on time?"

"All right. There was a time when I spoke to them about payments."

"You spoke to Albert Wallace?"

"No, I spoke to his son, Michael Wallace."

"Was it an amicable meeting?"

He shrugs.

"I was making enquiries. He was responding."

"How did it end?"

"We got our money."

She looks at him carefully. Would he as a young man stand firm with Michael Wallace or was it the other way round?

"Even though they were going through a bad patch?" she says.

"It happens."

"What about you? How was your business doing?"

"We were all right."

"But you were dependent on this job. It was a big job. You couldn't afford to lose their business?"

"We can never afford to lose any business."

"You did other work for the Wallaces?"

Again his recollection is hazy.

"I don't remember the details."

"But there were other Wallace developments?"

"I believe so."

"One good turn always deserves another."

He shrugs.

"We all have our ups and down. It's the nature of business. Things picked up for them. There were no more... difficulties."

"So you helped each other?"

He doesn't respond. During the interchange he's veered between aggression and accommodation. He knows more. Now's the time to speculate.

"So, at a later time the boot could be on the other foot?"

"Meaning?"

"They had difficulty paying, but you were also short of work..."

"I didn't say that."

"But you were weren't you?"

Another silence.

"So in exchange for waiting for payment Michael Wallace promised to use your firm for any further work in the future. No tendering, you just get the work."

Further silence.

"But there was more wasn't there? More than promises for the future, something more immediate, something on a particular day?"

He shuffles uncomfortably.

"You were on site on the day of the accident, weren't you?"

He stares at her intently. This woman knows. There's nothing to be gained from further denial.

"Yes, all right, I was there earlier in the day, before the accident."

"And Michael Wallace was there?"

"I don't know."

"What do you mean, if you were there why don't you know?"

"Because, as I said, I was there before the accident. I only heard about it later."

"You'd left the site?"

"Yes."

"This was an arrangement, wasn't it? You were meant to be away, you and others?"

"The foreman and I...we both had other duties on that day."

"You left the site and knew Michael Wallace would be there later?"

"No. I couldn't know. I wasn't there."

"But Michael Wallace wanted to see John Renshaw?"

"He may have done."

"In fact Michael Wallace wasn't there to see you at all?"

"I've told you. I wasn't there. I'd left."

"As did the foreman...on your say so and you knew Michael Wallace wanted to speak to John Renshaw?"

"I don't know what was said."

"So you know they'd met."

He grimaces and sighs deeply. He's fallen into her trap. Or would he have done anyway? She already knows.

"Did you ask Wallace later?"

"Can't remember. Anyway I don't know what was said."

"This was the day of the accident. You must have said something."

"It never came up."

"Michael Wallace's presence on site on that day was never mentioned during the investigation."

"Why should it have been if he wasn't present when Renshaw fell off the scaffolding."

"You don't know that. As you say, you weren't there."

He stares again, no longer shuffling, but though immovable his eyes betray his fear. A mixture of verifiable information, guesswork and pretending to know much more than she does has been successful, but it's as far as she can go with the 'accident.' After so long there's nothing more to be proved. Keith Renshaw's campaign has shown that.

Despite their later success, the Wallace operation was in financial difficulty in 1965, which may have been the stimulus for a suspect 'arrangement' between Henry Dugger and Michael Wallace, but it's only circumstantial. If Michael Wallace witnessed the accident, let alone was involved in manslaughter or murder he's bound to deny it and it seems there are no other witnesses. Henry will never admit he arranged for himself and others to be away from the site. Supposition isn't proof.

She asks about his general relationship with the Wallaces. He's evasive again, but not very smart.

"It was a purely business relationship."

"Why would it be anything else?" she says suspiciously.


Jenner watches the lunchtime local television news despondently. It was inevitable somebody would talk and the identity of the woman attacked last night is revealed. Any short term advantage of concealing Arlene is gone and all the press will descend like a plague of locusts. Arlene is no longer writing the story. She *is* the story and the attacker knows where she is. That could loosen her tongue, telling all she knows or it could make her even more intractable. He scans her latest *Courier* article again. She said it was published without her consent 'in that form.' Yet if she was only in the newspaper office for a short time, saw no one and spoke to no one, how can she tell from her hospital bed?

Jennifer goes to Keith Renshaw. He's surprised to see her, saying he's 'already talked to her boss.' It's a slightly charged atmosphere, which will be difficult to ease up. She says her visit is only intended 'to tie up loose ends.' She's not expecting to discover anything new, but the conversation will turn out to be more than mere 'loose ends.'

He's taken aback when she expresses interest in his father's movements in the period after his 'return' from Brazil and repeats what he told Jenner. Initially John Renshaw didn't do very well and took some time to 'settle down.' He doesn't go into details.

"But eventually things improved?" she says.

"It took some time," he says guardedly, "We were strapped for cash."

"But he got a regular job. Things looked up?"

"I suppose so."

He's subdued and his voice is dull. They both know what's to come. She watches him carefully, remembering what Jenner told her and noticing the papers and magazines on the table. Hopefully, he'll not drag out his 'campaign notes,' but the subject can't be avoided.

"After all," she says, "He got the job with the Duggers."

"Yes," he says sullenly.

"I wanted to ask you about your family's relations with the Wallaces."

He looks up, surprised.

"You mean the shop people?"

"Yes. We know Karen was acquainted with Simon Wallace."

"Don't know of him. I've already told your chief inspector all I know about her close friends. My family has no connection with the Wallaces."

This is too quick and too adamant.

"That's not quite true, is it?"

He looks at her quizzically with raised eyebrows.

"Your father, John and Hilda Wallace were both in the same shelter during an air raid in May 1941. It was a church hall and subject to a direct hit. Your father survived, Hilda didn't."

"I don't know anything about that. Anyway it's hardly a connection. Must have happened to many people in the war, stuck for hours in air raid shelters. It doesn't mean they knew each other."

"Perhaps not, but there's another connection. The building site where your father was killed in 1965."

It's as if the door of an oven has been suddenly flung open and the intense heat rushes into the room.

"The Duggers were the builders. They were responsible," he says vehemently.

She glances nervously as he gets up and goes to the cupboard. That must be where he keeps the dreaded press cuttings and correspondence on the 'accident.' Pre-emptive action is called for.

"The Wallaces were the clients," she says, then more quickly, "One of the them, Michael Wallace was on the site on the day your father was killed. He went there specifically to talk to your father. Why do you think that was? Was there bad feeling between them? Could Michael Wallace have been responsible for your father's death?"

Keith turns and looks at her directly. For a moment it unnerves her. It's how Henry Dugger looked at her. A cornered animal, frightened but defiant. He sits down. At least she'll be spared the 'campaign' documents.

"The Duggers, they…" he begins.

"It's possible none of the Duggers were actually on site when the accident happened," she says.

But Keith won't be deflected from the thrust of his long campaign.

"Is that what they told you?"

"Why would Michael want to speak to your father? He was not involved in the management of the development. What could it have been about?"

"I know nothing of these things."

"Your father and Hilda Wallace were both caught up in the air raid with tragic consequences for her. Could there have been suspicions about Hilda's death?"

"Suspicions about what?"

Jennifer swallows hard. This is not going to be easy.

"There were not many survivors from the direct hit on the church hall. Albert Wallace, her widower might have questioned why and how John Renshaw was one of them. His children may have continued that suspicion. When Michael Wallace discovered your father was employed on the site of his firm's development he might have wanted to confront him over those events in the war."

"Are you saying my father had something to do with this woman's death?"

"The Wallaces might have thought that."

"What possible reason would my father have to do such a thing? She was a complete stranger to him."

"You're sure they didn't know each other?"

Keith explodes.

"This is a scandalous assertion. The Duggers have put you up to it to avoid prosecution for their negligence. My father had nothing to do with this woman's death any more than the Wallaces had anything to do with his death. It's the Dugger's you should be after!"

"I'm not investigating your father's accident."

"Then what's this all about?"

"It's about finding a reason for someone wanting to harm your daughter."

"And you believe that's because of the death of her grandfather fifty odd years ago?"

"Or maybe something even earlier than that."

Jenner examines the CCTV footage for the night of the attack on Arlene. It's not good. There are no cameras close to the *Courier* office. The nearest is at a pub on the opposite side of the road. It's set at the wrong angle towards the near pavement and takes in only a peripheral view of the entrance to the newspaper office. There's a fleeting passage showing Arlene walking out of the office. She takes a few steps along the pavement, but then a passing bus obscures the whole view. It moves painfully slowly. By the time it's gone Arlene has moved too far out of shot. He examines the pictures many times, but no one else can be seen in the crucial seconds before the bus appears. No one is hovering, no one is approaching, the attacker must be waiting, watching, but can't be seen. No one is around until immediately after she's attacked when presumably he's got away and well out of sight. Jenner has nothing conclusive.

All Arlene's family and colleagues are seen. No one has any idea who might wish to harm her. Everyone who can be identified at the scene *after* the attack is interviewed. No one saw anyone or anything untoward. Even the bus, it's driver and passengers are identified and statements taken. More blanks. No one has any recollection of even seeing Arlene, let alone any possible attacker. Enquiries at the pub also draw a blank. Unfortunately no one the worse for drink or needing some fresh air or creeping out for a quick smoke. Everybody inside, oblivious to what was going on outside.

The timing is unbelievable. A relatively busy street at that time in the evening yet in those crucial seconds no one was around. Whoever did this knew when and where to strike and planned the attack carefully. The only redeeming element is that plenty of people were on the scene quickly enough to ensure she could be got to hospital. He must have seen someone coming and made his getaway. That's assuming murder was the objective. Jenner isn't so sure. Arlene's injuries were bad, but not life threatening. Someone intending to kill her could have finished the job, like poor Sarah Murrell. Are the two attacks unrelated, two different attackers or even three if Karen Renshaw is also considered? Was it a gruesome warning and if so why?

With all current lines of enquiry already in hand and no immediate progress, Jenner is drawn into the problematic confines of the past. Once more he examines the old files on the spate of wartime robberies, attributed to the rogue Ronald Calthorpe. Inevitably this leads to a delve through the general documents on the blitz and especially those of the dreadful air raid of $8^{th}/9^{th}$ May 1941. He recalls again the 'evidence' Ettie and Jennifer gleaned from Karen while in her coma. Finally, he considers the 'observations' of the recently deceased Wilf Sanders as recounted to Ettie by his granddaughter, Arlene Bates.

He cannot interrogate any of the 'witnesses' (except possibly and hopefully Karen at some future time) particularly Wilf Sanders, assuming his 'statement' is correct and not some foolish concoction by Arlene. On balance, while she can't be wholly trusted and is probably slightly unbalanced he's prepared to believe what she's said. Much of it synchronises with Ettie's 'sensations' of Wilf on the train. Besides, if there are elements of romanticised claptrap Ettie would have filtered them out.

One thing about Wilf's 'story' can be independently verified. Jenner has the old railway timetables for 1941. Assuming Wilf did catch the later train from London and it was reasonably punctual, this coincides with the current train, scene of recent events, sighting of the ghost and Karen's attack. It also pinpoints Wilf's arrival time in Nottingham. From this he works out how long it would have taken to travel to the 'Cross Keys' pub, then on to the church hall, establishing a fairly precise timeline for Wilf's movements.

Jenner's calculation accords with the known time the church hall received the direct hit. So, although he can't question them he has two witnesses with direct experience of the events, Wilf and the young prostitute, Milly Fielding. He compares her statement with Arlene's account from Wilf. They both saw a survivor emerging from the bombed out building, but there's a disconnect. This is understandable. In confused and fast moving situations witnesses often report conflicting impressions. This would have been even worse in wartime. The blackout meant the area was in almost total darkness and there would have been heightened shock and panic after the bomb fell, allowing little time to accurately identify anyone escaping from the carnage. In a fleeting glance people might distinguish quite different features. Wilf saw quite a short man, thin and wiry with a slight limp whereas Milly saw a slightly taller man and didn't mention a limp. How reliable is Milly's description? It was very dark and she may have been otherwise engaged at the time.

However there's little doubt they both saw the same man. Milly gave more details of his clothes while Wilf's account, though less detailed was similar. Both said he wore a hat and was moving quickly, though only Wilf talked of a 'running man.'

Wilf didn't hang around. He's not mentioned in any of the reports. There were more important things to consider that night and in any case the man was quickly identified as John Renshaw, though this was some hours later and after the all clear had sounded. Again, that wouldn't have been unusual. In such a prolonged and heavy raid the emergency services were severely stretched. Protracted rescues or people being temporarily taken in and not immediately reported meant not all casualties were immediately identified nor all survivors successfully located. Renshaw was not only a survivor, but one relatively unscathed. There are no reports of him being injured. Where was he immediately after he escaped from the devastated church hall basement?

Jenner lets it go. His suspicions about the Renshaws in general, particularly John's mysterious adventure in Brazil and equally peculiar return are no more than vague suspicions. There's another matter more compelling. The files indicate Milly actually mentioned seeing *two* men. If John Renshaw was one, who was the other? When all victims and survivors were accounted for, her account of seeing two men was discounted. Milly was on the scene much earlier than Wilf and presumably taking every opportunity afforded by the dark streets and alleys to more effectively pursue her occupation. Could the second man she saw have been Wilf? What if he arrived earlier, perhaps around the time of the explosion? Like Milly he would take cover as best he could in the street. He must have remained for a little time because like Milly he saw John Renshaw escape from the church hall.

Wilf never mentioned seeing the explosion, but such a traumatic event, bearing in mind his continuing 'guilt' over the years, may have been too much for him. It was too painful to recall, but was it even feasible? Jenner checks his time calculations. It would have been possible for Wilf to have got to the 'Cross Keys' and then on to the church hall *before* the bomb fell. But what if Milly saw this second man *after* the bomb fell, but before Wilf arrived? So, if this man was not Wilf, who was he?

There's one final thing on which he needs to be satisfied. Ronald Calthorpe continues to fascinate. Jenner must find everything about him before the sudden and dramatic end to his career on that fateful night. After a half hour he's almost completed his research. He's taken extensive notes and is about to finish, then wonders how many other such characters flourished during the war? Despite the country pulling together against the common enemy there was an increase in crime, especially robberies and black market rackets. He gets out other files for the same period. After studying the information on other cases he's taken aback.

An MO, remarkably similar to Calthorpe appears in a spate of robberies during the rest of 1941 and into the following year. It could mean many of the unsolved cases, attributed to Calthorpe were not committed by him at all. That would explain why it was difficult to produce the evidence to convict him. He simply wasn't responsible, which is why such a run of burglaries continued. Another explanation is that others closely studied his expertise and emulated his methods after his death.

He feels some disappointment. It seems inappropriate and even somehow dishonourable for such a worthy adversary's record to be sullied by lesser villains. Then amidst all the other papers he unearths the report of a robbery in the suburbs on the night of 8$^{th}$/9$^{th}$ May and no more than a half mile from the church hall. The complainant, a certain Dorothy Matthews, like many others had left her house to go to a nearby shelter. She returned to find she'd been robbed. It had all the hallmarks of what Jenner would otherwise label a typical 'Cathorpe job.' So, the rogue was at work right up to his abrupt demise? Mrs. Matthews was not always conscientious in seeking shelter. It was a large house with a cellar, which she often used during a raid or (as she brazenly told the investigating officer) she remained in her lounge, refusing to be 'driven out by bloody Hitler.' No doubt in the future she was more prudent. From the file she comes across as a very precise lady. Her departure and return times to and from the house are carefully recorded. Jenner is about to close the file. Then it hits him. The time period during which her house was burgled is on the same night, but well *after* the bomb hit the church hall.

Jenner considers all the implications for several minutes. The speed with which a copy cat burglar was in action so soon, on the same night that Calthorpe was killed seems utterly *unwholesome*.

Jennifer goes to the Wallace office. Michael is indisposed, apparently having gone down with a sudden winter cold - in the spring! Jennifer has a good idea why.

"Simon is in," the secretary says, "You can see him."

It's not part of Jennifer's original plan, but she's here now and it might be interesting. It's just over two weeks since their last meeting. Then he was amiable, but reluctant to admit a close relationship with Karen. This time he's polite rather than friendly. She gets a comfortable seat, but no drink is offered. Does he know about her conversation with Michael? He immediately takes the initiative and opens up before she can speak.

"Do you have any news of Karen? You'll have been to the hospital. There's been no mention of her in the paper. I suppose with… the other things they've lost interest and of course now that the reporter…she shouldn't be forgotten."

Jennifer is guarded.

"There's no change, but no worse."

"So, she's not been able to speak about it?"

"The doctors are optimistic. I'm sure she'll be able to tell us something soon."

She watches his reaction, but he only sighs and says, "That's good."

"Has your family always been on close terms with the Renshaws?" she says pointedly.

He's bemused.

"My family? I don't know what you mean."

"Karen is your friend."

"Yes, but that's me, not the whole family."

She lets it go for now and approaches from a different direction.

"You're very knowledgeable about the history of the firm."

It appeals to his vanity. He relaxes and smiles coyly. She continues.

"It's a fascinating story. I suppose even when you were very young it must have been exciting going into the shops, playing in the backrooms and stores?"

His smile widens.

"I was very close to my grandfather, Albert, the founder of the firm and my father always told me about the past. I like to think I know all there is to know."

"Your grandfather and your father after him grew the firm from small beginnings. You must have visited all the new shops when they were starting up?"

He nods sagely.

"Yes, it's been a success story and we're still expanding."

"But it's not been an uninterrupted story, has it? About fifty years ago when you went through a period of financial stringency?"

His smile is gone.

"Yet the firm recovered and you've never looked back."

He relaxes again.

"Of course, that was after the terrible accident in 1965."

He stares warily, just as his father and Henry Dugger did.

"Naturally you know the details. What do you know about...?"

"I can't add anything to what you've already been told," he says forcefully."

"What I've already been told?"

"From my father."

"Yes, I see. Your father must have spoken about it, a fatal accident is always tragic and..."

"It's a long time ago."

"Your father visited the building site on the day of the accident. He could have been meeting John Renshaw. There was no one on site from the Duggers' management, not even the general foreman so..."

He intervenes with what has become a familiar phrase throughout the day.

"I know nothing about this. I don't even know where the accident took place."

"Really, when you often visited sites including new developments, you don't know the shop now on the same site?"

The same familiar phrase.

"It's a long time ago."

She knows he knows she knows he's lying, but there's nothing to be gained from ploughing the same furrow. She returns to general relations between the families and he nervously reverts to Karen, ending with "But my concern for Karen has nothing to do with any of this."

She announces the interview is over. He's visibly relieved, even relapsing into small talk, commenting on the tension in the city, how arduous these enquiries must be for her and what long hours she must be working. For a moment she even wonders if he's about to make some kind of personal overture.

Then, as she gets to the door and seemingly on impulse, she says, "What do you know about your grandfather's first wife, Hilda?"

Caught unawares, he struggles for an answer finally saying he 'never knew her.'

"But you must have heard about her?"

"Not really. What does this mean?"

She recounts the air raid, Hilda and John Renshaw.

"She was killed. He survived."

"So?" he says.

"Such a devastating event in those harrowing times. The sort of thing that pulls families together."

His reply is quick, cold, dismissive.

"I don't see how."

"Might your family have blamed John Renshaw for Hilda's death?"

He explodes.

"That's ridiculous. How would he do such a thing...and why?"

Jenner, Jennifer and Ettie convene at his flat. Ettie is subdued and says nothing while they exchange the results of their enquiries and research. Despite what the doctor told him Jenner can't shake off his scepticism of the attack on Arlene, saying it could still be part of a 'put up job' and 'there's more to that woman than it appears.'

Ettie agrees, though for different reasons.

"The mystery will be solved in the past You're right to examine the old police files even though they seem to deepen the mystery rather than lead to its solution. You've talked about Wilf Sanders, but all you have has come via Arlene."

"Why would anyone want to attack her?" he says.

"Because she's getting too close to what Karen knows," Jennifer says.

"What's that?"

"The past," Ettie repeats.

"Then why the hell doesn't she tell us? I know more about the damned past than she does!"

He expands on his researches, dismissing what Arlene has said and wrote as 'confused ramblings.'

"It's not what Arlene actually knows," Jennifer says, "but what the attacker believes she knows."

He muses on his burrowing into the past with visions of the war, Hilda Bates, John Renshaw and Calthorpe, then says "We have to get into the mind of the attacker. How are the Bates', Renshaws and Wallaces connected?"

"The key is in the past if only we could find it," Ettie says.

"You've not got any *feelings?*" he says, without irony.

"I can't shake it off. Nothing specific, but all day it's been getting stronger. Something is going to happen. It must have been similar when you were ferreting through those files, there must have been times when you felt you were actually there?"

"Yes, it stays with you."

"It's not left me either and it *will* show itself."

"When?" Jennifer says.

Ettie has been speaking dreamily without looking at them. Now she turns directly to Jennifer.

"Soon, today, tonight."

There's a long concentrated silence. Then Jennifer talks how she put to Simon Wallace that John Renshaw might have been responsible for Hilda's death.

"Nothing like jumping in at the deep end," Jenner says, "He denied any knowledge, of course?"

"Hilda was Albert's first wife. His second wife was Simon's grandmother."

Jenner snorts derisively.

"Doesn't matter. Albert Wallace lost Hilda. He must have been devastated. That sort of tragedy permeates families throughout the generations. My grandmother lost two infant children forty years before I was born, but I always knew about it."

He's quiet for a few moments, then continues.

"Everything about that air raid bugs me. Things not quite right…What if Hilda wasn't killed by the bomb at all? Then there's that rogue, Ronald Calthorpe, what if he wasn't killed?"

"He survived a direct hit?" Jennifer says incredulously.

"John Renshaw did. What if Arlene believes Karen was going to say Wilf killed Hilda? Hence, Wilf's continuing references to his guilt and the further information he blurted out just before he died. Arlene would be anxious to cover up her grandfather's crime while Karen could be just as determined to stop her doing so."

"That's a big leap," Jennifer says.

"We have their previous encounters over conservation versus destruction."

"It's not the same. You're basing all this on assumptions about their relationship when one of the parties is refusing to talk and the other is in a coma."

"There's another potential player. Remember it's the Bates', the Renshaws…and the Wallaces. If Wilf killed Hilda, Simon Wallace might also have a motive for attacking Arlene."

"He denied any knowledge of Hilda."

"I'm sure he knew about Hilda being killed in the air raid, but what if Karen wound him up about Wilf? We know he and Karen were probably closer than he admits and if he was previously involved with Arlene, he might feel…"

Jennifer is unconvinced.

"More assumptions. We need something solid and how does Sarah Murrell fit into it?"

"She was known to both Karen Renshaw and Simon Wallace."

"So the two attacks and the murder are linked. One killer involved in them all?"

"Not necessarily Arlene Bates," he says, "If she's deranged…"

"Another giant leap," Jennifer says.

"I still believe…"

"No! No!" Ettie cries, "You're not going to solve these present enquiries until we've unlocked the past. That's where the answer lies."

"And we're not going to do that until we've properly questioned Arlene," Jennifer says.

Jenner's telephone rings. He answers.

"Yes it is…When?…I see…and was there an objection? …Yes, all right…"

He replaces the telephone.

"We're not going to be able to talk to Arlene Bates immediately. She's just discharged herself from hospital against medical advice."

"Where's she gone?" Jennifer says.

"The hospital doesn't know."

"But I do," Ettie says "The past is showing itself... tonight."

The telephone rings again. Jenner answers.

"But you've just said...Has she?...You're sure of that?... Something else?...What more...It did?...and...yes...Good God!"

He replaces the receiver and sits in silence.

"Well?" Jennifer says at last.

"Arlene was overheard talking about the site of the unexploded bomb at Sharp Road."

"Then we must get there."

"Of course."

"There's more, isn't there?" Ettie says.

"I'm afraid so. The bomb disposal team were working on the bomb when it apparently slipped in the ground and is now very unstable," he says, pauses then continues, "they say they saw a ghost and left very quickly."

# 11

JENNER begins the day with an early visit to Keith Renshaw before going on to the hospital where he talks to the constable on duty at the ward. Then, against his innate inclinations and Superintendent Emmins' better judgement he announces there'll be a statement. Emmins calls it a press conference, but such an open ended, uncontrollable exercise would never sit easily with Jenner. Comfort for journalists is not a high priority. The press are forced to wait impatiently at the hospital entrance

There are bound to be questions, not all of which can be ignored, but if they can't be avoided, maybe they can be jockeyed to his advantage? The 'statement' therefore stretches to something more, though from the journalists' point of view rather less than a full 'conference.'

It's better to begin with good news.

"Karen Renshaw's condition has been steadily improving and I'm pleased to announce that she's come out of the coma."

He pauses deliberately. The announcement is welcomed, but has to be fully absorbed. A flurry of questions follow, so many he appears confused, deliberately fiddling with and scanning his paper (which has virtually nothing written on it) until the questions subside.

"All right, all right," he says, seemingly forced into an answer, "She will therefore be going home tomorrow evening."

More questions follow about her condition, but no reporter picks up Jenner's choice of words, which carefully avoid any reference to Karen being 'discharged.' He appears ruffled again, allowing the questions to pile up without organising and directing them so he can respond. Then, in consternation, he gives some stabbingly inadequate replies before retreating into bemused confusion again. With this apparently ineffective performance he manoeuvres the questioning, making it appear his next statement has been prised out of him.

"Miss Renshaw has expressed a wish to visit a place, which is of particular significance to her past."

One reporter asks where the place is.

"That's a private matter," Jenner says.

Surprisingly, at first no one asks what is the 'particular significance,' but then Arlene Bates is not present. Instead he's asked a number of times about progress on Karen's attacker.

"The investigation is ongoing," he says.

There are further attempts to open up discussion with references to 'continuing tensions' in the city, but Jenner simply repeats his bland statement. The emphasis shifts to the unexploded bomb. Is any action being taken following reports of strange happenings at Sharp Road?

"That's not a police matter," he says, "Expert bomb disposal staff are dealing with it."

"There's no one there now. The army have run away."

"The army have not run away."

"But they say there's a ghost."

"We don't investigate ghosts."

"But it's just like the predator the women have seen on the train."

Jenner grimaces.

"That's why the army ran...left the site," the reporter persists.

Jenner hesitates. He's come straight to the hospital from seeing Keith Renshaw. There may be a more up to date report on what's happening at Sharp Road. He assumes the army has not yet returned to the site.

"The site is secured and perfectly safe. The bomb disposal team have left the site for purely operational reasons."

"If the bomb is unstable and the army are not dealing with it, how can it be safe?"

"The site is secure," Jenner repeats, then "And as for any so called ghost...it's pure speculation...like the reported sightings of a man on the train prior to the attack on Miss Renshaw."

"You don't believe there was a man on the train? So who attacked Karen Renshaw?"

"I said there had been speculation *about* the man, linking him with this latest...appearance...that's quite different from a real attacker."

"Is this connected to the significant place in Karen Renshaw's past?"

"I've told you, there's no ghost at Sharp Road."

The reporter's question remains unanswered and Jenner has dismissed the 'ghost,' but the hint of a possible link between Karen, the train and Sharp Road has been established. More questions along the same lines will be ignored. Fortunately the next questions return to the state of the enquiries. Jenner repeats his bland reply, but one reporter poses it from a different angle.

"Surely the recent sightings both on the train and the unexploded bomb must be taken seriously?"

"I've already dealt with that," Jenner says curtly, "I'm not concerned with ghosts. I suggest you contact the psychical research society."

Jenner immediately regrets his remark. Anyone aware of his discussions and previous collaboration with Ettie might draw interesting conclusions.

"It may not be just ghosts," the reporter says, "A number of people have seen a man getting off the train and leaving the station."

"A man getting off a train is hardly a matter of concern," Jenner says.

"You know what I mean," the reporter says "The *same* man who was on the train, the one you call a ghost."

"I've never talked about ghosts," Jenner says irritably.

He's already tiring. The 'conference' is starting to get out of hand. The reporter persists.

"This is a new development. The gho…the man…has not been seen leaving the train before. There's great consternation throughout the city. What do you say to all the frightened women?"

Everyone is silent and waits for his response. Jenner hesitates. He would prefer the previous gaggling to have gone on, but still no one speaks.

"I say everybody should keep calm. We need to get to the real flesh and blood predator."

There's a short silence. Jenner is ready to leave, but it doesn't work. The babble erupts again, with a torrent of questions about the 'inadequacies' of the enquiry and public demands for it to 'move forward.' Arlene may not be here, but the strength of her tirades has not diminished. They are using her exact phrases!

He tries to ignore them, occasionally reiterating his pervious lame responses, but it only increases their cries for 'progress' and positive reassurance for the women of the city.

"When do you expect to find this man?"

Like a music hall comedian Jenner is anxious to conclude his performance without a too abrupt exit from the stage. In the rush to get here he's forgotten to turn off his telephone. It's now his saviour. He answers the call, then makes the announcement.

"I'm advised the bomb disposal team has returned to the Sharp Road site and the bomb is now declared safe."

It lessens the tension.

"Maybe it was the ghost that did it," somebody says waggishly.

At Sharp Road the unexploded bomb is rapidly becoming an urban myth in which perception is the only reality.

False rumours and flimsy assumptions abound. It's wrongly believed the supposed withdrawal of the army means the site is unguarded and folk are enticed closer to the site though no one returns to their homes.

The 'ghost' allegedly seen by the army is the subject of much whispering. Some, attracted by the intriguing story report seeing a 'strange man' walking in the distance, saying he was near the bomb, proving it's safe. But with the bomb's supposed 'movement' and conflicting views about its precise location how can they be sure? His presence might be making it even more dangerous

Opinions vary on site security, protagonists and doubters for every view. There was never a bomb in the first place. It was 'just a vein of very smooth rock.' But what is the 'large metallic object' and where is it now? There was a bomb, but because it's been 'slipping' more has been revealed, making it easier for it to be lifted from the ground and taken away by lorry to a safe place.

Despite what Jenner told them, reporters are finding it very difficult to get the essential facts. The police are maintaining a barrier, but either through ignorance or design give out no information other than it remains 'a restricted area.' When they ask to see an 'army representative' they're told it's not possible. Again it's unclear whether that's because they've been advised to say nothing or are actually unaware of the whereabouts of Major Phillips and his men. When they approach the council, local authority officers cannot help. Faced with the impasse they say 'the authorities are refusing to provide any information.' This exacerbates unease and anger in the local population, which the press exploits with even more corrosive pummelling from the residents.

In the midst of the turmoil a lone, middle aged woman breaches the barrier unnoticed. It shouldn't happen. The area is well cordoned with sturdy fencing and there's been no relaxation of police presence at the boundary. Afterwards the officers will deny leaving their post and say they never saw any woman come close, let alone get through. The whole barrier is examined. None of the fencing has been disturbed. How the 'mystery woman' was able to get so close to the bomb, let alone return unharmed is never solved.

Were she to be asked even as she went through, Ettie would be unable to answer such a question. For as she walked over the threshold of the barrier she passed not only into a 'restricted area,' but into another place in time. She's not chosen to flout the restrictions and expose herself to danger, but after two days immersed in the past she must follow, wherever her concentrations lead. She's heard the rumours. The bomb may or may not have been defused, but the soldiers definitely saw something. The truth lies between those fearing being blown to oblivion and those laughing at such a prospect.

She gets closer, neither afraid of the 'long metallic object' nor what sensations may surround it. The past draws, but doesn't threaten, protecting her from present dangers. She stops short of the main excavation. The 'diggings' have expanded well beyond the original pit of the archaeologists, leaving the ground unstable, both from the army's work and the unexplored cave network that lies beneath. She feels shaky and hovers for some moments, shifting her weight between her legs and stretching her arms out as if balancing on a narrow path. But her unsteadiness is nothing to do with the ground beneath.

The great 'hole' looms like a vast mouth, exhaling visions and impressions of another time, drawing her into the past. There's a low rumble. It gets louder. It's what she heard in the hospital. She puts her hands over her ears, but it gets even louder. She staggers a few steps, clutching the air as if she might catch some firm grip to hold her back. But then relaxes. She's as she was by Karen's bed, as she was in the train and at Sharp Road, to see, to hear, to learn. Whatever happens she'll not be harmed.

The noise stops. The disparate shapes gradually coalesce and she sees again the man she and so many other women saw on the train. She's at the station and sees him leaving the London train. She smells the smoke curling backwards from the locomotive and hears its steady rhythmic pulse as it waits for all the passengers to leave. He mounts the stairs towards the station exit. It must be Wilf Sanders. Then he's gone. The smoke thickens, enveloping the whole scene until station, train and all the people are lost.

Smothered in a grey, acrid fog, she thrashes her arms and turns to escape and though never moving, seemingly runs out of the darkness. She must not panic. If she calls for help no one will hear. It *will* pass. Don't allow confused impressions to dominate. Think on what you know you can control! She concentrates on recent events...her journey to Nottingham, her arrival in the city, meeting Jenner and Jennifer, in the hospital, seeing Karen Renshaw, sharing her visions, her talk with Arlene, what she told of...she's the great niece of...Yes, Wilf Sanders...he's the anchor of the past. Hold on to him, don't let him get away!

She calms and opens her eyes. The haze dissolves. She's at the rim of the great 'mouth,' quiescent now, unthreatening. How did she get here? Maybe she was running after all... unless...has the 'dig,' the bomb and all the past it holds come to *her*? The ground falls away abruptly. Her feet are right on the edge and she stares into an abyss, its bottom lost in a jumble of rock, soil and the army's wooden reinforcements. Dimly, she sees something smooth, catching the sunlight. Is it the bomb? She should be afraid and step back for safety, but instead she scrapes her feet along the brink, as if taunting whatever is below.

As if answering her silent defiance the haze returns and obscures the excavation. She stares into a smouldering, narrowing chasm, until the emptiness suddenly rushes upwards as if the giant mouth is closing, ready to consume her before she can break free! Less sure footed, she slides her feet away.

As soon as she turns her back on the excavation the menace leaves her. She walks towards the barrier, but then stops. She cannot see him, but the spirit of Wilf Sanders is close. He will shield her from harm. Yet another force spells danger. It swells, then tapers off only to advance again. Even with Wilf's presence she's not wholly safe. Will he desert her? Is this other power too strong for him? She could run back to the safety of the present, beyond the barrier, but that would be surrender without understanding. She's been summoned to digest the knowledge of the past. She must not let it beat her.

She turns again towards the excavation, but it's gone. Instead a large Edwardian building, constant hubbub from within, people talking, laughing, clinking of glasses, singing! Others enter and join the throng. It's a pub! There's a sign over the door, the 'Cross Keys.'

She takes a few steps but the noise quickly subsides and the pub is gone. The great 'hole' returns. She stops and looks around, but sees only a vast emptiness. The barrier seems much further away than when she first entered the site. There are no soldiers or police. She's isolated and her unease, now tinged with a pervasive unwholesomeness, grows. It's more than malign. It's evil. She cannot stay. Evil was done here. She must get back to the barrier!

But no. A positive energy, trying to get through. Wilf Sanders has not deserted her. He will counteract the malevolent. The noise and the pub return! She turns, stridently, hopefully. Then it's gone again. The great 'mouth' looms up. She turns away. If only she could see that anxious man who missed the early train! After a few steps the noise comes again. There's the pub, but in an instant it's gone again. The competing forces are battling out. It's too much. She quickens her pace. The joyous sounds from the pub return intermittently. She doesn't turn. She must get back!

Events are coming to a head, determined by all she saw and felt on the train and now here. It must come tonight.

Then she sees him, an agitated figure between her and the barrier. He's smiling, looking forward to his meeting. Then the smile is gone and he runs, as he ran at St Pancras. Running for something that cannot be.

He's gone. The pub is gone. If she was protected that protection is now too weak. She walks on, away from the excavation. A few people in the distance. A welcoming sign. She's not alone after all. She avoids the barrier. Maybe she can get through somewhere else? But the fencing is strong and high. It'll have to be the barrier. She sees a policeman. He's bound to ask awkward questions. She changes direction, some ninety degrees away from the barrier. She walks along the fence for a few yards. Her distress intensifies. There has to be a gap in this fence!

But there isn't. The malevolent atmosphere suffuses everywhere. She has to get on the other side of the fence! Any difficulty with the authorities has to be better than this. She turns again, towards the barrier. Amazingly no one is there and she gets through without being seen. Head down, she strides away quickly. Concentrating on the ground, she doesn't notice a man walking towards her and almost bumps into him.

She apologises and tries to turn aside, but he turns into her. She looks up anxiously, fearful she'll see some awful creature from the past. He's young with wide, inquisitive eyes, a slight smile and modern casual clothes. She rapidly assesses him, devoid of ill intentions, unthreatening.

"You've just come from the site?" he says, "What have you seen?"

The question jolts her. Perhaps he's not as innocuous as she first thought.

"Nothing," she says quickly, this time successfully side stepping him.

She walks on and tries to get away, but the happenings at the excavation have drained her energy. She stumbles and slipping on the loose earth and stones loses her balance, flailing her arms out wildly. He comes up, grabs her and stops her falling. Once steadied he lets go. She's breathing heavily as if she's been running.

"Are you all right?"

"Yes, yes," she says between breaths, "It will pass. I've…"

"…had a traumatic experience?"

She turns and nods. He may be young, but sensitively observant. Maybe someone to be trusted.

"Tell me what you've seen. Have you seen the man? Is he the same man as on the London train?"

She hesitates. There's too much to think over. She's not ready to talk. Her legs weaken and she feels them about to give way. She looks down. The earth seems closer, looming like the great 'mouth.' She shudders and stumbles. The man grabs her arm gently and steadies her.

"You need to sit down."

"No. I'm all right. It will pass."

"That's what you said before. Come, take my arm."

"No, I just need to rest for a minute or two."

She turns around. She feels she's walked a fair way from the barrier, but then she sees the fence only a few yards away. She staggers and props herself against it. The man follows, but makes no attempt to intervene. After a few moments she feels better as strength returns to her legs and her head clears.

"It might help if you talk about it," he says.

She's ready to send him away, but he's not alone. A dozen men and women form a semi circular group around her. She has her back to the barrier and can see no way to escape. She glances anxiously along the fence. A couple of policemen have spotted the group and are walking towards her. She looks back at the people. They look at her expectantly. She's like an actor, alone on the stage for the first time, wary and tremulous, having forgotten her lines and desperately trying to find a way through the wings.

"Let me through," she shouts.

The people are aghast, as an audience faced with a non performance by a rookie actor. No one moves to let her pass. The man steps forward and holds out his hand.

"Come with me," he says, "You need to get away."

She doesn't take his hand, but edges slightly away from the fence. He turns and walks towards the small crowd. She follows closely. Some people step back and they pass through.

"Tell me what you've seen," he says again as they walk quickly away from the site and into the street.

He gets to what looks like a large van.

"You can rest here, undisturbed" he says and opens a rear door.

She looks inside quizzically. The van has windows in the sides and there are seats in the back. It's more like a mini bus except for a shelf and electrical equipment on one side. Another man is sitting there and beckons her within.

"What is this?" she says.

"It's a radio car."

Now she sees the logo *Radio Forest* displayed on the side.

"I'm not sure, I don't wish to…"

"Those people are following," he says and points back to the site.

A couple of dozen people are gathered beside the barrier with many streaming off, pointing at the radio car and getting closer. A police van has arrived and officers are trying to clear people away from the barrier. Others accompany those making for the radio car.

"You've caused quite a stir," the man says, "Everybody wants to know how you got in and what you've seen. The police will want to talk to you too. You'd better get inside."

She turns to him suspiciously.

"And you are?"

"Mark Evans, I'm a reporter on Radio Forest. We can…"

"I've nothing to say."

"You should still get in. They'll be here soon."

She glances back towards the site. The police and at least twenty people are on the other side of the road. Even more are walking from both directions along the road.

"Okay, only for a minute."

Once inside the other man gets into the driving seat and starts up the engine.

"Where are we going?" she says.

"Do you want to stay here?" Evans says, nodding to the police and people now crossing the road, "We'll just go to a quieter place."

The car moves off, passing swarms of people on both sides of the road, rushing towards the site.

"Word's got out," Evans says.

"About what?" she says bewilderingly.

"Everything. You name it somebody says its happened, the bomb has been moved, the bomb has exploded, there never was a bomb, but most of all there's a strange man wandering around the site and a woman has got in and she's escaped."

"I've not *escaped*. I was only…well it was…"

"This'll do, John," Evans says.

The radio car parks in a quiet suburban street.

"You were only what?" Evans says.

"I'll get out now. Thank you for the lift, but I really must get on."

She opens the rear door and steps out.

"Give me an interview," Evans call after her, "If you don't talk to me, you'll have to…"

He breaks off. Ettie clutches the side of the car, staring blankly into the empty street as the terrible oppression she felt at the excavation returns.

"No," she says, "Not here, it can't be…this is not…"

She loses her grip and slides down the side of the car. Evans grabs her.

"John, give me a hand," he calls to the other man, who joins him on the other side of Ettie.

"This is not the place," she whispers.

"What place? What are you seeing? Is it the man you saw at Sharp Road?" Evans says.

"Better get her inside," the other says.

They gently steer her back into the car and settle her on a seat. Ashen white, her hand shaking slightly, her eyes fix on the opposite window. Evans looks out. No one's around, only ordinary houses and gardens. John reads his mind.

"There's nothing to see. It's in her mind."

"Where are we?" she says, suddenly leaning forward and looking up and down the street.

"Just far enough to get away from all those people and…"

"Just far enough," she repeats.

"It's better here where we can talk."

She goes to the rear window.

"I've been here before."

"You live near here?"

"No, no, but I've been here. There's a pub nearby isn't there?"

Evans grimaces. He looks to John, who nods.

"There's the 'Grapes," he says.

"The Grapes," she repeats, "I've been there."

She returns to her seat and looks at them, but her mind is in another place and time.

"There was evil there," she says.

"At Sharp Road, where the bomb fell?"

"In the past. There was evil."

"In the war, with the air raid? They were terrible times."

"It all happened during the raid."

Evans has absorbed Arlene's articles on the war and done his own homework on the blitz.

"You're right. War is evil. You felt what the people felt. All those long months of waiting, then the night of the worst raid, so many killed…you felt the evil of the bombing?"

Ettie doesn't answer, which he takes as assent to his question, but she knows otherwise. The evil of which she speaks is more than the carnage wrought by the luftwaffe.

Some colour returns to her cheeks. She turns to face him.

"But it'll be all right. Everything will be all right."

"You mean the bomb site? You felt the suffering, the damage, the casualties, the…"

"The casualty, yes…"

Evans persists, without fully understanding what she says.

"Can you describe what you saw, what you felt?"

"It can be all right."

"It will be safe?"

"Yes. It *can* be safe, but there's much to do between now and then. Tomorrow…"

"The bomb is unstable, but you *feel* it will be safely dealt with?"

"Safe?"

"Everything will be put right?"

"Put right? That's what's needed. Yes, it has to be put right."

"So, can you tell, me…?"

"I don't want to stay here. I must go."

She moves towards the door.

"No, no, we can go somewhere else, Mrs…?"

"Away from here?"

"Yes."

Ettie considers for a moment. She must get away from so close to where the church hall stood.

"Towards town," she says.

John starts the engine and they move off. Evans tries to ask more questions, but Ettie either ignores them or gives bland, unhelpful answers.

"Where do you live?" he says, "We can take you…"

"That won't be necessary. Just drop me off here."

They can take her all the way, but she's insistent. John stops the car She strides away and catches a bus into the city centre. Evans is disappointed, but he's recorded their conversation and returns to the radio station.

Jenner checks the alibis of all suspects both in the past and the present. He'll go over them later with Jennifer. He has the radio tuned to *Radio Forest*. It's only just audible. He doesn't want it interfering with his thoughts, but he needs to listen for any comments on his press 'statement.' The development at Sharp Road enabled him to extricate from further questioning, but once the press investigate the situation more thoroughly there's bound to be a reaction. It can't be long before there's a summons to see Emmins.

Make the most of the comparative calm It's a crucial period. How best to proceed in the next twenty four hours. Every path is risky. He tosses around the alternatives. Mistakes can't be rectified. Once started it can't be stopped. He has to get it right from the beginning.

Jennifer comes in and immediately opens up on his press statement.

"Does the super know you were going to say Karen has regained consciousness?"

"He wanted a statement that would reassure the public."

"People won't be reassured when they find out the truth."

"At least it'll take their minds off ghosts and ghoulies at Sharp Road."

She ignores the levity.

"When they find out…"

"That some fool says they've seen a man wandering around near the bomb? They'll forget that when they know the bomb's been made safe."

"Has it?"

"The army has returned to the site."

"They never left. That was just one of the many rumours, but it's still not secured."

"It will be."

"And what about Karen? She's not out of the coma. What about the hospital staff?"

"I've assured the consultant and ward sister this is only a temporary arrangement."

"How can it be temporary? You've said Karen is being discharged. That's not true."

"I didn't say she was being discharged."

"You said she was going home tomorrow."

"Not the same thing. The hospital staff have not been compromised."

"What about her family. Won't they be expecting her home?"

"I spoke to Keith Renshaw before the press statement."

"What did you tell him?"

He hesitates, then says, "I explained it to him. He understands."

She could ask what Keith Renshaw 'understands,' but lets it pass and poses an issue closer to home.

"You're sticking your neck out with Emmns. If - no *when* - he finds out there'll be hell to pay."

"I know what I'm doing."

"I hope so, for your sake. Then there's the ghost at Sharp Road."

He sighs deeply.

"I've already told you. There are no ghosts at the bomb site and even if there were they won't interfere with the investigation."

She's unimpressed with his sarcasm.

"Really? Whatever you say now, you weren't really dismissive of the ghost."

"I said we don't *investigate* ghosts."

"You didn't say the reports of a man seen near the bomb were irrelevant."

"I said there was no ghost."

"Which you said was just like the sightings of the predator on the train…"

"…*before* Karen was attacked."

"There's a difference?"

"I didn't deny Karen was attacked."

"That's not the point. You were being asked about the direction of enquiries. You said nothing."

"Exactly."

She shakes her head.

"I've been checking the alibis of…"

She shushes him and turns up the radio. It's a local news bulletin.

"*…according to the bomb disposal officer the situation is stable and further work can be carried out without delay, but he refused to give an estimate of how long it will take. Meanwhile a small number of residents on the edge of the restricted area have been permitted to return to their homes. The lord mayor thanked everyone for their forbearance and once more apologised for the continuing inconvenience, which he hoped will soon be over.*

'*The police have appealed for sightseers to refrain from visiting the area. Not just residents, but others from further afield have ignored the warning signs, arriving in large numbers in adjacent streets, causing major traffic hazards. The public is advised to take no notice of unsubstantiated reports of a strange man seen within the restricted area.*

'*Despite being guarded by police, a woman got through the barrier, getting very close to the unexploded bomb and the excavations. Groups of people rushed to the site, gathering by the fenced restricted zone. Many followed as the woman rushed away and in an exclusive interview with Radio Forest she gave her own account of what happened.*"

There follows a montage of clips of Ettie's responses to Evans' questions. Inevitably, this disparate collection presents her 'account' quite unlike what actually happened.

'...there was evil there...in the past there was evil...it all happened during the raid...but it will be all right...everything will be all right...tomorrow...'

Jenner and Jennifer listen in disbelief.

He mutters "Hardly an *exclusive interview*."

The announcer continues.

*"And now for some views from those around the site. We spoke to residents..."*

The gripes from the 'sightseers' are cobbled together in much the same way as the 'interview.'

"What about Ettie?" Jenner says, "Where did she go?"

"She's not been mentioned by name," Jennifer says.

"Not yet," he says disconsolately.

Then the announcer brings in Mark Evans.

*"Mark, you were able to speak to this mysterious woman. Did she say any more?"*

'No. She was very anxious to get away. She was badly shaken by what she'd seen. We had to help her get away from the site. We drove a short distance and at first she was calmer, but got even more agitated. Said she'd been there before.'

'Where was this?'

'Near a pub called the Grapes.'

'Who was she? Where did she go?'

'We don't know. She wouldn't give her name and she wouldn't stay'

"Thank you for small mercies," Jenner intones.

*"She talked about tomorrow and of course tomorrow is the anniversary of that terrible air raid during the blitz. There were..."*

Evans gives a brief summary of the events on the night of 8th/9th May 1941.

"What's he going to say now?" Jenner groans.

The announcer cuts in.

*"Are the authorities concerned something will happen on the anniversary? Surely they're not taking the stories of a ghostly man seriously?"*

*'I asked if they would be making the bomb safe tonight,' Evans
continues.*

*'You believe something will happen tonight?'*

There's a short silence, then Evans says, *'Who knows? No
one is saying anything, not the army, the council, the police.
People saw a man near the bomb, a ghostly figure some called him.
The woman says it will be all right tomorrow, but what if it's
not?'*

Jenner and Jennifer exchange perplexed looks. Then the
announcer comes in again.

*"We'll bring you any new developments on this story as soon
as we can and in view of what he's discovered, David Jeynes will
be back tomorrow evening interviewing investigative reporter
Arlene Bates. She's taken particular interest in the events at Sharp
Road and the alarming incidents on the London train. On that
front there is of course encouraging signs with the news Karen
Renshaw, the unfortunate woman who was brutally attacked will
be leaving hospital. In other news..."*

Jenner switches off the radio. Jennifer groans.

"There's your information on Karen. I told you..."

"I'm more concerned about Ettie," he says, "God, what
will Arlene Bates make of this?"

"You'll soon know. We only have to listen tomorrow night."

"Can't wait that long. We've got to find that damned
woman. Get on to the radio station. They must know.
Wherever she is she's still making trouble. All this cafuffle,
she'll have the whole town tuned into her tomorrow night."

"Including you."

"Not necessarily," he mutters.

He lapses into silence and introspection, then suddenly
erupts.

"And what was Ettie doing at Sharp Road, even worse
why did she allow herself to be shanghaied by that damned
reporter...what's his name...?"

"Mark Evans."

"…yes, him…and blurting out all that stuff about evil and the past and tomorrow?"

"…and everything will be all right."

"Whatever that means."

"Anyway, they were clips strung together to make an impression."

"What impression?"

"Not the one Ettie intended. It's easy to draw the wrong conclusions. Evil *where* and *which* past."

"None of it sounded very lucid."

"Neither would you be if twenty minutes of your words were cut and pasted into three."

"Why was she *rushing* away?"

"We only have the reporter's word for that. He said she was *badly shaken*."

"It would take something momentous to make Ettie run. I'll try her hotel."

"Arlene Bates aside, this so called discharge of Karen from the hospital…"

"She's not being discharged."

"All right, she's *going home* tomorrow. It's the same thing. She's not well."

"I've told you the medical staff are aware…"

"I can't believe they've gone along with this. What about her family, what did you say to Keith Renshaw?"

"I advised him of developments so that he was aware before he heard from the media."

"She can't leave the hospital. What could you be thinking about?

"Quite right," Jenner says, "She won't be leaving the hospital. You will."

"What?"

"You're about the same age, same height, similar build. A near perfect Karen look alike."

# 8<sup>th</sup> May

Jennifer's enquiries at the radio station are unsuccessful. All their contacts with Arlene have been by telephone. They assumed she was still working from the *Courier* offices, but that was not the case.

"She's in hospital," the editor says.

"She discharged herself."

"Did she? Must be at home then."

But she isn't. There's no answer from her telephone and when Jennifer calls she gets no response at her flat.

"Not seen her for weeks," a neighbour says, "Isn't she in hospital?"

"She came out two days ago."

"I've not seen her."

"She may have gone to her aunt's place."

The neighbour looks puzzled. She knows nothing about an aunt. Arlene's only known relative is Richard Bates, her father, but he doesn't live locally.

"Do you know where he lives?"

"Couldn't say. She was sometimes away. I assumed she was visiting him, but she never said. Never mentioned her mother. I think she's gone. She mentioned her grandmother, but she's gone. Then there was her grandmother's brother, name of Sanders, but he's…"

"….gone? Yes I know, Wilf Sanders, died quite recently."

The neighbour shrugs.

"Can't help you then."

So Arlene is as elusive as ever. Jennifer returns to the radio station and gets the approximate time when Arlene's programme will be on the air.

"She won't be in, though. Some people prefer to be interviewed…"

"…by telephone?"

"Yes."

Jennifer returns to the police station. Jenner grunts impassively on being told she's not found Arlene. There are more important things and he's completing the final arrangements.

"What about Ettie?" she says.

He opens his palms and shakes his head.

"Not in her hotel. They've not seen her since early this morning. I can't spend the day chasing round the city even if I knew where to look."

He checks his watch, then repeats the briefing he gave her this morning. She sighs wearily as he goes over it again and again.

"There's no need to worry," he says.

"I'm not worried."

"If course not. Now, you remember…"

"You've been over it umpteen times and I have a good memory."

"Yes, yes of course," he mumbles.

She picks up the bag by the door.

"Yes," he says, checking his watch again, "You *do* realise I can't be with you at the start. We have to maintain…"

"…strict authenticity? I remember."

"I'll see you later."

She goes out to change, emerging a few minutes later and nodding to him through the glass.

He watches ruefully as she goes through the outer office, wondering if his scheme is safe and whether it will work. He worries about Jennifer, but she's sensible and strong. There are officers at the hospital and others strategically placed. He would like to be there himself, but his presence would not go unnoticed and could ruin the plan. He goes over everything once more, arduously checking and double checking. In the end he's satisfied…at least as far as it's possible to be.

The time has come. He switches on the radio, only desultorily listening to the early evening 'smooth' music. It's meant to be 'relaxed,' something he definitely is not, though with his mind elsewhere it could never achieve its objective. The music stops. The announcer gives the time. Jenner again checks his watch, which only serves to remind him of Jennifer.

Tonight there'll be a discussion with a 'special guest.' Merely a 'discussion,' not an 'interview,' and no reference to the guest in the studio. Arlene is built up in a sycophantic introduction as 'our local crusading and fearless journalist.' So fearless she's conveniently ensconced in some unknown location, unlikely to be rigorously questioned. As for 'crusading,' Jenner can vouch for that. The scars on his back have yet to heal.

The announcer talks of her 'well known campaigns' over 'conservation' issues and her more recent 'enlivening' articles about wartime Nottingham. He pauses before mentioning the recent 'tragic events' on the London train and the 'continuing difficulties' at the site of the unexploded bomb. What follows is not even a 'discussion,' let alone an interview, a few questions for clarification rather than analysis and generally dismissed.

As soon as she speaks it's clear from the slightly hollow sound that Arlene is at the other end of a telephone line.

*"All the recent happenings are connected. The tragic events on the London train and the unexploded bomb at Sharp Road are interlocked. Remember the ghost who was seen on the train? He was searching. He's still searching."*

The announcer intervenes.

*'The predator?'*

Arlene cuts him off curtly.

*'I'm not talking about a predator. The man on the train was searching..."*

The announcer tries again.

*'He was searching for a woman?'*

Arlene ignores the question.

*'He never found what he was searching for. Everything is connected, but the bomb is the pivot. It's where it all began and where it'll begin again. Be prepared. Remember tonight,*

the 8$^{th}$ and 9$^{th}$ of May is the anniversary of that terrible air raid. It will happen tonight.'

The announcer tries one last time to talk about the predator. Arlene is silent for a moment.

Her frustrated sigh is heard over the telephone, then she says, 'Karen Renshaw leaves hospital tonight. That's enough.'

'But what of the predator?'

The telephone line goes dead. Arlene has rung off.

"You damned fool," Jenner says, "You'll never get the answers you want like that. Should have had her in the studio."

The embarrassed announcer makes some lame excuse about 'technical difficulties' and resorts to a musical interlude.

Jenner switches the radio off, muttering "They'll not get her back tonight."

From hiding, she uses the newspaper and the radio station while evading both.

There's no mention of Sarah Murrell, just as she was reluctant to talk of her with Ettie. Her tone is different both from her articles and his talks with her. More like a lecture. Even questioned by a more competent interviewer she wouldn't have been deflected from what she was determined to say. The same direct, unexplained assertions, but delivered without her usual sensationalism. Her 'performance' no longer makes him angry nor influences his plans, though whatever happens tonight, *she* is involved. He remembers her article.

*Something the police ought to know.*

And he knows, but knowledge is not enough. He needs evidence. No time for troublesome meetings with superiors. Emmins and Davies may joke, sometimes even flatter him about 'unconventional' methods, but there'll be no endorsement in advance. However much they rely on 'abnormal' factors, he has to trust his gut suspicions,

He checks his watch. Jennifer should be at the hospital by now. It's the time Wilf Sanders will have arrived on the London train.

At the hospital the next shift is beginning and nurses are entering at reception. One of the uniformed figures is inconspicuous. Jennifer is nervous, but determined. Clutching her bag, she moves quickly to the lift and up to the ward. She's relieved. No other nurses are in the lift, no need to parry embarrassing questions. She remembers what Jenner told her about alibis. All the arrangements are in place.

She arrives at the ward and goes into the nursing office.

"There's been no change," the ward sister says.

"Still in the coma?"

"Yes."

"What's the prognosis?"

"She's stable. Are you hopeful of progress tonight?"

"Yes, if we're right" Jennifer says enigmatically, then, "Have there been questions?"

"A few. The rota's been changed. Only the more sensible staff are on duty and the doctors have been discreet."

The ward sister emphasises 'sensible' with a wink, then adds, "I'm afraid I've had to blame your chief inspector if anyone seems doubtful. He'll have to be blamed even more after tonight when it's known she's still in the ward."

"That may not be necessary," Jennifer says, then checking her watch, "Where can I change?"

"In here. Her clothes are in the locker. I'll make sure you're not disturbed."

The ward sister leaves, closing the door behind her. Jennifer discards the nurse's uniform and takes out Karen's clothes. She also has others provided by Keith Renshaw, still wondering how Jenner convinced him to cooperate. If it doesn't work…best not to think about that. She knocks gently on the door. The ward sister enters and whispers 'all clear.'

No one is around and Jennifer slips out unobserved. She slows in the main hospital corridor, carrying her bag and walking with the cautious deliberation of someone who's just emerged from a coma and recovering from a major assault. She makes no attempt to conceal her supposed identity and in the lift even chats with visitors. The more canny of them will surely understand who she is.

She crosses the entrance foyer with the same slightly affected gait and confidence. Outside a taxi awaits. It's right on time. She gets in, almost shouting her destination so anyone will be bound to hear.

Then 'Karen Renshaw' leaves the hospital.

# 12

JENNER isn't a regular listener to the evening Ron Grant Show. He's not a fan of 'phone in' discussions. 'Ill informed criticism' of the police in recent programmes has done nothing to disabuse him of 'ignorant fools exchanging forgettable opinions with equally mindless halfwits.' But tonight they replay Ettie's 'interview' and as he listens he fills in the 'gaps' between her cut and pasted statements, each time drawing additional conclusions. Mark Evans said they stopped near the 'Grapes' pub. He didn't follow it up, but Jenner understands the significance. Everything fits with his plan. He's surprised Arlene didn't mention it. Did she hear Ettie's 'interview' before her own? He constantly checks the clock on the wall. Jennifer must have just have left the hospital, but it seems much longer. He's sure…isn't he?

He leaves the radio on low volume, in case something interesting is reported and returns to his notes, re-examining wartime events until confident every aspect reinforces his analysis. Finally, he flicks through his notes on John Renshaw's 1965 accident. Until now it's been no more than an exaggerated obsession by Keith Renshaw, a tangential event to the main investigation. Keith is a whinging chip off the dubious old block, a son refusing to accept the death of his enigmatic father, the mysterious 'failed' adventurer from Brazil. He's about to put it down, but on re-reading Jennifer's interviews with the architect, Douglas Cunningham, the Duggers and Simon Wallace, the 'accident' is no longer a sideline. It's directly connected to the wider relationship between the Wallaces and the Renshaws.

Then the radio jerks back his attention and he turns up the volume.

*"We have back on the line, Arlene Bates, the investigative journalist who was with us less than an hour ago..."*

Ron Grant tries to grab the initiative, inviting Arlene to comment on 'what's happening at Sharp Road,' but she has her own agenda.

*"Karen Renshaw is leaving hospital this evening. That's good news, but as the detective leading the investigation has said* (Jenner gulps expectantly) *she'll want to visit a significant place in her past. That...'*

*'You've previously made trenchant comments on the effectiveness of the police investigation. What's your view now?'*

Arlene cuts him off abruptly.

*'I didn't come on to talk about that. I was talking about the significant place in Karen's past. I believe that place is where the air raid struck that night in 1941.'*

*'A place that was bombed?'*

*'Of course,'* she says, with undisguised irritation.

*'You're talking about the biggest raid, the anniversary of which is tonight?'*

*'Naturally.'*

More irritation, but Ron has done his homework.

*'Many places were hit, so...'*

*'Obviously a place of importance to Karen.'*

*'But she was...'*

*'Not born?'* Arlene says with a deep sigh, *'Of course not, few of us were, but while she wasn't there, what happened was of great consequence in her life.'*

*'But where are you talking about? Bombs fell all over the city.'*

She's silent and he answers his own question.

*'It's the site at Sharp Road, isn't it? Karen is going to the unexploded bomb?'*

She repeats her vague assertions. He gets frustrated. There's a futile exchange with Ron wondering whether there were any casualties at the 'Cross Keys.'

"Of course there were no casualties," Jenner cries out, "The bomb never went off!"

Ron gibbers on about subsequent damage to the surrounding area, from which the pub was damaged and only partially rebuilt.

"Get back to that night!" Jenner shouts.

As if he hears him, Ron returns to Karen. Arlene obliquely implies Karen will make for the bomb site. Why does she believe that? She's previously told Jenner Karen told her something of 'direct personal relevance,' while denying a 'personal' relationship. But what did she say to Ettie? He checks his notes.

*'I have a personal interest...there are memories of those days in my own family.'*

Arlene was referring to her great uncle Wilf, but everything is interwoven and 'personal interest' could also mean her relationship with Karen.

Arlene is reluctant to get into specifics and, despite Ron's persistent prodding deflects the discussion away from Sharp Road.

*Family connections are everything. The ghost or whatever it is will be revealed.*

Does this mean the connection between the Renshaws and Wilf and Hilda?

*'This is the night, 8^(th) May. Everybody must be ready. It's the right time, the right place.'*

Thwarted by Arlene's fuzzy generalities, Ron tries to draw her into a definite position, but she's more comfortable on hazy ground and won't be hemmed in. Jenner isn't surprised, her imprecision only further fuelling his suspicions. Knowing she has a vast audience she ranges over murkier, indistinct prognostications, getting more and more frantic and incoherent.

*...immediate...the past...anniversary...tonight...right time... right place...family...connections...*

Ron tries to intervene, but her stream of trembling foreboding is impossible to shut down. Jenner imagines thousands of listeners shaking their heads in bewilderment, fascinated but anxious, many thinking she's deluded, he's not one of them. Even a raucous fool can spout with insight.

Everything she says is couched in the past and as the interview continues he drifts into imaginings of that other time. He's in Sharp Road and somewhere else he doesn't recognise. Dark and noisy with low rumbles and sudden flashes of light, just above the urban horizon. People rush past, desperate for shelter and safety. The war is around and within him. Then he's suddenly wrenched from the oppressive reverie and is back in the office.

"My God," he shouts, "she's sussed it!"

It's a nerve filled journey from the hospital. Jennifer looks out the taxi's back window so many times she loses count. Several times she spies a car, which seems to be following, only to discover it's disappeared when next she looks. Perhaps he's clever. Hanging back behind a bus, then overtaking again at it's next stop. It's a trick she's played herself many times. Best done with more than one surveillance vehicle and ideally using vans. It doesn't always work with sharp eyed hunters like herself. She recollects several cases when…

…She stops reminiscing. The job to be done needs her full attention. But concentration is debilitating. The taxi takes an inordinately long time, though it's really only minutes. Soon enough she'll reach Sharp Road where her real anxieties will begin. She checks the destination, asking the driver if he knows it. He's an older man and replies sharply. There's no street in the city he doesn't know. She settles back, resisting the temptation to steal more glances out the rear window. It'll only increase her unease. Besides, doesn't she want to be followed?

The taxi drops her at the end of the road. A gentle stroll to the site will calm her. It's eerily quiet and she sees no one. She's nervous and walks faster, but then feeling more buoyant slows again...she's experienced and determined... but this is a job like no other. There are parked vehicles, but it's otherwise deserted. She gets to the unguarded barrier. Where is everyone? It's not right. There should be other officers...but then they should also be concealed. Even so, she would be aware of their presence. Is she losing her grip? She looks back. There's no one, yet senses she's not alone.

Jenner tries to focus on the present. Sarah Murrell was killed because of what she knew. Is that connected to her gambling? Someone with money troubles? People who gamble can be in financial difficulties. No one comes to mind. Jennifer saw all Sarah's contacts. They didn't really discuss it. He should have raised it before she left or even earlier, but things have been moving so fast there wasn't time. That's the excuse he gives himself. He needs to talk to her, but he can't...not now...for all intents and purposes she's in the past...along with Sarah Murrell and almost anyone else...so he joins Jennifer in the past...in the blitz.

Arlene's startling descriptions and the harrowing old newspaper and police reports surge over him, rising up and parading like the ghosts of Banquo's descendants in a long remembered school performance of Macbeth...Wilf Sanders, John Renshaw, Hilda Wallace, Ronald Calthorpe, Milly Fielding. No longer drab names in dusty documents, but real people, with real faces, dressed for their parts in real clothes, trudging and scurrying through darkened streets, illuminated by explosive flashes from the wings, with backstage rumbles of aircraft and booms of falling bombs.

They're alive! And creep into his office only to be processed downstairs by a wily custody sergeant like Saturday night drunks or unsavoury characters arrested on suspicion. But separating the wheat from the chaff...? Now the officer is no custody sergeant, but a detective, weighed down by unsolved petty crimes and a perennial hunt for a persistent, but elusive burglar...his wartime predecessor, Inspector Ted Carlin, trying so hard yet failing to bring the indefatigable Ronald Calthorpe to justice.

The images remain as he pulls out his research notes, gleaned from hours in the file room and library. He fixates on a running man without a name. He goes over Milly Fielding's description recorded verbatim by Carlin. It doesn't accord with Arlene's account of her great uncle. Wilf Sanders is not the running man, but could it fit someone else?

As a well known local shopkeeper, Hilda Wallace's funeral was reported in the newspaper. There's even a photograph of the funeral party and Jenner can easily pick out her husband, Albert Wallace. His image matches what Michael Wallace said of his father. The report mentions Hilda's 'bustling business,' her shop providing 'a vital and vibrant service to the community.' On Hilda's death it passed to her widower. Therefore what became a successful retail empire was not founded on Albert's entrepreneurial skill, but on that of his wife. This casts Albert in a wholly different light and makes Jenner very uneasy.

Milly's description of the 'running man' is not the only misfit. Both she and Wilf Sanders saw John Renshaw emerging from the bombed out church hall, but there are differences in their descriptions. This was of no significance at the time. There were more important matters to be dealt with on that terrible night and any inconsistencies could be dismissed as understandable misperceptions in a confused and fast moving situation. Besides, both Wilf and Milly were bystanders, neither survivors nor rescuers at the church hall. Of the two, Milly's account would be the more likely to be discounted, but Jenner isn't so sure.

He's used to dealing with divergent descriptions of the same event by separate witnesses, but senses this is different. Could Wilf and Milly be seeing two different men? It all hinges on who was at the church hall at the relevant times. He makes a few assumptions, accepting everything Milly said was correct, that she saw all the separate men she said she did and that one of them, despite having no immediate explanation was Albert Wallace. Milly was in the area of the 'Grapes' pub when people were entering the church hall basement shelter. She saw both Albert Wallace and John Renshaw. Up to now Jenner has only taken into account John Renshaw. After the church hall was hit, both Milly and Wilf witnessed people emerging from the carnage. How can the dissonance between Milly and Wilf's accounts be explained?

Ettie and Jennifer 'saw' a running man from the comatose Karen. Yet Wilf made no mention of him to Arlene. Jenner carefully calculates Wilf's movements from the time he arrived in Nottingham from the London train, got to the 'Cross Keys' and from there to the 'Grapes.' He couldn't have arrived *before* the bomb dropped, but Milly had been in the area for some time, pursuing her usual activities. Her description of the 'running' man tallies with what Jenner knows of Albert Wallace. This explains why she saw two men.

Jenner now makes one of those leaps of supposition sometimes necessary in an investigation. Ettie and Arlene both assert Wilf was looking for someone. Ettie says he was agitated. He first goes to the meeting place, the 'Cross Keys,' but is late. Arlene says he was looking for a woman. He goes on to the 'Grapes.' His arrival is after the bomb has destroyed the church hall. The memory of what he found remained an open wound filling him with guilt for the rest of his life. He had to be meeting someone who was killed in the church hall. Could it have been Hilda Wallace?

In which case he's likely to have known Albert. If Wilf arrived early enough to see Albert, that memory would also have remained with him and he would be likely to have told Arlene, but he didn't. So, if Wilf arrived too late to see Albert, it means the 'running' man left the scene very soon after the bomb dropped. If he was a survivor he was a very lucky one who needed no help and was very anxious to get away without delay. Milly said the 'running' man did nothing to help. Unlike some of the other survivors he must have been uninjured. This 'evidence' was ignored at the time.

Like Milly, Wilf saw Renshaw. Or did he? Their descriptions are totally different. Milly saw two men after the bomb fell. She saw the 'running' man and Renshaw. Wilf only saw Renshaw. The few survivors are well accounted for. Albert or whoever was the 'running' man may have got out before rescuers arrived, but by the time Renshaw emerged he was properly recorded. Now Jenner makes his second leaping supposition.

There's a more serious difference between Wilf and Milly's descriptions. They both saw a man leave the shelter, who was assumed to be Renshaw, but only Milly saw Renshaw enter the shelter. What if the man she saw enter and the man she saw leaving were different? Before the bomb struck she would have time to fully perceive the man who entered. In the dimness and confusion after the shelter was destroyed she would assume a man leaving, wearing the same clothes, was identical to the man she saw entering.

Tonight Jennifer will leave the hospital dressed as Karen and in the dimness, with clever movements she could be taken to be Karen. She's pretending for a purpose. Ronald Calthorpe was killed in the church hall during the air raid. Or rather it was assumed it was Calthorpe. Like Jennifer as Karen, a man wearing the same clothes as Renshaw could easily be taken to be Renshaw and a man killed in the shelter wearing Calthorpe's clothes and carrying his identity documents could be assumed to be Calthorpe. The inconsistency between Wilf and Milly's descriptions of 'Renshaw' was a minor detail, ignored at the time. It was assumed the survivor emerging from the bomb blasted church hall was John Renshaw, but what if it was actually Ronald Calthorpe?

Jenner returns to his notes on Calthorpe's criminal career. There are a few references to the man, which could match with Wilf's description, but not with Milly's. If it was Calthorpe emerging from the church hall devastation then Wilf, who had not seen Renshaw enter, actually saw Calthorpe whereas Milly, remembering rather than seeing, 'saw' Renshaw.' That explains why Wilf and Milly gave different descriptions.

A man found dead in the destroyed church hall, wearing Calthorpe's clothes and with his papers was assumed to be Calthorpe, yet later on the same night someone with the same MO as the 'dead' Calthorpe broke into the house of Dorothy Matthews. Calthorpe was a wily rogue, but not a killer. The bomb probably killed the 'real' John Renshaw. Calthorpe, a canny opportunist took advantage of the situation, switched clothes and identities and emerged not only as a survivor, but as a 'new' man. Carlin's subsequent investigations contain a passing reference to the bomb on the church hall, but it wasn't followed up. Carlin missed the significance of the inconsistencies on the night of $8^{th}$ May 1941, but then he wasn't looking for a burglar in an air raid shelter.

It explains the apparent continuation of burglaries similar to Calthorpe's exploits, after his 'death' in the air raid, but they stop at the end of the war. Perhaps, he too was scarred by the night of $8^{th}$ May and the trauma finally caught up with him? More likely, no longer shrouded by blackout and darkened streets, he was less confident of evading capture and sensed retribution closing in? Either way he decided it was time to move on. So followed the mysterious later life of 'John Renshaw,' his unexplained flight to Brazil and equally perplexing return.

Milly therefore saw three men, John Renshaw going into the shelter, Ronald Calthorpe leaving after the bomb blast and Albert Wallace, the 'running' man. It would be good to talk to Milly, but like so many others she disappeared, never to be heard of again. Did she continue her professional activities, perhaps making enough money to retire and live in outward respectability somewhere in the suburbs? He'd like to think so. Or was she killed in another raid, perhaps taking too little care, sedulously pursuing her calling, her fate buried with the rubble and the carnage?

After so long Jenner can only make assumptions. Two deceptions took place that night under cover of the air raid and the destruction of the church hall. One led to the 'rebirth' of Ronald Calthorpe and for a time the continuation of his nefarious activities. The other killed Hilda.

Albert Wallace was supposed to be out of town that night. No one expected him to be with Hilda, but what if he was there? Milly saw him leaving...running...why was he so eager to get away? He inherited his wife's business and on that foundation built an even more successful enterprise, but was it him rather than the luftwaffe that killed Hilda?

Had Albert discovered Hilda's affair with Wilf and was bent on bitter revenge? Did he arrive unexpectedly in the shelter and there was a row? Or was it more cold blooded? Does a gambling connection run through the past as well as the present? Albert was moving in some shady circles. Was he already experiencing 'financial difficulties?' Did he covet Hilda's small, but profitable shop to solve his problems? Maybe he'd already approached her and she'd refused to get him off the financial hook?

Jenner's leap into the darkened past casts Albert Wallace as the villain of the raid, but was Wilf's 'guilt' conditioned not by arriving too late, but getting there earlier? Jenner's calculations on his movements on that fateful night are based on Arlene's version of events. What was really behind Ettie's vision of an agitated man at St. Pancras? Was his distress not because he was late, but because he had to stiffen himself for what he would have do if he was early? Was he, not Albert the 'running' man? He may well have been running from the bombed building, distraught after learning of the death of Hilda.

So, if Wilf killed Hilda, what was his motive? Did he want to end a clandestine relationship that had no future? In which case, why not just walk away? Or was there some other terrible secret he couldn't live with or at least not with Hilda? It's not only what was, but what's believed to have been. If Arlene believes Wilf was responsible she'll not want his memory besmirched. Does Arlene believe Karen was going to reveal Wilf as Hilda's killer? Tonight will she finish off the job she botched on 13th April? Karen was attacked by a man, but if a man can masquerade as another man, surely a woman can masquerade as a man? What will be Arlene's move tonight? He recalls again her mysterious phrase.

*Something the police ought to know.*

What did she really mean and more importantly, how has the attacker interpreted those words? He'll believe she knows who he is and is ready to expose him. All will be determined by events in May 1941. So he must take action tonight. So much for the when, what of the where?

His plan is centred not on the 'Grapes' and the church hall, but with an assumed confrontation at the 'Cross Keys' site, reinforced by Arlene saying the unexploded bomb is the pivot. Officers will be able to apprehend the perpetrator and protect Jennifer, but what if that's wrong? Should they be where Milly was, the 'Grapes,' across the road from the original site of the church hall? Then there's the timing. He's based everything on Wilf getting to the 'Cross Keys' not the 'Grapes.' Arlene referred to 'right place, right time,' fitting with his original calculation, but now they could be in the wrong pace and at the wrong time!

His head reels in confusion, getting deeper and darker as he fears for Jennifer. Then he begins to wonder whether his assumptions have been made on the wrong suspect.

Ettie agrees with Arlene's radio broadcast. The bomb is the 'pivot' of what is to come. That means Sharp Road can be resisted no longer. She expects others to be drawn to the site, but on arrival finds few people and no journalists. The air is quiet, but suffused with hidden energy, an oppressive pall like the stillness before a storm. It gets stronger as she walks towards the barrier. A few police are at the edge and she slinks out of sight, carefully skirting the perimeter, imbibing the atmosphere from every direction. She'll be at her most effective from an outward vantage. It will be for others to tackle what unfolds within.

Now she feels them. Unseen, unheard, but as real and as palpable as the visions she absorbed from Karen's coma. They are earlier than she anticipated. The time nears. There must be no delay. She looks round anxiously. Soldiers have arrived. She goes over.

"What's happening?" she says to the nearest police constable.

"You need to get away," he says, "The army disposal team are returning."

"What are they going to do?"

"Deal with the bomb."

"No, no," she says anxiously, "They must not touch it."

"It'll be quite safe."

"No, no. It will mean…"

"You'd better get back," he says, gently steering her away from the barrier.

She steps back. This can't be. Where is Jenner? She phones his mobile. Locked in a whirlpool of inaction he ignores it. Then she tries the landline number. Still he prevaricates until at last shaken out of his vacillation he picks up and grunts a feeble 'hello' into the receiver.

"Where are you?" she says.

He's momentarily taken aback by her questioning strident voice.

"Where? Er, yes, I'm…here…"

"In the office?"

"Yes."

"You need to be here."

"Here being where exactly?" he says, gradually pulling out of his whirling reveries.

"Sharp Road, the site of…"

"…the unexploded bomb."

"They've all been wrong."

"Wrong about the place?"

"Wrong about the bomb. The army disposal people are back. There's been an awful mistake. They've assumed… but they're wrong. It was never said the bomb was safe. They're clearing the area again. They've crossed the threshold."

"Someone has entered the site? Who do you mean?"

"I felt it. They've crossed the threshold."

"Have you seen Jennifer?" he says, suddenly very alarmed, "She should be there by now."

"I've only just got here."

He gets up from the desk. With one arm trying to put on his coat, the other holding the receiver he shouts, "No one should be there, it's the wrong place!"

"What are you talking about?"

The wrong place, the wrong time. The phrase hammers!

"You're sure Jennifer isn't there?"

"I'll look for her."

"Could she have gone to the 'Grapes' pub?"

"Why should she be there?"

"Everybody needs to be at the 'Grapes.' That's where…"

"No, no, no. This is the place. They don't know what they're doing. This is where it's going to happen. You have to be here and now!"

"What's going to happen?"

"They are here. They…"

The man in the old clothes stares directly at Jennifer. He opens his mouth slightly as if to speak, but closes it again. His lips curl slightly at the edges with the beginnings of a peculiar half smile, half grimace, a meld of anguish, question, warning. Then he wrings his hands in apparent pain, an overwhelming guilt. Jennifer has seen him before, through Karen's room. It must be Wilf Sanders. Why is he here? He belongs on the train, but is no 'predator.'

It's not just him that's out of place. She's moved only a short way, but looking back it's already difficult to make out the barrier. She puts it down to the dark evening and cloud filled sky obscuring moon and stars. Yet surely she should see the vehicles, the shapes of buildings, but there's nothing. No street, no soldiers, no wide excavation where the bomb should be exposed, no forms of any kind, only an impenetrable blackness, almost solid in intensity and now no barrier, as if she's not at the bomb site at all.

She walks on. It's only in her mind. It will clear. The stress of the anxious taxi ride, over concentration on the task, what she may find, how she'll manage, it's all too much. De-engage. Remember why you're here. Slow the mind, quicken the senses, be more aware, less reactive. She turns back and forth, side to side quickly checking her clothes. They've not changed. She's relieved. They're Karen's clothes. As they're meant to be. Stay alert. He has to be here, following, waiting, ready to appear at any moment.

But where is *here*? It's no place, just blackness, a terrible dream of nothingness. She never realised before how nothing could be so much more frightening than something. Not just an unfamiliar place, but unfamiliar in time. Where is Wilf Sanders? How can he protect her? He's in the past. This is not the past. It's no time.

Consumed with what she sees or doesn't see she's not listened. Now she does. In the loneliest barren place, let alone in the heart of the city, there's always some sound, some sign of life however small, flying, crawling, creeping things, the soft sigh of the breeze, the distant hum of the night. Not even the restful sound of silence...nothing... unnerving as any resonating explosion.

Then she hears it. Softly at first, then gradually increasing in volume until the clamour cascades over her. A raucous medley of humanity and so joyously recognisable! Talking, laughing, arguing, singing, loud, chaotic, how she wallows as it enfolds her! Then she sees dimly. It's the pub, but which one? The 'Cross Keys,' where he came from the station or the 'Grapes,' full of revellers who will scurry across the road to the church hall shelter when the air raid siren sounds?

She approaches, eager to join the throng. Inside, she looks for Wilf, moving between the tables, but cannot find him. She goes outside. Perhaps he's still on his way? She'll talk to him, but what will she say? The sounds from the pub recede. Someone's nearby. It's not Wilf. She's uneasy.

The phone in Jenner's office goes dead. He tries to call Ettie back, but it won't connect. As he struggles with the second sleeve of his coat the receiver slips noisily to the floor. He picks it up, replaces it on the desk, then moves to the outer office, barking instructions for everyone to get to Sharp Road as fast as possible. Still convinced it's the wrong place he despatches a couple of officers as a contingency force to Wisden Street, the 'Grapes' pub and the site of the church hall.

His agitation doesn't abate during the journey. He's taken Arlene's wild assertions too seriously, the movement of her great uncle Wilf Sanders and her obsession with the bomb as the 'pivot' of tonight's inevitable operations. His plan is unravelling, the villains of past and present slipping away. But now a more pressing objective. Jennifer's in danger and has to be rescued!

Enlivened by Arlene's broadcast, he assumes hundreds will descend on the area and rounds the last corner, sure to see a large group milling around the site, held back by harassed officers. Instead there are only army trucks and police vehicles, the nearby streets deserted except for small clusters of people huddling close to the empty houses like sentinels. A few stare suspiciously as he passes by. There's a low rumble of subdued conversation, similar to the sound in his recent imaginings.

Beyond the parked vehicles a few officers and soldiers are at the barrier. There's little activity and he can't find the superintendent. The constables are of little help. He mentions the people along the road and is assured they are well outside the 'restricted area.'

"Where are the other officers?" he asks, only to be met with blank stares.

"Have you seen sergeant Heathcott?"

No one has seen her.

"She's meant to be here, you must have seen her!"

He phones the station to find where the others are, but can't get a consistent signal. The soldiers can't help. They're 'awaiting orders' and neither Major Phillips nor any other senior officer is available. He tries his phone again, but the signal is dead. One soldier says they've had similar difficulties. He approaches the barrier. A couple of constables stand in his way.

"You're not going in there, are you, sir?" one says.

"Is there a problem?"

"We have strict orders to let no one through except army personnel," the other says.

He glares aggressively, about to ask on whose authority they're acting, when one of the soldiers, a sergeant approaches.

"They're quite right, sir" he says with cheery firmness, "I'm afraid you can't go in."

"Are you in charge?" Jenner says.

The sergeant studiously ignores the question. Other soldiers join him.

"I'm looking for one of my officers, Detective Sergeant Heathcott. Are you sure no one has seen her?"

"This is a restricted area. No one has been permitted to enter. The unexploded bomb…"

Jenner notes the 'correct' response. Has there been an unpermitted entry? Could it be Jennifer?

"There's not a lot going on," he says ungraciously.

"We have our orders, sir," is the curt reply.

Then a police car arrives and several officers come over.

"Where the hell have you been?" he says.

"Lost our way," one says sheepishly.

"Lost your way?" he says incredulously, "How long have you lived in this bloody town?"

"Odd thing, sir. We were on our way here, then suddenly...it was very peculiar...we ended up at Wisden Street near a pub called the 'Grapes.' I know it sounds weird, but..."

"All right, all right," Jenner says quickly, "You're here now, so get about it."

*We ended up...near... the Grapes.*

The phrase echoes ominously. Even inanimate vehicles are going to where they're all meant to be! Jennifer could be carried away there just as these other officers were. It may be weird, but it's real! They should all get over to Wisden Street as fast as possible.

Then he sees Ettie, standing behind one of the army vehicles.

"How did you get here?" he says.

"The same way as you, except you've been taking your time."

"Sorry about that. I've had to carefully think through all we need to do. Have you seen..."

"Fortunately, there's been precious little happening about the bomb. I keep telling them it's unstable, but they don't understand. They mustn't touch it!"

He fiddles with his phone.

"It won't work," she says, "None of them will. Not now."

He curses and shoves the phone into his pocket.

"Have you seen Jennifer? "I'm afraid she's gone to Wisden Street."

"You sent her *there*?"

"She was meant to come here."

"There should still be time."

"Not if we have to go Wisden Street."

He explains the plan, which he may have miscalculated and how the events are more likely to work at the site of the church hall where Wilf Sanders was to meet Hilda Wallace.

"The bomb has always been the catalyst," she says, "It will be so again tonight."

"That's what Arlene Bates said on the radio."

"That doesn't mean it's wrong. This is the right place. Besides, if what you've set in motion is correct, your quarry will follow Jennifer."

"But where is she?"

"One of the soldiers saw someone matching her description. He doesn't know where she's gone, but I know and... (she nods to the area beyond the barrier)...I've felt... presences."

He's in no mood to take up her last point.

"How did she get in, with all these soldiers and our own officers? They stopped me."

She shrugs.

"You're very relaxed about this," he says, stamping his feet and gaping forlornly towards the excavation, "She could be in great danger. You said yourself the bomb is unstable."

"Because I was worried they would touch it. They don't know, cannot know, what they're doing."

"Touch it or not, Jennifer is in there."

"Isn't that where you want her to be?"

"Not like this. Not if the bomb's about to go off, with nobody in authority able or willing to take action, not if we're in the wrong place!"

"They have no control here...not in 1941. It was a very different place then and..."

"But there's an unstable unexploded bomb!"

Ettie takes him by the shoulders.

"Events are moving as they moved this night in 1941. What's already in motion can't be stopped."

"But the bomb…"

"As long as no one touches it she'll be protected. It didn't explode in 1941, unlike the one at the church hall, another reason why we can't be there."

Another military vehicle arrives and Major Phillips walks to the barrier. He speaks to the soldiers and constables. Jenner turns back to Ettie.

"How did she get through the barrier?"

"Those from the past have passed unnoticed. You sent her to reveal the mystery of the present, but once here she was conferred with the same shield and like them passed unobserved."

Jenner watches the movements around the barrier, unconvinced by Ettie's relaxed confidence.

"I can't put all my trust in the past. I'm going in."

He strides to the barrier, at first unseen. Then the soldiers bar his way.

"We may have to evacuate this whole area of the city," Phillips says, "You must stay back."

"You mean a controlled explosion?" Jenner says.

"It may be necessary. As you know…"

"Or uncontrolled one. I can't wait for that!"

With a deft and muscular strike he pounds the side of the nearest soldier who, winded and unbalanced falls to the ground. Jenner steps over him, gets across the barrier, breaks into a run and is quickly well away towards the excavation and the bomb.

Jennifer must get away from the man. The strained silence returns, all sense of direction submerged as the overwhelming blackness comes down again. Which way, the barrier, the pub? She chooses the pub, but it's gone. It must be where the excavation and the bomb lie. She can see the ground immediately in front and around her, but not beyond as if she moves through a darkened room with a lighted candle.

The illuminated space increases and she runs faster, hearing only her feet crunching the ground, her heart pounding. She stops and takes quick deep breaths. It reminds her of Karen's deep breathing in the hospital. She can see further now and in the dim light makes out the diggings, the barrier, distant houses and the encircling barrier. What she saw and heard earlier was an overworked imagination. Focus on the task in hand.

Nobody is here. Where are the other officers? The excavation is ahead. Despite the danger she's drawn. Better not get too close. She may have to handle this on her own. What was the barrier is now only a shadowy shape and seems further away. There's some activity. One, two three, four, five people talking. No one looks towards her, but if she shouts surely they'll come to her rescue? It gets darker again. Their forms blur. She can no longer make them out and cannot hear them. Yet another imagined presence, a trick of the diminished light?

She trudges towards the bomb. The newly excavated ground is exposed, but hard, her steps falling heavily with dull thuds. She kicks up the stones and looks down, the better to keep her balance. Her eyes now better adjusted, she looks up, straining to make out the hazy forms and distinguish the 'hole' and diggings through the murk. It's too far away. The shapes jump. She's wary, slows and stops to concentrate. After a few moments she's sure. This is no trick of the darkness. A figure is in the distance and it gets closer. She suppresses her fear. This is why she's here. She must stand her ground.

"Come back!"

She turns around. Another figure approaches from the gloom. She's caught between the two. Go on or remain? This could be the confrontation, but which one can be trusted?

"Come back, Jennifer. They're here to blow the bomb. It's not safe."

She recognises the voice. Jenner comes closer, but though relieved she doesn't move towards him.

"No, I have to see it through," she says.

"I've checked out all the alibis. What the Wallaces said is…"

He breaks off, stops and stares wildly at the figure behind Jennifer.

"So," he says solemnly, "*She's* here."

The figure in the distance is Arlene.

"You were right," Jenner says, "My suspicions about Albert…"

"That's the past," she says.

"Yes, but it also…"

He breaks off. Jennifer turns and walks towards Arlene.

"How did she get here?" he mutters, then loudly to Jennifer, "Wait!"

Jennifer keeps walking forward.

"Remember she's a suspect," he calls, "She'll think you're Karen."

His warning is ignored, but does it matter? It's what's intended. Jennifer appearing as Karen. But without support she may be walking into…Jennifer reaches Arlene. They stand a few yards apart, staring blankly without speaking, as if looking at complete strangers, their eyes darting continually, suspicious travellers at a foreign border, assessing whether to enter. Arlene's clothes are unfamiliar and old fashioned while her hair is oddly different. Jennifer struggles to understand. The woman she sees is straight out of a 1940s war film, but why does Arlene scrutinise her in similar fashion? Surely she recognises her? Or does she also see someone else, ignoring the face and concentrating on the clothes?

Jenner's words resound. *She's a suspect. She'll think you're Karen.*

Jennifer must be on her guard. Arlene will be afraid 'Karen' will divulge Wilf's guilt. But this is not Arlene, any more than she is Karen. Each is clothed to fit someone else. The more Jennifer looks the less she sees Arlene. The noises she heard earlier return, softly at first then getting louder… talking, laughing, chinking glasses…the pub.

She turns round and round, but there's only the empty diggings, the distant barrier and the imminent hole where the bomb awaits. Yet the sounds of merriment continue and she feels the 'Cross Keys' as real as the gritty ground beneath her feet. Now she hears the siren followed by the low rumble of aircraft, draining of glasses, gathering of possessions, scurrying feet, anxious exchanges, running to shelters. Yet there's no pub, no people, no one except this woman a few feet before her.

Now there's Hilda Wallace. Arlene has become Hilda. No longer standing, but sitting impassively as if at a table though there's no table. She glances up and across, occasionally tapping her fingers on the invisible table, checking the time on the invisible pub clock. She waits, but he doesn't come. The background noise of the pub returns, but she doesn't hear it. Her mind is elsewhere. She gets up and walks away, her image gradually fading until it's no more.

Jennifer looks around again. Perhaps Arlene is returned, but there's only the blackness. Then she sees a man approaching. It must be him who came towards the pub earlier. She's ready to run, but this isn't the same man. This is Wilf Sanders and she's not afraid. The sounds of the pub return, muted, but recognisable. Wilf comes closer. He looks beyond her and she turns to see the 'Cross Keys.' He keeps staring, but not at her, at the pub.

"I was late that night and I've been paying for it ever since. It was my fault. If I'd not been late…when I came you were gone. The die was cast at this damned pub."

Jennifer turns to back and side to side. Is he talking to Hilda? She still hears faint sounds from the pub, but no one is outside. It falls silent again and the pub gradually recedes. A woman appears. The same woman she saw before. It must be Hilda…no, it's Arlene…but those clothes…she could be Hilda. Jennifer walks towards her, about to call out, but suddenly she's gone. Jennifer turns back. Wilf is still here, immobile, still staring beyond her to where the 'Cross Keys' stood. Jennifer turns, but the scene changes again. It's a church, no a church hall. There are people, they are…

…a wild howling clangour pervades the air. Jennifer shoves her hands tightly over her ears. More and more people in the street, rushing into the church hall, down to the basement. The siren continues, then subsides, replaced by dull rumbles, getting louder and louder, black sky pierced by searchlights, rapid flashes in the distance like mini suns in accelerated rising, ominous aircraft drone becoming a menacing roar. They are here. The bomb will fall. She must escape…

"Come away, Jennifer, he's here. Get away!"

Jenner? What's he doing in 1941? Wilf Sanders is not with him. Are they now at Wisden Street?

"You must go too," she calls, "This place will be an inferno!"

Jenner gets closer.

"I know it all now. I've gone over Milly Fielding's statement, what she really said. You see…"

He jabbers on about files and reports and how they ignored Milly. Jennifer isn't listening. She's turned back to the street. There's a young woman at the corner, watching as she is watching, making no attempt to go into the shelter. Wilf isn't here. But he can't be. He was too late for the 'Cross Keys,' too late to get here and save…

"…He's here. You must beware of Albert Wallace. …"

It's Jenner's voice. What does he mean Albert Wallace? No, it's Hilda Wallace…but she's not here…she's already in the shelter and Wilf is too late…

"Not in the church hall," she shouts.

Jenner comes closer.

"What church hall?" he says, then insistently, "I've cracked his alibi. He wasn't in Derbyshire that night. He could have been at the church hall. It means…"

The church hall? Jenner is taking no notice of the furious scene. He can't see it! He's almost upon her, his hand outstretched, but she won't move. This is the place, it's where…

"Albert Wallace is here. You must get away!" he shouts.

An enormous boom surges with a grating pummelling over everything. It's the bomb. It's hit. Jenner tries to grab Jennifer, but he can't see her. The ground shakes, the air filled with choking dust. The site has collapsed. Jennifer is flung to the ground as it heaves and buckles under the enormous force of dislodged rock and earth. She lies inert as the dust gradually settles, covering her in a fine grey film. The silence is unnerving. Such a major rupture is bound to have disrupted the bomb. Fractured and sundered the fuse must be activated and she waits for the inevitable explosion. The chilling silence continues, a few minutes seemingly interminable. Perhaps the bomb has lodged in some precarious fissure, rent open in the diggings. But it's a charged illusion. The fuse ticks on. Soon it will set off the explosive. But maybe she's lucky. The ground is already cracked and split. When the explosion comes it may only cause superficial damage, flinging its fragments up and over her position…but even if she survives the explosion, the shock waves will rain down the jagged fragments. At least a wholesale explosion will be quick, but showered with such deadly…

She gets up. Jenner is gone. The church hall, Hilda, Wilf and the frenetic world of 1941, all gone, leaving only the troubled present.

"You'll not escape now."

Simon Wallace stands a few yards away, glaring with a malevolent smirk.

"How did you…?" she says.

"I've been with you ever since you left the hospital. We have unfinished business to transact, do we not, Karen?"

With the borrowed clothes and through the dismal, dusty air it's easy for Simon to 'see' Jennifer as Karen. She could correct him, but she's here to expose Karen's attacker. Better to continue the illusion. She's isolated, but Jenner and other officers will protect her. They must be close. But they're not.. Simon speaks.

"You've spun them a catalogue of lies, as you did with me, but isn't that with all affairs? Our relationship was a sham. We were suspicious, both out to get as much as we could from the other."

"You're very cynical," Jennifer says.

Behind his back she catches sight of a distant flash, like lightning though she knows it's not. Then faintly, distant rumbling and occasional booms, no natural storm, very much a man made one.

"You were determined to humiliate me, calling it 'exposing.' The papers would love that."

The noises have gone. No more sudden flares in the sky, however distant.

"So you were out to…" she begins provocatively, but breaks off.

Very faintly the same chinking, chattering sounds from the pub. Two figures appear behind Simon, a man and a woman, both in 1940s clothes. The woman is the harassed figure in the pub, but the man is not Wilf Sanders. Simon babbles on.

"All businesses have their financial difficulties."

The figures disappear and the pub sounds fade.

"That's not why you pursue me, you…"

She breaks off again. Wilf Sanders appears behind Simon, walking grimly towards him with his half smiling, half scowling expression. Then he's gone.

As they talk the same figures, Wilf, Albert, Hilda and the sounds of the pub and the bombs come and go. At first it unnerves Jennifer, but gradually the images and sounds comfort her. The past is desperately trying to interrupt the present. Only Jennifer sees and hears them. Obsessed with his onslaught on Karen, Simon is unaware of anything else.

"Karen was finding out whether your family was involved in her grandfather's death," Jennifer says.

Simon is baffled. Why does 'Karen' speak in the third person? Jennifer notices and immediately corrects herself.

"I mean I was only trying to find…your family, your father, your grandfather they were involved in my grandfather's death. The so called accident in 1965…"

"I don't know what you're talking about. You were out to…expose me…as you'd call it. You acquired confidential information about the firm. You were uncontrollable. You were even jealous of Arlene and…"

"Ka…I…was never jealous. Your affair with Arlene was much earlier and over long before."

He's ready to counteract her, but hesitates. She speaks of Arlene with a strange detachment. In any case he doesn't like to be reminded of past failures and reverts to the more comfortable subject of the firm's 'legitimate' financial problems. She lets him talk. If she can keep up the pretence of 'Karen' and manoeuvre his uncontrolled babbling he's bound to implicate himself. Then Jenner can…

But Jenner isn't here. An invisible barricade has been thrown around her, a boundary over which Jenner cannot cross. She's alone. Yet not so, for as Simon recounts with incriminating detail the various financial 'deviations' of he and his father, Wilf Sanders appears once more in the background and the faint chatter of the 'Cross Keys' leaps through the air. It emboldens her to challenge him directly.

"Is that why you killed Sarah Murrell?"

"I didn't know…"

"You knew her. She worked for your firm and…"

"You never mentioned this. You were only concerned... Wait a moment, you couldn't know...you're not Karen."

Jennifer steps back. However much she's in danger as 'Karen' she may be even more vulnerable as herself!

"But I do know you" he says, "I've seen you... somewhere..."

"You're just like your grandfather. He was a gambler and gambled with much more than money."

"My grandfather...?"

"Albert Wallace, the founder of the firm or should I say the thief of the firm for he stole it from his wife, Hilda."

She expects another denial but Simon is speechless.

"Sarah was not only a good accountant, she was an expert gambler. You were just a pathetic and failing amateur in comparison."

He bridles at the insult. Jennifer may be guessing, but he doesn't deny it.

"You owed Sarah a lot of money. It all went back to the time she worked for you."

"No," he says quietly, "It wasn't like that. The money..."

"She was demanding payment and there were financial irregularities, which she threatened to expose. You attacked her at the station."

"No, no, not me," he shrieks, "It was that bloody ghost. He did it. All those women kept seeing him on the train. It was him!"

"No one was killed by a ghost, but it was a convenient cover. The ghost, the predator, call him what you will was blamed for the attack on Karen."

"My God! I know now. You're that bloody detective. What are you doing wearing Karen's clothes?"

"So you admit you attacked Karen?"

"I couldn't have done. I was away from town on that day. I was in Leicester."

"Yes, but not into the evening."

"I couldn't have been on the train," he stumbles, "I was at a meeting."

"You can't confirm you were there for the whole evening."

"I was in Leicester."

She lets it pass. If Jenner says he's blown Simon's alibi that's enough. She sees Wilf, then Hilda, then Albert, each for a split second. Then they're gone.

"Your grandfather also had financial pressures. He too was a gambler. Like you not a very good one. He owed a lot of money and in the company he kept he'd have to pay it back very quickly. Hilda kept a tight control on her business. Her shop was doing well. She wasn't going to risk its future prosperity bailing out her husband's impecunious card playing. So there was only one way he could get his hands on the shop and the money to pay off his debts."

"I told you before. I know nothing about my grandfather's first wife."

"You've heard of Hilda."

"Hearing of her isn't knowing of her."

"Enough to know your grandfather killed her."

"She died in an air raid. She was sheltering in a church hall. There was a direct hit."

"So you do know. She died in the air raid, but not because of the bomb."

He laughs, but nervously.

"This is ridiculous."

"What about Karen's grandfather, John Renshaw, killed in a supposed accident on a building site in 1965?"

"There was no supposed about it."

"John Renshaw figured things out - just as Sarah Murrell did - and he was prepared to go public unless he was paid off. Isn't that it?"

"Keith Renshaw's been doing plenty of stirring up ever since."

"Your grandfather Albert knew only one way to resolve his problems. He or your father killed John Renshaw. It was no accident."

Simon moves closer, muttering "She had to be dealt with. It couldn't go on."

"She?" Jennifer says, "You mean Hilda?"

Simon doesn't answer and continues muttering, all the time getting closer to Jennifer. She retreats, nearer to the subsiding ground around the bomb. Something is slipping... something metallic. The side of the bomb is clearly exposed. Simon still comes on. Jennifer turns and runs.

He pursues her, shouting, "I have to pay them. You'll give me the money."

He gains on her.

"But I'm not Hilda," she calls.

"No," he says, "You're Karen."

She runs faster and suddenly bumps into Ettie, who steadies her. Between gasps for breath, Jennifer tries to explain.

"He was in... the past...then they were there and...he was back in...the now...they were gone...then...he thought I was Hilda...no...Karen...then me and..."

"I know, I know," Ettie says, "The past is pressing on the present."

"He said the ghost was..."

"I heard."

Ettie pulls Jenifer behind her and faces Simon. He stops and glares aggressively.

"Who are you? How did you get here?"

"You can't invoke the past," Ettie says, "It won't be moulded, it's power's too great for that. Assign your misdeeds to a ghost at your peril. You won't be forgiven."

Simon gapes nervously, the colour draining from his cheeks as he thrusts a defiant but fearful jaw.

"I'll get you like I'll get her. I'll have the money."

"He's Albert again," Jennifer whispers.

"She was going to blurt it out, take advantage of me," he says, pointing a wavering arm towards Jennifer.

"Now he's Simon," she whispers.

"You'll have to face the vengeance of those you've wronged!" Ettie shouts, "There's no escape!"

Simon staggers back a few steps, his arm still outstretched and waving from side to side, which makes him lurch as if he's drunk.

"Go back! You don't belong here!"

His arm no longer points directly at either Ettie or Jennifer, but to their side. They turn to see a woman standing a few yards behind, dressed in 1940s clothes, but now besmirched with dirt and dust. Arlene speaks...or is it Hilda?

"Ettie's right. The past draws me. It draws us all and it tells us. Your grandfather killed his wife and ruined Wilf Sanders life."

"You mean her fancy man," Simon shouts.

"I mean my great uncle."

"Been carrying on with him for months. I had to do something."

"Albert again," Jennifer whispers.

"Hardly surprising," Arlene calls, "How could she live with a man like Albert? A wastrel, up to his neck in debt, mixed up with nasty characters like Sydney Moorwell."

"Only Sydney would help me," Simon mumbles, then more loudly "You wouldn't give me the money."

"I was right. You did kill her!"

Simon is confused. Is he talking to Hilda or Arlene?

"No, no, no! I didn't kill anyone. I didn't attack anyone."

"Now he's himself *and* Albert," Ettie says.

He stamps around in a small circle, flinging his arms, punching the air and continually shrieking "I didn't kill Hilda! I didn't attack Karen!"

"See what I mean?" Ettie says.

"You did, you did," Arlene calls back, "Confess! You went to the church hall. After the bomb dropped there were only a few survivors. You were one, Hilda was another, but you made sure she'd never get out the shelter alive."

He stops and looks between them in turn, muttering vaguely, his only coherent words "I had to get the money" and glancing at Arlene saying "You don't know what you're talking about, you're unstable."

"One of those survivors is Ronald Calthorpe!"

They all turn to a different, strident voice. Jenner stands a short way behind Jennifer and Ettie.

"He's in the church hall basement. He knows about Albert's problems, but in his line of business it's often better to keep things to yourself. He sees Albert kill Hilda, then getting away. That might be useful insurance for the future. Besides, he needs to melt into the night. So he exchanges his identity with one of those killed by the blast. From then on the man everyone calls John Renshaw is actually the notorious burglar, Ronald Calthorpe.

'Life isn't easy for him after the war. They are hard times. He gets a job with a local builder, the Duggers. They are working for the Wallaces. One day he sees the head of the firm on site and recognises the man he saw all those years before in the church hall shelter. It's an opportunity he can't ignore. He can always use extra money. He approaches him, but Albert has ways of dealing with 'financial difficulties.' A convenient accident is staged and Albert's latest problem is nicely sown up."

Simon listens, open mouthed and wide eyed, his arms and legs shaking uncontrollably. Before he can say anything, Ettie takes the initiative.

"The past is unforgiving. Your only hope is to be totally honest."

Simon starts perambulating again, shaking his head and muttering disjointedly

"You have to be honest, Albert," Ettie calls.

Simon reels around, holding his head with his hands. Behind him figures appear intermittently, Wilf, Hilda, even

Ronald Calthorpe, but not Albert. The others gape at the constantly changing images.

"It's coming," Ettie says, "the final merging of past and present."

Simon puts down his hands, stops moving and standing rigidly still, stares at them with unfocused eyes.

"That night is like no other. I'm in Derbyshire seeing my mother. I often get back late because I can be gambling nearer home. I hear Sydney Moorwell is after me. I owe him a lot of money and he isn't the sort of man it's wise to keep waiting. So I avoid the usual place and don't go home either."

Simon breaks off, looks around as if for inspiration, takes a few deep breaths then carries on.

"I'm desperate. I'm wandering around. The sirens sound. I see Hilda go into a church hall basement, which is used as a shelter. Why isn't she at home? I've suspected she's been up to something when I'm out of town, but there's nothing definite. Anyway, she's alone. I follow her."

He pauses, then jerks around, alternately glowering at Jennifer and Arlene. They are his nemesis. He must destroy them. He turns first to Jennifer.

"Your grandfather got all he deserved. John Renshaw was blackmailing me. He had to be put down."

Simon or rather Albert might well be talking about an ailing dog. Then he rounds on Arlene, though speaking as if to Hilda.

"While you…skinflint…you wouldn't give a miserable penny to a beggar…you're in my way…you have to be got rid of."

He pauses, ordering his thoughts, then says, "Why do you care? Your great uncle enticed her away from me. He deserved a life of desolate guilt."

He moves closer. Arlene retreats further into the diggings.

"Not too close!" Jenner shouts.

She stops and Jennifer joins her. Simon laughs. It's forced and hollow. He sways from side to side, alternately turning between the two women as he shrieks.

"You can't touch me. I'm from the past. Of course I got rid of Hilda and that wretch John Renshaw, but his family kept prattling on about the accident. Keith Renshaw was a total bore. Then you…Karen…you had to be stopped."

"You attacked me on the train," Jennifer says.

"Of course, I did," he snaps with irritation as if chiding a foolish child, "but I was disturbed…stupid women interfering. It doesn't matter now. You'll go the same way as Hilda."

He gets closer to the main excavation, where two sides of the bomb are now fully exposed.

"No one can touch me," he bawls gleefully, "I'm Albert… from the past. You're not…I couldn't let you reveal all the information about the firm, Karen. You had to go the way of…"

In his befuddled confidence he hasn't realised how far he's strayed from the others and now stands right up to the bomb. Jenner calls to him.

"Simon, it's unstable. Get back!"

"I'm not listening to you, copper," Simon laughs.

"Get back," Jenner says to the others, "Quickly as you can. Get back!"

Everybody retreats, leaving Simon alone, leaning against the bomb.

"Can't touch me, not even this lump of metal. I'm in the past!" he shouts, laughing.

He kicks the bomb. The others reach the barrier as a deafening roar and boom, part blast, part cracking surrounds and closes over the site. Their last view of Simon is with the figure of Wilf Sanders standing beside him smiling broadly

### 9th May

*'Last night two sources of terror and alarm came to a bizarre conclusion when the man dubbed 'the predator' was cornered at Sharp Road, site of the unexploded bomb.*

*This brings to an end the city's six weeks of fear and anguish with the mysterious appearances on the evening train from London, culminating in the vicious attack on a passenger on 13<sup>th</sup> April and the murder of Sarah Murrell only eleven days later. Simon Wallace, grandson of the founder of the 'Home Comfort' chain of stores, confessed to the attack and murder.*

*As police closed in to arrest him he ventured too close to the unexploded bomb. This caused a major landfall. The whole bomb was then fully exposed and miraculously did not explode, but Wallace was engulfed by the landfall and killed instantly.*

*On further inspection this morning, the army discovered the bomb to be much smaller than originally believed and it was successfully removed to another location, where it was made safe in a controlled explosion.*

*Chief Inspector Derek Jenner, leading the investigation, paid tribute to his officers and especially to Detective Sergeant Jennifer Heathcott who accosted Wallace at the site. He also acknowledged the assistance of Arlene Bates, of the Courier and Ettie Rodway, a psychic investigator in identifying the crucial importance of the site to Wallace.'*

The *Courier* article doesn't carry her by line, but bears Arlene's unmistakable mark. It leaves a number of unanswered questions, some of which are answered in the following weeks. Others remain mysteries for all time.

The previous night everyone was sure they'd escaped not a 'landfall,' but the explosion of a 500 kilogram bomb. Yet it was neither an explosion nor such a large bomb. The army disposal team is dumbfounded. They were convinced it was a 'big 'un.' After the bomb is removed the site is thoroughly searched. Simon's body, which was completely buried is recovered and examined. It shows no signs of blast injuries. One of the soldiers sums up their collective bafflement.

"It's as if the other bomb was never there at all."

They are similarly perplexed by the collapse of the unstable site. It could be explained by Simon's foolish contact, causing further movement, which in turn initiated the landfall. In a later Courier article the 'psychic researcher (a title Ettie abhors) is praised for successfully 'predicting' the landfall rather than an explosion.

Karen comes out of the coma as if she's never been in it, fully recovered, though continuing for several weeks to have 'visions' of the events of 8<sup>th</sup> May 1941.

*Home Comfort* and the other Wallace stores inevitably face a new round of 'financial difficulties' as more details of Simon Wallace's violent activities emerge. Within a couple of months her grandfather's 1965 'accident' is subjected to a new enquiry. During the investigation Michael Wallace learns to be less dismissive of Keith Renshaw's 'campaign.'

Within a year Jennifer's courage and prowess is rewarded with promotion to detective inspector. Though Jenner's reputation as a successful investigator of 'peculiar' cases is further enhanced, he takes no comfort or pride in it. His two sources of greatest satisfaction, the resolution of Hilda Wallace's murder and especially the effective closure of the file on Calthorpe's robberies can never be publicised. He intimates it's time for him to 'retire.' Only a few people take him seriously.

For her part Arlene never again mentions her great uncle, though she always sees the events as the turning point in her later very successful career. In her articles and despite many questions she never speculates about what she shared with Ettie.

The Sharp Road site is developed. There are occasional reports of a lone figure in 1940s clothes, but never threatening and with a wry smile. For Wilf Sanders is the real victor with his ultimate revenge on Hilda's killer.

# More books by the same author are available from timelinkpublications@gmail.com

## *Out of Time*

*Out of Time* is a riveting quest, combining mystery, thriller, detection, historical drama and the interplay of past and present.

International financier Sarah Layman wants to discuss a 'mystery' with freelance journalist Carla Diemer. She won't say what it is except it has nothing to do with finance. Carla arrives to find Sarah dead and is immediately embroiled in a murder investigation led by the dogged Chief Inspector Jenner.

Carla links up with psychic investigator Ettie Rodway, who has also been approached by Sarah. Joining them is a maverick historian, obsessed with a lost Anglo Saxon Chronicle and Carla's dubiously motivated father. Their perilous search of revenge, discovery and intrigue spans 1200 years, from the perilous wetlands of eastern England to the shrouded hills of the west and even to America, pitting them against forces of power, greed and deception.

From the 9th century they must find a ring, a sword, a brooch and a belt. They may solve the mystery, but also unlock immense unpredictable powers. With friend and foe difficult to disentangle they are swept into the swirling currents of a distant age where fearsome warriors fight out their bloody inter family feud, penetrating to the heart of origins and identities.

Confronted by ruthless adversaries intent on the same discovery further deaths follow, the hunters become the hunted and they realise the Chronicle is much more than an obscure historical document. Once the magical powers are invoked, all the pieces have to be fitted together against a frightful deadline in which Time itself could be the ultimate victim.

ISBN 978-0-9557928-1-6

# *Cross Cut*

*Cross Cut* is historical novel meets thriller, ricochetting through time, keeping the reader guessing to the end with its dark alleys, riots, foreboding tunnels and caves, gaslit docksides, terrifying train journeys and nerve racing pursuits across town and country, vividly recreating the desperate world of the past.

Is Bernard Weston dead or alive ? How is his disappearance connected to the campaign to reopen the brooding and abandoned *Cross Cut* canal ?

For DCI Jenner a routine missing person enquiry quickly turns into something more sinister with the present dislocated against the turbulent background of 1840s Nottingham. Trusting his instincts he teams up with Ettie Rodway with her psychic insight and is forced to adopt unconventional methods. Combining their skills of intuition and deduction produces a powerful partnership, but this is stretched to breaking point as they try to avert disaster.

Looming ominously is the foreboding atmosphere of the canal with its shrouded secrets and the fearful power of the tunnel to reach across time. Can Jenner trust his gut feelings and take a path he's reluctant to go down? How much can Ettie risk her own safety to help him ? Can they unravel the crime only in the present or must they step into the past ?

ISBN 978-0-9557928-0-9

# *Wake Us Tomorrow*

Film director Chris Pleasant's project to bring the story of the 1381 Peasants' Revolt to the screen is running into trouble, disturbed by peculiar interruptions and appearances on the set.

Meanwhile psychic Ettie Rodway is approached by Warren Grover, convinced he has made contact with one of the Revolt's local leaders in St. Albans. Arriving to find Warren has been murdered, she mounts her own enquiry, overlapping with DCI Jenner's own investigations.

But Warren's death is only the beginning as events in past and present frighteningly come together. Unpredictable forces are unleashed and a mysterious 'falling man' is constantly seen in the area.

There is a further murder, the victim linked to a re-enactment, staged by Warren in 1981 on the 600th anniversary of the local Revolt.

The pivotal anniversary draws near again. They are beset by a renegade outlaw from 1381. Is the film changing from pretence to a dreadful re-run of the real past ? Can present mysteries only be solved within the frightful events of 600 years ago ?

ISBN 978-0-9557928-3-0

# *Vanishing Point*

Just two weeks after local artist Jose Pearsall rushes to complete in one day her four paintings for the annual art exhibition, she discovers the body of famous television personality Carina Fennell on the beach. The same evening Kelly, a strange young woman grabs attention when she not only 'sees' Carina in one of the pictures, but is adamant that she is moving !

The normally uneventful resort of Darrasea is suddenly the centre of national interest, the bizarre scene compounded that night when the picture is stolen and the cheque for a second of Jose's paintings bounces !

Jose is furious and pursues the buyer while tracking down Kelly, the mysterious 'interpreter' of her paintings, a trail that will unravel the paintings, but put them both in danger and lead to a second murder.

Throughout is the unpredictable seafront, its varied characters inhabiting the pubs, cafes and hotels, but above all the ever changing beach wherein lies the ultimate key to the mystery.

ISBN 978-0-9557928-5-4

# Rivenland

*Rivenland* is a tense story of detection, intrigue and mystery set against the shattering conflict of the English Civil war.

Captain Matthew Fletcher is seriously wounded and teeters between life and death. He recovers, but permanently disabled he cannot return to active service in the Parliamentary army. Instead he reluctantly accepts an assignment to assist local magnate Jospeh Manning investigate strange disturbances in the village of Harringstead.

He arrives to find Manning's steward murdered and the local minister convinced it is the work of witches, while the village is ripped apart by land disputes and family feuds. Needing to find one of Manning's servants and his daughter's secret lover, Matthew is pulled back to war torn London, full of rumour, conspiracy and peculiar religious sects.

Assisted by his streetwise ex – corporal Ezra, he delves into the seedy underworld, is driven into the hands of the desperate 'clubmen' and has to confront disturbing reminders of his own past.

As tensions reach fever pitch in Harringstead he wonders whether one of the 'witches' conceals dangerous secrets. Following another murder, he is accused of being a Royalist spy, relentlessly pursued across town and country and seized by an old enemy from the army.

ISBN 978-0-9557928-4-7